THE NEXT CONTINENT

ISSUI OGAWA

THE NEXT CONTINENT

ISSUI OGAWA

TRANSLATED BY JIM HUBBERT

HAIKA SORU

SAN FRANCISCO

THE NEXT CONTINENT
© 2003 Issui Ogawa
Originally published in Japan by Hayakawa Publishing, Inc.

English translation © 2010 VIZ Media, LLC

HAIKASORU
Published by
VIZ Media, LLC
295 Bay Street
San Francisco, CA 94133

www.haikasoru.com

Ogawa, Issui, 1975-
  [Sixth continent. English]
The next continent / Issui Ogawa ; translated by Jim Hubbert.
    p. cm.
"Originally published in Japan by Hayakawa Publishing, 2003."
ISBN 978-1-4215-3441-1
I. Hubbert, Jim. II. Title.
PL874.G37S5913 2010
895.6'35--dc22

                                                              2010001667

The rights of the author of the work in this publication to be so identified have been asserted in accordance with the Copyright, Designs and Patents Act 1988. A CIP catalogue record for this book is available from the British Library.

Printed in the U.S.A.
First printing, May 2010

CONTENTS

———◆◆◆◆◆———

BOOK I:
FEASIBILITY STUDY AND DRAFT PLAN, 2025

BOOK II:
ENGINEERING EQUIPMENT, TRANSPORT, AND SITE PREPARATION, 2029–2033

BOOK III:
FINAL SHAKEDOWN, 2036–2037

BOOK I

FEASIBILITY STUDY AND DRAFT PLAN, 2025

CHAPTER 1
PROJECT SITE AND INITIAL PLANNING

[1]

A SERIES OF distant booms reverberated through the bridge of the deep submergence shuttle *Leviathan*. Startled out of a light doze in the rear jump seat, Sohya Aomine opened his eyes. "What's that?"

"It's a school of *anguiras*, sir."

The pilot pointed toward the quartz viewport from his seat at the controls. Countless thousands of bizarre fish the size of a finger were swarming up from the depths.

"Eel fry, sir. In Japan we only see the adults. They say the breeding grounds are in the Mariana Trench. What are they doing way out here? This is amazing."

The pilot was struck with wonder at the hordes of willow-shaped fingerlings flooding through the cone of light from the ship's halogens and back into the inky darkness. Sohya glanced around the bridge uneasily. "No, that's not what I meant."

"I'm sorry?"

"Didn't you hear that?" said Sohya.

"They're striking all over the hull. Sounds a bit like rain, doesn't it?"

"No. There was something else." Sohya listened closely. The sound

11

that had awakened him, almost like the low-frequency pealing of a temple bell, seemed to have vanished. Or maybe it was back, like a distant echo? Switching his attention momentarily to the shower of fish outside had left him disoriented. "I'm going to have a look aft."

"You shouldn't miss this, sir. We may be the first to witness it."

"We had to use ultrasound to keep those things away during construction." Sohya grinned at the astonished pilot and went into the passenger cabin.

Leviathan's forty VIPs seemed to have settled in following the excitement that had prevailed during boarding. Half of them dozed or looked about to nod off. The rest perused magazines or chatted quietly with seatmates. They seemed little different from airline passengers, blithely unaware of the hostile environment just outside the metal walls of the compartment. Everything in the windowless cabin seemed peaceful. With no portholes, there was no view; there would have been nothing to see anyway. *Leviathan* was two thousand meters beneath the surface.

Looking good, thought Sohya with a sense of satisfaction. If this nervous group of VIPs could feel so relaxed, the transition to commercial operation should be trouble free. A group of elementary school students would be hard to keep quiet in this environment, but otherwise the experience seemed unlikely to spark anxiety in the average traveler.

Sohya looked toward the rear of the cabin and stopped in surprise. In the last row, at the end of a long line of heads showing above the roomy seats, a small white beret peeked out, almost concealed by the head of the passenger one row forward. *A child? What's going on...* Then Sohya remembered that children hadn't been banned—just not invited, as far as he knew. *She must be with one of the VIPs.* A thatch of snow-white hair rose above the next backrest. Yes, someone else must have brought her along. Nothing to worry about.

In point of fact, there should have been nothing to worry about at all, at least not from Sohya's standpoint. His employer was Gotoba Engineering & Construction, the builders of Dragon

Palace. Sohya did not answer to the five-nation development consortium that operated the undersea facilities and the shuttle subs. Operational safety was the responsibility of the consortium, which at this precise moment meant the pilot. Safety had been a priority in the shuttles' development and construction long before the first weld. And even had Sohya been prone to worry, he was in no position to fix a mechanical problem under two kilometers of ocean.

Still, the twenty-five-year-old engineer could not shake a feeling of apprehension. Sea trials had gone smoothly, and the vessel was no longer his responsibility, but he still felt that this was his boat. In any case, he was not heading for Dragon Palace to attend the soft-launch party. The last inspection before handoff would occupy every available minute of his time. Right now he had a glitch to track down.

He refocused his attention and moved slowly down the aisle toward the rear of the cabin. A well-dressed male passenger in the second row—Sohya guessed he was a member of the Philippine delegation—looked up. "When does coffee service begin, please?"

"I'm sorry, the soft drinks distributed before boarding were the only service on this run. Drinking water is available anytime." Sohya gestured to a small dispenser recessed into the seat back in front of the passenger, whose silent frown suggested he had been expecting more than tap water.

Sohya continued down the aisle at a measured pace, wondering if bringing stewards would have been a good idea, but in a moment his attention returned to the sonic anomaly.

Leviathan's layout was straightforward: bridge forward, passenger compartment in the center, power plant aft. Nearly all of the ship's machinery and control hydraulics were contained inside her twenty-one cylindrical meters of high-tensile steel. Two rudder propellers projecting from the stern provided the only source of propulsion and steering. This seamless, primitive shape was required if *Leviathan* was to withstand the two-hundred-atmosphere overpressures at this depth. Her only means of ascent and descent were the ranks of ballast tanks arranged in three independent arrays—forward, amidships, and aft—along the underside of the vessel. Compressed air injected into the tanks expelled seawater and provided positive buoyancy; drawing water in to expel the air brought the sub lower. Other than the turbopump for compressed air, the sub's buoyancy system used no machinery of any kind.

This streamlined, compact design was not without its drawbacks. Compared to a thruster-equipped submarine, response was slow and pitch control limited at best. The design was adequate for the stable, slow currents of the deep ocean, but three passengers moving forward or aft was enough to affect the sub's trim. Providing drinking water at the seats would hopefully limit movement about the cabin. Sohya's leisurely pace was also intended to ease the pilot's efforts to maintain trim.

Sohya was concerned that the sonic anomaly he heard might signal a design flaw. Gotoba Engineering had acquired the basic design for *Leviathan* and her sister ships—*Kraken* and *Sea Serpent*—from Mitsubishi Heavy Industries, with modifications and design enhancements implemented during construction. The original plans were meant for shallow-water undersea tourism at one hundred meters or less. For deep submergence, passenger viewports were eliminated, and the hull material was switched to the same dependable high-performance alloy used in the outer shell of the Palace domes. The real challenge was building a compressor capable of forcing air into the ballast tanks at ambient pressures far greater than those near the surface. A solution was finally found by licensing hydrogen-turbine technology developed for rocket engines.

The Mitsubishi engineer assured Sohya that the turbine design had been verified by multiple tests to destruction (in other words, explosion) and was thoroughly reliable. Sohya was not completely convinced. In fact, compressor problems had detained *Leviathan* in port for three hours today after her sisters departed.

Still, even if they were actually forced to halt and wait on the sea floor, two identical vessels were available for rescue operations. The passenger compartment was designed as an independent unit; no critical power or control circuits were routed through that section of the boat. A blue whale could rest on the compartment without causing a leak. Whatever the origin of that sound, it was not a matter of life or death—at least in theory. But Sohya could not afford to be complacent. He knew too much.

Only one man-made structure is fail-safe: the structure no one builds. Any existing structure is inevitably subject to failure. Years earlier, Sohya had heard an English automotive engineer drily make this observation, and with these words echoing in his mind, he reached the rear of the passenger compartment and the door to the aft service area.

As he put his hand on the latch, he was stopped by a pure, high voice, like the strings of a harp.

"I saw the sound. Right here." He glanced down to his right. A pair of sparkling round eyes, like a puppy's, met his.

It was the girl. Her large pupils in the shadow of long lashes were calm, open, and direct. Straight black hair flowed out from under her beret, framing smooth white cheeks and falling almost to her waist. A black sailor jacket with a broad white collar, a white flared skirt, ankle socks, spotless loafers. The overall effect, down to the beret, suggested the uniform of some private academy. She sat with knees aligned, one small, balled fist resting on them. To all appearances, a girl of good family, perhaps twelve or thirteen years old.

Sohya took three of the five seconds of silence that ensued to observe and draw conclusions. The other two seconds went into analyzing the girl's statement, but he still had no idea what she might mean.

"What's this all about?" he answered at length. The girl pointed to the water dispenser with a graceful flick of the finger.

"I saw the sound right there."

"What sound?" Without thinking, Sohya had raised his voice. He glanced quickly around. None of the passengers seemed to have noticed. He leaned forward and said quietly, "What kind of sound did you hear?"

"Booming sounds. Like someone kicking an empty oil drum."

"Why are you telling me this?"

"Oh...didn't you leave the cockpit because you saw it too? You came back here right after it happened." She looked down at the floor, contrite, but Sohya nodded. The timing matched. She must have heard the same sounds. He hadn't imagined them.

"Look, thanks for letting me know. Do me a favor, okay? Let's not tell anyone." He started to enter the service compartment but was stopped again, this time by the old man.

"Just a minute, my friend. I don't think my granddaughter is finished yet."

Sohya winced. "I'm sorry, I'm really in a hurry." The old gentleman had a neatly trimmed white beard to match his thick hair and was dressed in a white three-piece suit accented by a red bow tie. He reminded Sohya of the life-size mannequins found outside a certain chain of fast food restaurants in Japan. As if to complete the effect, the old man was wearing the right sort of heavy, black-framed glasses. Despite his somewhat loud attire, he had an air of refinement similar to the girl's.

Sohya hadn't changed his tan Gotoba work jumpsuit in three days and was starting to feel a bit out of place. But this was no time to defer to wealth. "I'll come back when I'm done and you can tell me all about it."

"Now look here, young man. This little girl's ears are quite sharp. Or shall we say, her sense of pitch. Either way, it will pay to hear what she has to say. You have my personal guarantee."

"I'm not sure who I'm speaking to here, but—"

The man cut him off. "Go on, Tae. You heard something that worried you, isn't that right?" He gave her hand a squeeze. Sohya felt himself sliding toward a confrontation when the girl spoke up.

"Grandfather, don't be so insistent. I think this man has important business to take care of." She lowered her eyes timidly again.

Now Sohya was trapped. He sighed and squatted next to her seat. "Okay, I'm listening."

"Very good, young man. A true gentleman always bends to the requests of women."

"Don't preach, Grandfather," said the girl. Then to Sohya: "Thank you. I know you must be very busy."

He bowed slightly, caught up in the formality. Then something the girl had said struck him. "You said you saw the sound, not heard it. What did you mean?"

"Of course I heard it. But I saw the little faucet shake too."

Sohya stared at the push-button water dispenser in front of her. Below the faucet was a simple cup tray. The faucet operated only with a cup in the tray, but water would continue flowing as long as the button was depressed. The system was not protected by an antivibration compensator. But why would it be? And why would the faucet move enough to be visible to the naked eye?

"Do you see it shaking now? The ship's drive makes things vibrate a little too, you know," said Sohya.

"No. That's different. When I heard the sound, the faucet shook ever so slightly."

"Are you sure?"

"I'm sure. I know what I saw." Tae peered at him intently. For a few moments, Sohya searched his mind for an answer. The pipes feeding the water dispensers extended under the compartment floor into the rear service area. From there they junctioned to a pipe that rose to the ceiling, where the water tank was installed. There was no pump, no control valves—the whole system was gravity fed. To simplify sanitation maintenance, the pipes were separate from the electrical conduits and climate-control systems. If some sort of impulse were traveling down those pipes, it meant the tank was involved.

Sohya turned this over in his mind. *The water tank...how did we implement that, anyway?*

Mitsubishi's original shallow-depth plans had storage for a communications buoy where the water tank was now located. When the boat was submerged, the buoy would float topside on a cable tether, giving the pilot a communications link to the sub tender. This was not an option for *Leviathan*, which had to be capable of dives exceeding two thousand meters. Instead, a compact, ultra-low-frequency transmitter was installed on the hull, making communication possible even in the depths of the ocean.

So the tank was installed where the buoy was originally going to be stowed. Was that the problem?

As he considered the possibilities, Sohya froze. There would be some space between the buoy and the compartment walls—enough to accommodate a tiny amount of compression when submerged. At two hundred atmospheres of overpressure, even the ultra-high-strength steel hull would shrink by a few percent. All interior compartments and fittings were designed to take such shrinkage into account.

The tank was attached to the pressure hull. That meant hull shrinkage would directly affect the tank, and the system did not incorporate control valves. There was no overflow outlet. So the tank design did not allow for significant pressure shrinkage; but that was not a flaw. With a bit of free air space in the tank, the pressure would be neutralized.

Still, there was no operating protocol in place for limiting the amount of water in the tank. And if the tank were filled completely…

His thoughts were cut off by a shout coming from a few rows forward. "What the hell?!"

The next moments passed in slow motion. Sohya sprang to his feet and ran. The problem was no longer theoretical. He could hear water gushing under high pressure before he reached the seat of the well-dressed man who had asked for coffee. Perhaps the passenger had decided water would be better than nothing at all; in any case, the moment he pushed the dispenser button, the cork was out of the bottle. Sohya yelled back, "Don't take your thumb off the button! Keep pressing!" At the same time, he reached out for the nearest water dispenser. But he was too late.

"Damn!" The passenger took his thumb off the button. A sharp bang immediately reverberated through the compartment—exactly what Sohya had tried to prevent by opening another escape route for the pressure. *Water hammer!*

Bringing the surging water to a sudden stop created a high-pressure shock wave that propagated throughout the plumbing system in seconds. That transient spike was far outside the design limit of the dispensers. In the next instant, forty faucets in forty seat backs blew out of their sockets, spewing like fire hoses. The compartment was instantly plunged into pandemonium. Some of the passengers tried to escape by climbing up on their seats. A few were literally blown into the aisles as they tried to stand up. Sohya shouted, "Keep calm! We're not flooding!"

No one paid attention. The screaming, praying, and terror continued unabated. He rushed back aft. The girl was holding on to her beret with one hand and trying to divert the water with the other. He reached out to her. "You okay?"

"Yes. My clothes are soaked, but I guess this is one way to do the laundry." She tugged at the hem of her dress and forced a smile. Her unflappable demeanor in the midst of this confusion was contagious. Sohya grinned.

"You're cooler than you look. You think this is the way to do laundry?"

"Not with seawater. But it's fresh..."

Sohya was thunderstruck. A bizarre inspiration flashed through his mind. He turned to the compartment and bellowed:

"Drink it!"

Instant silence. Some of the VIPs stared at Sohya as if he were crazy. He seized the opening.

"Go ahead! It's not salty. It's drinking water. We're not flooding!" A few of the passengers unfroze and began hesitatingly scooping water into their hands.

"He's right!"

"It *is* fresh water!"

"So what's going on? Did someone light up?"

"No sprinklers on board," said Sohya. "Just a plumbing problem. Naturally, smoking is still prohibited."

With this attempt at humor, Sohya managed to gain everyone's attention. He explained that the water tank had overflowed. With only fifty liters in the tank, the water would soon stop. Since the weight of the water was merely shifting from one place to another, buoyancy would be unaffected.

Sure enough, as he was speaking, the flow of water slowed and stopped. The passengers began to calm down. They were distinguished representatives from companies and countries around the world, and no one made a fuss once it was clear there was no danger—other than the one complaint Sohya was expecting.

"I went all the way to Savile Row for this suit. Will I have to ruin a four-thousand-euro suit whenever I use this shuttle?" Again, the coffee service guy. Sohya was appropriately apologetic and promised to ensure that compensation would be made.

Once the passengers had calmed down, Sohya went to the service compartment. A shock strong enough to blow off the faucets would not have affected the pressure hull, but the tank had to be checked. As he passed the last row, Tae's grandfather spoke up.

"Mind if we take a look?"

"Be my guest," Sohya answered stiffly. He was not used to looking after passengers but was too tired to object. He opened the door to the service compartment and walked past the circuit boxes and CO_2 scrubbers toward the back of the small room. He stared up at the tank. It was a simple sheet metal box, but the sides had ballooned outward, as if something had detonated inside it. Tae stood next to him, gazing up and nodding. "So that noise was the sound of this box expanding. I'm sorry," she said.

"For what?"

"I should have told you sooner. Then no one would've gotten wet."

"You don't have to apologize. I should've at least tried to make sure *you* didn't get wet."

"No need to take it so hard," said the old man. "You're not one of the crew, are you?"

"No. I'm with Gotoba Engineering. We built Dragon Palace and the three shuttles."

"Then this isn't your problem. Well, no—I guess it is. But it's not important. You handled the situation perfectly. 'Drink!' That was a stroke of genius. 'Drink!'" The old man laughed briefly. "And your name?"

"Sohya Aomine. I work for Gotoba's Engineering Task Force."

"I'll remember that. Let's be going, Tae."

"Yes, Grandfather."

The old man took the girl's hand, and they headed for their seats. Sohya called after them, "I'm sorry, but who are you?"

"Oh, you'll see us again soon enough. Who we are isn't important right now. Perhaps you'd better get your passengers some towels?"

This obvious measure had escaped Sohya completely. He hurriedly returned to the passengers to explain how to access the blankets under their seats. Back on the bridge, he met a barrage of questions from the pilot, who had had to stay at the controls throughout the entire incident.

By the time Sohya finished his explanations, *Leviathan*'s navigation lights had pierced the darkness to reveal a number of gigantic egg-shaped domes laid out in a geometric pattern on the ocean floor. It was Dragon Palace, the multipurpose undersea city of the Spratly Islands.

[2]

TWO THOUSAND KILOMETERS south of Japan, in the South China Sea between the Philippines and Vietnam, an archipelago of more than 650 reefs, atolls, and islands lay like pebbles scattered across the ocean surface. Since the end of World War II, the Spratly Islands had been the focus of a struggle for territorial rights between China, Taiwan, Vietnam, the Philippines, and Malaysia.

The prize at stake was not the insignificant bits of land peeking out above the sea. It was the vast, deep-ocean oil fields in the surrounding waters. The islands had been used as an anchorage since the time of Ming dynasty Fleet Admiral Zheng He, and China's territorial claims were the most insistent. The Chinese had surveyed the area and estimated that it held as much as two hundred billion barrels of oil, nearly as much as Saudi Arabia's known reserves. In fact, since the end of the twentieth century, Malaysia had been producing millions of cubic feet of natural gas every day from offshore platforms. That enormous treasure lay beneath these waters was a certainty.

During the first two decades of the twenty-first century, oil had become increasingly precious, and friction between the five nations surrounding the Spratlys had intensified. They began competing to build structures on the islands, and occasional exchanges of gunfire erupted between rival patrol boats. In 2018, after eighty-five crewmen died when a Chinese frigate exchanged fire with a Philippine missile cruiser, the five nations decided the situation had become too dangerous.

By this point, the overall international political climate had turned toward reconciliation and cooperation. The wars between the United States and the Islamic world during the first decade of the century had subsided after an undignified American retreat forced on the president by public opinion. Since then, use of military force in pursuit of national aims had fallen out of sync with the international political climate. No matter how great the value of the Spratlys' oil, the idea of going to war over it was unacceptable. The five nations agreed to set aside long-held grudges and find a path to peaceful cooperation. They formed a joint consortium to develop the Spratlys, and after casting about for a way forward, they agreed to start with a joint construction project that had no connection with resource exploitation. The project would serve as a symbol of their commitment to avoid armed conflict.

The consortium issued a call for competitive submissions from urban planners and civil engineers around the world. Proposals ranged from amusement parks and resorts to a peace memorial, a network of enormous spans to link the islands, and even an eight-hundred-meter observation tower looking out over mostly empty ocean. The winning proposal was Dragon Palace, Gotoba Engineering's vision of a multipurpose undersea city.

Officially, there were two reasons for choosing Gotoba. Because of the islands' stunning coral atolls, many of the proposals related to tourism. But the Gotoba plan was unique in combining surface recreation with an undersea leisure facility. As Gotoba's planning division put it: "Close by the shallow waters surrounding the islands, the continental shelf drops off to a depth of two thousand meters. Along with the coral and aquatic life of the atolls, these deeper waters contain rarely seen abyssal fauna. Research into these little-known life-forms can only be carried out here."

The second reason was that the undersea facility could be useful for surveying the sea bottom. In addition to the three passenger shuttles, Gotoba's plans for Dragon Palace included a long-range commercial exploration sub. The combination of undersea base and exploration sub would allow detailed exploration of seabed resources, an endeavor difficult to coordinate from the surface.

There was also a hidden agenda behind the Spratly Islands Development Consortium's selection of Gotoba's proposal: the desire to exclude Western companies, which submitted more than half of the proposals, from any involvement. Even if they could no longer rely on military power to help enforce the spread of globalization, the West was still wedded to the old economic strategy: seize any opportunity to tie national markets into a global network for the ultimate benefit of a small number of investors. To combat this, Japan was the perfect partner—a diplomatic superpower that had abandoned its experiment with militarism, had preserved its constitutional commitment to peace, and was strictly neutral. Construction had begun in 2021. The project had three main components. The first, subject to careful environmental assessment, was expansion of the diving resort on Swallow Reef to accommodate more tourists and researchers. The second component was mooring facilities for the shuttle subs, complete with a floating dry dock. Finally, the undersea city: seven thirty-meter domes, two kilometers down on the seabed and five kilometers off Swallow Reef.

Once construction began, another reason for choosing Gotoba Engineering became clear to the consortium: no other company could have handled the job.

Drawing on the expertise of engineers who had precisely positioned the anchorages for the world's longest suspension bridge in the fast-flowing currents of Japan's Inland Sea, Gotoba's engineers placed the six-hundred-ton footing blocks for the domes on the seabed without breaking a single stalk of coral. In a mere six months, they completed the floating dry dock for maintenance and repair of *Leviathan* and her sisters with components and materials sourced exclusively from the consortium partners, accommodating their different languages and commercial customs in the process. To oversee this task, Gotoba tapped a maritime logistics expert who, during the Persian Gulf War, had managed the routing of tankers from the North Sea and the Gulf to Japan without delaying a single liter of oil.

But the real tour de force was the placement of the seven domes on the seabed. The domes were built in Japan, sealed, and towed all the way to the Spratlys. The sight of these enormous concrete structures moving through the ocean like icebergs was unforgettable. But when Gotoba's handpicked team deployed a five-thousand-ton sea crane to place the domes on their footings with an accuracy of fifty centimeters—controlling everything from the end of two kilometers of cable—the consortium knew it had witnessed a superhuman feat of engineering. After the two-week operation was completed, Gotoba's project supervisor just smiled. "The submerged tube tunnels in Tokyo Bay became our reference point. Those tubes were laid over the Yurakucho Layer. That's softer than tofu. We had to take our competitor's senior engineer out to the best club in Ginza. The evening cost us a fortune, but what he told us was enough to tweak our approach."

Gotoba Engineering & Construction Co., Ltd. What sort of entity was it? How did it assemble such a crack team of engineers? How did it develop its techniques? As the rest of the world began to sit up and take notice, people were astounded at what they discovered.

Gotoba was behind the enormous Sahara Regreening Sector project—complete with an artificial precipitation generator—in a region where year-round humidity stood at zero. Gotoba erected the pitchblende refining facility for uranium extraction on Antarctica's East Ongul Island, where temperatures fell below minus forty degrees. They designed and built the year-round Upper Atmosphere and Cosmic Ray Observation Facility on the Abruzzi Spur of K2—the world's second-highest peak, in the Karakoram—with a twenty-five-kilometer aerial tramway access system that boasted a 4,400-meter free span between ropeway towers, the world's longest. In the field of extreme-environment engineering projects, Gotoba was matched by no organization on earth.

The company's president was fifty-seven-year-old Takumichi Gotoba. Born toward the end of Japan's high-growth era, he majored in earth science at Kyoto University. In the early 1990s, during the heyday of Japan's economic bubble, he joined a top construction firm. After working on planning for some of the futuristic projects that were so commonly proposed in those heady days, he quit and spent the next three years networking a broad range of movers and shakers inside and outside the industry.

In 2000, he founded the company that bore his name. Since then, this brilliant manager had applied his formidable expertise in civil engineering and applied technology, as well as his carefully nurtured personal connections, to build a leading specialist construction company in a mere twenty years.

As Dragon Palace approached completion, it came to light that the Taiwanese representative for the Spratly Islands Development Consortium had known Gotoba well during his days as a foreign student in Japan—they had bunked together in a tiny apartment for two months because the man was penniless. This fact was kept out of the papers, but no one in the consortium viewed it as a conflict of interest. It was obvious that Gotoba Engineering was the only entity capable of carrying the project to a successful completion.

Now Dragon Palace, a symbol of five nations' desire for peace, was about to go into operation far beneath the South China Sea. The next chapter in the Gotoba saga was about to begin.

———◦•◦•◦———

LEVIATHAN QUIETLY SETTLED into the docking trench in the seafloor below Dome I, the gateway to the complex. The sub's two-hour journey ended when sixty air lock bolts snapped into place around its debarkation hatch. Submersible robots moved around the ship, examining the hull. Eventually, shuttles would be able to use an air lock dock in Dome VII, which was still being outfitted. This would allow manned maintenance at normal atmospheric pressure.

Sohya was first off the sub. He hurriedly briefed the waiting hospitality representatives—all in Hawaiian shirts to add to the resort atmosphere—on the unwanted cold shower the guests had just endured and ensured they would have first-class treatment at check-in. Then he quickly left. He had much more on his plate than leis and towels.

First he buttonholed one of the shuttle operations personnel to inform her of the incident. Next he visited the tourism manager to describe the unusual sighting of eel fry on the way to the complex. Then he made his way to the environmental control room to request a manned inspection of *Leviathan* by surfacing the boat ahead of schedule in Dome VII. But he was rebuffed by the supervisor on duty, who objected that there was not enough atmosphere in the dome to carry out the procedure.

All three subs faced the same danger, but the best way to address the problem was to carefully inspect the vessel where the problem occurred. Sohya's background was architectural engineering, but since joining Gotoba, he had been force-fed a wide range of knowledge from other engineering disciplines, and he knew that a submarine was a structure with a far lower safety index than a building. A well-designed building might be immediately usable after a major earthquake, but a submarine was different. He was determined to perform an inspection.

As he argued his case with the Malaysian supervisor, they were joined by Takasumi Iwaki, a short, tough-looking middle-aged man wearing a Gotoba uniform. He said brusquely, "Where've you been, Aomine? I've been looking all over for you."

"Mr. Iwaki, we have a problem. The water tank design is flawed. I want to do a visual inspection of the hull."

Iwaki was the head of Gotoba's Special Projects Task Force and Sohya's boss. The task force was a standing unit responsible for assembling and managing specialists from other departments for unusually challenging projects. Though it was small and independent, the task force held division status, and its members were known as Gotoba's "shock troops" for their rapid-response capability. As chief, Iwaki was naturally endowed with formidable intelligence. After hearing the bare details of the problem from Sohya, he nodded and raised his wrist to tap out calculations on the touch panel of his wearable computer. After a few moments he looked up.

"We brought one of the power units down early. The electrolytic oxygen generator is already in place. Use the spare power to generate atmosphere and get the rest of the water out of the dome. Keep the O_2 tanks in reserve. It'll take you twelve hours, but the VIPs are spending the night anyway."

The environmental control supervisor started sputtering. "Are you sure? We aren't scheduled to run the full power output test till just before oil exploration starts. If you do it now, you'll scramble my whole timeline."

Iwaki stared at him calmly. "Better to get it out of the way. It'll make things easier later. Just move your timeline forward."

"But that will throw us out of sync with the entire—"

"It's fine. I've already reconciled the plan." Iwaki held out his wearcom for the supervisor to see. The man groaned.

"Okay, everything fits. But the plan has more than two thousand dependencies. How...?"

"Gotoba knows how to handle changes on the spot. This is routine. Leave it to us. All you have to do is follow the revised master plan and open Dome VII."

The supervisor pulled out his phone—Iwaki had already emailed him the new timelines—and began contacting his counterparts in Materials Supply and Operations. Iwaki pointed to the exit. "I'll handle this. Better get moving."

"To Dome VII?"

"No. Dome V, the theater. The president's looking for you."

"Gotoba?" Sohya gulped. "What does he want with me?"

"I didn't know before, but I do now. It must be about your little incident. Just be careful."

Sohya gulped again. "Okay." He hurried toward the tube that gave access to the other domes.

The theater on the first floor of Dome V was the largest single space in the complex. As the name implied, its main purpose was for screening films, but it could also be used for staging plays, as a restaurant, or as an event space.

Today the theater was hosting a party to celebrate the completion of major work on the complex. Sohya and Iwaki still had a daunting amount of work ahead of them, but the hotel dome, deep-sea aquarium dome, and convention dome had already begun operations. As he walked into the theater, Sohya saw more than a hundred guests from the consortium nations enjoying a stand-up meal. Some of the passengers from *Leviathan* were there too. Apparently the hotel's express dry cleaning services were up and running.

Sohya spotted Gotoba almost immediately. He was standing in the center of the room, a broad-shouldered, vigorous-looking man with a drink in one hand. When Sohya saw him with the old man and the little girl from the shuttle, he understood why Gotoba was looking for him.

Since joining the company, Sohya had spoken to the president scarcely half a dozen times. He nervously fastened the top button of his uniform and approached.

"Mr. Gotoba? I'm Aomine."

"Ah, there you are." Gotoba smiled at him broadly. Sohya did not relax. The president was known for putting people at ease before suddenly lowering the boom. Rumor had it that real praise was dispensed with a word or two and little expression; that was when you knew he really meant it.

"Mr. Toenji here tells me you showed some quick thinking on the shuttle today. I'm proud of you."

"Thank you," Sohya answered.

"Do you have a solution worked out?" Gotoba was still smiling, but Sohya sensed that a casual answer would not do. He paused, then said calmly, "A temporary overflow outlet to limit the level of water in the tank. These will be installed on all three vessels right away. Once the shuttles are on the surface, we'll add proper drainpipes and pressure gauges, followed by another round of sea trials."

Sohya thought that would be enough, but Gotoba's expression did not change. He was a scientist as well as a businessman. Clearly Gotoba had an answer of his own already. Sohya hurriedly added, "And before we leave, we'll upgrade all the insulation on the nearby circuits. The water from the overflow outlet could cause a 220-volt short. That would be hazardous."

"Yes, that should do it." Gotoba cocked an eye at Sohya and nodded expressionlessly. So the rumor was true. A moment later Gotoba's jovial expression was back. He turned to the old man. "See? Everything's under control. No need to worry about the trip home."

Toenji smiled. "Goodness, we're not worried," he said with a casual wave of his hand. "I've heard about your company and its achievements. It seems the reputation is well earned. The most advanced technology, the best people. If that's the case, I might even be able to use you."

"Well, thank you for that," Gotoba replied with a smile. "What did you have in mind?"

"Oh, it's right up your alley. I need you to build me a structure. Very difficult location. Only Gotoba Engineering can handle it."

"What kind of location? We've worked in blistering heat and freezing cold, at high altitudes where a man can hardly breathe, and deep in the ocean under crushing pressure. I was looking forward to a slightly less challenging setting for our next project," Gotoba said, still smiling.

"Then I'm sorry. My project has all of those things." Toenji seemed to be joking, and Gotoba was about to repay the favor when he noticed the old man's eyes twinkling strangely.

"All of them?" asked Gotoba.

"Correct. Temperature from minus 120 to plus 160. Atmospheric pressure, oh, a hundred-billionth of that at sea level. It's the kind of place where I'll need your help."

"I don't understand."

"Tae?" Toenji looked down at the girl, who was holding a glass of orange juice. With her free hand, she pointed at the ceiling. "There!"

They all glanced up. The ceiling was fiber-reinforced concrete, with a blown ceramic surface. Gotoba and Sohya were baffled.

"The moon." Toenji smiled, as if enjoying a particularly choice joke. "Care to consider it?"

Gotoba and Sohya stared at each other, speechless.

[3]

THE DOOR OF the airbus opened. From the moment Sohya stepped out onto the moving walkway, he was immersed in hot, humid air and the faint smell of foliage. Light perspiration immediately started under his long-sleeved shirt. He murmured to himself, "Summer in Japan..."

"Huh?" said Iwaki, a few steps ahead of him. He looked back at Sohya, who was wiping the nape of his neck with a handkerchief.

"The smell. The humidity. I notice it every time I step off the plane. It's nice to be home, but it's not exactly Swallow Reef, is it?"

"You smell something?" answered Iwaki. "You're pretty sensitive." He began sniffing the air intently. Sohya walked past him toward Customs and Immigration. Maybe the smell was a trick of his senses, but the air enclosing him was like a steaming towel. The only other place he'd encountered this kind of humidity was the Amazon.

He felt the sense of homecoming again at the immigration gate, which was little different from the wicket in a train station. Armed security personnel were a thing of the past. Japan had managed to break free from the endless economic competition between Asian nations that had reigned during the late twentieth century. It maintained its primacy in industrial technology through national commitment. There must have been hidden broad-spectrum cameras, metal detectors, and other high-tech observation devices all over the airport. But to the eye of the visitor, there were no heavy-handed security arrangements. Even though the world as a whole had become a much safer place, the atmosphere around the gate struck Sohya as especially peaceful.

"Eyes, please." The immigration officer leaned out of her glass booth at the gate and held a device like a cordless shaver in front of Sohya's face. The device trilled softly as it scanned his retinas, and an ID number came up on the display in the booth. The officer glanced at the screen, pulled Sohya's passport from the slot below the display, and held it out with a smile. "Welcome home."

The whole procedure was almost as simple as buying something in one of the convenience stores that used to dot every city block in Tokyo, but Iwaki always bridled at the inefficiency of it. Over Sohya's shoulder, he muttered, "Airports should catch up with the times. When I ride the train, all I do is walk through a gate, a high-resolution camera scans my face, and the fare comes out of my account."

"Not good enough for an airport," said Sohya. "Those systems miss one or two faces in a thousand. Japan Rail loses a few yen, but in an airport it could mean missing a terrorist or letting someone enter illegally."

"A human can recognize a face even if the traveler shaves his head," added the officer. "And we don't malfunction. Eyes, please." She held the scanner up before Iwaki, who muttered that machines make mistakes because the people who build them make mistakes.

"And that, Takasumi Iwaki, is why we use machines *and* people here. Have you lost a little weight?" The officer looked from Iwaki to the video in his passport. Iwaki frowned. "Too much spicy food."

The officer smiled. "Welcome home." She held out the passport.

"See? People are necessary. Who wants to be greeted by a machine?" quipped Sohya, and turned to the officer. "Is the air conditioning down? It feels like thirty-two degrees in here."

"It's cold in the plane. We're at twenty-nine degrees. If it hits thirty, the air conditioning comes on. We apologize."

"So it's like this outside?" pressed Sohya.

"Yes, we're just using the ventilators. Mustn't waste energy. Next, please."

Sohya exited the gate, slightly surprised. So the smell was coming from outside after all. It suddenly occurred to him that he'd always passed through this airport in winter. The winds blowing off China washed gently over New Haneda International Airport, floating in Tokyo Bay off Odaiba.

The men picked up their baggage and headed for the monorail station, but the walkway to the platform was blocked by construction. They stepped outside the terminal. Sure enough, the temperature difference was negligible. Paradoxically, the roar of jets arriving and departing from the airport's two runways almost made it seem cooler.

Looking northwest toward the center of the city, they saw what appeared to be a forest of gigantic, moss-covered tombstones topped by flashing red aerial warning beacons. Beginning around 2015, the practice of sheathing high-rise buildings with living vegetation had become widely popular. In addition to cooling the urban heat island and improving energy efficiency, people seemed to like the unusual, beautiful effect.

Sohya and Iwaki walked the short distance to the monorail platform.

"It's not just cool today, is it? They've basically shut the air conditioning off in the terminal. Global warming is trailing off," said Sohya, impressed.

"Here and around the world," answered Iwaki. "It was like this when we changed planes in Hong Kong."

"Climate change was such a big deal when I was little."

"Yes, and because of that things are getting better now. We helped out too, with the Sahara project."

"It would be great if we made a difference," replied Sohya. They boarded the monorail. As the train pulled out of the station, the enormous spaces of Tokyo's waterfront spread out before them.

The construction industry had changed profoundly in the past two decades. Before, construction companies had built buildings, erected bridges and dams, and laid endless miles of asphalt. Nature's domain was carved away, and the human domain expanded ceaselessly. As often as not, self-interest was behind all this development: the interlocking networks of influential people who depended on the profits from construction made sure that it continued unabated.

But that mindset had changed. Of course, the human domain had to expand. Global population growth had slowed, but people in the developing world were seeking more space and a higher standard of living. To give people a better life, farmland, factories, and modern homes continued to be necessities.

Still, construction did not just mean replacing nature with the man-made. The construction industry had the potential to enlarge nature's domain as well. The Sahara project was just one example. Gotoba Engineering had planted huge numbers of drought-resistant plants such as eucalyptus trees, then built a rain-generation facility for irrigation. Today the Sahara was slowly reverting to what it had been before the construction of the pyramids: a vast green region. Some of the inhabitants disliked the new, more humid climate. But across the globe, the flora and fauna that mankind had begun exterminating four millennia ago were beginning to rise again.

This restoration of the planet was not just taking place far from human habitation. It was promoted in the middle of large cities. Sohya watched the metropolis moving past as the monorail slid along, suspended in the air. Houses, buildings, warehouses, and factories were covered with lush foliage. Water-retaining polymer sheeting was widely used as a covering for roofs and walls. It was cheap and durable, and it protected the underlying structure against moisture. And thanks to a well-conceived system of government subsidies for such technology, the polymer was widely used. Protruding from the greenery at uniform intervals were rank upon rank of glittering, silvery purple mirrors pointing toward the southern sky—photovoltaic panels. With an efficiency of better than 50 percent at the earth's surface, these panels provided energy at less than nine yen per kilowatt hour—cheaper than power from an oil-fired power plant—and had become as widespread as foliage sheathing for buildings. Gotoba Engineering did not engage in residential construction, but virtually no structure was built without solar panels.

Political reform had accelerated the industry's transformation. The biggest change was the elimination of fixed electoral districts. Instead of standing for election from defined regions, candidates for the national Diet ran as representatives of local communities. Campaign pledges were posted on the web, and the entire nation voted on each candidate. Regional politics was left to local government instead of the central government using the power of the purse to meddle in local affairs. National office meant responsibility for national issues and diplomacy. Most politicians who relied on personal and financial connections lost their seats, and this led to the extinction of the old construction industry's vested interests and its struggle to gain advantage by backing handpicked elected officials. Politicians who used the industry to funnel funds for wasteful construction to the countryside disappeared from the scene.

Old-school construction companies were unable to survive amid the changes. One after another they went bankrupt. At the same time, environmental and technology projects and the revolution in energy production meant the construction business was healthier than ever. Nimble start-ups able to ride this new wave had grown into large concerns. Gotoba Engineering was one such company. Today, Japan was in the midst of an economic growth renaissance.

Since the completion a year previously of the Edogawa Riverbed Renewal project, which facilitated the treatment of wastewater with microorganisms, the waters of Tokyo Bay had reverted to their original crystalline blue with startling speed. As Sohya gazed out on the sparkling waters, he was struck by how bright the future seemed. Yes, life was good.

Yet, something about the current era smacked of stagnation. Sohya remembered the speech Takumichi Gotoba had given the new employees when he joined the company: construction is progressive. Harmony with nature? By all means. Restoration of the environment? Very necessary. But ultimately, construction means creating the new. Past generations had used this power in a way that harmed the planet. This generation would use that same power to repair the damage.

But what about generations to come? Would they be as active in maintaining and tending the biosphere? If every corner of this little planet were made amenable to human habitation, would the construction industry lay down its tools?

"No," was the president's aggressive answer. "Construction will never end. Even if there are no commissions, we ourselves can create projects. We have the capability to propose, initiate, and execute projects that would be impossible for almost any other organization. The proof stands today in the Sahara, in Antarctica, in the Himalayas. These projects are monuments to the power of human will made real, to the next stage in human history."

Gotoba was famous for bombast, especially when motivating new employees. Probably 80 percent of what he said was exaggeration. Yet as Sohya listened to the president gradually being carried away by his own rhetoric, he was deeply moved. Who knew what they might build next?

Sohya was more than blessed with the passion of youth, but for all that he was still levelheaded by nature. He found much to agree with in Gotoba's words, but those views were only natural for someone in the industry. Others would see things differently. Construction was merely a means to an end. Gotoba and companies like it had a role to play only when people required it. That was what they needed—huge challenges to test the very limits of their ability.

"Hey! We're here." Iwaki shook his shoulder. Sohya opened his eyes. He must have fallen asleep while contemplating the scenery. The monorail's doors stood open at the platform at Shimbashi Station. This new station had just opened eighty meters below the surface of Tokyo Bay.

"Hurry up. Get your things," barked Iwaki.

"Are we transferring here?"

"No—yes, we just pulled into Shimbashi Station. Aomine is with me." Iwaki was in the middle of a telecall on his wearcom even as he stretched on tiptoes and tugged at his luggage in the overhead rack. Sohya was nearly a head taller. He reached up and took down the luggage. "Head office?" he asked.

"Yes. Yes? Yeah, I'm coming straight in. Aomine has to stop off at home."

Sohya leaned toward Iwaki. "I don't have to go home." Iwaki held his hand up for silence. He nodded several times and ended the call.

"Go ahead, go home. Sounds like the meeting is going to take a while. My wife is used to me going straight in."

"I don't have a wife to worry about," protested Sohya.

"Aomine. You've been out of the country for three months. There must be someone waiting for you."

Sohya had never seen this warm, fuzzy side to Iwaki before, but it was wasted on him. They stepped out onto the platform. "Look, no one's waiting for me."

"You're kidding." Iwaki's eyes grew large with surprise behind his thick lenses. "What have you been doing with yourself? In this kind of job, you wake up one day and you're past forty and still single."

"Come on, Mr. Iwaki. How did you find a wife?"

"My wife was in the industry, and we just—look, forget that. Really…so you don't have anyone yet?" Iwaki shook his head. "Just get yourself back home. Repack your bags and come back to the office."

"Excuse me?"

"Looks like we're sending you out to the field again."

"Overseas?" asked Sohya, astonished.

"You could say that," said Iwaki with an odd expression. Sohya stopped.

"What does that mean?"

"That's a direct quote. Don't ask me, I don't know what it means either." Sohya stood for a moment in blank bewilderment. Iwaki clapped him on the shoulder. "Now get going." Sohya ran to catch the train home.

＊＊＊

HE WAS SOON home: an apartment in Ogikubo, on the west side of the vast metropolis. A few minutes later he was back at the station with newly packed bags, but a downed power line had paralyzed the train service. He had no choice but to grab one of the hydrogen-powered cabs that were authorized to use express lanes throughout the city.

As he rushed through the entrance of Gotoba headquarters in Shinjuku, an alert receptionist directed him not to the sixth floor where the task force had its offices, but to the twelfth floor main conference room. *It's something big*, thought Sohya. He usually participated in conferences via the interface at his desk. Face-to-face meetings were strictly for limited-access discussions.

When he reached the floor, he found Iwaki, the other division heads, and President Gotoba huddled in a tight knot at the opposite end of the large room. They seemed to be in the middle of a heated discussion with someone sitting in one of the high-back conference chairs, but the chair was facing away from Sohya.

Noticing him standing near the door, Iwaki quickly strode over, looking impatient and irritated. "What have you been doing?"

"The trains were stopped, so I took a cab. Is the meeting that urgent?"

"New project. Unbelievable."

"We got something big?" Sohya excitedly tossed his bags in a corner. Iwaki motioned him to sit at the oblong conference table, which was equipped with monitors set flush with the surface. Iwaki punched his wearcom, sending data to Sohya's monitor.

"Remember Mr. Toenji?" said Iwaki.

"Toenji..." Sohya was momentarily nonplussed.

"The launch party."

"Ah, right." Sohya nodded. "Mr. Kentucky."

"What are you talking about? He's Japanese." Iwaki raised an eyebrow.

"No, go on. He just reminded me of somebody. So what's going on?"

"Doesn't the name Toenji mean anything to you? Well, I didn't recognize him right away either. He's the chairman of Toenji Group."

"The amusement park Toenji?"

"The amusement park and a lot more." Iwaki pointed to Sohya's monitor, which now displayed the Toenji home page. "The group's main business is their wholly owned subsidiary—ELE, Eden Leisure Entertainment. They run Tokai Eden, the leisure resort near Nagoya. The construction budget was 160 billion yen. They get seven million guests a year. The park is huge. Only Tokyo Disney World and Universal Studios Japan do more turnover. The group has subsidiaries in the hotel and travel business, fast food, magazine publishing, entertainment programming, music, you name it. You must have seen some of their promotions."

"I know Eve and Adam," Sohya answered quickly. "I have a friend who's up on all that stuff. Toenji's characters are more popular in Japan than the ones from overseas."

"They're a major ice-skating sponsor—" Iwaki started to go on, but Sohya rubbed his temples. "What's this about?"

"The group has 1.25 trillion yen in assets. Sennosuke Toenji is the founder and chairman."

"So that's who that old guy was. I'd almost say he doesn't look the part, but then again..." Sohya had a hard time grasping the concept of all that wealth concentrated in one man. The numbers were too large. Iwaki droned on, all business.

"He's fond of scotch and likes to surprise people, but that's not enough reason to travel all the way to the Spratlys, even if he does have the money. Do you remember what he said down there?"

"The moon." Sohya found himself quoting from memory. Iwaki nodded, but Sohya was blank. "So what about it?"

"He wants Gotoba to build a base there," said Iwaki.

"He can't be serious."

"It looks like he is. ELE sent us a formal request." Iwaki punched the keyboard on his left wrist, and the display switched to a document titled REQUEST FOR CONSTRUCTION. "It's not a design solicitation. Nothing specific yet. We don't even know what they plan to do with it. But they did send this. They want a facility to accommodate ten people indefinitely, with future expansion for up to fifty. Feasibility studies, design, development, transport, execution, even initial operations management—they want us to handle everything, in coordination with ELE. The timeline is ten years. The budget is 150 billion yen."

"But...I mean..." Sohya's head was swimming. He held his hands in front of his chest and waved his fingers absently. "Is any of this possible?"

"That's what we're trying to figure out." Iwaki pointed to the group at the other end of the room. The discussion was proceeding more quietly than before.

"We can discuss it, but is it doable?" repeated Sohya.

"Humanity reached the moon decades ago." The deep voice cutting across the room was that of the president. The division chiefs stood around him with expressions ranging from resigned to dazed. One by one, they took seats around the conference table. Gotoba stood at the end of the table.

"I was a year old on July 20, 1969, when Armstrong and Aldrin walked on the surface of the moon. It was possible then. It can't be impossible now." Gotoba spoke slowly and quietly, intent on convincing his listeners. "The Chinese have a small base there already. But everything has been the work of governments, not private enterprise. Our quick review today indicates that this project is well within our reach. Wouldn't you think so, Sando?"

"Well, yes. So it seems." Tetsuo Sando was Gotoba's Technology Development Division chief. He was also a visiting professor at a major institute of science and engineering. Sando stood with one balled fist on the conference room's large display monitor, his face raised toward the ceiling. His eyes were closed. "Near-vacuum conditions. Huge temperature ranges. Ionizing radiation. Extreme conditions of every type. Build and maintain a facility in such an environment? Yes, we have the expertise. Robotic operations, remote surveying, communications, power transmission—we're very comfortable operating remotely via telepresence. We have experience building special-application construction equipment from the Spratly project. Obviously we would have no energy-supply problems. Solar radiation will be intense and abundant, with no intervening atmosphere to speak of.

"The question is transport. We need more time to study this, but concrete can be produced using surface material, so the heaviest and bulkiest of the necessary construction materials is up there waiting for us. Sending payloads into space has become fairly routine. I think current launch vehicles can lift payloads up to around twenty tons. Assume twenty-ton payloads of materials and machinery. Planning should not be difficult. Yes, twenty tons will do nicely. Gravity is one-sixth of Earth's, so we won't need heavy-lift equipment."

Sando lowered his head—what hair he had left had gone completely gray—and opened his eyes. He stated crisply, "I would say this project is feasible."

"There it is," said Gotoba as he surveyed the room. "To build a base on the moon. What a project!"

Not *construct*. Build. Suddenly everyone in the room understood. In the mind of this man of rare imagination and dynamism, equipment was already crisscrossing the moon. The outlines of the base were steadily emerging from the surface. The vision was complete in every detail. His mind was made up. This was how the Saharan, Antarctic, Himalayan, and Spratly projects had started: with a single, definitive statement of unshakable intent.

"This is Gotoba Engineering & Construction's next challenge. I take it there are no objections?"

No one uttered a word of dissent. Far from it—faces relaxed. Some of the division chiefs began shaking with anticipation, the kind of trembling that seizes soldiers before an assault. This was why they had entered the extreme construction field—to execute large, difficult projects. It was what they lived for.

"Then we'll do it!" Gotoba had both hands flat on the table. He exhaled loudly, as if the project were already complete. Suddenly he stared across the room at Sohya. "Aomine!"

"Sir!" Without hesitation Sohya leapt to his feet, back straight. At the next words he nearly collapsed back into his chair.

"You're going to the moon."

"Wha-at?" Sohya's jaw dropped.

"Site evaluation is first. Go see what it's like. As I said, the Chinese have a base there. They send a shuttle up every year to resupply and rotate personnel. The next launch is only a month from now. We'll handle the arrangements. I want you on that shuttle."

"To the—me? Why moon?" Sohya scrambled his grammar in his excitement. "I mean, I'm too junior. There must be someone else. From another division. I don't have the background or the qualifications. It's not that I'm afraid to go. But—"

"Young people get the tough assignments. Your division will lead the charge once things get rolling. And who said you're not qualified? You don't need a diploma to travel to the moon," said Gotoba.

"But, sir, you hardly know me."

"I chose you because I've witnessed what you can do. And Iwaki is not a man to keep anyone but the best under his wing for three years." Having dismissed Sohya's stammered protests out of hand, Gotoba leaned forward abruptly. "Anyway, it's what the client wants."

"Senno—I mean, Mr. Toenji?" The chair that had been facing in the opposite direction the entire time swiveled around. Sohya nearly groaned. "Tae?"

White beret and collar were set off, as before, by the girl's long, jet-black hair. She smiled. "Nice to see you again, Mr. Aomine. My grandfather asked me to go with you. He's too old to travel to the moon. He wants me to travel in his place and see what it's like. Grandfather doesn't want me to go alone, and he was wondering who could go with me. Then we met you. We both agree you're very trustworthy."

"You're going to the moon?" This was really too much for Sohya.

"That's right. It's so interesting—Did you know there's a junior discount for space travel? The less you weigh, the less they charge. For the first time, I'm glad to be kind of skinny."

Gotoba cut in. "The fare for you is two billion yen. Miss Toenji's ticket is a billion. Three billion for two, round-trip. The client is footing the bill. We're counting on you, Aomine."

"Three billion…for a site evaluation…" Sohya lapsed into speechlessness. His silence lasted so long that Gotoba added, as if playing his trump card: "Look, Aomine. If *you* won't go…"

The unspoken part of Gotoba's statement struck home so sharply Sohya thought for an instant he had actually heard it. *If I were you, I would go. In fact, I* will *go.*

There was no way Gotoba could go. He was the heart and brains of the company. And since he could not, he was trusting Sohya with everything. Of course, Sohya could not refuse, nor did he want to.

The power of Gotoba's trust was like a slap that brought his confusion and doubt into sudden clarity. He straightened up. "I'll go."

"Then it's settled." Gotoba nodded with satisfaction. "We'll be working on the details till you get back. I'll expect a comprehensive report."

"Yes, sir."

"Good. This conference is over," said Gotoba. "Get moving!" He slapped the table. Everyone rose to their feet. "Starting now, Gotoba Engineering & Construction will mobilize to build a base on the moon. It will be a ten-year marathon, but we'll see it through, no matter what. Give it everything you've got!"

The roar that came in reply was a chorus announcing the birth of the Next Continent project.

CHAPTER 2
OPERATIONAL STATUS OF EXISTING FACILITIES

[1]

TAE SQUINTED THROUGH the quartz window of the *Chang'e* spacecraft, atop China's Xiwangmu 5 space station module. "I can't see the surface too well. It's all blurry," she said from her perch on Sohya's lap.

"You have to focus both eyepieces," answered Sohya.

"I did. But it's still blurry."

"Here, let me try." Sohya reached for the forty-power Nikon binoculars. He peered over her shoulder toward the lunar surface, adjusting the knobs on each eyepiece and trying to gain a consistent focus at a variety of distances. He got the same results as the girl. The stark black-and-white outlines of craters and valleys slowly scrolling past the window refused to come into focus. Focusing the eyes to compensate just made the strain worse. Tae, her head beneath Sohya's jaw, looked up.

"See?"

"You're right. Maybe it's foggy down there."

"There's no air." Tae giggled. She knew when Sohya was joking. For a thirteen-year-old she was surprisingly mature.

After they had struggled for several minutes with the binoculars, Commander Feng, in the center couch, interrupted his discussion with Flight Engineer Ma and turned to Sohya. "There's a trick to it. Give me those for a minute."

Feng held the binoculars in front of the window and released them. They floated in the free-fall conditions of lunar orbit. With the tip of his index finger, he gently tapped the binoculars two or three times, rotating the focus knob slightly without displacing the instrument.

"Take a look now. Be careful, don't bump them."

It was not clear what he had done, but when Sohya looked through the floating optics, he cried out in surprise. "I can see!"

"Really?" asked Tae incredulously.

"Clear as a bell."

"Let me look!" She raised her head to look through the glasses. Her long hair was gathered into a bun on her head, but her bangs brushed an eyepiece. The binoculars began to rotate slowly. She whined in frustration and grasped them. Sohya said to Feng, "How did you do it?"

"With the naked eye you can see the surface moving slowly under us. Right? But our altitude is one hundred kilometers, and our speed is about 1.73 kilometers per second. That's twice as fast as a rifle round. Looking down with forty-power binoculars is like being 2.5 kilometers from the surface. The angular velocity of your field of vision is magnified by small hand tremors. That's why everything ends up blurred." He moved the tip of his finger around Tae's head. "We're orbiting once every 1.9 hours. Give the binoculars the same orbital period and they'll track the surface for you. Tae, do you think you can do that?"

"Just focus the eyepiece a little, right? I'll try." She parked the binoculars in front of the window and made several attempts to bring the surface into view, using the tip of her finger to rotate the eyepieces, but was unsuccessful. "This is hard!" she pouted. Feng laughed.

"It takes a while to learn. The Russians taught us, but it took us a while too. Manage it before we land and you'll be a certified taikonaut." He went back to his predescent checklist.

Though they were based on a Russian design, the Xiwangmu modules were the pride of China's aerospace program. The China National Space Administration—CNSA—had sourced its manned space technology from the Russians, improved on it, and produced its own spacecraft. The prototype for Xiwangmu was the Soviet Salyut space station module, originally developed in the 1960s for missions to the moon. Thirteen meters long, with a mass of eighteen tons, Salyut was impressively large, but its descendant was more famous: the orbital science station Mir, launched in 1986. Mir consisted of five fourteen-meter cylindrical modules, all based on the Salyut design, arranged around a central spherical docking node. Descendants of Salyut were later incorporated into the International Space Station. It was a classic design, reliable and easily configured.

The key to China's successful construction of humanity's first manned moon base in 2020 was her development of Xiwangmu based on the Salyut design. These large modules offered ample living space and could be used to ferry taikonauts and supplies to the moon, where the modules would be lowered to the surface. In effect, that is what China's lunar base was—Mir modules sitting on the lunar surface. In each of the past four years, China had sent a Xiwangmu to the moon and used it to enlarge the base, which they christened Kunlun. This was Sohya and Tae's destination.

Four days earlier, they had lifted off with the two-man Chinese crew from Jiuquan Launch Center in Inner Mongolia aboard a *Chang'e* spacecraft. The *Chang'e* was also based on a Russian design—*Soyuz*—and carried by a Long March III launch vehicle.

At first, Sohya and Tae's participation in the mission was in doubt. With his usual drive and network of connections, Gotoba set about securing places on *Chang'e*, but was only able to obtain one. And that seemed to be that. Each new Chinese crew relieved those already on the moon and remained there till the next Xiwangmu arrived a year later. But Sohya and Tae were scheduled to return at the first opportunity, which meant that at least one base member would be forced to extend their stay for an extra year. This would create numerous operational complications. For the Chinese to grant permission for even one place on *Chang'e* was a huge concession.

One place on the three-seat spacecraft should have meant one passenger, but thanks to Gotoba's negotiations—and a well-timed cash transfer of three billion yen—the Chinese found a solution. Tae would travel into orbit sitting on Sohya's lap.

At first this seemed absurd. Nothing of the sort would have been possible with NASA, given the Americans' famously strict adherence to procedure. Yet the idea was not that outlandish. Sohya was of average build, and Tae was a slender girl. The Chinese crew members were not very large either. The prototype for *Chang'e* was the *Soyuz TM* spacecraft, and although *Soyuz* was designed for comparatively small cosmonauts, the combined weight of Sohya, Tae, and the two Chinese differed little from that of three Russians. The problem was not the number of passengers but their combined weight.

In the end, it proved easier to proceed than to worry about theory. The launch went flawlessly. The *Chang'e* with four passengers aboard withstood the acceleration and shock of launch and reached Earth's orbit safely. When they arrived there, Xiwangmu 5, successfully launched twenty-four hours earlier, was standing by. Xiwangmu's primary mission at this point was to carry a large payload of supplies to Kunlun. The module was equipped with the detachable second-stage booster needed to insert its considerable mass into a lunar transfer orbit.

Conditions were more comfortable once they docked with the waiting Xiwangmu. Though packed with supplies, it was still far more spacious than their three-couch capsule. The four voyagers went through the forward docking hatch and spent the three-day trajectory to the moon aboard Xiwangmu 5.

The *Soyuz TM* stack consisted of three components: an orbital module, a descent module in the middle, and a service module with engines astern. The *Chang'e* replaced the orbital module with a return module for the journey from the moon to Earth.

Once in orbit around the moon, the spacecraft detached from Xiwangmu, rotated 180 degrees, and redocked with the return module pointing forward. It was then detached and parked in orbit. Once on the surface, *Chang'e* was detached, and Xiwangmu was joined to the other base modules.

To return to Earth, the *Chang'e* from the previous mission was used to reach orbit, where the return module was waiting. This ensured that the base crew had a recently maintenanced spacecraft if an emergency forced them to leave the base.

After using the *Chang'e* service module to reach lunar orbit and dock with the waiting return module, the taikonauts headed back to Earth, where the return and service modules separated and burned up in the atmosphere. On the moon leg of the journey, the *Chang'e* weighed twenty-seven tons; the only thing to reenter the atmosphere was the three-ton descent module.

Now Xiwangmu 5 was in a slightly inclined orbit around the moon, preparing to descend. In case an emergency required them to abort and head back to Earth, the crew had moved from Xiwangmu to the descent module. The stack had rotated 180 degrees, and the return module was parked in orbit. Now *Chang'e* could separate from Xiwangmu at any time. Xiwangmu's slow rotation, necessary to passively distribute solar heat, had stopped. With the descent module's engines pointing in the direction of travel, all that was required now was to fire them for a powered descent.

Commander Feng snapped his checklist binder shut. "Beijing Control, *Chang'e*. Return module separation complete. Ready for powered descent. Request permission to proceed."

Radio waves from *Chang'e* sped toward a trio of data-relay satellites in geosynchronous Earth orbit. Feng's voice was handed off to Beijing Aerospace Command and Control Center, which at this moment was on Earth's far side. These relay satellites allowed communication with Flight Control twenty-four hours a day. For the Apollo missions of the sixties and early seventies, NASA had been forced to construct satellite tracking stations in far-off Spain and Australia to maintain contact with its astronauts when the United States was facing away from the moon.

Ten seconds later—including the three-second lag required for radio waves to make the round-trip—the flight controller replied. "Affirmative, *Chang'e*. You are cleared for powered descent to Kunlun Base."

"Roger. Beginning powered-descent sequence." Feng turned to his passengers. "Ready?"

"Wait!" Tae was looking intently through her floating binoculars. Sohya looked out the window and saw what had caught her attention. On the surface directly below, something glinted at the dividing line between glistening dark volcanic ash and brilliant white lunar surface. Sohya could just make out a tiny cross, like rice grains laid end to end. It was Kunlun Base, in a valley southwest of Mons Hadley on the eastern limb of Mare Imbrium. NASA's *Apollo 15* had landed in this area, and this part of the moon's northern hemisphere was familiar to the Japanese as the space between the right-hand of a pair of rabbits pounding rice paste in a mortar, and the mortar.

"I see it! It's in focus!" cried Tae.

"Beginning powered-descent sequence. Commencing attitude maneuver." Feng engaged the sequencer to increase lateral acceleration. The surface slipped from sight as the stack rotated. Tae puffed out her cheeks in frustration. "Just when I get it to work..."

Feng chuckled. "Too bad, we couldn't confirm it. This one doesn't count. You'll have another chance on the way home." Feng and Ma calmly continued with the landing sequence. "Attitude maneuver complete. Initiating descent burn." Sohya felt slightly pressed into his flight couch. The binoculars landed on Tae's chest and her body took on weight, pressing down on him.

Xiwangmu was moving backward, its engines slowing its orbital velocity.

"First descent burn complete. Surface velocity, 1.6 kilometers per second. Descent angle, nominal."

"*Chang'e*, please confirm correction for Imbrium mascon."

"Beijing Control, I've just sent you the radar altimeter correction factors."

"Thank you, *Chang'e*, we have the data. When is your next burn?"

"Beijing Control, we are looking at initiating next burn in approximately forty-five hundred seconds. Will apply correction just prior to burn. Third burn after ILS acquisition."

"Ah...*Chang'e*, we'd like you to rerun your center of mass and thrust vector calculations with your backup computer. If the solutions are inconsistent, we'll bring you in manually."

"Roger, Beijing Control."

This is routine for them, thought Sohya. The assurance that seemed to pervade the Chinese approach to spaceflight, from adding a passenger to using weightlessness to steady the binoculars, made it hard to believe the Chinese had flown into space for the first time early this century. This was only their fifth manned moon mission, but they had sent astronauts into low earth orbit over twenty times. The payoff in depth of experience was evident.

He glanced at Tae. She seemed to be studying every move Feng was making at the controls. Sohya spoke to her in Japanese. "Scared?"

"A little. Why do you ask?"

"You seem worried about the controls."

"I'm sure the commander knows what he's doing."

So what is she looking at? thought Sohya. *She can't be interested in the flight controls or the hardware.* Over the past month, Sohya had discovered that Tae was extraordinarily precocious for her age, but it was hard to believe she could grasp anything about the functioning of a spacecraft. Even Sohya found it hard to understand.

He could feel the beating of her heart through her back. His own heart was also pounding. Both of them were rather—no, very—tense. Feng and Ma were seasoned veterans, but that wasn't the point. Watching them control the spacecraft's descent was stressful in itself. The procedures were bafflingly complicated. One mistake and they would probably be smashed to bits on the surface or torn apart to float in fragments in space. If not, they'd undoubtedly suffocate. Just thinking about the consequences made calm impossible. Tae must have been thinking the same thing.

They watched silently. The only sounds in the capsule now were those of the commander and the flight engineer as they confirmed each adjustment.

Reducing its orbital speed caused the stack to descend. The only way to do this was to fire the engines directly against Xiwangmu's orbital path. Firing the thrusters directly away from or toward the surface would change the shape of the orbit but would not enable them to land. So the stack was moving backward and firing its engines straight ahead.

Still, touching down was not a simple matter of using the main engines. The distance from first descent burn to landing was several thousand kilometers. With three separate burns, they had descended close to the surface from an altitude of one hundred kilometers. Once Kunlun Base reappeared on the horizon, its guidance signal would be acquired. Then the ship would gradually be brought to a vertical attitude while following the signal in toward the base.

Too close an approach to the base risked collision with the modules, so the landing site was one hundred meters away. Once the stack was positioned over the site, the engines were fired to keep it suspended. The engines would then be gradually throttled back until contact with the surface was made.

The stack was now vertical. As he lay in his flight couch, Sohya felt a hard vibration beneath his back. Tae's body sank into his. Sohya braced to support her thirty-odd kilograms, but just as gravity seemed to have restored a small amount of weight, Commander Feng said crisply, "Touchdown."

Sohya and Tae exchanged glances as they experienced their new weight, different from that on Earth.

"Sohya, I'm not very heavy, am I?"

"You never were, but right now you feel light as a feather."

"Crew IV is here to greet us," said Ma as he switched a monitor to one of the external cameras. Two figures wearing orange space suits were bounding over the surface in large skipping steps. Each odd-looking step covered five meters and lifted them off the surface for two seconds.

"So this is what one-sixth G feels like," marveled Sohya.

"Well, we're on the moon, you know," replied Tae.

Her matter-of-fact response, instead of the excitement one might have expected, made Sohya burst out laughing.

[2]

MAN-MADE SATELLITES first reached Earth orbit in the 1950s. People of that era assumed that by the following century, space exploration would be in full swing. Cities would be built on the moon and Mars. Humanity would travel freely between Earth and space. *Apollo 11* seemed to be the curtain-raiser for the coming space age.

But today, in 2025, fewer than forty astronauts were at work outside Earth's atmosphere. Four out of five were in low orbit—below five hundred kilometers—at the aging and soon to be de-orbited International Space Station or at the barely funded Vardhana Orbital Experimental Facility, operated jointly by the Indian Space Research Organization and the European Space Agency. Of the remaining 20 percent, three were represented by the crew of mankind's first manned mission to Mars, mounted by NASA and JAXA, Japan Aerospace Exploration Agency, in 2023. But the crew had miscalculated their orbital insertion and missed the opportunity for a descent to the surface. Now they were on their way back to Earth, having accomplished little. The final three astronauts in space were the crew of Kunlun.

Humankind's push into the solar system, a dream since the last century, had hardly begun. Two factors were behind the delay.

The first was the daunting expense. America's Apollo program had cost $25 billion in the 1960s. Even in 2000, the cost to put a ton of payload into orbit ranged from four hundred million to one billion yen. Furthermore, the percentage of successful launches was less than satisfactory. Most launch vehicles failed to promise 99 percent safety even on paper, and the real failure rate reached several percentage points. There was certainly little prospect that anything like the one in a million odds of a catastrophic commercial-airline accident could be achieved. Enormous expense had gone into raising the safety margin of launch vehicles to where it was today. New technologies and materials were applied first and foremost to improving safety. Achieving lower operating costs took a backseat. By 2025, the cost to put a ton of payload into a three-hundred-kilometer orbit above the earth was more or less stuck at three hundred million yen.

But there was another factor, more deep-rooted and fundamental, blocking the road to space: the lack of an objective.

Why go there? During the Apollo program, there was a simple answer: to beat the enemy. In the sixties, Khrushchev's Soviet Union and Kennedy's United States were at the height of the Cold War. Rocket development was an urgent priority. That technology would allow direct strikes on enemy targets with nuclear warheads. Even after the development of intercontinental ballistic warheads, the motivation for space development was the pursuit of national prestige. With one launch after another, the two superpowers had embarked on a titanic struggle to seize the advantage. Development leads amounting to little more than a few months shifted back and forth. Ultimately, the Americans pulled away from their Soviet opponents and ended the competition by putting men on the moon.

Skylab. Salyut. The U.S. space shuttle. The Soviet Buran shuttle. Space Station Freedom. Orbital station Mir. Each program, successful or not, represented a boast of national strength carried out with one eye on the other superpower. But this competition had ended along with the Cold War. Other powers—Europe, Japan, India, China—caught up and began fielding their own launch vehicles. In the process, national prestige as a driver began to fade.

But by that point, the energy to reach the moon had already been exhausted.

At the turn of the century, the collapse of the Soviet Union had boosted American power. The anarchic forces of free market capitalism were in full control. Everything was evaluated from the standpoint of costs and benefits, and space exploration could not escape the reigning mood. The basic goals of scientific progress and human advancement fell by the wayside while investment was channeled to launching satellites that promised a return on investment. Internet-communications satellites. GPS satellites for car navigation. Earth-observation satellites for detailed mapping services. Earth orbit was crowded with them.

In contrast, budgets for "unprofitable" scientific missions were cut one after another, and proposals for launching manned missions were regarded as wasteful at best. Construction of the International Space Station, touted as a symbol of East-West cooperation, was delayed at the outset, thanks to Russia's chaotic transition to capitalism. Some even mocked the ISS as a program in search of a concept. Then technical problems forced a gap in the resupply schedule by aging space shuttle and Soyuz spacecraft, and the ISS went unmanned for six months. It was a humiliating setback for a program that boasted it would deliver a continuous presence in space.

Clearly, the problem was the lack of a fundamental justification for space exploration. The barrier was the fact that humans did not truly need to leave their home planet. If funds spent on space programs were channeled to social welfare, education, promotion of international peace, and environmental preservation, the planet would be that much better for everyone. This was the position of the antiexploration faction. It was, without a doubt, a valid position.

The proexploration faction struck back with facts of their own. If making our current habitat more comfortable removed the need to go elsewhere, why did humanity spread across the planet in the first place? Since it had left the forests of Africa two million years ago, the species had constantly been on the move. The Arabs voyaged with their dhows along the coast of Africa to India. The Mongols subjugated Asia. The nations of Europe vied to send ships across the seven seas. The Japanese attempted to expand into Asia as a whole. And all despite having a place to call home. For most of its existence, Homo sapiens had been a species moving ever outward.

But there was a huge hole in this argument. It explained the motivation of those who wanted to keep moving, but it did not justify demanding help from those who preferred to stay home. Each side was talking past the other. The debate always seemed to end in pointless mutual denunciation.

And so time passed, and the species remained earthbound.

But there were those who realized that the entire debate was purely academic. As things stood, they were like islanders without a boat arguing over whether they should visit the next island. If a boat was available, those who wanted to go would go. If cost was an obstacle, all that was required was a profitable boat. With enough boats, even profitless voyages would become a possibility. That is, if there were some way to send humans into space profitably.

People had been making efforts to do that for some time. In 2001 the Russian space agency had sent a self-made millionaire to the ISS for twenty million dollars. This was neither the first nor the biggest deal of its kind. Before that, a Japanese television station had sent a journalist to Mir, and an American soft drink company had offered a ride on a spacecraft as a prize in a sales campaign. Many plans for space tourism, offering anything from a few minutes to a few hours of low-altitude spaceflight, were on the drawing boards in America, Europe, Japan, and elsewhere. Many of these concepts were too far-fetched to be taken seriously, but others were well within the realm of possibility.

A proposal by a Shanghai travel agency probably represented the peak of space-tourism planning. The plan was to send three tourists into space for four orbits—half a day of genuine space-flight—using a launch vehicle and spacecraft supplied by China, which had already mounted six successful manned missions.

Then just before the launch, the plan collapsed. The Chinese government's condition for using the *Chang'e* spacecraft for a civilian flight was that the launch be combined with the testing of a device—a weapon, according to some rumors—that was to be attached to the exterior of the spacecraft. At the last minute, CNSA announced that for reasons of national security, the windows of the capsule would be covered during the flight.

The three space tourists were looking forward to experiencing Yuri Gagarin's famous words—"The Earth is blue. How wonderful…It is amazing"—and refused to accept the Chinese demand. The fare was twenty million dollars, and no one else was willing to pay such a huge sum. And that was the end of the plan.

People around the world who were waiting expectantly to see this concept move forward were extremely disappointed. The dilemma was this: the best technology was controlled by national space agencies with no interest in helping stage pleasure excursions into space. Private enterprise had the dreams and the plans but no spacecraft, and the cost to obtain one was far beyond their means. Few were willing to pay the enormous fees required, and making the business a paying proposition involved walking a very slender tightrope.

The history of commercial spaceflight planning was a succession of concepts appearing and disappearing, of proposals submitted and shot down. A feeling of helplessness began to overtake those who understood the situation even superficially. Perhaps national space agencies and the enormous resources they commanded really were the only way to get off the earth.

For years, resignation continued to spread. Technology advanced, nations grew richer, the time seemed ripe for reinvigorated space exploration, but the experts were unanimous: it was not yet feasible. If only the cost could come down a bit more. If only technology were slightly more advanced. If only people were a little more affluent...

Two lines on the graph—the cost of space travel and what the average person could afford to pay for it—seemed forever poised to cross, but did not. And people who dreamed of a new age waited with a forlorn hope that someone would find a way to make it happen.

But although no one had noticed, the future of space travel was about to arrive.

[3]

A SIMPLE ARM-AND-WINCH arrangement was all that was necessary to lower *Chang'e* onto the lunar surface next to the upright Xiwangmu 5. The operation appeared dangerous but was not unusual for this type of spacecraft. The Russians regularly used a robot arm a few tens of centimeters long to maneuver modules nearly the size of Xiwangmu into place at Mir's spherical docking node.

The four crew members were in their suits and had finished the prebreathing period to avoid decompression sickness. Feng depressurized the command module, and one by one the new arrivals climbed through the hatch and down onto the surface of the moon. Tae was first to emerge, jumping lightly down onto the surface. Feng, Sohya, and Ma followed. Sohya watched as the occupant of the tiny orange space suit raised her arms in a long stretch.

"Wow, that was tough! My joints hurt."

"Those are your first words? The first Japanese to set foot on the moon?"

"What?" Tae turned to look at him. Her large pupils were just visible behind her gold antiglare visor.

"There's live television coverage of everything we say. President Gotoba sold the rights to help pay for the trip."

"Really? But it was so cramped in there." The fact that more than one hundred million people in Japan and around the world might be listening seemed the furthest thing from her mind. When it was decided that the seating arrangements dictated that Tae be the first to climb down onto the surface, Gotoba's PR chief started salivating. He guaranteed huge fees for even a bare audio feed. As it turned out, Tae's first words were likely to generate complaints. The Chinese government, for one, would want to know where she got off calling their spacecraft "cramped."

"This suit is tight and hard too. It pinches. A skirt would've been more comfortable," joked Tae, continuing to blaze a trail through the history of Japanese space exploration with another pedestrian quip. It had cost 15 million yen to modify a Russian Krechet M space suit to fit her. Still, it was not made for comfort. The Krechet was much more flexible than the previous-generation Orlan M suits, but the joint material was better than three millimeters thick—difficult enough for an adult to flex, much less a girl of Tae's size.

Commander Feng stepped firmly down onto the surface, turned, and raised a hand toward the camera. "Beijing Control! This is Feng. Leaving my footprints on the moon, I add another shining chapter to the glorious history of the People's Republic. I am honored to be here."

That's more like it, thought Sohya. He folded his arms across his chest and nodded. But Feng's words might not have had quite as much impact coming after Tae's remarks.

Jiang and Cui, the two base members who came to meet them, saluted Feng. "Commander," said Jiang, "we are ready to reorient the cargo vehicle."

"Very good. Aomine, Tae—please stand clear."

The two passengers moved away from Xiwangmu, and the Chinese astronauts began the difficult post-landing procedure. The cluster of modules comprising Kunlun Base was one hundred meters away. The cylindrical units were joined at a central core, like the petals of a flower. Xiwangmu 5 would be linked to the end of one of these modules. But before the giant module, tall as a five-story building, could be transported to its final position, it had to be laid on its side. On Earth, this would have called for a crane. The moon's low gravity, however, allowed for alternative procedures.

"Mass distribution data received, Commander," said Jiang. "Ready to deploy shock mat."

A flatbed automated moon rover, looking like a low-slung buggy, approached the landing site. Jiang hoisted a white, pillow-shaped object off the rover—it was nearly as wide as his outspread arms—and placed it on the surface. He squatted by the object, triggered a switch, and quickly moved away. In an instant, the "pillow" inflated explosively to a drumlike shape five meters across.

"It's just like a pancake," exclaimed Tae.

"It's a shock-absorbing mat. A gas cartridge takes care of inflation," said Sohya.

"Is that where the module is going to fall?"

"That's right."

Feng operated a remote control. A small, bird's nest–shaped thruster near the top of Xiwangmu began firing. The module started to list like a huge tree being felled. Feng immediately applied full power to the opposite thruster, minimizing Xiwangmu's lateral motion. It took a full twenty seconds for the huge cylinder to topple over onto the mat. Jets of gas erupted around the perimeter of the compressed cushion. Sohya muttered skeptically, "Pretty basic. What happens if they miss?"

Feng's voice came over his headset. "We never miss. Thruster control is completely automated. Xiwangmu is built to withstand this sort of handling. The mat was originally designed to raise overturned battle tanks. Compared to that, Xiwangmu's three and a half tons of effective mass is light as a feather."

Feng toggled the remote, and gas began slowly escaping from the mat. Xiwangmu quietly settled onto the surface. The Chinese walked around the module, visually inspecting to confirm that no projecting elements had been damaged.

"This might seem primitive to you," continued Feng, "but believe it or not, NASA used the same method to drop a probe onto the surface of Mars. It functioned flawlessly. Compared to that our method is quite gentle, don't you think?"

"How do you transport it to the base?"

"Simple. Watch."

The four astronauts moved to the vehicle and rapidly fastened thin wires to reinforced attachment points. Their practiced motions suggested previous experience in a low-G training pool. The anchored wires were joined in a bundle and attached to a winch on the rover. Sohya asked in disbelief, "Are you going to roll it? You can't be serious."

"That's exactly what we're going to do. Any objections?"

"No. But isn't that extremely risky? What happens if it snags on a rock? Or a wire breaks? Or you punch a hole in it? Just one mishap could end your plans to stay for another year."

"The first Xiwangmu was positioned to avoid those problems. We chose a flat area free of rocks that might interfere with later modules. Since then we've attached three more modules without a hitch. Even if we're unable to move a module, there's no need to abandon it. We just leave it in place as a stand-alone unit. Going back and forth will be a little inconvenient, that's all."

The rover shuddered as power was applied but barely seemed to be moving. Since it was smaller and lighter than a compact car, very slow speed in hauling the huge Xiwangmu might have been unavoidable. Still, it looked like the two-week lunar day would be over before it reached the base.

Feng confirmed this. Connecting the module would take at least till the end of the lunar day. Sohya felt a strange admiration: after four thousand years of history, the Chinese could be amazingly patient.

"We carry out the transfer in units of one revolution. Today we level the interior floor and we're done. Let me show you to the base—then I must return here." Feng motioned toward the cluster of modules partially buried in lunar regolith. Sohya and Tae began walking toward them. Suddenly Sohya noticed that Crew IV member Cui was staring at them. Feng scolded him. "Cui! Stop wasting time. The only one who'll suffer is you!"

The man turned to his work, but several times his glance drifted back to Sohya and Tae.

<hr>

THE SOLAR DAY on Mare Imbrium was perhaps a third over. The surface was bathed in dazzling direct sunlight. With no atmospheric scattering, the flat surface scintillated in pure white. The dividing line between light and shadow on the distant Apennines was stark, but portions of the base in shadow could just be made out in the reflected light from the surface.

Out in space, the sun was perhaps thirty degrees from the zenith, surrounded by a fierce corona. Earth loomed hugely overhead, divided into equal portions of light and darkness. The stark clarity of surface, space, and Earth created an impression of intense three-dimensionality.

Sohya and Tae kept looking around at the landscape as they walked toward the base. Several times they stumbled. When they reached the air lock at the end of one of the modules, Tae murmured reluctantly that she wanted to see more, but Feng assured her there would be plenty of time for that later. They would be here for a week, and part of their stay would include observing operations on the lunar surface.

They climbed a collapsible stairway and entered the manhole-shaped air lock about two meters above the surface. Each time the air lock was used, a certain amount of atmosphere was lost, so Sohya and Tae squeezed in together. There they waited for the air lock to be repressurized from the inside.

Once pressurization was complete, the inner hatch opened, and they removed their helmets. Base Commander Peng, the third member of Kunlun Crew IV, was waiting for them clad in a light T-shirt.

"Guests from Japan! We welcome you to Red Phoenix, the Kunlun Base lunar-surface research module." Images of their arrival were being transmitted to Earth via a camera mounted on the ceiling. As if conscious of this, Peng grinned broadly and extended his right hand. Sohya assumed an appropriate smile and shook his hand, but Tae ignored him. Instead, she looked around and sniffed the air doubtfully.

Sohya whispered in Japanese, "Tae, don't forget your manners."

"It smells like a ramen shop in here."

"What?"

"The smell. I don't like the smell of cooking oil." She frowned. Sohya hurriedly plastered on a smile again and tugged at her, forcing her to shake hands with Peng. Once the base commander's large hand enclosed her glove, she finally looked at him. In slightly stiff but clear English, she said, "I'm very happy to meet you, Commander Peng."

"Welcome, Tae. Is something bothering you?"

"Well, it smells kind of—"

"Tae," Sohya broke in, "it can wait. Let's get these suits off."

"But..."

"Yes, that's a good idea," said Peng. "You've been suited up since you transferred into *Chang'e*. You must be tired. And we've got some time before Cui hands off to Feng and comes back." As he spoke, Peng moved toward the wall rack. Suddenly he slipped and, with a comical grab at the rack, barely prevented himself from falling. He clucked his tongue in frustration and looked up at the video camera.

"Beijing Control, I'm terminating the feed for a few minutes. Tae needs to remove her suit." Peng entered a command on his wearcom, and the camera's indicator light went off. Without the observing eye, Peng's smile disappeared. "Now you can change," he said in a businesslike tone.

Tae looked down at her suit and murmured, "Where do I go to change, again?"

Beneath their suits, Sohya and Tae were wearing just a spandex liner garment crisscrossed with thin tubing for coolant circulation. They would need additional clothing once they were out of their space suits.

"Uh-oh—our gear is still in Xiwangmu. We can't get to it right now," said Sohya.

"Then you can use something of ours." Peng went toward the rear of the module. Once he was out of sight, Sohya murmured, "That must've been embarrassing, losing his balance in front of the whole world."

"The floor is wet." Tae pointed. Sohya looked down at his feet. About two-thirds of the module's cylindrical interior was above the floor, which was composed of aluminum-alloy panels. The mesh panel was slick with some kind of liquid. Sohya traced the leak with his eyes and saw it coming from a patched pipe on the wall. He touched the liquid with a fingertip.

"Feels like glycol or something similar. Coolant for the air-conditioning system. Not very tidy for the base entrance."

"Sohya, I'm getting this weird feeling," Tae whispered and grasped his hand. As he looked around, Sohya knew what she meant.

The entire space was a jumble of equipment. Peng's suit hung on the wall, along with digging tools, a crowbar, something that looked like a metal detector, and various other pieces of equipment, all of which seemed to have been carelessly stowed. Some of the gear was broken or damaged. Bundles of cables drooped from half-open cabinet doors like dead snakes. Several pipes were rusted, seemed about to come loose, or showed signs of having been patched here and there. Some of the pipes had been repaired with metal tape. The LED illumination panels in the ceiling were darkened with what looked like soot, and the mesh panels underfoot were gritty with lunar regolith. There was a strong odor of cooking oil and something else—a sweet smell, almost like honey. The module was large, probably thirty-five square meters, but the heaps of gear and materiel made for a gloomy and claustrophobic feel. Suddenly Sohya understood.

"I get it. Maybe he shut the camera off to hide all this. It looked a lot tidier in the PR video we saw."

"It did. Sorry, but this looks like a junkya—" Just then Peng emerged from the rear of the module carrying two folded bundles of clothes. Tae fell silent.

Sohya's bundle consisted of a previously worn cotton shirt, trousers, and underwear. Tae unfolded her bundle and stared. "Is this from a flea market?" She was looking at a white, gownlike garment that would have reached to the knees of an adult. The gown could be closed with strings in front but was otherwise completely unadorned. And like Sohya's garments, it showed signs of having been worn recently.

"It's a med-lab gown," said Peng. "I'm sorry, we don't have anything here for children to wear. I thought maybe if you tied it around your waist, it might look like a Chinese dress."

"Tae, there's no washing machine on the base. Now that I remember, there's an unmanned supply ship every four months. It brings clean clothes. Until then they have to make do with what they have."

Tae gripped the gown, looking as if she were fighting back tears. "So where's the changing room?"

Peng and Sohya looked at each other, then turned their backs at the same time.

"I'm sorry, Tae. We've never had a woman on our base before."

"We won't look. Promise."

The men heard a huge sigh and the sounds of Tae hurriedly changing out of her space suit.

[4]

THE BASE CLOCK was set to Beijing standard time. By the time Sohya and Tae were out of their suits it was already one o'clock in the morning. A full-scale welcoming ceremony was planned for the following day, so they had a simple meal and tumbled into their sleep-station hammocks in the habitation module. When they awoke next morning, they found that Feng, Ma, and Jiang had already left to work on the Xiwangmu transfer. As they were finishing a breakfast of congee and deep-fried rolls, base engineer Cui joined them. He had apparently finished his work for the morning and offered to give them a tour.

"Kunlun Base is currently composed of four Xiwangmu modules, oriented toward the four points of the compass and several supplementary modules. Everything connects through the Topaz node."

Cui pointed to a manhole-sized hatch at the south end of the habitation module with bundled hoses and tubing of all sizes snaking through it. The hatch opened into a spherical docking node originally intended for use in space. The node was 2.5 meters in diameter with identical hatches on all six axes.

"Yesterday you entered through the main air lock on the south module, the lunar-surface research module. We call it Red Phoenix. The west module, White Tiger, is the life sciences module. The east module is Azure Dragon, where we do medical studies. Azure Dragon is also the docking point for the unmanned supply vehicles. This north module, the habitation area, is Black Tortoise. The *Chang'e* emergency-escape orbiter is just outside."

Before breakfast, Tae had taken a pair of scissors to her gown and produced something that almost looked like a one-piece summer dress. Now she went to the Topaz hatch and peered into the passages leading to the other modules. "Is this the whole base? It's about the size of four buses. You spend a whole year here?"

"I think the floor area is bigger than it looks," said Sohya. "I remember the specifications said three hundred square meters."

"You must mean the habitable volume. That's three hundred cubic meters," corrected Cui. "In zero gravity, the walls and ceiling can double as floor space, so volume means something. But here we have gravity, even though it's only one-sixth of Earth's, so the metric we use is floor area. Leaving out shelving and subfloor space, the total area of the base is about 160 square meters."

"A hundred and sixty meters of floor space...Yes, that's enough for a family of three," said Sohya. "But then again, you have all this equipment." Sohya was trying to understand the base arrangement in terms of his construction background. That was his mission; his number one goal was to understand Kunlun as a structure.

Cui glanced at the time readout on his wearcom. "Wherever you live, that's home. Space isn't much of a problem. Black Tortoise has everything people need for life." Cui spread his arms wide toward the space around them. The ceiling was nearly three meters above the floor, the width of the room was three meters, its length nearly fourteen meters. Cui walked along, pointing to various devices along one wall, as Tae and Sohya followed.

"Advanced oxygen generator. Two CO_2 scrubbers. Climate control keeps the base temperature at a constant twenty-four degrees Celsius. Power supply units are connected to the external solar panel array, which provides plenty of power. The water-treatment device lets us recover 60 percent of the water we use. We have 220 different food items and enjoy a varied diet. With an always-on, high-speed comm link with home, we can watch as many movies as we like. That control panel on the wall allows us to control all the important devices on the base. The sleep stations up top provide personal space. And most important of all, we have this."

Cui pointed to the table around which they now stood, near the north end of the module. It served as a meal table but could be converted for other uses with extension panels. Cui placed both hands on it. "This table is where the three of us gather and socialize as a family. It's important for promoting group harmony."

Cui's delivery reminded Sohya of a sales pitch for a new housing development, but he was still impressed by the man's sincerity. He decided this was a good opportunity for some questions. "This is such an advanced installation. The structure must be quite something too."

"The structure?"

"The framework. Let's see...the insulation. Seismic reinforcement, that sort of thing," said Sohya.

"Oh, I understand. Of course, very advanced. The pressure hull is comprised of two layers of three-millimeter aluminum alloy over five-millimeter ribs. We've added Whipple panels and a layer of regolith on the exterior to protect against micrometeor strikes—"

"Hold it. Three millimeters?"

"What about it?"

"Well, I mean..." Sohya was nonplussed. On Earth, a metal structure with such thin walls might be usable as a storage unit. Any rigid-frame structure, whether made of wood or steel, required a certain thickness, if only for insulation. For a box frame structure with load-bearing walls, an even greater thickness would be required. Of course, Sohya was well acquainted with monocoque construction in aircraft, cars, and ships, but even so, three millimeters of aluminum skin was just too thin.

"Is that enough? What about heat and cold?"

"Of course, the environment gets very hot," replied Cui. "The sun is up for fourteen days. It's dark for the same amount of time. During that cycle the outside temperature ranges from 160 degrees Celsius to minus 120 degrees. The outer skin is covered with a heat shield, but that alone isn't enough to keep the inside temperature constant, so we circulate coolant to the hull during the day to maintain constant temperature."

Sohya remembered the network of pipes next to the outer skin that he'd seen in the air lock.

"You don't have to worry about structural strength either," Cui continued. "Material strength is proportional to the cross section, but with one-sixth gravity we make do with one-sixth thickness. And there are no moonquakes to worry about."

"What about the foundation? Where the module contacts the surface."

"Each module is wedged with rock to prevent rotation, but that's just in case."

In other words, the modules were just sitting on the regolith. Maybe the rock wedges could be considered a type of mat foundation, but without measures to prevent the modules from settling unequally. Gradually, Sohya realized what sort of structure the base represented. It was nothing more than a temporary installation. He was amazed it had lasted even a year.

"This is a permanent facility. Shouldn't it be built to higher specs?"

"Not practical." Cui shook his head. "Mass limits apply to everything brought to the lunar surface, you know. Oxygen, water, food, solar panels, and other life-support supplies get first priority. Next are supplies required to carry out our research mission. As far as structural aspects of the base go, the minimum is enough."

"Of course, when you improve the quality of a building it usually adds more and more weight," said Sohya.

"Mr. Aomine? Is there something about this base that concerns you?" Cui's eyes narrowed as he regarded Sohya, who was deep in thought.

"Oh, nothing," Sohya said casually. There was something about Cui—he was the tallest and brawniest of the base crew—that made him difficult to approach. Sohya was beginning to feel uncomfortable around him. It would probably pay to avoid sounding critical.

"If you're satisfied with this orientation to the habitation module, shall we move on?" said Cui, glancing again at his wearcom. He stared at Sohya and Tae. Sohya suddenly realized that Tae, usually so full of curiosity and questions, hadn't said a word during Cui's explanation. She stood with her hands clasped in front, looking down uncomfortably.

"Tae, is there something wrong?" asked Sohya.

"I-I haven't been to the toilet since we got here."

This was thoughtless of Sohya. The previous night before going to sleep, he'd gone to get an explanation of the toilet's location and how to use it, but Tae had been too shy to bring it up.

"Mr. Cui, is there a toilet?"

"Of course. It's on the other side of that clothes rack." Tae nearly jumped in the direction Cui pointed. She peeked into the toilet, which was about the size of a tiny closet, and wailed. "The walls are so thin!"

"Don't worry about smells, it's ventilated," Cui reassured her.

"It's not just smells. I mean, the sound..." she murmured feebly. Cui and Sohya had nothing to say. "We'll wait for you in the node," said Cui. "Call if you need help."

"Okay."

The two men passed through the command center on the south side of the module, which was crammed with monitors and control equipment, and entered the Topaz node, the intersection of the four base sections. There they waited. After a few minutes, Tae appeared, her cheeks slightly red. Sohya recalled her expression from the night before, when she was about to remove her space suit. "Did everything go well?"

"Of course! I studied the manual before we got here!" she said heatedly, touching something at her throat. Sohya realized it was a wearcom suspended on a chain. She was absently fingering the tiny keyboard.

Suddenly the node was plunged into darkness. Tae yelped with fear. Sohya reflexively embraced her from behind to shield her. He had had a number of close calls on construction sites, but as his mind raced and he tried to remember the escape route, he suddenly felt a chill run down his spine.

Having put himself and Tae in the hands of the base members, he had forgotten that death was only inches away in this place. There was no escape route. The only way to escape was via the *Chang'e* spacecraft, and Sohya had no idea how to operate it. Iwaki never tired of saying it: keep the worst case in mind at all times. Sohya bit his lip as those words came back to him. He had been careless.

"Cui, where are you? Should we head for the backup vehicle?" Cui should have been right next to him, but when Sohya put out his hand, there was only empty space. Sohya exhaled sharply with frustration and started to go back into the habitation module.

There was a click, and light returned. Cui was leaning into the node from the west module, joining two cables.

"Sorry. One of the power connections came loose."

"Really? Is that all it was?" asked Sohya.

"Yes. The cables have to be easy to disconnect, in case we need to seal off one of the modules."

"Sohya?" Tae was trembling against his chest. "Is—is everything all right?"

"It looks that way. A cable just got loose." He stroked her hair. Cui came back through the hatch.

"We were scared. You could have said something," said Sohya.

Cui looked away. "Really? It was just a minor problem."

"Does it happen often?"

"Not often, no. Come with me." Cui checked the time on his wearcom again and turned his back. They followed him uneasily into the next module.

WHITE TIGER, THE life sciences research module, was comprised of two banks of multilevel racks lined with plastic cases in a variety of shapes and sizes. Some of the cases were brightly illuminated with air lines leading into them. Others were opaque and sealed against the light. Countless tubes and cables snaked among the cases. The room was filled with the hum of an air compressor. It looked just like a familiar business back on Earth. Sohya realized what it reminded him of: a pet shop.

Cui pulled a case down from one of the racks and showed it to them. "A New Zealand rabbit." Inside the case, a plump rabbit lay curled in a ball.

"Oh, it's cute!" Tae reached for the lid, but Cui stopped her.

"We're keeping it in a germ-free environment."

"You brought this all the way from Earth?" asked Sohya.

"No, we brought this specimen's grandparents up in the form of fertilized eggs. This is the fourth generation. We want to see how they breed and develop in low-G conditions."

"It's the real rabbit in the moon," said Sohya. "Where are her parents?"

"Once they breed, they're no longer needed, so we eat them."

"Oh no...so that's going to happen to this little one too?" Tae's eyes opened wide. She put her hands together in an attitude of prayer and bowed toward the rabbit. Cui replaced the case and went to another rack.

"These are plants. We cultivate sixteen kinds of edible plants, mainly grains and legumes. We're already harvesting barley as a staple year-round. The aquariums over there contain black tiger shrimp, tilapia, and other aquatic life."

"You're prioritizing food sources?" asked Sohya casually. Cui frowned slightly.

"Yes, there is that tendency. But of course, we're doing pure science too. Some people have criticized Chinese space exploration as too practical, but that's not at all—"

Cui was cut off by an electronic beeping from the far side of the module, like an alarm clock. Peng called out, "Damn it, I'm out of time. *Qian shao xia ren* is off the menu for tonight."

"*Qian shao*—you can make Szechuan shrimp?" Tae called back. After a few moments, Base Commander Peng emerged from behind a worktable half-hidden by one of the racks, scratching his head. "Well, yes...after I dissect the specimens we've raised."

"I love Szechuan shrimp."

"I'm sorry, but I've got to move on to my next task, so I won't be able to harvest shrimp today. Cui, can I ask you to look after our guests? I didn't finish the quail and the rhizopus fungi. The seaweed's gone bad—you can discard it."

"Yes, Commander," said Cui.

"Carry on then." Peng spoke into his wearcom. "Beijing Control, Peng is moving to Black Tortoise CO_2 scrubber maintenance." He strode away. Cui asked Sohya and Tae to wait as he attended to Peng's remaining experiments. Sohya realized why he had not seen Peng since early morning.

"It must be a lot of work to keep all these life science experiments running."

"It takes up a third of our time. Excuse me," Cui said as he moved quickly past with a container of seaweed. Sohya and Tae flattened against the wall to let him go by. In a few seconds he was back. He took a bag of something that looked like animal feed from beneath one of the floor panels and began scattering it inside several cases containing quail.

"What a job," marveled Sohya.

Soon the timer on Cui's wearcom began beeping. "Oh well," said Cui as he replaced the cover on the case he was about to open. "It's time for my medical experiment in Azure Dragon. Why don't you come along and watch?"

"What about the fungus?" asked Tae, pointing to the case.

"Don't worry, they won't die." Cui shelved the case and walked past them. They climbed through the hatch and into the node, then through another eighty-centimeter hatch into the eastern module. Passing repeatedly through the narrow hatches was becoming a bit of a chore.

The interior of the Azure Dragon module was the most complex space they had yet seen. Perhaps "complex" was a little too complimentary. The space was crammed with food and equipment boxes, waste containers and devices, and tools and components stacked on the floor and hanging from the walls and ceiling. Amid all this clutter was something that looked like a conveyer belt, a bicycle with no wheels, and some spring-loaded exercise gear. Tae looked stunned. "You could get lost in here," she whispered.

"Don't drop anything," said Cui. "We'll never find it. This is where the automated supply vehicles dock, so we use it for storage." Sohya and Tae could see another hatch at the opposite end of the module and beyond it a space that looked like a dark cave.

Cui stood on the conveyer belt and removed his shirt. He unhooked several cables tipped with electrodes from a device on the wall, attached them to his naked chest, and donned a mask with a hose leading to another device. "What's that?" asked Tae.

"Cardiopulmonary-function check. We have to do this every day, along with the training. The low-G environment has a negative effect on muscular and cardiovascular function. The treadmill and the stationary bike are ergometers to measure the work we do while exercising." He began running on the treadmill.

"Can't you get exercise out on the surface?" asked Tae.

Cui answered at intervals as he paused to catch his breath. "EVAs are hard on space suits...It's hard to get efficient exercise... Anyway, we have to use this equipment."

"So this is the only exercise you get? What about tennis, or a horizontal bar, or swimming?"

"We're not...doing this for...pleasure."

"Do we have to exercise too?" said Tae.

"Fifteen minutes should be...enough...You won't be here...long anyway. We have to exercise...for an hour."

"You have to look at the wall for an hour while you run?" Tae furrowed her brows. Sohya put a hand on her shoulder.

"Tae, he's busy. Let's talk about it later. We should do some exercise too." Sohya pointed to the stationary bike. Tae mounted the machine doubtfully. Sohya picked up a spring-loaded chest expander and extended his arms against the resistance. The springs creaked where they were attached to the handles. Cui looked over at him. "We haven't...used those...for a while. Be careful."

But before he had finished speaking, the springs separated from their attachments with a metallic squeal. A blur shot past Sohya's eyes as he reflexively drew in his chin. The springs crashed against the opposite wall. "Whoa!" he shouted.

"This is rusted too!" cried Tae. She was red with exertion, but the pedals were stuck fast.

"It's not rusted—you have to adjust the torque." Sohya helped her lower the resistance.

After fifteen minutes of exercise, the pair poked around the module as if it were a yard sale while they waited for Cui to finish his running quota. Twice Peng entered the module and hurriedly grabbed a cylinder similar to tanks used for diving.

There were around twenty of these tanks along the wall. Sohya took one down to examine it more closely. "SFOG" was stenciled on the tank.

Solid Fuel Oxygen Generator, Sohya thought. Why would the base need a supplementary oxygen source?

THEY HAD SEEN all four modules. This completed their tour of the base. Sohya still had to take photographs and write up a report for Gotoba, but their one-week stay had just started. Though they had not come just to examine the base hardware, they still had plenty of time.

It seemed there was nothing left for them to do that day. They were in no position to help the crew; they had received only the most basic training before leaving Earth and had no idea how to perform any of the base tasks. The only way for them to keep from getting underfoot was to kill time in a corner of the habitation module.

"Sohya, look at this." Tae brought a cup of water. She had rearranged her hair from the bun on her head to braids.

She tilted the cup back and forth with her wrist. It slopped back and forth in the glass with a slow, syrupy motion.

"Isn't it weird? It looks alive."

"Careful you don't spill it," warned Sohya.

She spilled it. The water suddenly shot over the lip of the cup in a long sheet of fluid that rose higher than her head, like a jellyfish. The tongue of fluid broke into droplets and splashed lazily over the floor panels. Tae dropped to the floor so quickly her braids pointed at the ceiling. "Oh no!" she wailed. "I'm sorry, I didn't think it would go so high. Where's a cloth to wipe it up?"

As they searched for a cloth, Jiang stuck his head through the entry hatch. His work moving Xiwangmu 5 was finished for the day. As soon as he noticed what was going on, he yelled, "What have you done?"

Jiang nearly did a somersault coming through the hatch. He grabbed a towel from the garment rack and covered the pool of water with it, carefully wiping the floor as if desperate to get every drop.

"Fresh water is precious! Who said you could do this?"

"It's not fresh water," said Sohya defensively. "It's from the shower." He pointed to the stall farther back in the module. Jiang sighed deeply.

"Oh, I see. In that case it's okay. We can replace it."

"Can't you recycle water for drinking too?" asked Sohya.

"Sure, but recycled water tastes bad." Jiang wrung out the soaked towel over the inlet to the recycling unit. "There was a hole in the distillation unit. The E. coli count went through the roof. We have to add tons of silver nitrate to kill the bacteria. The water isn't undrinkable, but the supply ships bring water that's much tastier."

This was the first opportunity Sohya and Tae had had to speak to this young man, the youngest member of the base team. He seemed much more open and approachable than Cui. Sohya decided to risk a question.

"Have we done anything wrong? Cui doesn't seem to like us much."

"Oh, he's just stressed, that's all. We've been away from home for a year. We're all homesick."

"Really?" marveled Sohya. "I thought you all had this burning desire to fulfill your mission."

"Of course we do. Otherwise we could never manage this." Jiang shrugged and looked at his wearcom. His face lit up. "Finally—time for the evening meal. That's the best stress reliever. It's my turn in the kitchen tonight. I'll show you what good cooking is all about."

"What's on the menu?" asked Tae.

"We can off-load supplies from Xiwangmu now, so we're going to have a feast. Camel hump fried in oil, stir-fried abalone—"

"Is that why the base has this smell?" said Tae, jabbing a finger in the air.

Jiang nodded. "It's too bad we can't ventilate better. Whatever we can't scrub stays in the air."

"Doesn't that put an extra load on the life-support system?" asked Sohya.

"Lighten up," chided Jiang. "The Russians actually smoked cigarettes on Mir. Well, I better go get things ready." He clapped Sohya on the shoulder and went out through the hatch. Sohya was openmouthed with amazement. Jiang was completely different from his nervous counterpart, Cui.

Tae looked delighted. "This is the best thing so far!"

"Didn't you say something about not liking oil?"

"It's the smell I don't like. Chinese food is good every now and then. I think I'll give him a hand." She left through the hatch, smiling with anticipation. Sohya shook his head. What kind of an operation was this? He wasn't sure.

[5]

THE DAY AFTER the festive welcome party, the work of off-loading supplies began in earnest. Sohya and Tae's weeklong stay on the moon was based on the time required to complete this work, not on any accommodation by the Chinese. They knew nothing about lunar operations, but a week was enough to learn about the base. They observed the crew's activities very closely.

Each day started with a wake-up call from Beijing Control at 0600. Work started at 0800 and ended at 1800, with a two-hour lunch and rest break in between. An hour of physical training was supposed to be followed by two hours for dinner and private time, then an hour of prep for the following day, with lights out at 2200. But the real schedule was mostly very different.

The crew was up much earlier than 0600. Breakfast was sometimes just a hurried snack. The extra time gained was largely devoted to monitoring and maintenance of the life-support systems. The rest of the day tended to proceed according to plan, but it was difficult to complete everything in the time allotted. It was often necessary to break early from one task and hurry on to the next.

The evening meal was punctually observed. In fact this was the only part of the schedule that was. Like clockwork, the five Chinese strictly adhered to the two-hour meal period, but there was no private time afterward. The crew never observed the scheduled start of the sleep period at 2200. Instead of private time, they worked late into the night on facility repairs, harvesting the experiments in White Tiger and preparing for the next day. Once, around four in the morning, Sohya woke to use the toilet and heard the animated voices of Peng and Cui coming from White Tiger, audible over the round-the-clock *basso profundo* hum of fans heard everywhere on the base. It sounded like an argument.

And after every task was finished, there was communication with Beijing Control. Cui had been constantly checking his wearcom during that first day's tour not only to monitor the time but to send text updates to Beijing. His refusal to do updates via voice link reflected his irritation with having to do them at all. This was not hard to understand. He even had to contact Control when he visited the toilet.

Yet there were times when Cui set aside his usual dour mood. One evening after dinner, Ma suggested they watch a movie together, and Cui revealed another side to his personality.

The movie was not streamed from Earth; Ma had carried it with him on a memory card. It was not the kind of entertainment Beijing would have transmitted via one of their communications satellites. It was an erotic comedy from Hong Kong. Tae looked away in confusion. Sohya was embarrassed for her, but Cui paid no attention. For a short time, he became a different person, exploding with laughter throughout the film. Still, the rest of the time he was difficult to approach, while Peng and Jiang were easy to deal with.

After several days, the reason for the irregular scheduling suddenly dawned on Sohya.

A huge amount of the crew's time was monopolized by repair work. Each crew member was occupied with something during waking hours, but a third of the work was devoted to repairs to the cooling system, the air and water purification devices, and the base power supply. Next in terms of demands on their time came looking after the creatures and harvesting the experiments in White Tiger. These tasks clearly limited the time available for other scientific work, so the only solution was to skimp on sleep. Even the crew's strict adherence to the evening meal schedule was an artifact of the overburdened working day. Without at least an unhurried evening meal, they would not have been able to cope with the pressure.

It seemed to Sohya that Kunlun Base was barely holding together, or at least operating at the limits of its capacity. The coolant leak they saw that first day proved to be a daily occurrence, and a sweet smell wafted throughout the base from pools of ethylene glycol beneath the floor. The solar panels installed outside the modules were exposed to direct sunlight with no intervening atmosphere to reduce its intensity, so the older panels were beginning to sustain damage. This sometimes pushed the base's power supply to dangerously low levels. As an outsider, Sohya might never have noticed this, except for something that occurred just after they had bedded down on the fourth day.

Sohya was about to doze off when he heard a crash and opened his eyes. The endless whirring of the purification fans and the droning of the reverse osmosis unit made for a surprisingly noisy environment, and it was never easy to sleep. Sohya drowsily opened the door to his sleep station to find Peng lifting a familiar-looking tank from the floor.

"Still working, Commander? Don't you guys ever get any sleep?"

"Sorry to disturb you. Please go back to bed," said Peng. He glanced at Sohya and tightened a valve on the tank. Sohya heard a loud click and without thinking, asked, "It says 'SFOG' on the tank. What does that stand for?"

Peng shook his head slightly, looking uncomfortable. "So you noticed that. It stands for Solid Fuel Oxygen Generator."

"Oxygen generator?" Sohya said sleepily. "Are we short on oxygen?"

"Of course not. Everything's fine. We do this all the time."

"Oh, okay…" Sohya climbed back into his hammock and closed his eyes. He needed the sleep.

When he woke the next morning, he collared Jiang to ask about the oxygen generator. The young taikonaut smiled wryly.

"You're right. That's not standard procedure. We normally generate oxygen from electrolysis. SFOG doesn't need electricity. It heats potassium chlorate to generate oxygen in emergencies. Commander Peng probably noticed we didn't have enough power to keep the oxygen level nominal."

"Are we going to be okay?"

"It's a temporary problem. The base is crowded right now."

Sohya had learned that not only the power supplies were stretched to their limit. He was also impressed by the crew's calm in the face of potential disaster. The reality behind their government's patriotic promotion was that the base was barely functioning, and only thanks to the tireless work of the crew. Keeping Kunlun going had almost become the crew's sole reason for existing.

The afternoon of the sixth day, Sohya and Tae suited up and ventured outside onto the surface. The moment they emerged from the air lock, Tae called out in amazement. "Wow! Look how long the shadows are!" The two-week lunar day was nearly over. The sun was hanging just over the horizon. Instead of the colors of sunset, the shadows of the base and of Jiang's legs seemed to stretch endlessly, razor sharp over the plain.

Jiang pulled his excavation tool from the regolith. It looked like a standard shovel, but Sohya assumed it must be specialized. Surely the Chinese would not bring anything less all the way to the moon.

"What sort of tool is that?" Sohya asked.

"It's just an ordinary shovel," said Jiang.

Deflated, Sohya and Tae watched as Jiang walked to White Tiger and began shoveling sun-drenched regolith against its side. Regolith was banked against the third of the module closest to the docking node, apparently piled there by hand. Over and over, Jiang scooped regolith against the module in a monotonous rhythm. "I'd ask you to help if we had any extra shovels," he said. "In this gravity, it's easier than it looks."

"Why are you doing that?" asked Sohya.

"Protection from charged particles. The moon doesn't have a strong magnetic field like the earth does. Solar proton events and cosmic radiation are a constant danger. For short-term visitors to space like you, drugs give enough protection. But if you stay for a year, cumulative exposure gets to be a real problem."

"What does the radiation do?" asked Tae. "Does it make holes in the base?"

"Holes? No. It can cause cancer though."

"Cancer!" she said fearfully. Jiang smiled.

"Don't worry. In four years, we've completely covered the habitation module. As long as we go there when we get a solar storm warning, we're fine. Before Crew III finished covering it, they had to take shelter under the water tank."

"So the life sciences module comes next, because of the creatures inside." Sohya looked up at the four-meter-high module. Regolith was piled against it to a height of only about eighty centimeters. It was like using a spoon to bury an elephant. "At this rate, it looks like it's going to take ten years to finish."

"Including the new module, we plan to have it done in twelve."

"Wow. That's...a pretty long-range plan," mumbled Sohya. Tae picked up a discarded solar panel and made as if to help Jiang dig, but he stopped her.

"No—you might cut your gloves on the edge. And be careful, there's a lot of trash around here."

They took a closer look at the surface around them. An intermittent trail of objects of all sizes extended outward from the module's dump hatch—canisters of exhausted drying agent, discarded electronic components, even the mummified remains of animals. Some of the detritus was close to the module, but other pieces were some distance away.

"There's a trick to evacuating the air from the dump chamber. If you release the outer hatch with a little atmosphere inside, the trash flies out nicely. Too much atmosphere and the decompression might damage the hatch. It's fun to get it just right and see how far you can shoot the trash. My cooking-oil toss holds the Crew IV record, at 15.55—"Jiang looked toward the garbage trail and stopped. "Uh-oh. Somebody beat me. That's a seaweed cultivation case, isn't it? I guess Cui's the new record holder."

"How can you do this?" yelled Tae. The two men wheeled in

surprise. She stood with hands on hips as if defending the lunar surface. "Don't you remember what we did to Earth? And now you're doing the same thing here?"

"Well, we can't take it back with us," said Jiang. He resumed his leisurely digging. "It's all we can do just to get supplies up here. We can't even take back the trash, much less anything of value from the surface. You should see the other side of the base! When a new resupply vehicle is ready to dock at the medical science unit, we use the leftover propellant in the old one to blast it a short distance away. That's twelve vehicles in four years, scattered all over the place. If you could get them back to Earth, collectors would pay a fortune."

"I mean, this whole base…" pouted Tae. "It's falling apart, it smells, it's in the middle of a garbage dump. Can't you do something about it?"

"That's a little unfair," Sohya interrupted. "Everyone here is working hard to help humanity push into space. It's going to be a bit jerry-rigged in the beginning. They're using their knowledge and ingenuity to deal with the problems in a positive way. Don't you think that's impressive?"

"But Grandfather said that was the wrong way to do it!"

"Mr. Toenji?" asked Sohya, baffled. "What did he say?"

Tae suddenly looked away. "I can't talk about it yet. I promised. I'm sorry."

Something that Sohya had not given much thought to before suddenly loomed as potentially significant. He had always assumed that Tae had been imposed on him so an old man could give his beloved granddaughter the trip of a lifetime. It was the kind of indulgence not uncommon among the wealthy. Still, it was out of proportion for an indulgent whim. It was hard to believe anyone would casually hand over three billion yen to fund a pleasure trip, even someone with personal assets several hundred times that. And it would not be surprising if Tae had been given some sort of goal. But even so, what sort of responsibility could she be expected to fulfill? As Sohya pondered this question, Jiang spoke up.

"You're certainly paying enough, Aomine. I'm not sure we're worth it though." Jiang was shoveling faster now.

Sohya was briefly speechless. "Isn't there something more important for you to be doing here? Geological research? Gathering samples? I'd like to know more about soil testing—"

"Crew II's data is in the computer, complete with visuals. I'll give you a copy later."

"What about Crew IV's research?"

"We're not doing any."

"You're not?" Sohya was dumbfounded.

"That's right," Jiang said simply. "With only three crew members, and with these facilities, there's nothing left to research. We've done everything. We tried making concrete out of regolith, but there's no water ice anywhere around here, so there's not a lot we can do. Maybe at the south pole…Anyway, whatever it is we might be doing, we haven't got the people, the equipment, or the funding."

"Then why are you here?"

"Maybe because they can't afford to send a bulldozer to bury the modules."

Jiang's cynicism was understandable. Beijing Control rode herd on the crew with a schedule controlled to the minute. Of course, even manual labor was important if it helped protect the base. Still, what was the point of such a minutely choreographed schedule?

A short distance away, Tae was playing at stepping on her own shadow. One set of shadows danced happily in the silence. Another shortened and lengthened in a monotonous rhythm. Sohya was lost in thought.

[6]

THEY WERE UP early the next morning. It was departure day.

The crew rose even earlier than usual and furiously began making launch preparations. There was nothing to retrieve from

Xiwangmu 5, but research materials and several hundred commemorative boxes had to be loaded into the *Chang'e* spacecraft. The small boxes contained shards of regolith, Chinese flags, and cards postmarked by the taikonauts. Back on Earth these "postcards from the moon" would fetch high prices. Sohya had seen something similar at Dragon Palace. He had never been able to understand this passion humanity seemed to have for setting up post offices on mountain peaks, at the bottom of the ocean, and on other planets.

Sohya and Tae were carrying very little. The Gotoba plan assumed the production of concrete from regolith, but simulated regolith had already been synthesized on Earth from Apollo-era samples. A bigger question was the load-bearing capacity of the surface. Sohya had already obtained the needed information from Jiang and transmitted it to Earth. The rest of the video and audio data was loaded into Sohya's wearcom, which he used as a camera/recorder.

Those four who were going home today had a more important task to complete. They had been able to spend the Earth–moon leg of the journey in Xiwangmu 5. But during the three days till touchdown in the Gobi Desert, they would be confined to the *Chang'e* spacecraft, and unfortunately the toilet had been removed to make room for extra payload. Not that it was impossible for male taikonauts to satisfy physical requirements in space, but evacuation would require the use of plastic bags, an exceedingly embarrassing procedure considering that a young girl would be on board. They would have to use drugs and the weightless conditions to help weather the three-day journey. Tae in particular was deadly serious about obtaining a detailed explanation of the drug and its effects.

Naturally, the most important task was the handoff of the various base responsibilities. The crew formed pairs—Peng with Feng, Jiang with Ma—to jointly confirm the condition of the equipment and ensure that nothing had been overlooked. Cui, however, had little to do and idly wandered around. It had fallen to him to stand in for the Crew V member whose place had gone to Sohya and Tae.

He would be spending another year on the moon.

Like it or not, the two Japanese felt his glance falling on them from time to time. The situation was unfortunate. Cui's resentment at being bumped by two feckless tourists was understandable. Still, they had hoped to get to know him better.

They had no idea how impossible that would be.

* * *

WITH LAUNCH PREPARATIONS complete, everyone gathered in the Black Tortoise module. Crew III's *Chang'e* was waiting at the north end of the module. After launch, the plan was for the remaining crew to move the latest *Chang'e* into position—the service module's landing gear was equipped with treads for this purpose—where it would stay for the next year, ready for an emergency departure if needed.

Peng, Jiang, Sohya, and Tae were in their space suits. Feng, Ma, and Cui faced them in the usual work clothes. Once again the camera was feeding images to Earth in real time. Peng stepped forward.

"We depart Kunlun Base with an abundant store of precious research accumulated over the past year. We have no doubt that we leave the base in capable hands. Please strive to maintain this base for another year, as the pinnacle of the glorious scientific achievements of the People's Republic of China and humanity's farthest outpost."

"We humbly accept this duty," said Feng, "and pray for your safe journey home."

The exchange was formal and conventional but emotional just the same. The two commanders shook hands. Scientists Jiang and Ma exchanged similar words. Then all eyes fell on Sohya. He had assumed something like this would take place and prepared accordingly, but the thought that he would be heard in more than a hundred countries was still daunting. He cleared his throat.

"This is a magnificent facility. I have the deepest admiration for the dedication and passion you bring to the advancement of science. The lunar environment was thrilling. I almost wish I were staying longer. I leave with the hope that you will enjoy life here on the moon over the coming year." Sohya shook hands with Feng and Ma, but Cui ignored his outstretched hand. It suddenly occurred to Sohya that he had neglected to praise China. Perhaps Cui had taken offense?

Sohya looked at him and froze. The man's expression was terrifying. His eyes were blazing. He was biting his lower lip as if the honor of his parents had just been trampled on. Sohya was struck dumb.

Sensing the situation, Peng quickly turned to Tae. "Miss Toenji, would you like to say something?"

"What? Oh, sure. The food was really good. Much better than we get in Chinatown back home."

The others laughed nervously. Sohya was relieved. At least it now seemed unlikely that Cui would follow with more high-flown phrases about the People's Republic.

Jiang glanced at Cui, urgently signaling him to begin. Cui gulped as if swallowing something hard and opened his mouth.

At that instant there was a loud bang, like a gunshot, from somewhere inside the base. Everyone froze and stared at each other. Perhaps ten seconds passed.

Then the cry of an alarm sounded. They flinched again. Almost simultaneously the two commanders shouted, "Pressure warning!" and sprinted toward the Topaz node, with Ma close behind. Jiang sprang to the equipment control panel. He took one look at the numbers streaming across the display and yelled, "Pressure drop! Azure Dragon! Cargo docking hatch sealed! Node junction nominal! It's not the air lock. Whipple shield—it's a meteor strike!"

Jiang's words were barely audible over the keening of the alarm. Feng and Ma, already out of the module, almost certainly could not hear him.

"Cui! Take care of her!" Sohya pushed Tae toward him.

"Sohya! Wait!" she called out, but he was already running, diving through the hatch to follow the others. He had trained for just this sort of emergency. The damaged module had to be identified immediately and sealed off.

But Peng, Feng, and Ma had not heard Jiang. Each had entered a different module, frantically searching for the location of the breach. Sohya found Peng in Azure Dragon, standing in the middle of a maze of supplies and training equipment. "Where is it? Where's the breach?" he shouted.

Sohya yelled back. "Here, Commander! It was a meteor!" Peng looked up at the ceiling, searching for where the meteor had hit. He saw it almost instantly. There was a circular hole, about three centimeters across, in the corner of one of the semiconductor illumination panels that covered the curved ceiling. The hole was surrounded by white mist, the signature of adiabatic cooling in the presence of an enormous pressure differential.

Sohya looked up and froze. He was seeing something no human had seen before: the black emptiness of naked space—with nothing between him and it.

As Sohya stood rooted to the spot, Peng did something astounding. "There it is!" he shouted. He flexed his knees and jumped with all his strength.

"Peng! No!" Sohya cried out.

Peng pressed his upper right arm against the hole. Even under the moon's low gravity, his mass was over ten kilos. With the fingers of his free hand clinging to a gap between two lighting panels, he struggled to hold himself in place.

"Don't worry! The suit will hold. What's the pressure? And shut off that alarm!"

Sohya called to Feng, who was looking through the hatch.

"Peng is blocking the breach with his arm! What's the pressure?"

Feng shouted, "Jiang, pressure!"

"Nine oh seven!" Jiang called out. "Down more than a hundred millibars in two minutes. At this rate we'll lose all pressure within twenty minutes!"

"Is it still falling?" yelled Feng.

"Passing nine hundred! Wait…back at nine hundred now and holding. Looks like it's stabilizing."

"Good! Shut down the alarm!"

Suddenly the base fell silent. Sohya rubbed his ears to stop the ringing. He looked up at Peng.

"Pressure stabilized at nine hundred millibars. What do we do now?"

"Get putty sealant and some kind of metal panel—anything will do. Wait, I need some support first. Get a length of drainage tubing from Red Phoenix."

"No—it won't go past the angle. I'll check White Tiger!" Sohya brushed past Feng, who had just entered the module, and hurried into White Tiger where Ma was still searching for the leak. Sohya repeated Peng's orders and pulled a long length of conduit off one of the experiment cases. He carried it back through the node. Feng was opening the valves on one reserve oxygen tank after another. Sohya pushed the conduit against the hard torso of Peng's suit, giving him extra support. The flexible fabric on the arm of the suit was not designed to stand up to one atmosphere of pressure. Apparently his skin, pressed against the fabric, was helping to seal the breach. Peng's face was drained of blood.

"I'm glad I put my arm against it. The suction is terrific. If I'd used the palm of my hand, I might have broken some bones," he laughed.

Sohya yelled, "Where's that putty?"

"Got it." Ma entered the module, kneading a large chunk of fiber-reinforced putty and carrying an aluminum panel under his arm. Feng boosted Ma up on his shoulders. Sohya tightened his grip on the conduit.

"Okay, peel him off!"

As Ma called out, Peng gripped the conduit. Sohya wrapped his arms around Peng's legs and started to pull, slowly increasing his effort against the powerful suction. It took all of his strength. Peng separated from the hole with a loud pop. The air around the breach flashed into churning mist. Ma slapped the putty-covered panel over the hole and began sealing the edges with more putty. Feng called out: "Jiang! Pressure!"

"Nine zero five…nine fourteen…nine nineteen! The tanks are working. The leak's stopped!"

The men sat down heavily on the floor. Every face was deathly pale, bathed in cold sweat. Peng massaged his arm through the suit. The contusion must have been terrible. It hit Sohya again: just outside this tube, which in its own way represented comfort, reigned a vacuum with tremendous destructive power. If Peng had not acted in time, those wearing space suits could simply have lowered their visors. Feng and the others clad only in work clothes would have been doomed.

Yet even Peng did not take the right course of action. If the hole had been much larger, his arm might have been pulled through. If the edges of the breach had been ragged metal rather than plastic panel, he could have lost part of his suit and a chunk of his flesh. And if there had been more than one breach in the hull, even entering the module could have been suicidal.

"You could have gotten killed…" Sohya's breathing was ragged. Peng just smiled and mopped his brow through his open visor.

"This base is ours. Our own people don't give us adequate support. The place is falling apart. But we'll defend it with our lives."

"How can you say it's falling apart?" said Sohya, momentarily chastened. "It's an unbelievable achievement."

Peng raised his eyebrows. "Drop the pretense. You don't believe that. It's obvious."

Sohya blushed. He had underestimated Peng. This genial taikonaut had seen right through him.

"The dreams and hopes of 1.8 billion Chinese—no, of the whole human species—are on our shoulders. Our presence here took a huge commitment of national wealth. Should we run away because of one meteor? And even if we wanted to run, where could we go?"

Sohya had been paralyzed with fear at his glimpse of naked space. Yet this man had confronted it without a moment's hesitation. He felt a yawning gap between the demands of the situation and his own reaction.

Peng turned to Feng, who was looking up at the aluminum panel. "It must've had a cross section of about twenty millimeters. The Whipple bumper would've vaporized it, but the gas jet punched through the hull. In Earth's atmosphere it would've burned up. If it had hit Black Tortoise or White Tiger, the regolith blanket would've kept us safe."

"I'm not so sure," said Feng. "I'm just glad it didn't hit the habitation module. In fact, maybe we're lucky it struck here."

"You'll have to do permanent repair work on the hull after we leave. Looks like you've got something else on your plate, Commander."

"It'll be good practice. Now we know we can handle a small strike without harm to the crew. We'll be fine." The two officers seemed almost casual about this brush with death.

As Sohya hung his head, almost overcome with exhaustion, Tae timidly peeked in from the docking node.

"Sohya? Is everything okay?"

"Hey, Tae. Hole's been patched, for the moment. Don't worry, the danger's over."

"Really? That's good news." She sighed with relief.

Sohya rose, went to her side, and gave her a hug. "Pretty scary, huh? Sorry I left you back there. I had to do what I could to help."

"I was really scared. Please don't do that again, ever. Maybe you didn't have a choice this time though."

"Commander Peng blocked the hole with his body."

"He what? No, I don't believe it..." Tae peeked out from behind Sohya and stared at Peng.

"It's true," said Sohya.

"I don't understand how he could do that." Her voice was calm, but she had begun to tremble. Sohya put his hands on her shoulders.

Jiang looked in from the Topaz node. "We patched the breach," said Feng. "What's the word from Beijing?"

"I shut down the comm," Jiang answered.

"Shut it down? Why?"

"I think you'd better come see for yourself." Jiang looked more embarrassed than worried. The others exchanged puzzled glances and reentered the habitation module. There they found Cui sitting on the floor, knees drawn up, arms hanging limply at his sides. He was shaking all over.

"Cui! What is it? Are you injured?" Feng leaned over him.

"Send me home...please..."

"What?" Feng straightened up in bafflement. Cui lifted his face. It was streaked with tears.

"Send me back to Earth! I'm begging you!" It was a howl of desperation. "I can't take this anymore, this...this desert of nothing but rocks and sun, this vacuum. Beijing doesn't know a damn thing about this place. All they do is order us around. Dig, dig, day after day, don't stop digging...Control doesn't give a rat's ass about us. Pedal the bike, work till you drop, just don't ask why..."

"Cui...?"

"I want to see my kids in person, not on a damn screen. I want to swim all day. I want to eat home cooking till I explode. I want to sleep and not dream all night. *And I don't want to die!*" Cui was screaming now, his cheeks flecked with crimson. He glared at Sohya, eyes narrowed, and stood up. "You! If it wasn't for the two of *you*, I'd be going back to the smell of cool, fresh earth. You goddamn Jap!"

"That's enough!" shouted Peng. Feng and Ma pinned Cui's

arms. "Look at you! You call yourself a taikonaut? You were selected over 18,000 candidates. Where are your guts and your courage?
Have you forgotten your oath?"

"I don't care. I just want to go home." Cui sagged against Feng
and Ma and sobbed like a child.

"Can you get him back in shape?" said Peng. "I don't think he's
far gone enough to send him home on the backup vehicle."

"I agree," said Feng. "The same thing happened on Mir. The
presence of our guests caused more work and stress. With the meteor strike, he snapped. He needs extended rest and more personal
family calls. That should be enough."

Tae gripped Sohya's hand tightly. He knew what she was
thinking. Cui was the cream of China's aerospace program,
and his drive and energy had seemed heroic until a few moments
ago. Now it had become something cold and inhuman.

Though he knew it was pointless, Sohya said to Feng, "We're
sorry to have caused such a problem. If there's anything we can
do—"

"Don't worry about it. Before launch, we all signed a contract
agreeing to stay here as long as necessary." Peng's voice was cold as
he looked at Cui, who had slumped to the floor again. "He should
be thankful. No one in history has spent two years on the moon.
He'll be a hero when he gets home, with two years of back pay
waiting. But we need your help."

He peered at Sohya and Tae, eyes bright. "We hope you'll keep
this confidential. We are a very proud people. We'll do anything to
save face—even shut down the link with Beijing, which is strictly
forbidden."

The two Japanese nodded quickly. "Of course." "I won't tell anyone either."

"Thank you. Then let's prepare for departure. I'd better check
my suit." Peng left the module. Sohya and Tae looked down at
Cui, who was silently weeping.

[7]

TAE TOOK A last look at the lunar surface from the quartz window of the return module they had left in orbit.

"What a dangerous world..."

"Yes," said Sohya. "Too dangerous for me." He looked out the window, his head next to hers. "Those men down there are willing to sacrifice their lives. They're heroes. They give their all for their country, and they're all alone. It's almost scary to think how noble that is."

"It won't work that way." Tae spoke in Japanese. Sohya looked at her. She was rapidly inputting something into the wearcom pendant she wore around her neck. Since they had arrived on the moon, she had been using it during most of her spare time.

"What are you writing?" asked Sohya.

"It's my report for Grandfather." She only glanced at the high-resolution display from time to time as her fingertips darted across it at dizzying speed.

"Kunlun Base was cramped, smelly, and scary. The crew had to work all day and never had time to really rest. They had almost nothing to look forward to or make them happy. The only people who can handle that are people doing it for their country. Regular people can't."

Sohya frowned. "Isn't that a little too pessimistic? You don't want your grandfather to cancel his project, do you? Have you changed your mind about building a base on the moon?"

"No. Not at all." She shook her head resolutely. "The moon is way more amazing than I thought. They showed us the layout of the base before we left, so I had an idea of what we'd find. But that's not what I want. I want to build something different."

"Are you the one who decides what to build?" said Sohya, mystified.

"Oops." Tae gave him a childlike smile. The tip of her tongue darted out between her lips with happy embarrassment. "We better keep that confidential."

"Sure." Sohya let the matter drop.

Peng signed off his comm with Beijing Control. "Tae, after we touch down in the Gobi Desert, would you mind spending a week or so at CNSA's medical facility?"

She cocked her head and looked at him doubtfully. "I thought we'd get to go home right away."

"China sent a young person into space a few years back, but frankly, we didn't gather the kind of medical data we should have," said Peng apologetically. "And you've been all the way to the moon. Our scientists would really like an opportunity to look you over."

"See? I knew it." Tae puffed her cheeks in frustration. "Anyway, I can't say no, right? I mean, really. Just make sure they've got miso soup and some decent rice crackers from Japan. I only eat red miso. And I want deep-fried tofu in the soup."

"Well, I guess we can manage that," said Peng. He seemed slightly skeptical but passed Tae's requests to Beijing.

Sohya's amusement was interrupted when he heard Tae whisper to herself, "I won't give up." She looked down at the moon again. "It's just as beautiful and amazing as I thought. The white sunlight, the blue earth, and millions of stars floating in black space. And feeling as light as a feather...Let's do it. Let's build our base here."

Sohya still did not understand what she meant, but he said nothing.

AFTER THEY TOUCHED down, Sohya was also subjected to a battery of medical tests. He could hardly refuse, given the favor the Chinese had extended in allowing him to go, so along with Tae he played the role of docile guinea pig.

Surprisingly, he was detained longer than she was. Tae left for Japan after a week, while Sohya had to spend an additional three days stuck on the continent. Naturally, the ever-curious media was waiting for him when he got home, as were media from around the world, all of them jostling for interviews. Japan's first girl astronaut had given them the slip, and they were determined not to let that happen with Sohya. How did it look? How did the low gravity feel? What was the meteor strike like? Favorite food? Heightweighthobbiesspecialtalents? Seeing anyone? Are you and Tae more than just colleagues? No question was too personal. Tight-lipped Sohya told them to contact Gotoba Engineering's PR department, but every now and then he'd slip up and make a comment, such as that he thought Tae was cute, and that would just start the questions all over again.

Back in Japan at last, Sohya got off the train at Tokyo station, fed up and exhausted, to find Iwaki waiting for him behind the wheel of a company car. As Sohya got into the front seat, the first words from the Mobile Engineering Division chief left him stunned with surprise.

"One point two trillion yen."

The look on Iwaki's face, forbidding at the best of times, was even more serious than usual.

"A trillion?" Sohya's jaw dropped.

"A trillion two. That's Gotoba's bid to build a base on the moon."

Sohya sat back, trying to grasp a number that large. Suddenly it hit him. "Wait a minute. That's impossible. Toenji's budget was only 150 billion."

"During that first meeting, everybody was focusing on construction costs. Turns out the cost of getting it all up there is much larger. It costs at least five billion just to put a satellite in orbit. A hundred and fifty billion definitely isn't enough to build a base on the moon, not the way things are usually done."

"Of course. After all, it cost three billion just to send two people. Then again, I assumed that was because we had to pay top rates to buy our way onto that launch. That's not the rate we used to run the whole budget, is it?" Sohya paused as his boss's words sank in. "Did you say 'the way things are usually done'?"

"Yes. The Eden people claim to have a solution. I don't have the details yet. Some new type of rocket."

"Makes sense. A launch vehicle is something Gotoba can't bring to the table. Is that confirmed?" asked Sohya.

"Confirmed according to her," said Iwaki. "Right?" Iwaki jerked a thumb toward the rear seat.

"That's right," said a female voice. A woman Sohya had never seen before leaned forward and smiled.

"Who are you?" asked Sohya, thoroughly flustered.

She looked about thirty. Her hair—its translucent red coloring had recently become popular—was pinned up, leaving her neck bare. She was dressed in a fashionable, peach-toned suit and smiled brightly at Sohya.

"Reika Hozumi. Special Auditor, ELE."

"You're an auditor?"

"Yes. From now on, waste is our enemy. A half century of penny-pinching is how a little amusement park operator in Nagoya called Paradise Tours grew to become ELE, Eden Leisure Entertainment. Our cost-control expertise will be a powerful asset for Gotoba Engineering."

"Mr. Iwaki...?" After old man Toenji and Tae, Sohya was beginning to wonder if there were any "normal" people in ELE. "What about our auditors? Why does an outsider have to get involved?"

"Take it easy. This is how the client wants it. ELE saw the bid, and they haven't said no. They even said they were expecting it. They've already invested three billion. They're not bluffing. Gotoba is willing to take this as far as they want to go. Those are his instructions. You're going to Tanegashima."

"Tanegashima? The island?" Sohya was so startled he half rose from his seat. "I just got back from the moon. What am I, the Flying Dutchman?"

"Can't be helped. Tanegashima is where the launch vehicle is. ELE suggested sending you, but now Tech Development is pushing for you to go too. Sando thought your report from the moon was top-notch."

"You're just saying that so I'll shut up," said Sohya, morose.

"Maybe. It's not up to you anyway," Iwaki shot back. "Unless you want to find another job, better relax and enjoy the ride."

"All right, okay." Worn out, Sohya slumped into his seat. A chuckle came from the rear seat.

"You did a good job of cozying up to the chairman's grand-daughter, but that won't work with me," said Reika. "I hope you're ready."

"Cozy up to her? Give me a break," Sohya said tiredly. He was starting to wonder whether his real job was babysitting people no one else wanted to deal with.

CHAPTER 3
LAUNCH VEHICLE DEVELOPMENT AND
LAUNCH FACILITY

[1]

"HERE'S THE COFFEE, Boss. Whoa!"

Shinji Tai opened the door to the president's office and nearly lost his balance as the two visitors brushed past him. They marched off down the corridor without a word of apology.

"Hey, what about the coffee?" Shinji stared after them.

"Bring it here. I'll drink it."

Ryuichi Yaenami motioned to Shinji from behind his desk. The early autumn heat was still fierce on Tanegashima Island, but Tenryu Galaxy Transport's president was, as always, impeccably dressed. Today's suit was tailored Italian. His long hair—had it ever been trimmed?—swept over his head and shoulders like a lion's mane. Shinji set the tray of iced coffees on the table in front of the desk. Ryuichi grabbed one and gulped it down.

"Should I bring them back?" said Shinji anxiously.

"Don't bother. The whole thing's off. Norvalt's going with somebody else."

"What did we screw up? Their organ synthesis satellite went up without a hitch."

"We didn't screw anything up," Ryuichi said. "The launch team did the job perfectly—like always. They worked like slaves. Nobody slept for a week. You know what they accomplished."

Shinji nodded. He was the director of TGT's Advanced Research Department. "'Course, I'm not on the launch team. I wasn't even in the blockhouse yesterday. I was kicking back with a can of juice, watching everything from Takesaki."

"The control center? You jackass! Stay the hell away from the press. What if they start asking questions?"

"No worries. The only ones there were this NHK reporter and some deadwood from MEXT. No way would they recognize me."

Ryuichi's face fell. "No commercial broadcasters? Oh well. With only two launches a year they were bound to forget us sooner or later." His shoulders sagged.

"So what were the Norvalt guys unhappy about?" asked Shinji.

"'Not enough depth.' 'People who work without sleep for days on end are going to screw up sooner or later.' They want people who look more 'experienced.' More 'proficient.' They'll probably take their next launch to China or India," said Ryuichi.

Ryuichi slapped the table angrily. "What the hell do you expect? We don't have enough experience! We're lucky to get two launches a year. How do we work out the kinks? I'm busting my ass rotating our people into different jobs. Holding seminars with the old industry veterans. Anything to help the younger guys get seasoned. Anything!"

"Our competitors launch pretty much every month. I'm not surprised Norvalt thinks we're greenhorns." Shinji sounded dejected. "That's why we kill ourselves doing a good job, and it pushes our fees up. Higher fees mean less work. And that means less experience."

"It's a vicious cycle. God *damn* it! The least the government could do is give us their satellites."

"Now that we're privatized, they treat us like outsiders," said Shinji. "They send all their astronauts to NASA. Foreign rockets launch Japanese satellites. Get this—yesterday the guys from MEXT said it was amazing that Japan had developed the capability to launch such great rockets. 'Developed'? We've been building launch vehicles for thirty years. What's amazing is how little attention anyone is paying."

"What do you expect?" muttered Ryuichi. "They don't have a stake in the industry. We might as well be invisible. These bureaucrats should be chosen via the web, just like the politicians."

"On the other hand, we only managed to grab this facility because it wasn't making money."

"The place was going to waste. All they were launching were birds."

Ryuichi looked out the window. Shinji followed his gaze. TGT's headquarters looked out across a primeval forest of intense green. Mangroves thrived in pristine wetlands. The lush foliage rippled lazily in the offshore breeze. In the distance, TGT's launch complex rose from its cape jutting into the Pacific. The Vehicle Assembly Building, a gigantic white tombstone, shimmered in the heat like a mirage. Other than the flora and fauna, everything in the ten kilometers between the three-story headquarters building and the twin launchpads was under the control of Tenryu Galaxy Transport.

Ryuichi lit a domestic cigarette with a Longines lighter and absently blew a cloud of smoke. "Maybe it's time to get into the safari-land business."

"Or better yet, sell this place, take the money, and run."

The two men sighed.

Tenryu Galaxy Transport had been founded by Ryuichi Yaenami to offer commercial satellite launch services. TGT was now Japan's only rocket manufacturer and launch facility. Until the turn of the century, rocket manufacturing and launches were controlled by twin government entities, the National Space Development Agency and the Institute of Space and Aeronautical Science. The fact that TGT was now in control was the outcome of administrative restructuring carried out by Japan's government.

Deregulation, privatization, and cost reduction were the bywords of restructuring, and no exception was made for space development. In 2003, NASDA and ISAS had been merged with the National Aerospace Laboratory of Japan to form the Japan Aerospace Exploration Agency—JAXA. As if that wasn't enough restructuring, a large percentage of JAXA's staff was soon spun off to the private sector. Rocket development would now depend on profit and loss accounting, not the public purse. Inexpensive foreign launch vehicles would put Japan's satellites into orbit.

Until the waves of change hit, Japan's launch vehicles had been built jointly by NASDA, ISAS, and two giant corporations, Mitsubishi Heavy Industries and IHI. But space development was under MEXT, the Ministry of Education, Culture, Sports, Science and Technology. Following the government's mandate, the ministry slashed funding for NASDA and ISAS. Launching Japanese satellites and astronauts was left completely in American hands. With little work coming in, Mitsubishi and IHI backed away from space development, and the Japanese launch industry languished.

That was when Ryuichi saw his opportunity. The son of a wealthy businessman, he had been fascinated by rockets as a child. As he grew up, he watched in frustration as Japan's space program struggled to maintain its focus while China forged ahead and sent men into space. Like many of the sons of wealthy fathers, however, Ryuichi seemed unable to find his footing as an adult. He audited university aerospace lectures, worked as a parallel importer of foreign autos, managed to obtain a light aircraft license, knocked around Southeast Asia selling used industrial equipment, and generally drifted through life. Then five years ago, he had stumbled across Shinji Tai, and his path in life was set.

Shinji was a graduate student incubating revolutionary ideas in aerospace materials science. But in Japan's hierarchical academic environment, he couldn't get the funding or support to verify his concepts. One evening he was impatiently expounding his theories to several slower-witted friends in a local pub. Ryuichi was at the next table. He bought Shinji a beer, and in ten minutes the two men were off in a corner, deep in a discussion of Shinji's ideas.

Ryuichi was electrified. If Shinji were right, the course of history would be altered. But the young man had nothing he needed to pursue his ideas: no experience, no money, no staff, no time. At this rate, by the time he made real progress, some foreign competitor would be far ahead. Ryuichi vowed to help.

He moved quickly. After convincing Shinji to join him, he approached people Shinji recommended as capable and persuaded them to work with him. He liquidated several business ventures to generate working capital. When the grapevine brought news that Mitsubishi Heavy Industries was looking to sell their Space Development Group, he called in every favor in his Rolodex and actually succeeded in bagging it.

This was the beginning of Tenryu Galaxy Transport. Ryuichi's success in negotiating the deal with a colossus of Japanese industry—without powerful backers—and in navigating MEXT's bureaucracy to obtain approval for the deal sent ripples of astonishment through Japan's business circles.

After that, it was all downhill. Ryuichi intended to use TGT to implement the sort of drastic restructuring that old-line companies like Mitsubishi found impossible. Then he would put the business on a paying basis, gain experience, and wait for an opportunity to commercialize Shinji's theories. But it was far harder than he thought.

Simply put, there was no demand. Ryuichi planned to staunch the red ink of Mitsubishi's cast-off division by reorganizing it. But once it was under his control, he discovered that a bloated organization was the least of his problems. *There was no demand*. Under the wing of government, almost all of Mitsubishi's space-related revenues had arrived courtesy of the taxpayer. Ryuichi was forced to admit that getting out of the business was probably a smart move for the government.

Without official patronage, he had no choice but to go to the private sector for launch business. But this proved equally tough. The global market for satellite launches was around twenty trillion yen, which seemed a large enough number. But the telecommunications market—the source for most launches—was twenty times larger. Absolute demand for launches was limited. And unlike the telecommunications industry, where new ventures were continually sprouting up and disappearing, success in the launch business was critically dependent on having an established track record and the trust of your customers. There was little opportunity for a newcomer like TGT to grab a piece of the business.

Ironically, one of TGT's few selling points was the fact that it was ignored by its own government. The major players—including the national space agencies of America, Russia, and the EU—were strongly influenced by national defense and economic policies. This sometimes made them reluctant to service certain customers. By promoting TGT as a neutral party with no political or military entanglements, Ryuichi managed to keep just enough business coming through the door to keep from folding.

A typical "orphan" project was this September's launch of an H-3C rocket carrying an experimental satellite for a Swiss multinational pharmaceuticals conglomerate. Norvalt Pharmaceuticals was making major investments in the development of artificial organs for regenerative medicine, and the satellite was designed for microgravity cultivation of tissue for organ synthesis. Organs are three-dimensional organizations of cells, but in a lab culture dish on Earth the cells would only grow horizontally. Cultivating a three-axis structure called for tissue engineering; the cells had to be grown in an environment that allowed them to adhere to a framework of biodegradable polymer. The tissue could then be cultivated in a liquid matrix. But failure to create tissue with the required blood vessel density, along with structural distortions caused by convection in the liquid, was holding up future research.

In a microgravity environment, three-dimensional structures could be cultivated free of distortion. But Norvalt's attempts to do this had run into another roadblock. The cell line they were using was immortal, with enhanced glycolysis capability and viability in a low-oxygen environment—not unlike cancer cells. Most space agencies were extremely nervous about putting payload like that into orbit over their territory. NASA would not approve a launch without reams of documentation guaranteeing public safety in the event of an accident.

Norvalt's experiment, however, was meant to generate profit. Their competitors would be climbing over each other to get copies of the disclosure documents. This knocked the leading space agencies out of contention. At the same time, the few nations with a fledgling launch capability could not deliver the kind of low-vibration lifting necessary to ensure the functioning of Norvalt's delicate satellite.

TGT stepped up to fill the gap, and the launch went flawlessly. Like its H-series predecessors, the H-3C, first launched in 2019, was the cutting edge of the art and science of rocketry. Norvalt's twenty-two-ton satellite was the fifteenth successful launch for the H-3C, which carried it into orbit with an astonishing vibration ceiling of 100 dB. The final four-hundred-kilometer orbit had a variance of only forty meters. China's National Space Administration probably could have beaten TGT's seven-billion-yen launch fee by 20 percent. But thanks to meticulous vehicle and facilities maintenance, the Japanese company boasted a higher successful launch rate. Without a doubt, TGT delivered satisfactory service.

Yet Norvalt had just turned down a deal for additional launches. If the concerns they'd stated were real, they would probably take their next launch to a relatively experienced space agency—probably India or China. Chinese and Indian launch vehicles were crude compared to the H-3C, but with some investment in vibration damping, they could probably be made serviceable. Had Norvalt decided that the extra cost would offset the advantages of using TGT? If so, Ryuichi and Shinji had good reason to be depressed.

"Well, we're in a pickle now. There's nothing on the schedule." Shinji was stuffing himself with the sweet potato pastries, an island delicacy, that he'd brought in with the coffee. He knew TGT was in dire straits, but he was optimistic by nature and had boundless confidence in this man who had plucked him from academic obscurity. "What should we do?" he added. "Borrow money for another demo launch?"

Launching for the sake of launching was part of rocket development. Technology required honing, and TGT's hundreds of technicians and launch specialists needed to keep their skills sharp. Better to isolate and deal with problems on test launches than with a customer's payload. It allowed TGT engineers to tweak their designs and maintain their edge and motivation.

Of course, test launches didn't pay. Ryuichi was going to almost pathetic lengths to squeeze costs in an effort to ensure continued funding for employee motivation, which mostly meant drinking sessions. He'd recently switched his company car from an expensive foreign model to a used domestic clunker.

Ryuichi's usual comeback to Shinji's laid-back observations was humorous dismissal, but now he plunged a hand into his lion's mane and scratched thoughtfully. "There's one more angle. We've got some more visitors today."

"Oh? From where?"

"Japan. Gotoba Engineering, and Eden something. Some kind of park operator. Heard of them?"

"Sure, I've heard of Eden. Tokai Eden is right next to our Tobishima plant in Nagoya. What are they coming here for?" said Shinji. He shook his head. "An amusement park operator and an engineering company. What would they need a rocket for? Maybe it's some kind of ride."

"They sounded serious on the phone about putting something into orbit," said Ryuichi. "But they obviously know zip about rockets. I need you in the meeting. You're good at explaining this sort of thing to the uninitiated."

"Is that why you called me down from Tobishima? I thought I was just here to serve coffee."

"Why the hell would I need a scruffy mutt like you to serve coffee? My assistant's off today." Ryuichi stared at him and chuckled. Shinji's rumpled white lab coat was as much a part of his image as the president's tailored suits. It only made him look busier when it got dirty, and it saved him from explaining where he fit in at the company. He wore it everywhere. "Great hair, 'cept for the dandruff" was the saying around the office. Clean but rarely combed, it looked like a sparrow's nest. Behind gold-rimmed wire frames, his eyes seemed perpetually narrowed in amusement. Tall and stooped, he shuffled rather than walked. One could not exactly say he was handsome.

Ryuichi glanced at his gold wearcom—he used to have a Rolex, but the device on his wrist was now a lowly Seiko—and said, "They should be here about now. Is there a taxi outside?"

"What taxi? The taxi company went bust, remember? Didn't you send someone to meet them?"

"Damn! I totally forgot. I was too busy thinking about those Norvalt guys." Ryuichi snapped his fingers in frustration. Shinji was dialing the airport on his wearcom when the room was filled with the whirling boom of engines. The two men stuck their heads outside and looked up into a vast cerulean sky, far bluer than over the main islands.

"Whoa!" shouted Shinji. "Pretty swank, coming in a helicopter. See? There's the Eden logo."

"That's no helicopter. It's a Boeing tilt-rotor. They must've flown nonstop from Nagoya. That's why they didn't call from the airport. Shinji, you better clear the parking lot."

"Is it okay for them to land? This isn't a heliport. Won't air traffic control come down on us?"

"Rockets are a lot more dangerous. The control tower won't mind. Helicopters don't have a habit of exploding," Ryuichi deadpanned.

Shinji left the room. Soon TGT staff began streaming out of the building. As the tilt-rotor hovered motionless, employees ran through the propwash to their cars and began moving them to the periphery. A few moments later the small aircraft, each wing tipped with a single proprotor engine, floated down onto the parking lot.

First off the plane was a red-haired woman in a business suit, followed by a man who appeared younger than Shinji. The woman shielded her head with a briefcase but was buffeted by the wind and fell to the pavement before she was clear of the propwash. The man with her moved to help her up, but instead of accepting his outstretched hand she yelled at him. Apparently these two were not exactly on the same team.

Watching from the third floor, Ryuichi chuckled to himself. "Well, well. This should be interesting."

A few minutes later Shinji was back with the visitors. The woman had done her best to rearrange her hair. She assumed a winning smile and thrust a hand toward Ryuichi. The man did the same.

"Reika Hozumi, Eden Leisure Entertainment. This is Sohya Aomine from Gotoba Engineering."

"Sohya Aomine, Gotoba Engineering. This is Reika Hozumi from ELE."

The two spoke simultaneously, eyed each other suspiciously, and kept their hands extended. If Ryuichi was amused, he was also discouraged. This pair didn't look much like the saviors TGT desperately needed now.

"Ryuichi Yaenami. President of Tenryu Galaxy Transport." Ryuichi grabbed both outstretched hands and pumped them simultaneously. Realizing how ridiculous they looked, his visitors blushed.

"Very efficient. Egalitarian, even." Shinji was dead earnest.

[2]

HANDSHAKES OUT OF the way, they moved on to the formality of exchanging business e-cards via wearcom. Reika's French-made designer unit relied on a tiny touch panel and voice recognition rather than the usual panel/keyboard combo. Ryuichi briefly praised its refined design, but the tension in the air didn't ease. Both visitors seemed to have their guards well up.

As soon as everyone was seated, Ryuichi cut to the chase. "You said over the phone you wanted to send a heavy payload into space. How much mass are we talking?"

Reika answered without hesitation. She had already reviewed Gotoba's estimate and operational analysis in detail. Sohya was still not totally familiar with the plan and kept glancing at his wearcom.

"For Phase One, we'll need to launch a probe. That's two tons. Over the next ten years, we want to send around two hundred tons of equipment and materials."

"Two hundred tons? That's quite a lot." Ryuichi sat back and nodded. He tried not to look surprised. If the deal went through, this one client would be enough to feed TGT for the whole ten years. Then again, it wasn't at all unusual for clients to throw out a number like this early in the discussion. Then sticker shock set in as they discovered how much it would cost to launch their payload.

"In that case, you'd need at least nine launches, assuming efficient payload distribution. Our H-3Cs can put 23.5 tons into low earth orbit, so long as you allocate your payload according to that capacity..."

"And how much would the fee for nine launches be?"

"Well, launch vehicles are pretty much made to order," said Ryuichi. "They take a lot of craftsmanship. Building one can take several years. Foreign exchange fluctuations and new technology can affect the bottom line, so it's hard to quote an exact figure. But based on experience to date? Seven billion yen per launch. Nine launches…say fifty-five billion, give or take three billion or so. We save a bit on scale economies."

Sohya looked up from his wearcom and nudged Reika. "Too low."

"Perhaps," she said. "Maybe the metrics we used for our projections are out of date. Mr. Yaenami, how much could those costs vary in practice? Could they end up being, say, ten times higher?"

"Not a chance. Last century the yen went from 240 to the dollar down to around 80, so in dollar terms, yeah, the price tripled. But this is a domestic transaction, correct? There's no way the final price could even double."

Reika paused for a moment. "I'm sorry. We seem to have made a mistake. We assumed the costs would be higher."

Ryuichi smiled. "If we can give you what you want at a lower price, is that a problem?"

"No, of course not. It's just…Tell me, is there only one type of rocket? We thought sending a payload to the moon would require something different from what you have."

"The moon?" Ryuichi wasn't sure he'd heard correctly. "You want to put two hundred tons *on the moon*?"

"That's right."

"Two hundred—wait, what's the payload? Are you going to explore the surface?"

"We're going to build a base at the moon's south pole. A manned base." Sohya nodded.

Ryuichi was now speechless. His visitors had struck him as unsophisticated, but he hadn't guessed that they'd be crazy. So far he'd heard many outlandish proposals, all completely impractical. But for sheer stupidity, this latest proposal beat everything hollow.

Reika looked at him with a hint of nervousness. "Is getting to the moon harder than launching satellites?"

"Hard?" Ryuichi finally mustered a response. "You know how far away that is?"

"It varies between 356,000 and 406,000 kilometers," she answered brightly. "That's about a thousand times farther than low earth orbit. But there's no gravity in space, right? Once you're outside the atmosphere, we thought the distance wouldn't matter much."

Right. In other words, you dug out your high school astronomy textbook and brushed up for half an hour. And that's about all you know. Hey, wait a minute… As he groped for a diplomatic answer, Ryuichi suddenly realized that his other visitor looked oddly familiar. Wasn't this the guy from the evening news?

"Mr. Aomine? Are you the Aomine who went to China's moon base?"

"Yes, that would be me."

"Your training and orientation must've been quite a challenge. How much time did it take to get ready for launch? A year?"

"I'm embarrassed to say this, but we actually trained very little. We had to make the next supply mission, so a month was all we had. Other than the physical exams, all we did was train for basic emergencies."

Ryuichi groaned inwardly. *And this one's just a space tourist.* He was glad Shinji was here. He looked at his research director.

"Shinji, I think this would be a good time to explain something about rocket capabilities."

"Should I start with Goddard?"

"Better start with Jules Verne. No, just start anywhere."

Shinji nodded and turned to the visitors. Without further ado he said, "Do you know how fast a satellite travels?"

Reika answered immediately. "Seven point nine two kilometers per second."

Shinji nodded. "And why does it travel that fast?"

"So it can perform its functions efficiently, I guess. Like monitor the earth's surface. There's no atmosphere to slow it down, so it can go a good deal faster than an airplane."

"I see. Okay, maybe I better back up." Shinji scratched his

head and started in again. "A satellite travels as fast as it does to continue falling around the earth. The only reason it goes faster than an aircraft is because if it doesn't, it won't stay in orbit. A ball thrown horizontally to the earth's surface will hit the ground eventually. But if you throw it fast enough, it will keep falling around the curvature of the earth forever. You'd need to throw it at 7.9 kilometers per second. This is known as the first cosmic velocity."

"I see." Reika seemed slightly mystified.

"If you throw it even faster, it flies out into the solar system. This is the second cosmic velocity, *escape* velocity: 11.2 kilometers per second. If you want to reach the moon, you have to be traveling at least this fast. Please remember this number.

"Now, the gross weight of the H-3C launch vehicle is 520 tons. Do you know what percentage of that weight is taken up by fuel?"

Reika greeted this sudden shift in topic with puzzled silence. Shinji plunged ahead.

"Eighty percent, about 420 tons. This is called the fuel fraction. For a jet airliner the fuel fraction would be about 40 percent. Why carry this much fuel? Because the first cosmic velocity is so high. To use the usual comparison, it's eight times the speed of a rifle bullet or twenty-five times the speed of an airliner. You don't get that kind of speed from just any engine. A rocket engine is designed to squeeze the theoretical limit of power, or pretty close to it, out of the exothermic reaction of rocket fuel combustion. By feeding a huge amount of fuel into an engine like that, we can escape Earth's gravity—but just barely."

"So it's not possible to reach the moon?" Reika broke in, seemingly irritated at this long-winded digression. Shinji laughed and waved his hand, no.

"Of course it's possible. All I'm saying is that spacecraft travel at unbelievably high speeds. The differential between the first and second cosmic velocities is 3.3 kilometers per second. That's the extra speed you need to get out of low earth orbit. This differential alone is 12,000 kilometers an hour. So we'll have to carry even more fuel to boost ourselves up to that speed. And the weight of that fuel comes out of your payload."

"How much payload do we have to sacrifice to carry the extra fuel?"

"Eighty percent. That means you can carry about five tons to the moon," said Shinji.

"So the cost goes up by a factor of five?"

"I wish it were that simple. If you plan to build a base, you want to put your payload *on* the moon, not just in orbit around it. That means you need a lunar lander. The lander will account for around half the mass you can put on the surface. And there's another problem on top of that."

"What now?" Reika frowned.

"Look, I'm just telling you how it is," said Shinji.

Sohya spoke up. "The base will be manned."

"Exactly." Shinji smiled.

"The Chinese invested a huge amount on their Long March rocket to make it safe enough to carry passengers," said Sohya. "The total cost of our launch was almost eight billion yen, with four passengers and the twenty-one-ton Xiwangmu module. But no Japanese rocket has ever taken passengers into space, and the extra safety margin is going to cost us."

"That's right. We've successfully launched the H-3C fifteen times in a row. Based on the design, the expected success rate is actually 95 percent. Still, that's quite high. Ten years ago, 90 percent was considered enough. Launch ten, lose one. Launch fifty, lose three, maybe four. Failures are expected. Most of them take place early when your design is new. Japanese rockets have a low total success rate for the simple reason that not many have been launched."

"One out of every ten!" Reika was astonished. "Then how can we put people on them?"

"Well, we're talking about unmanned rockets. For manned flight, you have to work like the devil to get your reliability up to

98 percent, at least. Still, failures happen. NASA's space shuttle flew 150 times in forty years. They lost three vehicles, two with crews. If your chance of failure is about the same as winning a prize in a supermarket drawing, you can't operate commercially. You have to get your failure rate below 1 percent. But that's a tough one." Shinji scratched his head again.

"Take the LE-11 engine on the H-3C. Any engine running on LOX and liquid hydrogen is going to be a delicate beast, but the LE-11's two-stage combustion system is unbelievably complex. It uses dual 50,000 rpm turbines. Starting with its direct ancestor, the experimental H-2, then the production-model H-2A, the cluster-engine H-2C, the H-3 using the LE-11, and now the cluster-engine H-3C, we've brought the design as far as we can. That is, without TROPHY."

"Shinji!" Ryuichi cocked an eyebrow. Shinji's mouth snapped shut.

"So you see how things are," continued Ryuichi. "Sending people to the moon is a whole different ball game from launching satellites. If you want a crew of people with engineering equipment hauling building materials around on the surface, you can't bunk them in a telephone booth, the way NASA did with the Apollo astronauts. You need to build long-term habitats, rotate your crews, that kind of thing. The operational scale gets very big, very quickly." He turned to Shinji. "About how much total payload do you think they'd need to launch?"

"Well, if we use the Apollo program as a baseline…" Shinji's gaze floated toward the ceiling as he worked the numbers in his head. He brought his eyes level again and frowned. "Putting two hundred tons on the surface would require a hundred, maybe two hundred tons of support payload. On top of that, sending people there and back, even with current technology, you'll need about five tons of support payload per person. How many you were thinking?"

"We're planning for ten people in the beginning," said Reika. "Ultimately we want fifty people on the base."

"Say a hundred people or more over ten years, with rotations. That's five hundred tons. So you'd have to put eight hundred tons of payload on the moon. That's the same as putting four thousand tons into low earth orbit. A ton in low orbit runs a bit over three hundred million yen, so the total would be—"

"One point two trillion…" Reika's voice was hoarse.

Sohya stared at her. "See?"

"Yes, I do. That was the estimate. But for everything: payload, salaries, operations—not just the launches." Reika looked sadly at her wearcom. She and Sohya exchanged glances. Some shared sense of disappointment seemed to have brought them together for a moment. They lowered their heads.

Sohya whispered, "What are you going to do? That's way over your budget."

"Mr. Toenji gave me a trump card." Reika looked up and said innocently, "Everything we've been discussing assumes that we use conventional rockets."

"Well, of course," said Ryuichi. "But as I told you, the vehicle is the same for low earth orbit or a trip to the moon. The H-3C is all we can offer you."

"As of now. But we understand you've got a new engine on the drawing board."

"A new engine? No, we don't have anything like that."

"Something called TROPHY?"

Ryuichi and Shinji flinched in surprise. *Yes*, thought Reika.

"I believe it stands for TRansfOrming Power source HYbrid engine. We hear you're working on it right now. Why, Mr. Tai even mentioned it a moment ago."

"Where did you hear that?" asked Shinji, astonished.

"Shinji, would you *please*?" Ryuichi winced. But Shinji had already taken the bait.

"We're not at liberty to say." Reika smiled. "But are we in agreement that such a project is under way?"

"Yes, it does exist," said Ryuichi. "But we're not at the stage where—"

"Thanks for confirming it. If development is successful, we presume our costs would drop significantly."

"That would be speculation." Ryuichi stalled for time. He was scrambling to think through the pros and cons of the situation. TROPHY was extremely confidential. It might be TGT's sole long-term chance for survival. At the heart of the project were Shinji's revolutionary theories—theories Ryuichi was betting the company's future on.

It was his dream to someday apply those ideas to a launch vehicle. Yet if TGT's current dry spell continued, the dream might never be realized. That was something he wanted to avoid at all costs. The alternatives seemed to be getting government approval to seek outside investors or, in the worst case, selling the development rights to TROPHY. If they sold the rights, NASA or ESA could probably finish the work, but it would be impossible for Ryuichi or Shinji to share in the triumph.

Was knowledge of TROPHY something he could entrust to these two people? Perhaps they were industrial spies, posing as greenhorns? That seemed a real possibility.

Reika interrupted Ryuichi's train of thought. "It's not speculation. If TROPHY is feasible, we'll cover your development costs," she said as Ryuichi's jaw dropped. "Does that interest you?"

"Do you realize how much we're talking here?" said Ryuichi, returning to reality. "It costs ten times as much to develop a rocket as it does to build one unit. It can't be done for a billion or two."

"We're prepared to pay twenty billion if you can develop the engine. With economies of scale, TROPHY could cut today's launch costs by 95 percent."

"Where did you find all this out?" marveled Ryuichi.

"Boss!" Shinji slapped his forehead. "My master's thesis. My academic advisor posted the abstract on the institute's website.

Other than that, he hardly paid attention to it. Someone probably read the abstract and remembered it."

"It's always something, isn't it?" Ryuichi said with a sigh. "Well, I guess you're not just fishing."

He was in a quandary. His visitors didn't seem to be bluffing. He was no longer concerned about how much they knew. His foreign competitors probably had far more information concerning TROPHY and its workings than these two did. The question was, could he trust them to deliver? Did they really share his determination to go into space?

"I'll be frank," said Ryuichi. "You have to understand: if TROPHY succeeds, humanity's future will completely change. I'm betting everything I have on it. Give me your firm commitment to stick with this all the way to the end and not bail out when the going gets tough, and I'll do the same. Can you promise me that?"

Sohya straightened up and peered at Ryuichi, who was more than a dozen years older. Ryuichi couldn't help but smile at the fire in his eyes.

"If that's what you want, you have my promise. I'm sure my bosses will agree. In fact, I'll make sure they do."

Ryuichi was impressed. This young man had none of the cynicism so typical of others his age. They were on the same wavelength. Of course, Sohya's assurances didn't amount to a signature on a contract. But then again, his company wouldn't have sent him unless they trusted him to carry the ball. Ryuichi suddenly recalled that Gotoba's founder and president was a bit of an *enfant terrible* himself.

Reika had a different response, just as simple and straightforward. "If we're going to fund you, we expect a return on our investment. If this technology is going to change mankind's future, the demand will be enormous. As long as there's a possibility for that kind of return, ELE will commit to going the distance. Shall we discuss the allocation of profits?" Reika's fingertips floated over her wearcom.

I might have guessed, thought Ryuichi. *ELE is the client, Gotoba is the contractor. Of course the client is going to talk about money, not about some dream.* Still, if both his visitors had been prepared to move ahead without even trying to negotiate, that would have been suspicious indeed. The fact that ELE's representative was a blinkered bean counter couldn't be helped. Later, however, Ryuichi would discover that his impression was off the mark.

"Let's count our chickens later. First you'd better take a look at TROPHY."

"You already have a prototype?" Reika was astonished.

"If all we had to show you were blueprints, I wouldn't be making such a big deal out of it. Let's take a drive," said Shinji. He stood up. He wore a different smile now, the smile of a man whose quest was about to be fulfilled.

———————

TANEGASHIMA SPACE CENTER sprawled across more than two thousand acres of developed and undeveloped land on the southern tip of the island. After driving several kilometers through a wild forest, they emerged onto a beach edged by the ultramarine waters of the Pacific. They left the car and walked toward a strange structure, about ten meters high and thirty meters deep. A huge metal shutter, closed now, was set into the front of the building facing south toward the ocean.

It seemed to be a conventional warehouse, but the sides and rear were enclosed by high earthen embankments, like gigantic levees. A telephone pole stood at each corner. Steel cables were strung between the poles, enclosing the top, sides, and rear of the structure. To the south, between building and ocean, was another embankment, faced with concrete and sloping gently upward. It almost seemed as if an aircraft coming out of the warehouse could use the ramp to quickly gain altitude. Sohya easily walked up it and stood at the top, looking out over the ocean. "Looks like the catapult on an aircraft carrier," he called to Reika, who was standing at the bottom.

"I don't think catapults are this beat-up," she replied.

"Beat-up?" said Sohya. Reika pointed at his feet. He looked down at a huge grayish pink blotch, roughly star-shaped, in the center of the ramp. The surface seemed to have been blasted off in some spots. Looking closer, he saw that the concrete was roughened by fused particles of aggregate, all flowing in one direction like stalactites in a limestone cave. *Like the side of a building after a fire*, thought Sohya. But this was very different from the usual fire damage. The fused particles seemed to be straining upward, as if intense fire had flowed up the sloping surface.

"This way!" Ryuichi called from the warehouse. Sohya ran down the embankment and joined him.

"What kind of place is this?" he asked.

"Our SRB-R firing facility," said Ryuichi. "For testing solid boosters like the ones on the H-3C."

"Oh, those cute crayon things on the side of the rocket," said Sohya.

"You call several hundred tons of solid propellant 'cute'?" said Ryuichi.

"Could we dispense with the word games?" said Reika, frowning. Sohya shrugged, then realized what Ryuichi had just said.

"When you say 'test,' you mean you ignite those things right here?"

"That's exactly what we do," answered Ryuichi. He motioned to the shutter, then the concrete ramp. "The booster fires horizontally toward the ocean. The flame deflector guides the exhaust toward the sky. The solid propellant is rubber based. Imagine burning eighty tons of tires in a minute and forty seconds. The smoke is unbelievable."

"Do the boosters ever explode?" asked Reika.

"That's why we have embankments around the building. If there's an explosion, we at least want to funnel the blast wave upward. The steel cables are lightning rods. Fortunately we've never needed them so far." Ryuichi looked in through the service door. "Today it just so happens we've got TROPHY set up for an ignition test. Officially, we're doing a conventional SRB test burn. Shinji, open the shutter."

"Yes, sir." The voice came from inside. As the huge door rose, sunlight advanced along the floor and up across the business end of a strange-looking device. It resembled a wind tunnel with an exhaust slit like the maw of a shark. Shinji strolled out from among the technicians busily swarming around the engine. He extended his palm toward the device.

"This is TROPHY-E103. Pretty simple, don't you think?"

Sohya and Reika walked deeper into the building and began inspecting the engine, which rested horizontally on its test stand. Pointing out to sea, the nozzle was a simple box shape, unlike the bell-shaped nozzles of conventional rocket engines. There was little if any constriction between the silver-gray nozzle and the next section, which continued the one-meter square profile for another four meters, except that its cross section expanded gently, making it fatter toward the end. The far end of this section seemed to be a wedge-shaped air intake that could be constricted with a simple vent. The only other visible mechanisms around the intake were a few pipes that apparently served as sensors and actuators.

Beyond and in line with this was a hulking, bewilderingly complicated mass of tubes and piping, several of which extended into the intake. The cluster of piping looked like some gigantic, metallic internal organ. Neither Sohya nor Reika knew what to make of it, but as they approached it, Shinji said, "Everything from there on back is just the supply module for this experiment. It's not part of the final build."

"From where on back?" asked Sohya.

"From there. The square section is TROPHY itself." Shinji pointed from the nozzle to the wedge-shaped intake. The entire device was only seven meters long. Clearly a simple design, even suspiciously simple. The thing certainly didn't look like some new technology that was poised to change the world.

"You look surprised," Shinji said, as if he'd read their minds. He happily launched into his explanation. "This is TROPHY test engine three. As you can see, it's not a conventional engine. The lower section acts as a rocket engine, while the upper section is an air-breathing engine for use in the atmosphere."

"Air-breathing? For space travel?" said Sohya.

"A launch vehicle operates in the atmosphere at first, of course. That's where TROPHY functions as a ramjet—technically, a ducted scramjet. Outside the atmosphere, it operates as a straight-forward rocket engine. That's why we call it a transforming power source. Back at headquarters we were talking about fuel fractions, the percentage of a vehicle's gross weight accounted for by fuel. For a rocket, the fuel fraction is 80 percent, but you need more than two-thirds of that just to reach an altitude of fifty kilometers and a ground speed of 1.6 kilometers per second. All that fuel is consumed before you even leave the atmosphere. Cut the fuel requirement and you can carry more payload.

"We can't reduce the amount of hydrogen we carry, but the atmosphere has all the oxygen we need to get to space. By making use of this oxygen, TROPHY achieves an extremely high specific impulse."

"I don't understand," said Sohya.

"Okay. Roughly speaking, specific impulse is the number of pounds of thrust the engine can produce each second, per pound of fuel. The mass units drop out when we do the calculation, so we measure specific impulse in seconds. It's slightly complicated, but you can think of it as something like fuel efficiency. The practical limit for liquid-fueled rockets is a specific impulse of around 450 seconds. With TROPHY, we can get as much as four thousand seconds of specific impulse."

Shinji looked at Reika and Sohya as if waiting for them to be impressed, but they just stared blankly. He looked slightly disappointed.

"Scientists have been trying to break five hundred seconds of specific impulse in a practical rocket engine for half a century. Everyone thought it was impossible."

"That's quite an achievement." Sohya nodded, but he didn't really grasp what Shinji was saying. Reika looked at Shinji doubtfully.

"If a simple engine like this can break such an impossible barrier, why has it taken so long for someone to do it?"

Shinji brightened. "The design is simple, sure. But only TGT can fabricate the components. The type of air-breathing engine I mentioned just now is called a ramjet. An engine like this, which is capable of burning fuel in a supersonic airflow, is a faster variation of a ramjet called a scramjet. You see, if the air coming through the intake is faster than the speed of sound, it's nearly impossible to keep your fuel burning as it feeds into the engine. The shock wave blows your burning fuel out like a candle. And at high speeds, air friction generates tremendous heat all over the surface of the rocket. Conventional materials can't stand up to it. What makes TROPHY possible is a certain material I've developed."

Shinji placed his hand on the nozzle. Sohya suddenly realized that its outer surface was completely smooth, unlike the ribbed structure he recalled from other nozzles.

"This is it. We used a specialized cermet—a ceramic metal alloy. Metal is hard but not very heat resistant. Ceramics are brittle but stand up well to high temperatures. This material gives us the advantages of both. I discovered that cladding the engine with this cermet makes for efficient laminar flow control, and that gives you smooth fuel mixing and combustion in a supersonic airstream. So you can see why no one's succeeded in developing a practical scramjet till now. They didn't have this material.

"A scramjet's just the start. The alloy allowed us to make several revolutionary improvements. There's no need to wrap hydrogen cooling lines around the nozzle, for example. That makes manufacturing simpler, gives you a safer motor, and reduces weight all at once. The intake is simpler, lighter, and stronger. Our cermet will be used in the rocket fairing and body, so the vehicle itself will generate less drag when passing through the atmosphere—but we haven't built a test rocket yet."

"Mr. Tai…?" Sohya tapped Shinji on the shoulder. TGT's research director's voice had grown feverish, as if he were addressing a huge crowd. "We'll leave the technical details to you. Just tell me, what kind of rocket will this engine power?"

"One the same size as the H-3C but with ten times more payload," Shinji said casually. Sohya gasped.

"You mean instead of twenty-four tons, you'll be able to lift 240?"

"Yes. At half the cost."

"Half…" Sohya was in shock.

"Structural strength and manufacturing tolerances will no longer be a major issue. Parts will be fewer and simpler. I'd guess a single rocket will have around three hundred thousand parts. That's a tenth of what's needed now."

"That's…that's unbelievable." Sohya was beginning to grasp the significance of this engine. He said to Reika, "Did you hear that? You're going to make a fortune with this thing."

"I wonder." She pressed her palms anxiously against her cheeks. "There's something important I have to ask. Have you patented any of this?"

Shinji looked deflated. "Not yet. If we drop the veil and apply now, the rest of the world will discover what we're onto. But if we keep quiet, someone might beat us to the punch. We figured we'd apply once we had a working prototype. It's a real dilemma."

Ryuichi spoke up. "Let's do it now. It's time. With backing, we can make this happen. We don't have to keep it secret anymore. We should file defensive patents now to make sure no one gets the jump on us."

"Good idea," said Reika. "And you can start collecting patent royalties."

"This isn't about money," Ryuichi said. "Let's encourage everybody to use the technology free of charge. As long as they don't try to interfere with us, who cares who uses it?"

"Mr. Yaenami, you can't just give your technology away," scolded Reika.

"Why *not* give it away? If TROPHY becomes the world standard, space development will explode. There'll be hundreds of launches a year. The space age will arrive—at last. TGT will be fine. No one knows more about TROPHY's core technologies than Shinji. He's a materials scientist. If someone tries to replicate the technology, we can easily stay a step or two ahead. We'll be first to reach the moon, and Mars, and Jupiter, with hardly a backward glance at NASA or Roskosmos. And we're just a private company. It doesn't get any better than that!"

Ryuichi was beside himself with excitement. Reika goggled at him. Sohya tried to keep a straight face. "Reika, I think he's gotten the better of you. He's right, you know. Patent the technology and give it away. In the long run, you're sure to do better."

"Well, perhaps…"

Ryuichi stamped the floor triumphantly. Reika was appalled.

"Ready for ignition!" one of the technicians called out. "Please move to the observation bunker. You'll be able to see our one-gun salute from there."

"Right. I almost forgot!" Ryuichi said.

Everyone left the firing facility and walked the hundred meters to the observation bunker. The bunker was filled with telemetry equipment. Sheltered by its embankments, the firing facility was visible through thick layers of Plexiglas. Members of the test team began calling out data from the readouts.

"H_2 temperature and pressure, nominal."

"LOX vaporizer pressure steady. Opening valves one through eight. Injection system looks good."

Shinji spoke quickly, flushed with excitement. "The actual vehicle will use an SRB to boost TROPHY to its initial operating envelope. Today we're using a turbine to push a supersonic stream of oxygen into the combustion chamber while we monitor the operation of the rocket."

Shinji was not responsible for the rocket subsystem itself and was not involved in monitoring the telemetry console. Still, he stared through the window with as much intensity as if his entire concept depended on today's test.

"Five…four…three…two…one…ignition start. One…two…"

The firing facility seemed to radiate light. A tongue of blue-white flame shot out of the building and hit the deflector. The edges of the flame quickly stabilized, becoming sharply defined. The fire was supersonic now, hurling itself against the deflector with staggering power. In an instant, a cloud of white steam shot hundreds of meters into the cloudless sky.

The observation bunker was submerged in a roar so loud it seemed to be coming from the bowels of the earth. Ryuichi and Shinji stood with foreheads pressed against the vibrations of the heavy observation window, eyes on the flame. Sohya and Reika looked back and forth between the two men and the exhaust flinging hundreds of tons of pressure against the deflector.

The test was over quickly. The technician kept calling the count. After thirty seconds he ordered engine shutdown.

As the flame was extinguished, a cheer went up in the bunker. Ryuichi turned to Reika and yelled excitedly, "Now what do you think? Will you help her fly?"

"Yes, let's do it. I'm just glad it didn't blow up."

"Of course it didn't!" Ryuichi shouted. He grabbed her hands and pumped them up and down, shouting "thank you" over and over as Reika looked at him awkwardly.

Sohya was grinning when Reika freed herself from Ryuichi's grip and walked over to him, hands fluttering. She sighed. "Why are men always acting like children? He's just like the chairman."

"I'm no different," said Sohya. "I'd say Shinji's the same too."

"Well, it would be nice if you could contain yourselves." She looked at him with embarrassment.

He nodded sympathetically. "Look, don't worry about it. This project won't succeed if we don't start trusting each other. If it's all right with you, I'd like us to deal with each other openly."

"All right, but don't get carried away. I don't think we can afford to be overly familiar, given our respective positions."

"That works for me." Sohya's eyes twinkled as he nodded. Reika suddenly seemed overcome with fatigue. She looked at him and said, "Well, we've found a way to get to the moon. Now everything is up to Gotoba Engineering."

"You're in good hands," said Sohya. He had a brief vision of the men and women who had faced and overcome almost impossible obstacles. "We're all kids at heart too."

[3]

GOTOBA ENGINEERING'S DESIGN lab, in Shinjuku. This was the room that had spawned the plans for a bewildering array of specialized structures for extreme environments. A project screen came down from the ceiling. Sando, the head of Gotoba's Technology Development Division rose from his seat, shook his head, and smiled.

"No, we didn't generate the basic concept. That came from ELE."

Sohya was astonished. "You came up with the base concept?"

Tae smiled. "If we don't tell you what kind of base we want, how will you know what to build?" She was back in her "uniform" and seated with Sohya, Reika, and Iwaki in scattered chairs around Sando.

"So we decided how big the base should be," she said crisply. "That told us what kind of building material we'd need. The kind of building material told us where to build the base. We're leaving the details to your company."

"Oh." Sohya nodded, still mystified. Sando picked up the thread.

"ELE's design request included a basic concept. A crew of ten will occupy the base for the first year. This detail tells us two things. The base will be larger than Kunlun, and it will be permanent. This tells us the method of construction we'll be using: cast concrete."

"Is that the only option?" asked Sohya.

"We could go with metal alloy structures similar to what the Chinese have. We could use inflatable structures, even a volcanic cave. Alloy structures would mean bringing everything up the gravity well from Earth. Very expensive. The flexible elements on inflatable structures tend to deteriorate in the constant sunlight. Caves offer limited space and flexibility for expansion. So the alternatives have their disadvantages."

"Interesting," Reika muttered. She was taking notes with her wearcom, as if this were the first she'd heard on the subject.

"Concrete, on the other hand, has more than enough strength and toughness to withstand vacuum conditions. And only concrete can be produced on-site. This is a huge advantage. It's the ideal material for a base that will initially accommodate ten and ultimately fifty people. Aomine, what would you need to make cement for concrete?"

Sohya answered without hesitation. "For Portland cement: clay, limestone, and gypsum. For calcium aluminate cement, we'd need limestone and bauxite."

Sando nodded. "We can produce calcium aluminate cement relatively easily with moon rock, which is mostly anorthite. If we heat anorthite to around fourteen hundred degrees, the constituents we don't need for cement production will melt out. Further heating should yield something close to aluminate clinker. We should be able to produce it in a solar furnace. There are two other things we need to produce concrete: aggregate and water."

Sando lifted his teacup and sloshed the contents back and forth. "Here's the problem. There's none of this on the moon."

"Well, of course," said Reika. "It's nothing but a huge desert."

"Not quite." Sando shook his head. "True, there's no water on the surface. The moon is very dry, with almost no hydrogen in its composition. This is a consequence of the moon's formation. The giant impact theory posits that the moon was created around four and a half billion years ago after a collision between the primitive earth and a planet-size body. A large amount of the earth's mantle was melted and blown into space, where it coalesced as the moon. The heat of collision drove off most of the lighter elements in the mantle, including hydrogen."

"Then how do you propose to make concrete?"

"With water from somewhere else." Sando narrowed his eyes mischievously and chuckled. "Comets. A comet's core is like a slushy snowball. It contains large amounts of water. What do you suppose happens when a comet strikes the moon?"

"It blows apart and evaporates, I guess," said Reika.

"Right—if it hits where the surface receives sunlight. In twenty-four hours or so, the water molecules are broken apart and scattered by photons coming from the sun. But if the comet strikes where the sun can't reach, ice might accumulate on the surface."

"On the moon's far side then. Water could stay frozen there." As soon as she spoke, Reika realized her mistake. "But the moon revolves with the earth around the sun, so sunlight would reach wherever a comet would hit."

"Actually, no. The earth is covered with ice at the poles, where the sun is extremely weak. Sunlight is also limited at the moon's poles. Furthermore, the moon's axis is nowhere near as inclined as Earth's—it's tilted off the vertical by only one and a half degrees or so. Sunlight has never penetrated some of the craters at the moon's poles. If a lump of ice fell into a zone of eternal shadow—"

"But has that happened?"

"There's no reason to think it hasn't. We're talking about a several-billion year time span. Logically, there must have been such impacts. Since the temperature in these permanent shadow zones is 220 degrees below freezing, there could even be large amounts of accumulated ice."

"Fascinating," said Reika.

"Do we have confirmation of that?" Sohya's tone was challenging and skeptical. Reika was unused to arguing on scientific grounds and was easily convinced by "expert" opinion. Not Sohya; he was trained to accept logical arguments only when buttressed with facts.

Sando returned his gaze with a half-amused, half-frustrated expression, and shook his head. "Allow me to rephrase your question. What would we need to confirm it?"

"And…?"

"This goes back to NASA's Clementine lunar orbiter and radar data indicating the possible presence of ice at the moon's south pole. In 1998, the neutron spectrometer aboard NASA's Lunar Prospector also indicated the presence of polar hydrogen. At the conclusion of the mission, the orbiter was deliberately crashed into a crater near the south pole. NASA hoped the impact would raise a plume of water vapor that could be observed from Earth, but the experiment failed. No such plume was observed.

"Subsequent missions by the U.S. and Japan have also suggested the presence of ice, at least based on radar and laser data. So is this confirmed then? Strictly speaking, no. There are other ways to check for ice, including evaluation of near-infrared absorption spectra, X-ray diffraction imaging, construction of phase diagrams, and so on. Still, at some point you have to draw a line and say you've got enough data. Of course, the only way to be really certain is to bring back a sample."

His specialty was construction engineering, but Sando was a veteran scientist, thoroughly familiar with a broad range of disciplines. His explanation was beyond Sohya's ability to challenge, much less Reika's. Sohya conceded the point. "All right, understood. In other words, we can't start till we've confirmed the presence of ice."

"Yes. We need to put a probe on the surface. But for the moment, let's assume the ice is there. Two thousand square kilometers are in perpetual shadow at the south pole, with what some say is as much as six billion tons of ice. That's several times more water than you'd find in a large reservoir and certainly all the water we need to make our concrete. All this is in the proposal we received from ELE." He looked at Tae.

"The proposal was that detailed?" Reika looked confused.

"Hardly," said Tae. "After all, it came from ELE's planning division. I mean, even I can understand it. The difficult part will be figuring out how to do it."

"Out of the loop?" Sohya asked Reika coolly.

Reika looked down, flushed with embarrassment. "Only a few people at ELE besides the chairman were copied on the plan. All I had were the topline numbers."

Iwaki, sitting toward the back, grunted. Sohya looked round and caught a warning glance. If Tae was privy to things even Reika didn't know, then close liaison with her was even more important than they'd thought. But for a girl of junior high school age to be let in on the most confidential aspects of the plan also had its risks. Iwaki seemed to be indicating caution on both counts.

Reika regained her composure. "So Gotoba Engineering has a detailed plan?"

"Yes," answered Sando. "The rest of this presentation is about why you were right to choose us. Given the long time frame, we propose dividing the work into three phases. Phase One will use unmanned equipment to prepare the site for the arrival of humans." Sando called up a project flowchart on the room's wall-mounted display.

"To start, we'll launch a probe as soon as possible within the next four years. The probe will determine where we build. The site must be adjacent to a zone of permanent shadow with *in situ* ice, but the site itself must be in sunlight. Without sunlight we can't generate power. There must be easy access to anorthite for cement production. By the time the site is selected, we'll have developed temporary habitats to support manned construction work. These units will probably be similar to the modules used at Kunlun Base. Phase One will consist of site selection, dispatch of habitats sufficient for a crew of ten, and development of specialized engineering equipment. This phase will last for six years, until 2031."

A bar extended across the top of the screen as far as the six-year mark. Another bar now appeared below and extended past Phase One with what looked like ten times the number of milestones and processes.

"Phase Two: construction. The base will be progressively expanded, prioritizing elements needed to support a human presence: first a landing facility, then power generation, oxygen production, water supply, a concrete production plant, transport facility, and an operations center, in that order. Only after this infrastructure is in place will we be able to start building concrete structures, and only then will we be in a position to send up large amounts of engineering equipment. This phase will probably be the most demanding and challenging.

"The first task will be to prepare the site and build the landing facility for spacecraft arrivals. The exhaust from the landers will throw up a lot of regolith that will contaminate anything nearby. Next comes placement of solar power panels and laying of superconducting cables. Electric bulldozers and scrapers powered by these cables will collect regolith and ice, which will be transported by skid loaders. Concrete will be produced using a solar furnace, a roller mill, and a rotary kiln. A large amount of energy will be needed to melt the ice, so most of it will be crushed and mixed directly with the cement or aggregate. The concrete will be poured into carbon fiber–reinforced forms to make precast blocks. The blocks will be prestressed and cured for several days in a solar furnace, then transported to the site with a forklift or skip loader, where they will be assembled into structures. Then they'll be bonded to each other using a liquid water sprinkler, much the way the Inuit build their igloos. This is also how early Antarctic bases were created. Given the constant low temperature, an ice shield guarantees an airtight seal. It will also be an effective cosmic ray barrier."

Sando called up an artist's rendering of the base under construction. The base modules looked like extended Quonset huts linked together in a lattice formation. An inset showed the completed layout, which resembled a circuit diagram. Tae seemed slightly startled.

"The key to Phase Two will be constant feedback between Earth and the construction site," Sando continued. "Nothing on this scale has ever been attempted in vacuum conditions. Anything can happen. If a problem occurs, data must be relayed to Earth immediately, and the robotic engineering equipment must be capable of responding precisely. Operational and safety protocols will be established during this phase. With everything that needs to be done, the phase beginning six years out and continuing for two years after that will be the most difficult." The bar extending to 2033 ended, and below it, a new bar appeared.

"Phase Three starts when the concrete habitat facilities are complete. At this point, all engineering equipment will be on-site and operations will be standardized. There will be fewer vehicles arriving from Earth with equipment, and on-site operations will be the main focus. We'll continue expanding the habitats and the number of personnel while enlarging areas of the base for other uses and fitting out the interior of the structures. Around this time we'll also start receiving ELE staff as well as additional personnel from Gotoba. And others as well—"

Sando suddenly broke off his narrative. After a short pause, he began again.

"Phase Three extends to 2035. This marks the completion of the work Gotoba has been commissioned to execute. In ten years the base will be complete."

Sando's listeners murmured their approval. Sohya realized his clenched fists were trembling. The presentation had brought a sense of reality to the project that left him shaking with excitement.

Sando continued matter-of-factly, "Our equipment and materials projections are nearly complete. Assuming everything goes as planned, 189 tons of engineering equipment, construction material, fuel, provisions, water, and personnel must be sent to the moon. Say two hundred tons with contingent requirements. This is the total we propose to send."

"So that's where the two hundred tons came from," said Reika.

"Yes." Sando nodded gravely. "To deliver that to the surface, we'll have to put additional payload in orbit around the moon. Spacecraft will be needed to rotate personnel back to Earth. After adding in this additional payload, as well as the cost to develop and build the necessary engineering equipment, the total costs amount to 1.2 trillion yen." Sando looked at Reika questioningly. "But I understand ELE has discovered a magic method to reduce the launch costs by 95 percent."

"Yes, I saw it myself." Reika leaned forward as if impatient to present her views. "We have a solution. We discovered that Tenryu Galaxy Transport is working on a revolutionary new type of rocket. If it succeeds, we'll be able to send everything with just a few launches!"

"Not likely," said Sohya dismissively. "It wouldn't be practical to divide all the cargo needed for a ten-year project into just a few payloads. And the impact if we lost a rocket would be too significant. The launch vehicles will probably be smaller, which will make them cheaper. We'll launch twenty or thirty of them."

"Oh…Yes, I suppose you're right."

Sando was observing Sohya and Reika's exchange with deep interest. He smiled and nodded. "In any event, TROPHY will definitely improve our prospects. Good. This will make all of our hard work worth it."

Sando motioned to the rest of the large room. Everything was in complete disarray. In a mere two months, Sando's engineers had completed the design for an unprecedented construction project. Judging from the state of the design lab, it looked as if the task had consumed the mental and physical energy of the entire Technology Development Division. The room was awash in documents, maps, and printouts. Several of the younger staff were in the back of the room and under desks, immobile in sleeping bags.

Suddenly Iwaki, who had been silent till now, raised a hand. "Sando, I've got one concern. You said there'd be other people coming to the base. Do you know who they are?"

Sando furrowed his brows in puzzlement. "Guests, I suppose. In fact, ELE's specifications include the construction of several meeting halls, restaurants, and an unusual glassed-in room. Clearly the base is intended for VIPs of some sort." Sando noticed Reika staring at him and paused to cleared his throat. "Of course, we don't need to know everything. Still, the fact that we haven't been briefed on the intended use of such an extensive facility does make our job somewhat more challenging."

"Mr. Sando?" It was Tae. He looked at her, tolerating the interruption. Iwaki and Sohya leaned forward expectantly—but she changed the topic.

"When you decide where the base is going to be, I have a request."

"A request?"

"I want it to have a nice view."

"A nice view?" Sando, Iwaki, and Sohya looked at each other.

"So you do plan to bring tourists to the base?" asked Sohya.

"Tourists…Yes, tourism will probably be one of the uses," said Tae. Then she smiled. "Mr. Sando, I basically understand how you are going to build the buildings. But there's something you haven't talked about yet." It was unbelievable that such a young girl could have grasped Sando's complex presentation, but what she said next was even more surprising.

"Is Gotoba going to handle all the embellishments?"

"The embellishments?" Sando looked blank.

"Yes, like beautiful towers, bay windows, little paths with pretty arches, and fountains surrounded by flower beds. Of course, the walls will be white, but it'll be boring if everything is white, so let's use colors like green and pink for decoration. You can use templates for frescos, but will it be hard to make statues?"

"Listen, Tae," Sohya broke in, astonished. "What kind of a base is this going to be?"

"I told you, didn't I? A place ordinary people can enjoy." Tae stood and motioned to Reika. "Let's go, Reika. I have to report back to Grandfather."

"Ah, okay." Reika turned to the others. "Well, goodbye." The bewildered men watched her back as she left.

TWO DAYS LATER, a list of additional requirements arrived from Eden Leisure Entertainment that seemed to have little to do with a lunar base.

The document began with a list of stringent standards for the base's interior environment: temperature, humidity, ambient noise, vibration, odors, illumination, and more. These parameters were not to be maintained at some minimum level but within the optimum range for comfort. The minimum residential volume per occupant was fifty cubic meters—nearly three times the minimum considered necessary for a space facility—including ten cubic meters of private space. Living quarters for visitors had to be strictly separated from those for base staff. Meal service was to offer a choice of five cuisines: Japanese, French, Chinese, Italian, and pan-Asian fusion, with chefs and staff to oversee each menu. All equipment, piping, ducts, cables, and other infrastructure would be hidden inside the walls. Colors and furnishings were to be commensurate with commercial standards on Earth, and occupant safety had to be fully ensured by means of at least three different safety systems: an escape vehicle, space suits, and an emergency escape tunnel. These systems had to be concealed so as not to clash with the furnishings. Operating personnel were to be provided with a comfortable working environment to enable them to provide the highest levels of service to base visitors. Et cetera. Et cetera.

In all there were more than 150 of these stipulations. In effect, Gotoba was being ordered to build a first-class hotel on the moon. The engineer responsible for designing the habitat interiors, where most of the impact would fall, went into shock and sent up a distress rocket to his superiors.

"How the hell am I supposed to meet these requirements? You can't lay paint inside a space station. What about the fumes while it's curing? Resin-based wallpaper? Wood fittings? How do we handle off-gassing and flammability? I can't work with this!"

The complaints went all the way up the chain to the president, but he brushed them off and told his people to stop complaining. The engineer racked his brains and came up with the idea of polishing the interior walls, finishing them with a special compound that would reflect visible light the same way as a butterfly's wing or a peacock's tail, to create the effect of color without pigments.

Some of the requirements could be solved through similar kinds of innovation, but others would mean sending extra equipment and material. This would add directly to costs. And the 360 square-meter ball court—one each for guests and staff, "if possible"—would mean further expansion of the habitat area. Even Gotoba himself found this hard to swallow and was forced to summon Sohya to his office.

"Have you seen these new requirements? ELE wants a volleyball court *for the staff*. We'd have to add the equivalent of two new habitat modules. It would push the time required for Phase Two another 10 percent. Do you have any idea why they're doing this to us?"

"Maybe they're planning to send really athletic people," ventured Sohya.

"Very funny. These guys seem to think the moon is just another Polynesian island. They don't realize that it costs a million yen to send a volleyball. I want you to go to Nagoya, Sohya. Bow low. Try to get them to cut some of this out."

"Don't worry about the ball court. All we need to do is come up with a new ball game that doesn't take much space to play."

"Brilliant! I like it."

"Still, the specifications have gotten a lot tougher for some reason. I'd better find out why," said Sohya as he left the office. The one thing he'd neglected to mention was the author of the new requirements.

It had to be Tae; there was no doubt about it. That "report" she'd been working on during their moon trip had gone to ELE. That was probably the reason she'd been sent—to determine how the moon could be transformed from a place where humans struggled to survive to one that anyone could casually visit.

But even so, things didn't add up. The current plan assumed that the fare for one person to travel to the moon would be at least a hundred million yen, even with the new technology. If they received an average of four visitors a month—nearly a thousand people over the base's twenty-year operating life—they would still not even break even on the 150 million yen construction cost.

Did a base on the moon—with its sand and ice, black skies, and weak gravity—really have that kind of drawing power? It might for a short time, while the concept still had some novelty. But could it keep attracting people year after year? People willing to pay a fortune for a stay of just a few days?

And if not, what was the purpose?

To find out, Sohya traveled to Aichi Prefecture and the head-quarters of Eden Leisure Entertainment.

[4]

SOHYA RANG OFF his wearcom from his seat in the Nagoya-bound maglev express. Gotoba's liaison at ELE headquarters in downtown Nagoya was expecting his call. Instead of a meeting at headquarters with ELE staff, Sohya was told to proceed to Tokai Eden, where Tae would be waiting for him.

He transferred to the train for Leisure Land at Nagoya. Japan's third-largest amusement park was spread across seventy-five acres of reclaimed land where the Kiso River flowed into Ise Bay. The early autumn school-excursion season had arrived, and the train was overflowing with students of all ages.

Naturally there were no ticket vending machines at the entrance to the park. Just as in the train station, an overhead imaging system tracked people entering the park using face recognition. A few days later, a bill would arrive from the visitor's credit card company or financial institution. When the system was first introduced, some feared it would miss the faces of rapidly growing children, but that particular problem was solved by simple common sense. Preschool children would not be visiting the park on their own. All the system had to do was identify the parents' faces. For children visiting in groups, the system could simply identify the face of the teacher accompanying them.

Tokai Eden's monitoring system enhanced its accuracy by linking to visitor wearcoms with electronic toll collection signals, a system first commercialized around 2000 to automate toll collection for highways. Sohya realized this when he passed through the entrance and his wearcom emitted a short beep.

The wearable computer was a universal terminal crammed with nearly every conceivable electronic function that could be made portable. No adult was without one. It united the functions of a personal computer and mobile phone in a device that could be worn as an accessory—as a wristwatch, bracelet, or necklace, or embedded in a hair ornament or eyeglasses. One of its main functions was to link to mobile networks in the gigahertz band, which allowed user locations to be pinpointed with great accuracy.

Of course, the wearcom providers all made a point of advertising security features that would prevent complete strangers from tracking the owner's whereabouts. But here in Leisure Land, Sohya was on ELE territory.

He suddenly found his path blocked by two charming costumed characters, a boy and girl representing primitive humans wearing clothes made of grass. He stood puzzled for a moment, then heard that pure voice, like a silver bell, calling to him.

"Hi, Sohya."

When he looked around, her smile was blossoming just a few feet away. He was astonished that she'd been able to spot him among the hordes of students streaming past on both sides—but then he remembered that park security could track anyone with a wearcom. He scratched his head sheepishly.

"Hey there. You found me."

"Welcome to my Eden. It's good to see you."

Tae approached him with controlled exuberance, one sandaled foot toes-first in front of the other. Her black tresses hung loose as always, but instead of the uniform, she was wearing a one-piece Canton crepe dress that shaded from white at the neck to black just above her knees. With it she wore a cardigan and a broad-brimmed white straw hat and black, open-toed enameled sandals. She radiated girlishness and refinement without a single false note.

Sohya wanted to get right to the point, but before he could begin, she took his arm. "Come on."

"Where? I came to discuss the base plans."

"You're riding on the house today. I got you a free pass."

"To the attractions? But we'll be in line for hours."

"No, we won't."

It wasn't her insistent tugging so much as her intent expression that persuaded Sohya to give in. So he allowed himself to be dragged off, as if Tae were a little sister he'd brought to the park.

She was as good as her word; after all, she was the chairman's daughter. At each attraction, her pendant wearcom was a talisman that passed them through the service entrance and onto every ride. The Viking Ark, the Snake-in-the-Garden Roller Coaster,

Go-Carts from Hell—each attraction seemed inspired by a free-wheeling, if somewhat mordant, borrowing of themes from the Old Testament. And at each attraction their waiting time was zero. Sohya put up with two rides just to be social, but when the girl refused to give her attention to anything else, he gave up, relaxed, and gave himself over to the fun.

"Tae, you don't have school todaaaay?"

"Whaaaat?"

"School! Schoooool!"

"Aaaaaaaah!"

The wind howling past their pod on Kokytos, a gigantic roller coaster with a 140-meter drop, snatched her straw hat and sent it spinning off into the sunset over Ise Bay.

Back on terra firma, Sohya collapsed on a bench, gasping for breath. He felt something cold on his forehead and sat up. Tae was looking down on him, armed with frozen drinks. She motioned to a giant Ferris wheel.

"One last ride. The Apple Tree."

Their apple-shaped gondola climbed slowly, lit by the sun setting beyond the Yoro Mountains. For the first time that day—no, it must have been the first time ever—they were alone together. Sitting opposite her in the gondola, Sohya looked at nothing else for a long time.

If called upon, Sohya could honestly express at least 95 percent of his attitude toward Tae. He saw her as a bit too precocious, perhaps, but sincerely appreciated her openhearted nature. She was almost like a lovable younger sister.

The other 5 percent of his feelings were harder to get a handle on. At thirteen, Tae was rapidly leaving childhood behind, and Sohya felt a slight tenderness toward her that was new to him. Yet his respect for her overshadowed all else. In a sense, she was even intimidating. There was something about this girl that lay far outside the ordinary. But what? It struck Sohya that he knew almost nothing about her.

Tae watched the eastern sky deepen into night. Her lovely profile, half in shadow, was bereft of vitality, but not from the day's endless round of attractions. Some fatigue beyond her years seemed to suffuse her face.

"The lights are so cold." Her lips, like a tender blossom, moved faintly. Sohya followed her gaze.

The lights of Nagoya, the largest city in the Chubu region, were starting to wink on. The numberless tiny points of illumination seemed to display as many colors. Sohya placed his hand on the edge of the window and rested his chin there. "I see red and orange too."

"The colors, yes. But there aren't any lights out there waiting for me."

"Isn't your home around here?"

"I have a maid and some robots, that's it. Grandfather's almost never around, he travels on business so much."

"What about your family?"

"My...father is even busier than my grandfather."

Uh-oh. The way Tae said "father" suggested that she was reluctant to call him even that. The reason was not hard to guess. She hadn't mentioned her mother.

Sohya's attempt to change the subject didn't fare much better. "But you must be popular at school. You're very attractive."

"I'm already out of college. I was in California." Sohya couldn't think of a response.

"Sure, I have a lot of friends on the web, but none of them are within a thousand kilometers of me. Stupid, isn't it?"

"But I'm here."

"I thought you'd be nice enough to say that. That's why I asked you to come." She suddenly seemed almost frail, but her eyes were smiling. "That list must be giving you fits. I thought you'd come."

"It reflected everything you learned at Kunlun. You dropped a bombshell, that's for sure." Sohya's next question hardly needed asking. "How we build the base is completely up to you then, isn't it?"

"Yes. I told Grandfather I wanted that more than any-thing." She said it casually, as if the base were a doll she fan-cied. "A hundred and fifty billion is the most he can spend without authorization. He doesn't think Eden will make a profit. Reika was brought in so things would at least look proper. I feel sorry for her. The base was never intended to make money."

"Sounds like she got a raw deal."

"And you?"

"I'm okay, I guess." They looked at each other and laughed weakly.

"I just hope Grandfather lives another ten years so he can see it finished. I don't have any right to expect that. This is a fairy tale. I'm trying to see how grand I can make it."

"Why are you doing this?"

She paused. "Because I'm a special girl." She looked out the window at the sky. "I don't have what ordinary girls have. Instead, I'm a little bit smart, and I have, well, a lot of money. So I decided I should at least try to do something no one else can do. Some-thing no one else would try to do."

"And that means building a base on the moon?"

"I'm saying goodbye to Earth." Her tone was frightening-ly calm. "I won't have any regrets. Everything I care about is in cyberspace. I've experienced it all—friends, warm waters off Samoa, soft kangaroos in Perth, hot borscht in Moscow, cool winds off Kilimanjaro, slick whales in Koch, the tallest redwoods in Yellowstone, sweet cream puffs on the Champs Elysées. So there's no need for me to stay. I'm going to make a new place for myself as far away as I can go—the moon."

"So we're building a home for you on the moon?"

Tae gave him a sharp, quick smile, lips like a crescent moon.

"You're building a wedding palace."

Sohya stared. Tae stared straight back at him.

"Why do you think I would do that?"

He was baffled. "I don't know."

"Even if it costs a lot, people will come for a wedding. Celebrities will spend hundreds of millions of yen without a second thought. Even regular people will pay, oh, ten million."

"Isn't that only if they're from Nagoya?"

"Yes, I got the idea because I'm from Nagoya. That old stereotype has an element of truth to it; we do like big weddings. But the world is full of parents wanting to celebrate a young couple's new start in life. Two hundred million per person, minimum two couples. For four hundred million, they get a two-day, three-night wedding and honeymoon. People will definitely come for a honeymoon like that. Lots and lots of them."

Tae looked down at the park below. "Everything has to be perfect so the guests can enjoy themselves. Look at all the people who pay eight thousand yen to visit Tokai Eden. It's because we pay such attention to detail. We even use costumed characters to collect the trash. It has to be a place where people can have fun."

"That's why you want the base to be so luxurious."

"Yes." She nodded and fell silent, waiting for Sohya's comment, but he had no idea what to say. He sensed a gap between the audacity and detail of her vision and the idea of having a wedding palace as the core facility.

The gondola reached its apogee and began descending quietly.

"Sohya? When people set foot in a new world, what do they have to do to be able to say it belongs to them?"

"Belongs to them?" It was an abrupt question. Sohya didn't think too deeply before answering, "Raise a flag, or notify somebody."

"They have to be born there." Tae spoke with firm conviction. "A person can have the confidence to call a place their own if they were born there. A visit is just exploring. But if they get married there and make a baby there...then that place will really be theirs."

"Is that another reason for the wedding palace?"

"One of them. There are others." Tae fell silent again. She didn't seem interested in explaining further. Finally she spoke, but as if she were talking to herself.

"Two people fall in love…they come to a new place, they marry, they make a baby. Build a home, build farms, build a city. Maybe it won't be Shangri-la, but it's sure to be full of life. A big new world. Yes…like the American continent long ago. A new continent, but untouched by mankind."

"An unexplored continent. The sixth continent, like Antarctica," said Sohya.

"Sixth continent…Sure, not everyone counts five continents, but the Olympic flag represents five. Yes, the sixth continent. I like the way that sounds." A smile she seemed to have forgotten for a short time played across her lips. "Sohya, I'm going to use that name."

"Mm-hm." His mind was on something else.

"Tae, what's your role in that new world?"

She didn't answer immediately. Apparently the question had caught her by surprise. She glanced around nervously, then looked out the window, as if looking to escape.

"I wonder. I don't want to get married, myself."

"I see. So you don't have a boyfriend?" Sohya looked out the window.

"Sure. He's right here with me." She smiled mischievously.

Sohya laughed skeptically. "Me?"

"Is that bad news?"

"Of course not. I'm honored." Sohya extended his hand. She took it and unhesitatingly moved next to him.

That was the real beginning of their relationship. Still, Tae was mature enough for her age not to fall into a girlish infatuation, and Sohya was not naive enough to lose his head over a girl a dozen years his junior.

So it started serenely, without fanfare or any surge of romantic feeling—a smooth start to a relationship that would weave itself in curious ways. A girl on a journey, and a young man following close behind.

"I guess it's a bit soon for marriage?" said Sohya gently.

"Yes. I don't want to anyway. I'm still not sure where I fit in."

"No problem, let's give it time. I'll always be in touch. I think your plan's a good one."

Their gondola neared the ground. Tae was still looking at the eastern sky. A line of buildings, and above that the horizon with a silver disk peeking above it. Faint bluish white light—was it the moon or the lights from the park?—lit up Tae's face and made her look noble, like royalty itself. Like the moon's harsh mistress…

The phrase floated up from somewhere in Sohya's memory. Somehow it seemed he hadn't gotten it quite right. Still, he thought it captured Tae at this moment perfectly.

Let it be so, then. Let all the sentient beings of this world gather for a magnificent banquet in a palace between endless night and a sun that never sets.

Not for the politicians, or the people, or even the earth and its precious biosphere, but simply for the pleasure of a little queen.

What could be more sublime?

ON OCTOBER 1, 2025, Gotoba Engineering & Construction, Eden Leisure Entertainment, and Tenryu Galaxy Transport officially announced their joint intention to build Sixth Continent, a wedding palace on the moon.

BOOK II

ENGINEERING EQUIPMENT, TRANSPORT, AND SITE PREPARATION, 2029-2033

CHAPTER 4
SITE INVESTIGATION AND ANNOUNCEMENT

[1]

THE TILT-ROTOR TOUCHED down on the landing pad, twin turboshaft engines roaring. Two figures walked down onto the tarmac. One was a white-haired old man in a three-piece suit. The other was a girl about high school age, wearing a white beret and a blazer the color of the predawn sky. The old man raised his hand, signaling the pilot to stand by. The girl set off toward the proving ground.

They were in a huge clearing cut from a forest. Between the helipad and a group of prefab buildings stood a pair of single-story structures the size of gymnasiums. Alongside was a power distribution station, encircled by a high fence.

The core of the facility, however, was not the buildings. It was the huge area of sunken ground in the center of the site. The visitors had seen it from the air. The barren depression, hundreds of yards across, was dotted with mounds of earth several meters high and crisscrossed by trenches that looked like parched riverbeds. There was an area full of huge scattered boulders and many sheer escarpments.

These were not natural features. They had been created artificially to achieve some purpose. The proving ground was enormous, a rough square a thousand yards on a side. If the visitors did not know they were on Japan's main island of Honshu, they might have assumed they were in some remote foreign location. In the distance, rising above the trees surrounding the helipad, rose a titanic conical volcano: Mount Fuji. The proving ground had been carved from part of a training area for the Ground Self-Defense Force.

A Jeep met the visitors as they left the pad. They climbed aboard and headed toward the testing area. The road climbed a shallow rise. As the Jeep reached the top, the girl said to the driver, "Stop the car, please."

"You can see everything from the control center," said the driver. "The chief engineer is waiting."

"It's all right. Stop here," said the old man. The driver reluctantly stopped. The girl got out and the old man joined her. Seen from the top of the rise, the vast depression before them looked like an open-air habitat for wild animals.

Down in the basin were several small structures sunken halfway into the ground, constructed from concrete blocks and seemingly scattered at random. No two were alike. One appeared to be under construction; only a section of wall was complete.

A number of white vehicles resembling small bulldozers were moving busily among the buildings. Compared to normal bulldozers, they were broad and low-slung. The shank supporting the blade was slender; the treads were wide. There was no operator compartment. Sensor masts protruded from the spines of the vehicles like the necks of giraffes. At the end of the masts, multiple lenses of video cameras glinted in the sun. Slender cables, nearly invisible against the background, sprouted from the masts. One had to look closely to see that these cables led back to a thirty-meter tower at the edge of the depression. There were six robot bulldozers in the basin, all connected to the same tower. There must have been some tension on the cables, because instead of curving toward the ground, they extended to the tower in a straight line, making each robot look a bit like a dog on a leash.

There was little sound. Each bulldozer was about the size of a four-ton truck, but considering that six of them were moving about, it was eerily quiet. All that was audible was a low hum.

"Electric," said the old man to himself.

The driver left the Jeep and joined them. "Yes. Seventy-five kilowatt motors. The cables are superconductive. Can't use diesel power plants where these things are going. Electric motors supply nearly all the motive power. There's a lot more to our multidozers than that though."

"Is that what you call them?"

"Yes," said the driver. "Multipurpose lunar surface engineering equipment. As the name indicates, they fulfill multiple roles: as bulldozers, forklifts, rippers, trucks, road rollers, and snowplows. Today is their final prelaunch shakedown." The driver's chest swelled with pride. "Komatsu, Honda, and IHI developed them under our direction. It was a tremendous challenge, but we're very happy with the results."

"What was difficult about it?" asked the old man. The driver kept glancing at the black-haired girl, who kept silent.

"First of all, configuring them for low-gravity operation. One-sixth G raises the units' center of gravity by a factor of six. Even small variations in the terrain could make them flip over during normal operations. So we've kept them wide and low to the ground. There's also the vacuum of space. Naturally, any sort of internal combustion device is out of the question, as are air-cooled radiators. Heat will build up inside the machines, so we distributed Freon heat sinks inside the bodies. The vacuum also makes lubrication difficult. Any volatiles will evaporate, so all moving parts and bearings are self-lubricating. We used molybdenum oxide alloy plating with a very low coefficient of friction."

"And?" said the old man.

"Maintenance-free operation was another important consideration. We took great pains to design out structures that might fail. That's also why we avoided compressor-driven heat pumps or nitrogen-based lubricants. If we couldn't design out a failure-prone component, we made it easy to swap in a replacement. Every component of the robots you see, including the treads, can be repaired or replaced without tools."

"Very interesting."

"The biggest challenge was limiting the total weight to under five tons. That was an absolute requirement to meet payload limits."

"Is that why they look so flimsy?" The old man moved his hand back and forth at the wrist, like the neck of a snake. "Looks like those blades would snap with a bit of strain."

"Well, it wouldn't do to cut the weight too much. If the unit is too light, it will be pushed back."

"Pushed back? By what?"

"By the surface." The driver grinned. "Terrestrial construction equipment is massively built because it will be pushing heavy mass around. If it were lighter, it would just end up applying force against itself. This effect is even more marked on the moon. When that blade cuts into the regolith, it could just lever the machine off the surface. So we'll be using regolith as ballast to increase the mass. The dozers need the structural strength to stand up to heavy loading and still be light enough to make the journey from Earth. This is one area where we really showed what we can do."

"Interesting. Did you hear that, Tae?"

"Amazing." She nodded briefly, not looking particularly impressed. The driver scratched his head. Maybe the technical details were boring her.

The driver's wearcom beeped. He spoke briefly and turned back to his two guests. "The test is starting. What would you like to do?"

"We'll watch it from here," said Tae. She reclined on the hood of the Jeep. The old man stood next to her. The driver gave up trying to coax them to the control center and stood silently watching.

The multidozers had been moving independently but suddenly began moving in unison. Their destination was a pile of refrigerator-size concrete blocks at the edge of the basin. Forks emerged from the front of the machines, each one lifting a block. Then they formed up and began slowly moving forward in a column. But instead of using the blocks for construction, the robot vehicles headed toward the area of scattered boulders, which were around half their size.

Even in the area of boulders, the machines hardly slowed. Some of the boulders were too large to crawl over, but each time a dozer encountered one that was too large, it skillfully moved its treads alternately back and forth to maneuver through the gaps between rocks.

Then the lead dozer reached a boulder that was noticeably larger than the others. It was flanked by other boulders and there appeared to be no way around it. A dead end. The line paused for a few moments. Dozers 1 and 2 moved aside and placed their blocks on the ground. The two machines maneuvered back and forth repeatedly in the narrow cul-de-sac until they were side by side in front of the boulder. Once aligned perfectly, they extended their forks under the rock in perfect synchronization and gradually levered it off the ground. One dozer would not have been able to lift it. With two it was a different story. Their combined power tipped the boulder, and it rolled out of the way, opening a path.

The cameras on the sensor masts of the lead machines busily swept from side to side. Once they were certain they could move forward, the two robots retrieved their blocks, formed a line again, and moved through the gap as if nothing had happened.

The old man clapped briefly. "Very good, for remote control. It's not easy, is it?"

The driver chuckled. "That wasn't remote control. No human intervention. The multidozers are capable of self-directed action. The cables supply power only."

"So those are robots?"

"Initial construction will be carried out without a human presence. Even if we tried to control everything from Earth, it takes close to three seconds for signals to reach the moon and return. If there's an emergency—say, a landslide—we might not be able to respond fast enough. So everything is AI controlled. Developing the software was harder than designing the hardware." The driver watched the machines affectionately. Evidently he had been personally involved in their development.

"Our multidozers can work in perfect synchronization and respond independently to emergencies. That's a critical requirement for construction on the lunar surface, and it's the focus of this test. But we're not finished yet. The next hurdle is operation on sloping terrain. It's very easy to flip over on the moon."

The driver pointed to an embankment. Dozer 1 was already climbing it. The embankment was extremely steep, perhaps thirty degrees. The machines began moving horizontally across it, all at the same elevation, forks held level to avoid dropping the concrete blocks. Their agility was impressive. But after a few minutes, the line stopped again. A two-meter trench had been cut into the face of the slope.

"That gouge in the slope is wide enough for the multidozer to lose traction and slide down if it tries to cross using its treads. What are they going to do?"

Dozer 1's cameras scanned back and forth. At first it seemed to be at a loss for a solution. But once again the machines found a way.

Each dozer was equipped with a load bed. Dozer 2 raised its forks and moved forward, as if to place its block on the back of the lead machine. However, instead of depositing it there, it simply rested its forks on Dozer 1's back. It seemed to be calculating how much downward force to apply.

The two machines now started forward, maintaining the same attitude. Dozer 1's treads projected out over the trench and gained a purchase on the opposite side. It crossed over. Then, as the second machine's treads projected over the trench, Dozer 3 placed its forks on its back in the same way, adding the weight of its block. In this fashion the dozer line crossed over one by one.

The driver whooped with excitement. "Pressure from behind to generate more traction! Too much pressure and they'd fall, so they had to calibrate it. These multidozers are way more advanced than the previous generation."

"But what if they can't figure it out?" said the old man.

"Unless it's an emergency, they're programmed to stop and wait for instructions. That's what the old model had to do when it reached this point. They've really come a long way."

The machines continued across the trench. The last dozer extended its treads over the gap. This was going to be a bit tricky. There was no machine behind it to hold it against the ground.

Dozer 6 lowered its forks until they were level with the ground. Its forks projected beyond the block it was carrying, and it slipped them under the chassis of Dozer 5. Dozer 6 then lifted Dozer 5 slightly, increasing its own load. To compensate for its loss of traction, Dozer 5 carried out the same maneuver with Dozer 4, which was completely across the trench and had full contact with the ground. With the three machines moving as one, Dozer 6 was able to cross.

The old man murmured, "I bet they're smarter than people."

"We'll see," said the driver. "The last test is coming up."

The line had reached the end of the embankment and was back on level ground. There seemed to be no further obstacles. Instead there were several steel panels scattered across the ground, about four meters square.

The line reached one of the panels. The first and second dozers crossed over. When Dozer 3 was on the panel, the trap was sprung.

The panel split down the middle and opened downward. The rear three-quarters of Dozer 3 was directly over the opening. The machine tipped backward and began to teeter over the hole.

The other dozers, which had been lumbering steadily forward, moved with startling agility. Dozers 1 and 2 backed up rapidly, while the three trailing units sped forward, wedging Dozer 3 front and rear. The line froze, with Dozer 3 nearly suspended in space.

"This is the cave-in response test. Lunar regolith is a lot like dry desert sand. With vibration it can collapse, even where it's packed down. What will they do now?"

The situation resembled the trench-crossing test, but this new gap was too wide for the dozers to cross. Dozer 3 clearly could not get out of this one on its own. Somehow it would have to be raised. The multidozers began solving the problem in a straightforward fashion.

First, Dozers 2 and 4 used their clawlike rippers to grip the ground, locking Dozer 3 in position. Next, the lead and tail dozers dropped their blocks, circled to opposite sides of the line, and approached Dozer 3 at an angle, forks extended. They moved very slowly, seemingly wary of the possibility of a secondary collapse.

When they reached the edge of the gap, they extended their forks under Dozer 3. Dozers 2 and 4 then retracted their rippers and moved away, transferring Dozer 3's weight to Dozers 1 and 6. Then 3 was raised in a controlled manner.

The old man murmured as he watched the robots' complicated movements. "Aren't you worried about getting those cables tangled with all that maneuvering?"

"It's not a problem. The power supply tower can automatically reposition the cable linkage points."

"But what if one of the cables is cut?"

"The dozers have onboard fuel cells. They can move independently for short periods of time, enough to make their way back to the power pole to hook up with a new cable."

"Batteries. Just like toys."

"Batteries, yes, but they produce power by reacting hydrogen with oxygen. Fuel cells are superior to other types of batteries. They don't need charging, and—uh-oh…"

The driver stiffened. The old man squinted.

The treads on Dozers 1 and 6 were twitching back and forth,

slowly bringing Dozer 3 sideways and forward. Its treads had already gained some purchase on the dirt and were digging in. Dozer 3 was trying to add its own power to the effort.

Suddenly its right tread locked, perhaps jammed by a stone. The sound of its motor rose to a whine. Suddenly the entire right tread separated from the drive wheels with a clatter. Instead of stopping automatically, the drive wheels kept on revolving at high speed. Probably the vehicle had sustained some damage when it was pinned between the other dozers.

White smoke began pouring from the underside of the dozer. Apparently the heat of friction had ignited a fire. Now the other machines did something unexpected. Dozers 2, 4, and 5 moved away. Then 1 and 6, as if realizing nothing more could be done, backed away as well.

Bereft of support, Dozer 3 promptly plunged into the hole and out of sight. There was a dull crash, then a surprisingly violent explosion.

The girl had been watching intently. Now she cuttingly said to the driver, "They couldn't save one of their own. Don't you need to make more improvements?"

Slightly dazed, the driver struggled to answer, then gave up. At length he pulled himself together and spoke into his wearcom. He listened and nodded.

"Just as I thought. That wasn't a failure. The other dozers abandoned it intentionally."

"Why would they do that?" asked the old man.

"The fuel in their batteries is similar to rocket propellant. There's no guarantee it won't explode. Even if it doesn't, an accident involving one dozer may end up involving others. In marginal cases, the protocol is to abandon the vehicle in trouble so as to minimize collateral damage. The control center advised that this was not just a cave-in response test. Dozer 3 was sacrificed to evaluate whether the other units could exercise logic and determine when a triage strategy was needed."

"Abandon if necessary…" The girl scowled. No, she did not just scowl. She seemed to be having a complicated emotional reaction.

The driver studied her expression. "I'm sorry I didn't explain earlier. But it's not a system fault. On the contrary, the system is operating as intended. If you could just understand that—"

"Thank you." The girl nodded and returned her gaze to the testing ground.

The white dozers were on the move again, carrying their blocks toward the center of the proving ground, unconcerned over the loss of their comrade. When they arrived at an indicator on the ground, they began lining up the blocks to make a wall. The blocks were laid out with a surveyor's accuracy.

Apparently the test was over. The girl turned to the driver. "Let's go."

The girl and the old man got into the Jeep. The driver gave her a worried glance as he pulled back onto the road.

THE GREAT GLASS walls of the control center gave a commanding view of the testing area. Inside, Gotoba's engineers congratulated each other.

"Passed with flying colors! This went better than the assembly test. I never thought they'd ace the triage problem."

Gotoba's development process for robotic engineering equipment had been plagued with difficulties. From the construction of a chassis capable of withstanding the lunar environment to engineering attachments, power supply, peripheral gear, and the AI system software, everything had been a process of trial and error. After components had been developed, countless tests of everything from site preparation to block assembly were required.

The final stage was a failure-resolution test that presented the robots with an unforeseen situation. The test was designed to push their software/hardware integration to its limits.

Gotoba's multidozer development supervisor grinned broadly. "Now we can head for the moon with confidence. Those four years of suffering were worth it."

"I think you exceeded your goals," laughed Sohya Aomine, now a manager in Gotoba's Mobile Engineering Division. He would be overseeing the initial construction work remotely, from Earth. He shook the supervisor's hand. "But they won't be ready to roll for a while. Before that we have to perfect the concrete production system. They're still working on it down in Yamaguchi Prefecture, but they don't have the water supply figured out yet. They've got another 20 percent of the job ahead of them."

"I know, but the plans are finished," said the supervisor. "They've designed thirty-plus different systems covering all the possible ways water might be dispersed on the surface. They're bragging they can have a plant up and running within three months after they get the findings from Serpent."

"That's what I hear. Man, I mean—us, the guys in Yamaguchi, the Phase Two base people in Nagoya—everyone's working like crazy. Even I'm impressed at what this company can pull off, and I work here."

"It all flows from the top." The supervisor dropped his voice to a whisper. "Did you hear about the Choshi offshore gas field?"

"What's going on?" Sohya whispered back. The supervisor chuckled.

"Shinnisseki Gas is running into problems getting the methane sherbet up from the seabed. Gotoba's offering them the dozers."

"To work on the seafloor?"

"It's not so different from the lunar surface, an extreme environment where manned operation is difficult. It wouldn't be hard to retrofit them for undersea work. The boss is looking for ways to recoup some of our development costs."

"Who'll do the retrofitting? Everyone has their hands full."

"Gotoba will find a way. And he'll turn a profit. The boss is almost a god when it comes to construction engineering."

"A god, huh? Hey…" Sohya froze. A white-haired old gentleman and a young woman were standing in the control center doorway, looking out of place.

"Who's that?" asked the supervisor.

"Another god. Our sponsor, the chairman of ELE. That's his granddaughter. Go tell the guys to quiet down."

The supervisor hurried off to alert the rest of the team. Sohya walked over to the visitors and spread his hands in welcome.

"It's been a long time, Mr. Toenji. Nice to see you too, Tae— Miss Toenji."

"How've you been, Sohya?" Tae Toenji was seventeen. She smiled in a grown-up way and extended her hand.

Sohya shook it, a bit nervously. "Last time was in Paris, right?"

"Yes, when we showed our wedding dresses for the Paris collection and kicked off the Sixth Continent PR campaign. But we see each other all the time on the VPN, don't we? It hasn't *exactly* been a long time." Tae stage-whispered this last statement and smiled.

"But I only see your face on the web. You…you're taller."

"A hundred and fifty-nine centimeters. Maybe I won't be able to ride in the capsule if I get too much taller."

"*Apple* is designed to carry five NBA players. We even got an inquiry from Johnson Jr. Of course, he's already hitched…I mean, married."

"Mr. Aomine." Sennosuke Toenji leaned closer to Sohya. "You don't have to put on a show for me. Don't be so formal."

"So then, you know?" said Sohya, slightly embarrassed.

"I like to think of myself as close to my granddaughter. I know you're close to Tae as well. I don't think that's a bad thing. She's told you that she's the real force behind this plan, I believe. She wouldn't have done that if she didn't trust you."

"Mr. Toenji…" Sohya was at a loss for words.

"Don't worry about me. Officially, I'm in charge of this project. I do have a lot of interest in it. I was one of the ones who came up with the idea. But making Tae happy is just as important to me." Sennosuke gave Sohya a jaunty wink. "Now then, Sir Aomine, please give our princess her briefing."

Twenty-nine-year-old Sohya was not thrilled to be treated like a hero in an adventure comic, but he did relax a bit. Over the past four years he had seen very little of Tae in person. She had been busy working with Eden's PR team on the global campaign for Sixth Continent. In the process, she had become something of a media figure herself. But they spoke over Sixth Continent's virtual private network several times a month. Naturally, much of their communication was personal, and Tae would have felt guilty keeping this from her grandfather, who was nearly her only family.

Now that Sohya had official approval, there was no need for pretense. He relaxed and said, "You're a little late. If you'd come an hour earlier, I could've shown you the final multidozer test."

"We watched it from out there. The robots are amazing."

"You saw the explosion?" Sohya was caught off guard. "That wasn't a system failure, you know. We wanted to see if the bots' networked AI could calculate the trade-off between the loss of one member and potential damage to the whole team."

"Don't worry. The driver told us all about it."

Sohya heaved a sigh of relief. When he had first met her, Tae had been just thirteen, yet she could already speak fluent English and easily grasped the principles of spaceflight. But four years of globe-trotting had definitely seasoned her. Still, she hadn't lost her innocent outlook.

"I feel sorry for the robots though."

"Sorry? Why?"

"As soon as they're a burden, they're left behind. I guess it's efficient, but it's merciless."

"Well, there's no other way." Sohya remembered how upset she had been about the trash scattered across the surface around

Kunlun Base. "We can't take a single excess kilo to the moon, so we have to recycle everything usable till there's nothing left to recycle. But sometimes recycling uses more energy and resources than just discarding things. When humans are present on the surface, we'll have the flexibility to recycle a lot of waste, but when it's just robots…sometimes we'll have to discard a unit."

"I know. That's why we have to send humans. But I liked the way it was handled."

Sohya shook his head, confused. "You did?"

"Yes. I liked the lack of mercy. The coldness to leave others behind if necessary and go for the goal." Tae's expression had turned unnervingly hard. Sohya had seen this side of her before. It reflected her isolation, a girl who had abandoned the pleasures other women her age pursued to embark on a strange quest to build a base on the moon.

Then the carefree smile returned. "Listen, Sohya. Wouldn't you like to come to Tsukuba?" Here was something else that hadn't changed: her tendency to spring surprises.

"Tsukuba? You mean mission control?"

"Yes. Serpent lands today."

"Oh, right. That was today." Sohya scratched his head. The development supervisor joined them.

"Did you forget?" said the supervisor. "We were going to celebrate today's shakedown test with a live feed from Serpent as the main event."

"Oh…yeah. Guess my mind was on the dozers," said Sohya.

"So you *were* planning to go?" pressed Tae.

The supervisor slapped Sohya on the back. "In that case, we'd better turn him over to you. I'm sure he'd rather be with you at flight control than sitting in some pub watching it on TV with the guys."

Sohya blushed and looked down. Tae extended her pendant wearcom toward the supervisor.

"Where is your party being held? At Gotenba? Okay, I have it. And how many? Forty-five? Right, got it."

"What's going on?" asked Sohya.

"I hope you won't mind if I cover the costs."

"Wow, are you sure?" said the supervisor.

"It's because those white dozers are hardworking and very courageous. Have a good time."

The manager called out to the rest of the people in the control center. "Did you hear that, everybody?"

The team gave a cheer. Sohya was impressed with Tae's practiced way of handling people. It was hard to believe she was only seventeen. She took his arm. "Shall we?"

"Sure, but can we make it in time? The maglev doesn't stop at Tsukuba."

"Mr. Aomine, that's what aircraft are for," said Sennosuke.

Once again Sohya felt as if he were in the presence of people from another universe entirely. Filled with anticipation and hesitation, he followed them out of the control center.

[2]

SEVEN HUGE FLAT-SCREEN monitors arranged in two rows dominated the flight operations control room of Tenryu Galaxy Transport's Tsukuba Space Center. The upper-right screen displayed a constantly changing array of red numerals.

JST 2029 05 01 17:30:45
MET 59:30:45

The main screen, in the center of the lower row, tracked the course of a white sphere. Its path through space was designated by a bright blue line.

May 1, 2029, 5:30:45 PM. Following insertion into lunar orbit after a flight of sixty hours, Serpent—Sixth Continent's two-ton probe—was approaching the lunar south pole. The control room was responsible for spacecraft tracking and control as well as data acquisition. Twenty-eight control positions faced the bank of monitors, arranged in four rows, including Flight Dynamics; Guidance, Navigation and Control; Propulsion; Instrumentation and Communications, or INCO; Collection and Recovery; and Data Processing. The controllers stared tensely at their monitors. In the last row, TGT flight director Hideto Hibiki stared at the backs of their heads with a dour expression.

The tension was even greater than usual, and for good reason. Many aspects of this mission were extremely difficult or involved some unprecedented element. The launch of TGT's new rocket, Eve I. Sending a probe to the moon. Placing the probe into polar, rather than equatorial, orbit. A soft landing at the pole. Collection of ice samples. Return of the samples to Earth. All carried out by private enterprise. A test mission would not have been unusual for any of these elements, but none had been conducted. It was hardly surprising that TGT's staff was under tremendous pressure.

Still, nearly half of the previously untested hurdles were behind them. Eve I, the first launch vehicle equipped with a transforming scram rocket engine, carried the probe into Earth orbit. The second stage, equipped with a conventional LE-9S engine, executed a perfect translunar injection burn. The insertion into polar orbit was also successful. Now Serpent was a hundred kilometers above the surface, waiting for the command to initiate descent.

Sohya and the others entered the observation booth at the rear of the control room. The glassed-in booth looking out over the controllers was crowded with journalists. Among them was a figure that seemed out of place: a tall man in a worn lab coat.

The man waved to Sohya. "Hey, Aomine. I hear the multidozers passed the final test. Congratulations."

"We wrapped the shakedown sequence less than an hour ago. How'd you know?"

"Everyone knows. Sixth Continent's portal went live in April." Shinji waved his wearcom.

Sohya smiled. "The news is up already. Gotenba is really on the ball."

"No point in having a site if you don't update it constantly, and not just for the public. The project partners are on the VPN all the time, swapping information."

Shinji smiled at Tae, who was standing behind Sohya. She was the website designer and ELE's head of PR. It was her idea to have each participant in the Sixth Continent project input updates directly to the site rather than running everything through her. Shinji was right: to keep the attention of the public over the project's decade-long timeline, regular updates were essential. Tae's decentralized approach spared ELE's PR team a lot of work. The project participants liked it as well. It gave them a chance to describe their hard-won success in their own words and made for effective communication. In addition to Gotoba, ELE, and TGT, there were over two hundred Sixth Continent partner companies—aerospace, airlines, engineering, construction, electronics, machinery, physical and life sciences, tourism, and advertising firms. The VPN was indispensable for efficiently sharing information across so many entities.

Sohya brought chairs for Tae and Sennosuke and sat down next to them with Shinji.

"If you're up to speed I don't need to explain," said Sohya. "My group's work is finished for the moment. I can spend the rest of the day here. When's touchdown?"

"Another half hour or so."

"In thirty minutes our fingertips will touch the moon."

"Yep. We've been reaching for four years. We're just brushing the surface this time."

"Has it seemed like a long time to you?" asked Sohya.

"No. I'm having so much fun I don't notice the time passing. Don't tell me it's any different for you."

The two men looked at each other and burst out laughing. Perhaps because they were so close in age—the childlike materials scientist would be thirty soon—Shinji and Sohya had become fast friends.

"Another half hour." Sohya folded his arms and watched the displays through the booth's bay window. The blue line representing Serpent's orbit slowly extended itself across the map of the lunar surface. In a corner of the display was a six-figure number indicating the Earth–moon distance in kilometers: 389,121.

Now everything was up to the probe, a machine about the size of a compact car, thirty Earth diameters away from Flight Control. *Not much to inspire confidence*, thought Sohya.

Suddenly the control room began to buzz. GNC began calling out updates.

"Losing telemetry. Readout interrupted."

"Unable to access attitude control."

INCO called, "Switching high gain to omni…No response. Unable to reestablish link with orbiter."

Flight's response followed instantly. "Switch to CORE 3."

"Roger, handing over from CORE 1 to CORE 3…We have contact!"

"Telemetry recovered."

"Reacquired attitude control. Orbiter is responding to commands." The controllers sounded relieved. Hibiki didn't relax.

"Confirm telemetry and go back to high gain. Support Room Two, troubleshoot CORE 1."

The commotion died down, and tense silence reigned again. Sohya and the others exchanged glances—they had watched the short burst of activity with bated breath but did not fully understand what had just taken place.

"What's CORE 1?" asked Tae.

"It sounded like the communication link was broken. Shinji?"

"CORE 1 is a geostationary satellite that links the probe and Flight Control. There are three communications satellites giving full coverage of the moon. I guess there was a problem with one of them. Say, why don't we go in and ask?"

"Are you sure?" said Sohya. "That room's pretty crowded."

"Why not? We're with the VIPs."

Shinji looked over at Tae and Sennosuke, who blinked uncomprehendingly, then glanced at each other shyly.

"Grandfather, we should have ringside seats."

"All right, as long as we're not in the way."

With Shinji in the lead, the group headed toward the door leading to the control room. They showed their IDs to security and passed through. The journalists watching them go fumed with envy.

Shinji approached Hibiki, who was sitting in the last row of control positions. "Can we ask you a question?"

"Hold it." Hibiki held up a hand as he spoke into his headset. "Go ahead, Support…What do you mean, someone blanked our frequency? Cut the crap. Who'd be jamming us? Rerun the diagnostics!" he shouted into his headset, then glared at Shinji. "If I had the budget, I'd hire a public affairs officer," he muttered. "What is it?"

"Is there a problem with CORE?"

"We don't know whether it's a malfunction yet. But the probe is fine. Don't worry." Nicknamed "the Japanese Gene Kranz," Hibiki had worked on the H-IIC rocket and was one of TGT's most seasoned flight directors.

"Serpent's telemetry was interrupted, so we switched to a different frequency. That didn't help, so we tried a different comm sat and recovered the link. There are always two CORE satellites available at any time. Even if we lost all three, we have a ground link. There's nothing to worry about."

"Okay, thanks." As Shinji spoke, one of the controllers put a hand on Hibiki's shoulder and pointed at the console.

"Um-hm…what? Goddard Space Flight Center? The Americans?" Hibiki stiffened. The console phone was buzzing. Baffled, he picked up the receiver. Apparently it was an outside call. The conversation was short, with no visual. The call ended, and Hibiki slammed the receiver into its cradle. "Those bastards! Who do they think they are?"

"What happened?" asked Shinji in surprise. The other controllers swiveled in their chairs and looked questioningly at Hibiki. He ignored them and roared into his headset.

"Support Two! Cancel CORE 1 troubleshoot. Resume normal operation…What? I don't know. Maybe aliens are messing with the probe!" Hibiki lowered his voice. "Keep this quiet for now," he said to Shinji. "We've just been treated to a NASA prank. That was Goddard Space Flight Center."

Shinji stared at him, mouth agape. Hibiki seemed ready to bite the mic off his headset. "They used a satellite in CORE 1's line of sight to jam our signal."

"Can they do that?" asked Shinji.

"It's not hard if they pump out enough power on a frequency close to ours. Ever listen to the radio next to a freeway? You get a lot of interference from CB traffic. It's the same thing. All they have to do is point a high-gain antenna on one of their ATDRS comm sats at CORE. To change the satellite's attitude, they just use their gyros. No need to waste propellant."

"Yes, but…can they *do* that?" Normally mild-mannered Shinji's expression was uncharacteristically severe. "Serpent is entering its most critical phase. Messing with our communications now could blow the mission!"

"No. The interference only lasted a few seconds. And they just hinted at the solution. Of course, they knew we'd have it fixed by now. But just in case we couldn't recover the signal, they wanted to make sure we knew how—without admitting anything, of course."

"But why?"

"I told you. It was a prank." Hibiki frowned and muttered, "Probably a test of our emergency-response capability. They've been guiding spacecraft a couple of generations longer than we have, so they gave us a poke just to see how we took it. That's bad enough, but what really burns me is how soft the poke was. They must think we're amateurs!"

Shinji and Sohya exchanged glances. Tae was confused. "Does this kind of thing happen often? Interfering with another nation's space missions? If they pushed it too far, a huge amount of work could be wasted. It seems like a terrible thing to do."

"Don't forget—America's space program started out as a missile program." Hibiki looked weary. "All the major space powers' rocketry started with the military. The Soviets even put a heavy machine gun on one of their manned spacecraft. If they wanted to, these guys could attack us."

"Isn't that something that went out with the Cold War?" said Shinji.

"We're in a cold war right now with our competitors. The prize is the moon's water." Hibiki's words pointed to another problematic aspect of the mission. Building a moon base was not something that everyone everywhere would necessarily welcome. Certain parties with vested interests were already uncomfortable, if not in open opposition. There was even some opposition to TGT's engine technology, since many nations were eagerly working to develop new, cheaper launch vehicles using TROPHY.

"Don't forget, we're going after a gold mine here…Okay, we're getting close. Take a seat in the corner over there."

Hibiki broke off the conversation and turned to his console. Sohya sighed. "A gold mine. I guess he's right. The only reason we're going through the trouble of sending a probe is to find water. It's ironic. NASA just showed how important that is."

"If Serpent brings back samples, I bet they offer us a million dollars for them."

"No way. Ten kilos is all Serpent can carry. And we're paying for it."

"I'm paying for it, actually," said Sennosuke with an innocent air. He laughed quietly and turned back to the mission screens.

Serpent was scheduled to bring back no more than ten kilograms of lunar material—a stark testament to the difficulty posed by a round-trip to the moon.

Eve I was forty-one meters long and weighed 148 tons fully loaded. It was capable of carrying fifty tons of payload into low earth orbit, ten times as much as other vehicles of similar size. For lunar orbit, its payload was ten tons. But since this was Eve's first launch, the payload was limited to 20 percent of maximum: two tons. That determined Serpent's total weight and the payload it could ferry back to Earth.

Half the probe's weight was accounted for by the orbital module. This was the heart of the probe, containing the satellite bus—power supply, communications gear, and attitude controls—as well as the engine, propellant for insertion into lunar orbit, a small relay subsatellite christened Figu, and a remote-sensing system for surveying the lunar surface. Using the capabilities of this module, Serpent made several passes over the south pole, using lasers and a spectrometer to pinpoint promising locations for water ice.

The remaining ton of mass was accounted for by the landing module. After the landing area was selected, this module would separate from the orbital module, maintain communication with Earth via Figu, and land on the moon.

Half of the landing module's mass was propellant: nitrogen tetroxide and hydrazine. This would allow the module to hover over the surface and carry out a more detailed search for the best landing area. Once the area was selected, the module would fire its engine, lower itself to the surface, and collect samples.

The mission's goal was to explore the nature of the ice-bearing material. It was virtually certain ice would be found, but its form was unknown. Water molecules deposited over hundreds of millions of years might be distributed like snow or as frozen lakes with an overblanket of regolith. It might be buried deep beneath the surface or mixed with particles of regolith in a kind of permafrost. It might even lie in scattered basins separated by tens of kilometers free of ice. Scientists had proposed a variety of such scenarios. Before the water could be utilized, Serpent had to determine which if any of these models was correct.

Great care had been taken to configure the landing module so it could return with samples regardless of the nature of the ice deposits. First, Serpent had to touch down on an ice deposit. To ensure this, it was equipped with active sensors in everything from microwave to infrared frequencies, and it was equipped with drills that would allow it to access ice on, as well as below, the surface. To prevent the torque of drilling from rotating the lander in the weak gravity, the drills would operate simultaneously. If one of them were to break, a sample could still be obtained. Even if drilling proved impossible, a contingency sampler—a collection bucket fired onto the surface with a small explosive charge and then reeled back with a wire—could recover a sample by scraping the surface.

Serpent's collection hardware totaled around a hundred kilograms. More than half of the remaining four hundred kilos was propellant to send the upper half of the landing module, known as the return module, back into lunar orbit. The descent engine, landing struts, and sampling gear would all be left behind. The lunar escape velocity is 1.68 kilometers per second, around Mach 5. But because of the moon's weak gravity, attaining this velocity would be comparatively easy.

Once back in orbit, the module would execute a trans-Earth injection burn and leave the moon behind. The propellant it carried was required to take it to this point.

Now reduced to one-hundred-odd kilos, the module would re-enter Earth's atmosphere a few days later, deploy a parafoil, and glide to New Tanegashima Airport. Its final weight, after loss of its parafoil and the ablation shield to protect it against the heat of reentry, would be just over forty kilos. The weight of the sample was ten kilos.

This was the reality of round-trip lunar travel. One hundred and forty-eight thousand kilos launched, forty-odd kilos returned. To escape from the gravitational pull of two celestial bodies and make a journey of over a million kilometers, a huge amount of propellant was required for multiple engine burns.

Still, the terms of space travel could be improved. Eve had demonstrated only a fifth of its lifting capacity. This first mission incorporated many design approaches that were proven but not especially efficient—for example, using the same type of hydrazine engines that had served the Apollo program over half a century earlier. Optimizing these systems on subsequent missions with more advanced hardware would mean more efficient round-trips. Two Eve rockets would be launched simultaneously, allowing five passengers and a pilot to make the round-trip journey to the moon. Yet space travel would still be similar to a solitary, perilous journey across a desert in which one was forced to carry all needed provisions.

But the moon's water could turn everything on its head.

The moon receives continuous sunlight. Convert that sunlight to electricity, and water could be electrolyzed into oxygen and hydrogen, two extremely efficient chemical fuels for powering a rocket returning to Earth. Not only that, since the fuel required for the last leg of the journey need not be ferried to the moon, fuel requirements for the outbound leg would be that much less. It would be as if there were an oasis at the midpoint of the desert journey, waiting with provisions required for the journey's second half. Provisions that before were necessary just to supply the energy required to carry supplies to the midpoint would not be needed either. Travelers could set out across the desert with a deceptively light amount of baggage.

The moon's water would not only make concrete production possible. It would transform lunar travel as well as the viability of settlement on the surface. TROPHY was essential to make use of atmospheric oxygen for escape from the atmosphere, but carrying a heavy load of oxygen into space still imposed significant limitations. Oxygen could be recovered from the moon's regolith, but only through complex processes. Electrolysis of water was straightforward. Oxygen produced at low cost in large volume was the best news people living on the moon could have. There was more than the future of Sixth Continent on the line; space agencies around the world were closely monitoring this mission to see if the moon's water could be easily accessed.

At 1830, Flight Director Hibiki gave the word. "Separate LM. Initiate descent."

"Undocking LM. Starting descent." Then, "First LM descent burn complete. Serpent is in the corridor."

"Figu nominal. LM telemetry is five by five."

"LM passing moon's limb. Starting countdown to loss of signal. Five, four, three, two, one, LOS. LOS error, minus 0.2 seconds."

"Signal handoff to Figu."

"LM to auto control," said Hibiki.

"Handing off LM to auto control."

From now on, the lander would be engaging in critical maneuvers that could not wait for signals from Earth, so control was handed off to Serpent's own computer. Beyond that, there was nothing to do but trust the AI, the same program refined through four years of hard work and used by Gotoba's dozers. The software had already proven itself.

The landing module descended rapidly from its altitude of one hundred kilometers. There was no video feed; this would occupy too much transmission bandwidth. But the numerical data flowing in from the lander allowed the controllers to track its progress as if they were watching it with their own eyes.

"Twelve thousand…eleven thousand…ten thousand. LM is in permanent shadow zone."

"LM pitch over. Floodlights on. Ground radar on. Spectrometer engaged." The lander flew over several pitch-black craters. Everyone's nerves were taut.

"Getting solid returns. We've got clear absorption lines close to 2.15 microns near-infrared."

"Ice on the surface," Hibiki murmured, relaxing slightly. Checking for near-infrared absorption lines was the best way to confirm the presence of ice, but it required a light source. In the eternal darkness of the shadow zone, the lack of sunlight had made such investigations impossible. Serpent's floodlights allowed readings to be taken for the first time. Furthermore, it seemed the ice was not buried. "Verify ground radar telemetry," barked Hibiki. "I don't want to get this far and plow into a mountain."

"We're fine," said the GNC officer. "Readings from the last orbit confirm no areas of major elevation…Altitude eight hundred. Down at ten, fifteen forward."

"Scanning for touchdown point. Fuel consumption is running slightly ahead of schedule. Should we move up touchdown?"

"No. Let Serpent decide. I'd rather risk a few extra burns to avoid a hard landing."

"Roger."

"Tae, do you know what's going on?" Sohya saw the answer in her faint smile.

"Yes. It's going well, isn't it?"

"Seems like it." Sohya nodded and looked at the displays.

Then it happened. GNC raised the first warning. "We've got metal!"

"What?" Hibiki craned forward in his chair. "What metal? What's the data, what telemetry are you looking at?"

"Ah…I don't know, the radar spiked suddenly. Like bouncing off a car."

"Probably a flat boulder. Don't worry about little anomalies." But as Hibiki was dismissing the reading, shouting came from Flight Dynamics and INCO.

"LM pitch over complete! AI has initiated touchdown sequence!"

"Telemetry off nominal! Range finder spike!"

Again Hibiki responded instantly. "Terminate descent! Camera on! Altitude?"

"Eighty!"

"What's going on? Did Serpent confirm the touchdown point?"

"No. She skipped confirmation. She's proceeding with the landing sequence."

"What is that, a system error? Give me a visual!"

"That will use most of our bandwidth."

"I don't care!" shouted Hibiki. "Forget the spectrograph. If we go down, I want to see it with my own eyes!"

GNC brought the feed from the lander's belly camera onto the center display. The image that loomed into view was met with stunned silence.

Hibiki stared, face frozen in surprise. "What is that? Gold dust?" he whispered.

The image before them looked like flecks of gold scattered across the bottom of a river, or perhaps countless golden breakers whipped by the wind. Against a brown background, the fine particles spread endlessly, sparkling in the lander's floodlights.

Hibiki stiffened. "It's getting closer! Are we descending?"

"Yes! The hover command was ignored. Kill the autopilot?"

"No—wait! Velocity?"

"One point one down. Right on the money."

"Let her go!" Hibiki gave the command without hesitation. The lander's computer might be malfunctioning, but he decided to leave it in control of the descent. "Passing twenty. We're beyond the abort limit. On your toes, gentlemen!"

The controllers were huddled in front of their screens, faces drained of color. The lander descended smoothly toward the sparkling surface. It was hard to believe it might be malfunctioning.

The halo of illumination from the floodlights narrowed toward the center of the display. At the same time, the surface began to blur, concentric circles of pale dust radiating rapidly outward. The room started buzzing.

"Steam?" called out Hibiki.

"No. Ice crystals. The vacuum is too high to sustain the liquid state. The ice sublimates and freezes again instantly."

"Diamond dust!"

"Maybe dry ice?"

"She's touching down," said Hibiki. "Don't sink..." He swallowed hard. The room fell silent again. This was a worry. Even if the surface could not support the weight of the lander, it would be viable as long as it sank only as far as the landing struts. If the sinkage were any worse than that, there would be no liftoff.

There was no sound, but everyone imagined it: three landing pads making hard contact with the surface. That was how abrupt the shock of contact was. The image jerked. The stream of fog kicked up by the lander engine abated. The LM engine shut down on sensing contact. Fine white dust streamed in all directions in a classic parabola and slowly fell to the surface. When the rain of particles ceased, the image cleared. The surface was clearly visible.

The controllers were glued to their monitors. Then, as if coming to his senses, one of them began calling out the data at his position.

"Flight, we have contact! Elevation, zero. Slope, zero. Sinkage, zero. Touchdown successful."

"Success?"

"Success!" The room shook with triumphant cheering.

"Quiet!" Hibiki rose slightly from his chair and pounded his console. "Figu won't be overhead for long. There's no time for celebration. DPS! Disengage autopilot. Don't go to backup yet! GNC, check telemetry and diagnose the dropout prior to touchdown. C&R, deploy the contingency sampler. Then the drills! Hurry!"

The controllers began calling out a stream of status updates. After a few moments the Data Processing Systems engineer advised, "Telemetry analysis points to a dropout triggered by circuit noise."

"Noise? From where?" pressed Hibiki.

"Flight, I think I have it!" GNC put a ground radar plot on one of the forward screens. "The metal reading. That was clearly anomalous—the reflection was so strong it interfered with auto control. We didn't expect this. The circuits are well shielded."

"All problems are unexpected," snapped Hibiki. "Can you recover?"

"Primary, secondary, and tertiary system diagnostics are all nominal. Whatever it was, it was transient."

"Go to secondary just in case. Are we going to have the same problem on the way out?"

"No. We won't be using ground radar on the way back to orbit."

"All right then! Good so far…" For the first time, Hibiki sat back in his chair and took a deep breath. Then he turned to his visitors.

"Shall we take a look at the scenery?"

"By all means," said Sennosuke.

"Hold it. Aren't you Mr. Toenji?" said Hibiki, finally noticing the project sponsor. "Perfect timing." He grinned. "Take a look at your new continent."

He engaged the color CCD camera atop the 120-centimeter-tall lander. Something appeared on the main display, but the image was nearly dark. The lower half was a white blur.

"Is that a camera malfunction?" asked Sohya.

"No. The default sensitivity is very low. Once an Apollo astronaut fried his camera by accidentally pointing it at the sun. Let's bring it up slowly…" As he spoke, the image gradually brightened and sharpened.

The white portion was the surface, illuminated from the underside of the lander. The long shadow of a landing strut cut across a fine carpet of sparkling particles, like a ski slope at night. Beyond the circle of light lay impenetrable darkness. There was no sign of surface, horizon, or space.

Tae's voice broke the silence. "So this is the three-billion-year night of the shadow zone."

"Yes," said Hibiki. "Let's switch on the floods." The lander's two-hundred-thousand-candlepower LED floodlights flashed on. For the first time, the team saw where they were.

It was a titanic, naturally occurring coliseum. The floor of the crater was draped in glistening white, like a blanket of snow reflecting light in all directions. Softball-size rocks were scattered across the surface. A wall of jagged cliffs was visible just above the horizon. Hibiki panned the camera. The cliffs stretched unbroken around the compass. That must have been the crater rim. The lander had touched down in the center of the crater.

"Radar puts the height of the rim at 140 meters. If they're on the horizon, that makes the crater diameter four kilometers. How steep are those cliffs?" said Hibiki.

INCO answered, "Slope is thirty degrees. Might be difficult to lay cables from the solar array over the rim." If ice were detected where the lander touched down, the equipment to gather it would need power. To supply power in the darkness of the crater, solar panels would have to be set up outside the crater, where sunlight was available, and cables laid into the crater. One of Serpent's goals was to locate a crater where this would be feasible.

Then one of the controllers spoke up. He was looking at a detailed map of the terrain.

"This is too good to be true. The height of the rim doesn't matter. In fact, we're lucky it's so high."

"What do you mean?" said Hibiki. The controller was rotating the map. The controllers on either side of her were staring at it as well.

"The crater's elevation is slightly higher than average. It's relatively isolated. That means sunlight will strike all along the rim. If the rim were lower, the crater wouldn't be in shadow."

Hibiki was skeptical. "There must be other craters with that profile."

"Yes, but they're at least twenty or thirty kilometers across. They'd need panel arrays on opposite sides of the crater to maintain power as the moon rotates with the earth around the sun. Here the panels can be spaced around a circumference of twelve klicks or so. The cables can be shorter. People on the surface will have less ground to cover."

"This is prime south pole real estate!"

"Hold on, everyone!" Hibiki raised his voice again. "You're assuming we've got H_2O. Don't get carried away. That ice might be methane or CO_2." He was right. The excitement died down. "Start drilling. Save the celebration till we're finished."

"Will that give you the answer?" asked Tae.

"It's a simple test. We heat a sample in a chamber inside the lander. If the ice liquefies at zero and boils at a hundred degrees Celsius, it's definitely water. Now that we're on the surface, that's all we need to find out."

"Mr. Hibiki?" Sohya raised his hand. "Can I sit with the C&R team? I'd like to check the site statics."

"You want to watch the dynamic load test? That's right, you're a structural engineer."

A dynamic load test applied a standard shock to a pile inserted into the ground. The change in pile depth was measured to calculate the bearing strength of the ground, an essential piece of information needed before constructing a building. Furthermore, if the surface were composed of water ice, knowing the hardness of the ground would be useful in estimating the difficulty of digging to recover the ice.

With Hibiki's permission, Sohya approached the C&R team. The engineer was already drilling into the surface. "The load on the drill right now is thirty-two newtons—about the resistance of cork. The habitat modules won't be in any danger of sinking."

The second team engineer added, "Unfortunately, the ice is full of regolith. Not gravel, but particles of all sizes. Well, it's still permafrost. There's more than enough ice—oh shit!"

A warning flashed red on one of the subscreens. The controller sighed in frustration. "Drill one is jammed. We better stop drill two."

"A rock?" asked Hibiki, craning forward across his console to look.

"It's not a rock. But drill one is locked up tight. We won't be getting a sample from this one."

"You stopped drill two, right?" said Hibiki. "Okay, that's far enough. Bring it up."

Drill two was reversed and drawn upward. Images from the belly camera were still visible on the main display. One of the controllers said, "Look. What's that?"

Everyone looked up at the display. The room went silent.

The two drills were visible to the left and right on the display. The drill on the left was withdrawing from the surface. As it rotated, a substance resembling gold thread stuck out at all angles.

"That almost looks like coconut fiber," said Hibiki.

"The reflections must've been from this material. It looks pretty densely tangled around the drill."

"So what is it?" said Hibiki. No one knew; there was no way they could have known. Neither the moon's ice nor the comets that brought it were theorized to contain anything like these fibers.

Drill two was free of the surface. The C&R team placed several grams of material in Serpent's test chamber. The rest of the sample was placed inside the return module. The probe sent its answer within minutes.

"Melting point: minus 0.41 degrees Celsius. Boiling point is 99.22 degrees. That's it. The sample is water ice."

"From how deep?" asked Hibiki.

"About 2,850 millimeters. We were expecting it at four thousand."

"That means—"

"The moon has water," said Sohya. "The surface is soft enough for digging but strong enough to support engineering equipment."

"Congratulations," Hibiki said to Tae and Sennosuke. "You have everything you need, Mr. Toenji. There's nothing to stand in the way of Sixth Continent."

Tae looked at her grandfather. They both stood and faced the observation booth. Sennosuke borrowed a headset so the journalists could hear him.

"I want to thank you all, and I ask for your continued support. Now the real work begins."

The sound of applause gradually rose and filled the room. TGT was not applauding their own success, hard-won as it had been. By discovering water on the moon, their groundbreaking mission would become the foundation for an even grander vision. It was that vision they were applauding.

Tae looked at Sohya, who gave her two thumbs-up. Shinji joined in the applause. Their faces strobed white from the journalists' cameras.

The mission was not over. But for once, Hibiki waited a few seconds before shouting his next command.

[3]

FOUR DAYS LATER, Serpent touched down at Tanegashima with three kilograms of surface samples. Careful testing revealed their exact composition.

Fifty-five percent of the sample was water ice by weight. Another 40 percent was composed of regolith particles. The water contained small amounts of dissolved aluminum, calcium, iron, silicon, and other minerals from the regolith, along with minute amounts of glycine, serine, and other amino acids. This closely matched one of the proposed models.

Eons before, a comet composed of water and amino acids had struck one of the craters in perpetual shadow. The intense heat and shock of impact had vaporized the ice, blowing regolith upward and mixing the water vapor with it. But in the cold of perpetual shadow, the vapor quickly refroze and fell to the crater floor as ice. Comets are more fragile than asteroids—sometimes enough to be vaporized by the sun's heat—and rarely leave impact craters. The shallow depression created by the comet was soon covered by falling ice. This was the origin of the plain of ice and regolith within the craters in perpetual shadow.

The sample's remaining 5 percent was composed of those mysterious metallic threads, which proved to be an alloy of aluminum and silicon. Their composition did not differ from elements that could be found on the moon, but there was no known natural process that could create a threadlike alloy. Electron microscopy revealed a regular, tubelike structure similar to the branching structure of plant roots, but the tensile force applied by the drill as it snapped the threads had destroyed any fine structural detail. Clearly, the material possessed high tensile strength.

The threads also solved at least two mysteries: the strong metallic radar response and the jamming of the drill as it bored into the densely packed threads. Still, the material posed far more questions than it answered.

Gotoba was inundated with requests from scientists around the world for even a tiny sample of the material, but the firm decided to use two kilograms for experimental concrete production. The last kilogram would be donated to research institutions. This didn't prevent a storm of criticism from the scientific community—using samples with such research value merely for concrete production! But Gotoba was unperturbed.

The moon's water was indeed suitable for making concrete. That was all they needed to know. The team standing by in Yamaguchi Prefecture began working feverishly with a large local cement-manufacturing firm to design a production module that could process lunar permafrost containing 55 percent water and produce cement in a vibration kiln designed to operate at one-sixth G.

The first task in building a structure on Earth was site selection. Once the site was chosen, surveying and soil-bearing capacity tests were carried out. Serpent not only confirmed the characteristics of the lunar water but also answered the question of site selection. Sixth Continent would be built outside the crater—quickly christened Eden—on the side facing Earth.

Dynamic load tests were unnecessary. The moon had no alluvial soils, no active fault lines, and virtually no quakes. Though Sohya had worried about the simple siting technique used at Kunlun Base, the approach used by the Chinese was more than adequate.

Still, it would not do to replicate Kunlun Base. The Chinese had simply placed their modules on the surface, but Sixth Continent would carry out full-scale construction using concrete blocks. Leveling the site would mean moving large amounts of surface material. With no erosion from wind and water, the lunar surface bore the record of three billion years of asteroid impacts and volcanic activity. There were no truly level sites, but without one the robotic engineering equipment could not be put to best use. Base design would face major limitations.

"Space development" usually brought to mind rockets rising into the sky on pillars of fire or satellites with huge solar arrays. But aerospace-related activity was only one facet of space development. What was needed on the moon was nothing less than the engineering technology developed for construction on Earth. Manufacturers of launch vehicles and satellites might pretend to offer such expertise, but those claims were just talk. The lunar environment would quickly punish any half-baked development effort. What was needed was for construction engineering firms to start participating in space development.

That she saw this from the start was proof of Tae Toenji's genius. And Gotoba Engineering & Construction was the only organization capable of realizing her vision.

For a company with Gotoba's experience in construction for extreme environments, designing a base on the moon was straightforward. What they realized early on was that the engineering equipment was a far greater challenge. Multidozer development was a key step; once that was accomplished, one of the most challenging hurdles had been cleared.

In September 2029, TGT's Adam 1 heavy-lift launch vehicle lifted off with the first ten tons of cargo—half its rated capacity—for lunar orbit. The payload consisted of one multidozer and 340 square meters of solar panels capable of generating 150 kilowatts of electricity.

Four days later, the cargo safely touched down outside Eden

Crater. TGT's minimalist landing module had been given the un-prepossessing name Turtle. It was far simpler than the highly advanced Serpent lander—a simple metal frame with retro-rockets and a fuel tank, radio altimeter, GPS system, and communications antenna. It was designed solely as a mass-produced space truck capable of putting seven tons of cargo on the lunar surface.

On landing, Turtle deployed the solar panels with a spring-loaded device. The panels were deployed perpendicular to the sun, which sat just above the polar horizon. The flexible panel unrolled like a carpet four meters wide by eighty-five meters long, launched outward in a parabolic curve. As it unrolled, support struts on the back unfolded. The panel fell to the surface and landed on these struts with its power-generating side toward the sun. The entire deployment took all of ten seconds. The method was crude, but in the airless environment it was possible to precisely calculate how the panel would unfold. Spring-loaded deployment would play a major role in future cargo deployments.

The news that the moon held abundant supplies of water was greeted with widespread excitement. Second only in importance to water was generation of electricity. The multidozers were not equipped with solar arrays because this would hinder their movements. Instead, they would derive power from the stationary solar panel via a cable. At the moon's polar regions, the sunlight struck at such a low angle that vertical solar panels were the only way to generate a stable supply of power.

Once word came—"The panels are up!"—the success of the mission was assured. Now power would be plentiful as long as sunlight was falling on the deployment side of the crater.

With electric power, everything else was straightforward. The multidozers were tough enough to handle heavy work. Even if one flipped over, it could right itself by anchoring its ripper claw and using a lifting lever. The dozers were also intelligent enough to solve most problems they might encounter. Drawing power from the panel, Dozer 1 rolled off the lander and began moving surface material, the first step in base construction. An absolutely flat area was required for future landers, to prevent their engines from kicking up regolith and contaminating the solar array. In a pinch, the dozer was capable of shaking the panel to loosen any collected regolith.

The video feed from Dozer 1 showed no large boulders or ground fissures in the area, indicating that operations would go smoothly. Unfortunately, Dozer 1 itself could not be observed from Earth. Like Sir Edmund Hillary on Mount Everest, Dozer 1 could take pictures of everything but itself. Nevertheless, the images it sent as it vigorously moved about pushing rocks out of the way and packing the surface flat demonstrated that it was successfully fulfilling its objectives. The project teams, especially the staff of Gotoba Engineering, crowded around the monitors in a state of high excitement to watch the work in progress. For the first time since he had joined the company, Sohya even saw Takasumi Iwaki smile.

SHINJI TAI LOOKED out the window, then back to the monitor in front of him, comparing the views. "Yes, I guess that would make him happy," he said to Sohya.

Shinji and Sohya were at the Gotenba multidozer production facility and proving ground at the base of Mount Fuji. The facility also served as the control center for multidozers on the lunar surface. Shinji shuttled back and forth between Gotenba, Tsukuba, Tanegashima Space Center, and other research facilities, helping to maintain the virtual private network between the different project teams.

"I've only met him a few times, but Iwaki seems to like efficiency," said Shinji. "Sending robots to the moon is more efficient than sending people, so he should be happy with that."

Sohya was calibrating the telemetry data sent by Dozer 1 with the data coming from the multidozers at the proving ground.

"Now that you mention it, I remember him saying that when a machine makes a mistake, it's a mistake of the people who built it. If a machine's reliable, it's not necessary for humans to go to the moon."

"So why are we working so hard to send people there?" murmured Shinji.

"If you want a technologist's opinion, the answer is simple: because it's possible."

"Because it's possible? That's backward. First you've got to have a goal. What you want to find out is whether your goal is feasible or not."

"That's what most people would do," said Sohya. "Take Kennedy—he started the Apollo program before he even knew if a moon landing was possible."

Shinji smiled faintly and shook his head. "We're a different breed. If it's doable, we do it, whether it's necessary or not. Oppenheimer built the bomb. Genentech made Nellie and Mary, the first human clones. The last big general construction company built a tunnel under Tsushima Strait. Ethics and cost/benefit aren't in the equation."

"Are you saying Sixth Continent is another boondoggle, Shinji?"

"History books a hundred years from now may say it was the biggest folly of the twenty-first century—wasting precious resources to colonize a planet with no practical potential for development. We could just stick close to home and look after the environment."

Sohya frowned. Shinji added casually, "But folly is all right. Even folly can advance human culture. Even if Sixth Continent shuts down after a year of operation, it will have been worth it as far as I'm concerned—even if all we get out of it is pure technological advancement."

"You're more of a cynic than I thought."

"People who might be working on the next A-bomb should at least be aware of the possibility. I mean, look—are you certain this project is for the best?"

"Well, I'm like you. I can only see so far. But I agree with Gotoba's take on things. Progress means creating something where previously there was nothing. Building habitats for people on a desolate place like the moon is proof of that progress."

"Sounds like your take isn't that different from mine," said Shinji.

"You're right. We've both got swelled heads." Sohya chuckled. Shinji looked up from his monitor and stretched.

"With my personality, I could've easily ended up doing obscure research for some metal refiner rather than developing something revolutionary like TROPHY. But I'm not, thanks to Ryuichi. I have to hand it to him, he's got a lot of passion."

"I envy him. He's a straight shooter. I can easily picture what he'd think of this discussion."

"No, you're wrong about that," said Shinji before Sohya could say anything further. "He'd say, 'Young people shouldn't worry about other people's opinions. Don't think. Get moving!'"

"You're probably right." The two men laughed.

"Come to think of it, it's amazing that so many people with different viewpoints are working on the same project. Some of us want to test the technology, some of us want to build, and some of us just want to go there."

"You forgot one motivation. Some of us want to make money."

This caught Sohya off guard. "You mean Reika Hozumi? I guess money should really be the main reason. This whole thing is private enterprise. It's hard to think of a project less suited to making money though."

"As far as Reika's concerned, money's the only thing. Oh well, whatever it takes to motivate her." Shinji whistled as he began running a stress test on the link to TGT's Yokohama Data Processing Center. "Ah yes, money…"

As ELE's auditor, Reika was like a human calculator. Was she interested in anything else? Shinji glanced at Sohya a few times before speaking.

"I'd say you have less to worry about than anyone else on that account."

"What do you mean?"

"You have just the right balance of enthusiasm and doubt. I envy Ryuichi, but I also envy you."

"I'm not sure what that means."

"See?" Shinji laughed again. "That lack of self-awareness. Just what TGT's president preaches: no doubts."

"Thanks a lot," said Sohya. He pretended to be hurt, but in fact he didn't mind Shinji's ribbing. Representatives from space agencies around the world referred to him as "Professor Tai," yet he was as unaffected as ever, liked by everyone. Sohya felt fortunate to be able to work with a man like Shinji. He was certain that someday Shinji would be mentioned in the same breath with pathfinders like von Braun and Korolyov.

━━━◆◆◆◆━━━

TROPHY'S SUCCESS GENERATED a storm of calls and emails to Tenryu Galaxy Transport. As usual, many came from crackpots and clueless amateurs, but there were also more than three hundred serious offers from space development companies. Most of these feelers were for launch services using the revolutionary Adam and Eve rockets, for purchase of entire launch vehicles, or for TROPHY engines. But Ryuichi had to choke back his tears and refuse them all. Sixth Continent had booked all of TGT's launch capacity for the next six years. Ryuichi would be unable to service other clients for quite some time.

Launch vehicles and engine sales also presented problems. In 1969, Japan's Diet had resolved that the nation would use rockets only for peaceful purposes. But in those days, "rocket" meant "missile," and the resolution became an obstacle for exports. This Cold War holdover prevented Japan from exporting the LE-5A, its first domestically produced rocket engine. That was in 1988.

Japan's government had grown more pragmatic on such matters, but the '69 resolution continued to hinder space-related commerce, like a useless antique no one was willing to discard. Japan's bureaucrats winced at the prospect of exporting TROPHY. TGT might be a private company, but most of its facilities, technology, and personnel had formerly been under government control. In the end, TGT did not have the leverage to overcome bureaucratic resistance. If overseas buyers could not lay their hands on the real thing, they would have to examine published documents and attempt to build a TROPHY engine themselves.

Still, for a world groaning under the unbelievable cost of putting a payload into space—three hundred thousand yen to put a single gram into low earth orbit—TROPHY was a gift from heaven. For only 1.6 billion yen, an Adam rocket could put as much payload into low earth orbit—a hundred tons—as the Soviet Union's titanic N1 rocket.

In the seventeenth century, passage across the Atlantic in a sailing ship cost the equivalent of two years' wages for a laborer; jet aircraft reduced the cost to a few tens of thousands of yen. Now nations and corporations around the world were vying to develop TROPHY-equipped launch vehicles. The wheel was about to turn once more.

***

ON HER FIRST flight to Tanegashima, Reika Hozumi realized that her outlook on life had changed.

Until then, everything for her had been about numbers. As ELE's auditor, she had reviewed the expenses for every division. The only question on her mind was whether spending would yield profit. ELE was an integrated entertainment enterprise, but life on the inside was not all dreams and fantasy. Instead, just as the company delivered a carefully calibrated experience to its visitors, it stringently tracked each and every yen, reckoning its profits precisely. This was Reika's job. In her mind, if an activity did not create profit, it was nothing less than chicanery, even if it was positioned as service to society.

Then Ryuichi had thrown her world into chaos.

Profits? Unnecessary. Service to society? Secondary. The goal was pure flight. To Reika, Ryuichi's obsession seemed a frighteningly personal, almost childish hobby. Yet she could only be astounded that this hobbyist had taken on the government and giant corporations, built a private company as his personal vehicle, nurtured an astonishing new invention, and was now positioned to make enormous profits.

By working with him, her world had broadened. It was not only that Ryuichi was extremely capable. He was continually pushing forward, almost heedless of those around him. The passion, the psychological fire that animated him, burned brightly. Sometimes this energy was destructive. How many times had he bellowed at her when she'd tried to knock some sense into him with graphs, charts, and formulas? "That's beside the point!" was his mantra. Everything that stood in the way of successfully launching Eve, Adam, and *Apple* was irrelevant. Return on investment? Cost/benefit? Beside the point—things would work out in the end. And indeed they had, and he kept moving ahead, always confident that they would. In a sense, Reika saw him as wisely reckless.

So when Ryuichi said he'd be in the *Apple* capsule for the first training exercise of Japan's first manned spacecraft, Reika was hardly surprised. Instead she was concerned, and for the first time she worried about his recklessness and where it might lead, rather than simply viewing his seemingly rash decisions with contempt.

Reika got the news flash from TGT during an auditing meeting at ELE headquarters. It was then that she realized just how afraid she had been. There had been a wiring fault in the capsule—and a fire.

All that was needed to send her running out of the meeting were the words "capsule" and "fire." TGT's Tobishima factory was close to ELE. She rushed there in a taxi, but Ryuichi had already been taken to a hospital. When she arrived at the emergency room, Ryuichi had embraced her with his bandaged arms.

That was a year ago. Since then, Reika had come to realize that no woman before her had ever argued so much with TGT's president. She hadn't laughed at his dreams or stood noncommittally watching from a distance. She was the first to meet him head-on, the first to refuse to bend.

"I have to admit, it's fun having a worthy opponent." Ryuichi stood with Reika on the catwalk at TGT, looking down on the first flight-ready *Apple* spacecraft. "And you certainly are worthy, Ms. Hozumi. Hey, it's a compliment."

"Can't you find a better way to compliment me?" Reika sulked and looked away, then leaned her shoulder against Ryuichi. "And please don't call me 'Ms. Hozumi.' My name is Reika."

"Sure. Reika. As I said, I do enjoy catching hell from you."

"That is not a compliment!"

They watched the activity in the assembly room as they bickered. Surrounded by technicians swathed in clean suits, *Apple* awaited its baptism by fire.

IMAGES OF CONSTRUCTION on the moon were broadcast around the world. In a single day, the Sixth Continent website received an unprecedented 140 million hits. Viewers of 1,200 web dailies in 115 countries saw Dozer 1 lift the largest boulder on the construction site, dubbed Ayers Rock. Twenty-two toy companies requested permission from Gotoba Engineering to market plastic multidozer models. While they waited for an answer, pirate versions spread across Asia and South America.

Companies selling lunar real estate had been around since the last century; now there were companies purporting to sell homes on the moon. Lured by virtual tours and slick presentations, more than five thousand people made hefty down payments. The media assumed Gotoba Engineering was behind it—it was, after all, a construction company—and the company became a target of fierce criticism. After struggling unsuccessfully to explain that they were in partnership with two other companies to build a wedding palace, were not in a position to sell homes on their own, and were not going to build homes in any case, Gotoba's PR team threw up their hands.

Most of the victims were in the United States, where a class action suit was brought against Gotoba. The suit alleged that the company never made it clear they did not actually build homes. With Gotoba's PR people on the ropes, Tae brought in Eden's own experts to fight back. They mounted a campaign that adroitly positioned ELE as the victim and assembled their own legal team for a countersuit. Tae's deep pockets, her understanding of American ways, and her intelligence offset Eden's disadvantages at mounting a suit in a U.S. court. In three months, the complaint was reluctantly withdrawn, though the Americans refused to concede that Gotoba was blameless. But about half the members of the class action suit ended up applying for tours of Sixth Continent, and five hundred new Tae Toenji fan sites sprang up. The firewall on Tae's wearcom was strengthened.

———◆·▸◂·◆———

"EXCUSE ME. ARE you Tae Toenji?"

The maglev express platform, Tokyo Station. The man was in his thirties and wore a polo shirt and a nervous look. Sohya, walking behind Tae, quickly interposed himself between her and the man.

"I'm sorry. You're mistaken."

"Why, you're Sohya Aomine! So she must be Tae Toenji."

"I don't know who you're talking about."

Tae tugged at Sohya's sleeve and whispered, "It's all right, Sohya."

"Hold on." He turned to the man. "I'm sorry, but I need your name and wearcom number." The man identified himself as a high school teacher from Kyoto. Sohya input the information and snapped the man's picture with his wearcom. He had his answer in thirty seconds: the man seemed to be who he said he was. His sophomores were in Tokyo on a field trip, and he was acting as their guide. Sure enough, around a hundred young people in school uniforms were watching with great interest from a short distance. *They must have pressured him*, thought Sohya. *Well, he's not a deviant or a terrorist.*

The information came from ELE's security department. Two of their plainclothes members were on the platform at this very moment, carefully observing the scene. Gotoba headquarters was in the heart of Tokyo, and Tae used the maglev whenever she visited on business. Given her wealth and celebrity, a security detail was a sensible precaution.

But Tae did not enjoy having bodyguards, and it became Sohya's job to accompany her whenever she visited Tokyo. It was his idea, even though it took him away from work.

Having confirmed the man was harmless, Sohya bowed. "My apologies. Not everyone approaches Miss Toenji with good intentions."

"No—it's all right. You need to be careful."

Sohya stepped aside. The man looked at Tae and cleared his throat. "I'm sorry to trouble you. My students wanted your autograph. The only way I could stop them from mobbing you was to approach you myself. I'm sorry, I know we're bothering you."

"No, I'm flattered." Tae smiled and waved at the students. They burst into cheers of excitement. "Thanks for your support, everyone," Tae called. "I hope you'll visit my Sixth Continent someday!"

The boys whistled. The girls squealed. Other people on the platform began to stare. Tae waved to everyone, then spoke to the teacher. "You said something about a signature." The man held out a copy of the field trip guide. Tae signed it with a flourish.

"And, er…could I shake your hand?" Sohya moved to intervene, but Tae shook her head and grasped the man's hand.

"We wish you the best of luck," the man said. Tae thanked him. He seemed to be gripping her slender fingers harder than necessary. Sohya broke in. "I'm sorry, but we must be going."

"Mr. Aomine, could I shake your hand too?"

"Excuse me?"

"Your hand. Can I shake it?"

Baffled, Sohya extended his hand. The man's eyes twinkled like a child's as he gripped Sohya's hand with both his own. "You went to the moon! It's so great, I can't believe I'm actually meeting you. And now you're building a base up there. What an amazing feat!"

Sohya mumbled thanks. The man pumped Sohya's hand up and down, full of excitement. "Actually, the students are interested in Ms. Toenji, but I really wanted to meet you. I've been interested in space travel since I was a kid. I even made a stab at becoming an astronaut." He reluctantly released Sohya's hand. "We're all behind you. Good luck!"

Sohya struggled to assume his media smile and thanked the teacher again, who then rejoined his students. Sohya waved, but they didn't leave. They kept looking at him and Tae.

Sohya looked at his open palm, still warm from the man's grip. "I'm sorry I doubted him. I guess some people are just nice."

"Yes. They're everywhere." Tae's voice was toneless. Sohya looked at her. She glanced away. "Everyone is so nice. They want my signature, but they don't want to be my friend."

"What do you expect? You're—"

"Different. I know. So what does that make you?"

"I'm different too. Anyway, you don't have to be self-conscious around me," said Sohya.

"Of course I do. The security detail is watching you too."

"Yeah, I noticed that."

"You did?" Tae looked at him. Sohya smiled.

"I'm not dumb enough to think I'm trusted by the people who look after you. But that's fine. The security guys are like your accessories. They're just there for your safety."

Tae was silent for a moment. "That's what I like about you," she said.

"I know. I assume I'm still a candidate for boyfriend. Or am I out?"

Tae laughed lightly. "Let's just say you're still the number one candidate." Her smile finally returned.

"I'm glad I'm number one. I'll try to make sure I don't slip to second place. You know…if you had more friends, you might not be building Sixth Continent." Sohya looked at her questioningly. "You said you wanted people to be able to live on the moon, to make it part of humanity's world. But you also said there was another reason. What is it?"

"Another reason…" The arrival warning sounded, cutting Tae off. The streamlined maglev glided into the station. The doors opened in front of them. Tae looked back at Sohya. "I'll tell you next time. Let's say goodbye here."

"Okay. See you."

Tae took her seat in the first-class car. Sohya lifted his hand in farewell. She kept glancing at him. Sohya looked back at her and pondered.

The thousands of people working to make Sixth Continent a reality had diverse motives. Tae was the axis around which all these motives revolved. Yet it seemed that she herself had multiple reasons for pursuing the project. What she had let slip so far was somewhat different from what she was telling the world in her PR program. What was her true motive? Sohya still did not quite know, and she wouldn't tell him. He knew there was no point in asking again. She'd tell him when she was ready.

The departure buzzer sounded, and the express silently moved forward. Tae wasn't looking at him now. That was a bit of a worry.

ADAM 2 AND 3 delivered full payloads to the moon without incident: more multidozers and a unit called a bulk shooter,
a linear-induction drive conveyer system designed to hurl excavated soil over the lunar surface. Prepping and paving roadbeds
to transport excavated material would delay the project timeline.
Hauling regolith would consume large amounts of energy. The
most efficient approach would be to move only the material itself.
That meant hurling it across the surface.

Dozers 2 and 3 worked together to carry the bulk shooter,
which was also standardized at a weight of five tons, into Eden
Crater. Dozer 2's power cable snapped partway through the climb
over the crater walls, but once in motion, the multidozers were
able to electrolyze their internal water supply to make hydrogen
and oxygen for their fuel cells. This allowed Dozer 2 to make its
way back to the Turtle and retrieve a new cable.

The bulk shooter was safely transported to the center of the
crater. It threw permafrost excavated by Dozer 2 a full kilometer
at forty meters per second. Once solar panels were installed on the
crater's far side, power would be available round the clock. And
once the area around the Turtle was ready to receive the material,
the plan was to hurl it all the way out of the crater, a distance of
two kilometers.

The world was transfixed by images of regolith shot through
with golden threads fountaining across the lunar surface. Moon-
related fiction flew off the shelves of bookstores, from science fiction
by Arthur C. Clarke to works by storyteller Jules Verne, the founder
of the genre. Publishers rushed to meet demand with paperbacks
and comics, and representatives from Hollywood visited ELE. The
world was engulfed in a passion for anything relating to space.

Maybe it was because the world was now so interconnected
that strife between peoples had eased, armed conflict had

diminished, and the money and resources devoted to military aims were seeking somewhere else to go. Maybe it was because the emerging countries had become more skilled at diplomacy that aid to them had increased. Protection and recovery of their still-significant environmental assets had succeeded, and they were able to stand on their own feet economically, so the world as a whole had become more affluent. Maybe it was because China had closed down Kunlun Base two years ago, and people were hungry for the next big thing in space exploration. Maybe it was the dizzying speed with which new forms of entertainment were appearing and falling out of favor. The people of the developed world were waiting for something new to entertain them, and Sixth Continent was the ideal dream.

Whatever the reason, Tae's vision had become the focus of feverish worldwide expectation.

But not everyone welcomed the prospect of a wedding palace on the moon—those who had first sent men to another world. Those who had left twelve sets of footprints on the moon, carried out photoreconnaissance of every planet in the solar system, and boastfully regarded it as their territory. Those who constituted Earth's most elite and ambitious fraternity...

As far as NASA was concerned, they had not been beaten yet.

[4]

"WHY IS GOING into space so important?"

Reika kicked the tops of the little breakers along the beach with her bare foot, scattering a line of droplets across the tide's calm surface. Then she sneezed. Even on Tanegashima, the December weather was cold.

"Because it's too comfortable here." Ryuichi took off his jacket and put it around her shoulders. She whispered thanks and put her hand on her shoulder, where his hand was.

"What do you mean?"

"The earth is too kind to us. She protects us from space so well that we don't even need clothes. Otherwise we'd be dead."

"We still get colds."

They exchanged smiles and walked on side by side, carrying their shoes and socks, feeling the sand with their bare feet.

"I'm thankful for it, but I don't like being overprotected," said Ryuichi.

"Why?"

"I know what happens to people who are coddled too much. My brother was one of them. We came from a pretty rich family. He had three private tutors all through school. He made it into Tokyo University but spent all his time betting on horses and dropped out. He ended up blowing the family's wealth. I've seen firsthand how money comes. Also how it goes."

"I'm grateful to your brother then. Thanks to him, you're here with me."

"I think we would've met no matter what path my life took."

"Is it fate then?" she asked.

"No. I would've found you somehow." He held her closer. Reika didn't want to say it, but at last she had to.

"I wish you wouldn't go. When I think of you going into space…I can't bear it."

"I want you to bear it. Whatever it takes." Ryuichi stopped and looked up. Under a winter sky showing a few patches of blue, they could see the cape at Ozaki. "I've got to go. Four years ago it was only a dream. Even a year ago I never thought it would happen. But now—there it is." Ryuichi pointed at the Eve launch vehicle nestled alongside its service tower. Eve's unusual shape—its bulging upper stage atop a flask-shaped aerodynamic body—had earned it the nickname "the Mushroom." Forty-one meters in length and 148 tons fully loaded, it was 80 percent as long as the H-IIA with only half the weight, yet it could send ten tons to the moon, five times more than its predecessor.

The "mushroom cap" contained TGT's *Apple 3* manned space-craft, developed jointly with a consortium of Japanese companies including Mitsubishi Heavy Industries, Kawasaki Heavy Industries, NEC, and JAL. The capsule itself, a first for Japan, weighed two and a half tons fully loaded and could carry a pilot and five passengers into space. Improvements in capsule material and ablation shielding allowed it to carry five passengers, rather than the four originally planned. The trip to the moon would be made with the capsule joined to a two-ton habitat module roughly two and a half meters in diameter, a 5.1-ton landing module, an 8.3-ton return module, and two tons of supplies. The total payload was twenty tons and required two Eve rockets. Smaller than the Adam launch vehicle, Eve had been developed specifically for this purpose. Its smaller payload was offset by the high reliability required to carry humans into space. But reliability was only a matter of degree, as Reika knew well.

"*Apple 1* crashed, you know. The parafoil wouldn't deploy."

"It was a mess. Too bad. We got it into orbit, but the East China Sea was as close as it got on the way back."

"And you'd still go?"

"*Apple 2* made it. Ichiro was fine."

"You are not a macaque!" Reika looked up at him with anger smoldering in her eyes. "If I lose you…If we lose you…"

"The parafoil's been redesigned." Ryuichi held her tight, but his tone was casual. "And Eve's reliability is 98.5 percent. That's 5 percent better than Adam. So we lose two out of a hundred. But the capsule has an advanced escape booster to take it out of harm's way. I'm not going to get killed."

"You can't bet your life on a few numbers!"

"Come on. If I can't prove that the rocket's safe, who's going to do it for me?" Ryuichi's look softened, and he smiled. "Japan has never flown a manned spacecraft. No paying passenger who knows anything about space development would agree to go under the circumstances. It's time for me to step up to the plate and bet everything I have. If I come back alive, we'll hit the jackpot."

"Look at what you're risking."

"Look at the odds. If they weren't in my favor, I wouldn't be doing this. Odds of 98.5 percent isn't even a gamble. It's a sure thing. Stop worrying."

"I'll worry if I want to." Reika buried her face in Ryuichi's broad chest. "I know it's what you love, but I'm so afraid of your recklessness. When you had that fire, I thought my heart was going to stop."

"We've done detailed analyses of all the accidents we've had. That's why I'm confident. I know it's going to be fine."

"Why?" Reika raised her tear-streaked face. "Why do you *personally* have to go up? You don't want to build a base, like Gotoba. You're not tired of Earth like Tae. You have so much left to accomplish here. Why are you so obsessed with going into space?"

"I don't know." Ryuichi relaxed, as if a weight had been taken off his mind. "I just do. I want to face the vacuum of space. The cosmic rays. I want to tumble in zero gravity. I want to go into the cold, cruel black where there isn't even a microbe. That's what makes it worth going. Because it's cold and cruel."

"But that sounds so crazy. You're smarter than that."

"So I'm crazy. No, I guess I'm not. Humans are the only life-form that has gone into deep space. Our intelligence got us there. It's got to be intelligent behavior for a species to enlarge its habitat. I'm a life-form, a human. I'm also a man. I want to extend our habitat—to the moon, to Mars. To the stars if I can."

Reika began to sob. "I just don't understand that, no matter how often I hear you say it." She looked up again and kissed him. He grinned playfully.

"Astronauts have their own wisdom about this kind of disagreement. There's something I'd like you to do for me."

"What is it?"

"'You make the custard, I'll fire the engine.'"

"What?"

"*Apollo 13*. Frank Bormann said that to his wife just before a dangerous retrorocket maneuver on the far side of the moon. At least I think he did. My memory might be a little hazy there."

Ryuichi held her close and whispered, "I'm a man. I don't expect you to understand me completely. It's impossible. But I'm not abandoning you. Wait for me. I'll be back. If you do, I'll have a little bit more to live for."

"A little bit? That's not enough. I want you to think about me every minute."

"I will. From liftoff to touchdown."

They quietly embraced. Reika's wearcom beeped. She stepped away from Ryuichi and answered.

"This is Reika."

"It's Tae. Can I talk to you?"

"I'm outside. I'll go back to the office now."

"No, I'll come to you. I'm close by."

She ended the call. "Let's get our shoes on," said Ryuichi. Reika leaned against him as she dried her legs with his handkerchief.

"She's amazing. Scary, sometimes," said Ryuichi quietly. "She pretends not to know about us, but she obviously does." Reika blushed.

"I remember the look in her eyes when she heard about the rocket." He helped Reika put on her shoes. "It wasn't the look of some teenager discovering the wonders of spaceflight. It wasn't the look someone interested in astronomy or physics would have either. I should know. We get a lot of them at TGT."

"So how did she look?"

"Clear-eyed and looking off into deep space. Not the look of an astronaut—they're always facing toward Earth. This was different, like she wanted to leave the solar system. Frankly, she might be better suited to what I'm trying to do than I am."

"Don't say that. She's a very gentle person."

"I know. But that look seems to come from a place of hopelessness. She's always so distant."

Ryuichi looked up to see a black-coated figure walking grace-fully toward them across the sand, as if floating. He spoke quietly. "Aomine is the ops supervisor. They're close, I hear. I hope he can stand up to her."

"Stand up to her?" said Reika. "It's not as if they're on opposite sides. Sohya has a good heart. He's a little like you."

"Well, it wouldn't do if they got involved. Don't you agree?"

"Who can say?" Tae was getting closer, and Reika stopped talking.

Tae was in her usual monochrome mode: white beret, black coat, white skirt, and black tights. It might have been her prefer-ence in any case, but as her public profile had grown, she was becoming more conscious of style. She was known affectionately in the media as the "Oriental moon princess." Figures resembling her were a hot item in overseas toy stores, especially in the United States and the UK, and Tae had done nothing to stop it.

She walked up to them and said evenly, "Are you finished with your walk?" They nodded. "Then let's head back. You won't be able to go tomorrow if you catch a cold, Ryuichi. And I've got something important to tell you."

Tae and Reika were on Tanegashima to watch the launch. Tomorrow, Eve I would carry *Apple 3* into space, and Ryuichi would be a passenger. This would have been almost unthink-able for previous manned space missions. Astronauts normally had to undergo quarantine and training for several weeks be-fore their flight. But the *Apple* spacecraft was designed to carry untrained passengers. The fact that Ryuichi could take a walk on the beach the day before liftoff was a testament to *Apple*'s tourist-friendly design.

They set off on the walk back to TGT's offices, Tae leading the way. Ryuichi said, "I think I should apologize. Reika and I have been keeping things a secret."

"No need to apologize. What you do is your business." Tae's reply seemed to indicate that she was already aware of the relationship.

"I see," said Ryuichi, intimidated. He hardly felt guilty, but he did feel uncomfortable taking time away from work to be with Reika.

"What was it you wanted to talk to us about, Tae?" asked Reika, looking to change the subject. But Tae was silent for some time before she answered.

"NASA just held a press conference at JPL. They announced that they're going to build a 'moon city' on the lunar surface. It's 9:00 PM in Pasadena. They held the press conference late in the evening to coincide with the landing of their first probe."

"A *city*..." Ryuichi was at a loss. "That's the first I've heard about it. There weren't any rumors."

"I'm sure there weren't," said Tae. "I have a friend at Caltech. He was caught off guard too. They must've been keeping it under wraps till they could maximize the impact on our project."

"But how could they keep something so big a secret? A manned mission like that takes years of preparation," said Ryuichi.

"But they *were* prepared—for Mars."

Ryuichi and Reika were speechless. Tae was icy calm. "And they failed. Martian weather is very unstable. They discovered that a glide landing is much harder to pull off than they thought. Carrying enough fuel to land using retro-rockets would have added a huge amount to their costs. So Mars is beyond their reach, for the moment. But the moon is another story."

"Yes," said Ryuichi. "It would be easy with the kind of launch capacity they assembled for the Mars mission."

"Right. And people pay more attention to a simple, successful mission than a difficult, failed one. NASA has always been driven by politics. This was the president's decision. He doesn't want Asians to overtake the U.S. in space." Tae laughed cynically and said over her shoulder, "America plans to take their whole Mars exploration mission and convert it into a lunar settlement project. They'll have some catching up to do, but Congress will probably approve any needed spending. They'll have to cancel a lot of Mars research plans, but as usual they'll justify it by saying they're putting the will of the American people first. America still likes to dream of itself as number one."

"I hope you won't let this discourage you," said Reika, running up beside her. "A research base—whether they call it a city or not—is one thing, a wedding palace is quite another. This shouldn't have any effect on Sixth Continent." She put a hand on Tae's shoulder. Tae stopped to look at her.

"NASA's probe landed in Eden Crater."

Reika froze, thunderstruck. Ryuichi felt dazed. This was a declaration of war, pure and simple. Then Reika realized Tae was trembling with laughter.

"This is beautiful. They proved us right." Her large eyes narrowed with glee. She was laughing from deep inside, without a trace of irony, truly happy. She threw her arms wide, as if about to take flight.

"We'll give them a special welcome. Assemble the multidozers! Hang *Apple* flags from the power cables! Have the bulk shooter throw up an arch of regolith. Give them a proper reception. But," she said with a wink, "don't let them beat us."

CHAPTER 5
CONSTRUCTION AND EXPLOITATION RIGHTS TO THE LUNAR SURFACE

[1]

AFTER MORE THAN an hour wrestling with the control stick, *Apple*'s pilot released it and slumped, exhausted, onto his flight couch. He mopped the sweat from his face. Droplets of perspiration floated lazily across the capsule's two-and-a-half-meter width.

"It's no use. She won't budge."

"Hmm." Ryuichi closed the flight checklist binder and glanced up at the external display. He should have been seeing a vast stretch of blue ocean and white clouds. Instead the view was blocked by a silver-blue panel. Nothing was visible.

The spacecraft carrying Ryuichi and his pilot had been orbiting Earth for the past hour at an altitude of three hundred kilometers. The conical core capsule had life support for twenty-four hours in orbit, but since Eve was capable of carrying a larger payload, the cylindrical habitat module and the propulsion module with its fuel tank and solar array had been launched along with the capsule. The propulsion module—a stripped-down test version of the return module that would bring passengers back from the moon—had encountered a problem. One of its solar arrays had failed to deploy.

The problem was neither malfunction nor human error. Just after reaching orbit, *Apple* had experienced a small shock, and the panel had refused to unfold. The external cameras and sensing systems indicated that something—probably a tiny fragment of space debris—had punched a five-millimeter hole into the end of the oblong solar array. The impact had evidently torqued the gimbal at the base of the array. Now it wouldn't move, even after the pilot released the retaining pin. It was an unavoidable accident, not a design flaw. They were lucky the debris had missed the core module. Still, the collision had major consequences.

Ryuichi looked over at the pilot and said calmly, "Life-support systems?"

"Nominal."

"Communications?"

"Fully functional."

"Can we make it back?"

"No problem. Other than the array, all systems are go."

"What about the propulsion module test?"

"I'm afraid that's out of the question now," said the pilot.

"Then we're screwed," Ryuichi said with a sigh. "The media is going to be all over us. 'Sixth Continent spacecraft encounters problems on maiden flight. Crew unable to cope.'"

The pilot sighed and wearily rubbed his face. Ryuichi looked through the observation port above his head. *Apple*'s revolution had brought the shining blue planet into view. Earth slid past, replaced by the dark of space. At first there were only stars in sight, but then a white, delta-shaped spacecraft loomed starkly against the blackness.

It was space shuttle *Frontier*. NASA had been operating this new generation of shuttles since 2018. The "supershuttle" had a smaller payload than its predecessors—ten tons—because the design had been optimized for manned flight. *Frontier* could carry a crew of nine, two more than the original shuttles.

TGT had no experience with manned flight, and *Apple 3*'s launch timing and orbital path were calculated to bring it close to *Frontier*. In the event of a problem, *Apple* could request assistance. NASA had agreed but had an ulterior motive. The mission would give the Americans their first close look at this unknown spacecraft. Now *Frontier* hung suspended, a thousand meters ahead of them, observing.

"We kill ourselves getting this far," muttered Ryuichi, "and end up having to ask for help..." Scenes of the effort that had gotten them to this point flashed through his mind.

To say TGT's team had strained themselves over the past few months would have been putting it mildly. On top of his demanding responsibilities managing the company, Ryuichi had spent the last three months supervising the first launch crew's training. During this interval his sleep time was cut in half. And in the hours before launch, he had experienced the greatest tension and fear he had ever known. He knew better than anyone that the risk of a catastrophic failure was not zero.

Nonetheless, his efforts paled next to those of his staff. Failure was not an option for Eve's debut. Two thousand specialists from TGT and its subcontractors—triple the number usually assigned to a launch—had assembled a month beforehand to carry out round-the-clock maintenance and system verification checks. Though TGT had of course not made it public, more than a hundred personnel had collapsed from mental and physical stress, a third of them in the forty-eight hours prior to launch. The atmosphere at the space center the night before the launch was as tense as a military camp on the eve of battle.

Eventually operations would become routine. But for this launch, everyone and everything went right to the wall. Sending humans into space and bringing them home safely demanded untold amounts of effort. The blood, sweat, and tears expended by his team allowed Ryuichi to face the prelaunch photo session with a smile. Despite his instinctive fears, he was convinced the mission would be a success. Now this…

"We don't have a choice then. Better radio those guys for help." Ryuichi sounded despondent. "Call *Frontier*, ask them to approach and do a visual inspection of the array. We couldn't shake or twist it loose, but maybe they can come up with something."

The pilot opened a channel to *Frontier* and outlined the situation. Ryuichi was close to giving up. *Frontier* was not going to help them with its payload bay robot arm or with anything else for that matter. NASA had already stated that it would maintain a minimum distance of five hundred meters from *Apple*. A collision could cause explosive decompression. Just managing a close approach would cut into *Frontier*'s precious time in orbit. NASA had agreed to help only as long as its own mission would face no additional risks. Consequently, *Frontier*'s response was completely unexpected.

"Mr. Yaenami, they say they're going to provide assistance," said the pilot.

"You're kidding," said Ryuichi. "What else can we do?"

"Nothing. They're going to EVA over to us."

"I don't believe it." Ryuichi was stunned. TGT was still working on space suit development. They were in no position to conduct extravehicular activity even if they had wanted to. He signaled the pilot for silence. "*Frontier*, this is Ryuichi Yaenami. Did Johnson Space Center approve your EVA?"

"*Apple 3*, *Frontier* Commander Henderson. We're proceeding with a scheduled AMPU operational test."

"*Frontier*, what is AMPU?" asked Ryuichi.

"Advanced Manned Propulsion Unit. Tetherless EVA."

"So you have approval to approach?"

"No approval required, *Apple 3*. The test protocol allows us to take AMPU out to five thousand meters. Sit tight, we'll be with you shortly." *Frontier*'s commander sounded like he was planning a walk in the park. Ryuichi stared out the observation port in a daze.

In less than half an hour the shuttle loomed outside, nearly blocking the view of space. *Frontier* was now revolving in synchrony with *Apple 3*. A small oblong object separated from the shuttle. In what seemed a few seconds, it grew larger and resolved itself into an astronaut astride a slender tube, almost like a witch riding a broom. At the forward end of the tube were five gimbaled thrusters. The main motor and fuel tank were at the tube's other end.

The astronaut glided to within ten meters and gave his handlebar a slight twist. The vehicle's front and rear thrusters pulsed propellant in several directions at once. It turned side-on, like a motorcycle skidding to a stop, yet maintained its rotation relative to *Apple 3*. The simple, intuitive way the astronaut controlled his vehicle belied the complexity of the maneuver. Any movement during orbit would change the orbit itself. NASA's space scooter clearly had a sophisticated attitude control system.

The astronaut's EVA suit was also cutting-edge, a total departure from the bulky suits of the past. It had a sleek, streamlined look, accentuating the length of the astronaut's arms and legs. The pride of NASA, this hard suit required no user predecompression.

The astronaut was just outside *Apple 3*. He waved. "Sorry to keep you waiting. Flight Engineer Hardin, at your service. How about them apples?"

"That was a very impressive approach. Give us a minute and we'll roll over and show you the damage," said Ryuichi.

"Not necessary, *Apple 3*. I'd prefer to keep clear of your thrusters. Please maintain your current attitude. I'll just do a walk around." With that, Hardin nimbly flipped upside down and disappeared from view. The pilot put the external camera feed on the monitor.

The American darted around the capsule like a hummingbird, then dove beneath the habitat module, which was connected by a narrow waist to the propulsion unit. He whistled.

"Hello…looks like your problem is at the base of the array. The hinge is rotated and snagged. Engineers work hard to make these things snag-proof. This looks like something outside the design envelope."

"Can you do anything?" asked Ryuichi.

"You're not bringing this back with you, right? You just need power for orbit. Okay, let's see if we can free this. One, two…three!"

Ryuichi heard a thump from beneath his feet. At the same time, the panel blocking the external camera slid smoothly out of view.

The pilot shook his head. "That was quick."

Hardin chuckled. "Force-feedback thruster control. AMPU is rock steady. That's why *Apple* didn't kick me back."

The American reappeared outside the observation port and nonchalantly radioed the shuttle. "*Frontier*, Hardin. Picking went smoothly. The *Apple* looks delicious."

"Thank you, Captain," said Henderson. "You're thirty-two seconds ahead of schedule. Synchronize and proceed to next position."

"Roger, *Frontier*." Hardin waved.

Suddenly the significance of this exchange hit Ryuichi. "So you guys didn't report this to Johnson?"

"EVAs are part of normal operation," replied Henderson. "When we conduct them is up to me. Captain Hardin was, ah, previously scheduled to spend two minutes in your vicinity. And that's all he did, Mr. Yaenami."

"You mean this was an unofficial rescue operation?"

"We use that term when crew safety is at stake. Then everyone on the ground and in orbit works as a team to solve the problem. Shall I advise Johnson that we have an emergency?"

"Of course not," said Ryuichi with a reflexive shake of his head, though there was no video link. "We're grateful for your help."

"No problem at all, *Apple 3*. You're welcome to forget all about it," Henderson said casually and signed off. Hardin waved one last time and moved away.

Ryuichi and the pilot were drained. They floated about the capsule. "They completely had us. I didn't know what to say," said the pilot.

"They knew what they were doing. This is child's play for those people. We work like our lives depend on it just to get into space. We get up here and there they are, strolling around. Whistling." Ryuichi watched Hardin's receding form, eyes narrowed. "Those guys are the real deal."

———— ◆·•··• ————

THE 150-INCH MONITOR *is flat white, without detail. Gradually the brightness falls to reveal a rocket lifting off amid towering plumes of white exhaust. A caption at the bottom reads:* EVE I LEO MISSION LIFTOFF.

Cut to the interior of Apple 3. *A lion-haired figure in a flight couch, casually dressed in sweatshirt and jeans. Four other flight couches are occupied by test dummies: women and children. The man smiles and flashes the victory sign. The camera jiggles.*

Footage from a chase plane. Eve gains altitude at a shallow angle, like an aircraft, and disappears into the distance. An insert shows a CG image of "the Mushroom" leaving the atmosphere. When Eve reaches Mach 1, the solid boosters jettison, and TROPHY kicks in for the long, smooth, air-breathing leg of the flight, taking Eve to an altitude of sixty kilometers. As the rocket climbs along the curvature of the earth, it leaves the blue of the atmosphere and enters the black of space. The first stage falls away. The second stage accelerates Apple *into orbit.*

Capsule interior. At a signal from the pilot, the passenger releases his restraint harness and floats upward. He seems startled, then breaks into a broad smile. He pantomimes a cheek-to-cheek dance with an invisible partner. The reaction seems a bit over the top.

A different interior, spacious and cylindrical and twice as wide as the passenger's outstretched arms. The caption reads HABITAT MODULE. *The man takes a foil food packet from a drawer and punctures it with a straw. He "accidentally" lets some soup spill. The droplets float, suspended. He inserts his straw into one blob of soup after another and sucks them down.*

The toilet, at the far end of the compartment. The seat is formfitted for a complete seal. The man solemnly points to the two intakes—one small, one large—then to the antiseptic tissues for sterilizing the seat.

Undressing. The man changes into pajamas. He looks relaxed, as if he were back home at the end of a long day.

Sleeping accommodations. The man lowers a panel built into the wall of the compartment. A large, cloth-covered truss-frame structure unfolds like an accordion and extends to the other side of the compartment. The man walks to one end of the structure; from end-on, five hexagonal capsules containing beds are visible. The cross section looks like a honeycomb. Since everyone will sleep at the same time, the structure occupies most of the habitat module. The man floats into one of the compartments feetfirst, waves, and closes the opening with a curtain. The pilot, holding the camera, attaches an air line to each compartment. A subtitle explains that the lack of onboard convection requires the use of forced air.

After a moment the man emerges from his sleeping compartment. He stretches comically as if he's just had a good night's rest. Naturally this is not possible. The flight is only three hours.

After brushing his teeth, shaving, and tending to his mane of hair, the man changes back into sweatshirt and jeans. The compartment has two round observation ports. The man goes to each port and looks out, quietly absorbed in the view.

Cut to external camera view. A whirlpool of white clouds—a large low-pressure cell—sprawls across a dark blue ocean. The clouds hug the edge of the pressure cell like a floating Great Wall of China. The camera pans slowly toward the arc of the solar terminator. Suddenly the view is tinted purple, a gentle neon glow. The subtitle reads NOCTILUMI-NESCENT CLOUDS. *The spacecraft is moving through glowing clouds of ice crystals high above the earth's surface. The camera lingers for a long moment on the clouds and dissolves into a superimposed shot of the man's profile. His cheeks are wet with tears.*

A computer graphic representation of the reentry process. The space-craft's path is a sine wave over a Mercator projection of the earth. After a descent burn over southern China, and after jettisoning the habitat modules, the capsule descends on a northeast trajectory toward Japan.

Capsule interior. Lots of camera shake from the shock of reentry. The passenger grits his teeth but still manages a wave for the camera.

The view from a ground-based camera. A speck against the twilight sky grows larger: a red and white trapezoid with a capsule slung beneath. The pilot skillfully trims the parafoil slider, banks gracefully, and softly touches down on the landing cushion laid along three hundred meters of runway. The underside of the capsule is charred black. The landing crew rushes up and hoses it down. They open the hatch.

After a tense pause, the man's head appears. He climbs unassisted down onto the runway, pumps his fists in the air, lit by a storm of camera flashes, and roars in triumph. Reporters with microphones rush toward him. Face still flush with excitement, he gleefully answers their questions. The camera pans upward. A full moon is rising into the glow of twilight.

The video ends.

"That was the five-minute version of the promotion video," said Reika, standing next to the monitor. "We have a thirty-second version for prime time that went to terrestrial broadcasters worldwide. We're streaming this digest and an uncut three-hour version on the net—unedited, except for the assistance from NASA."

"The Americans haven't said anything about that, fortunately," said Takumichi Gotoba. "They're probably confident they're ahead of us. Still, we're not obliged to mention it. I don't see a problem leaving it out."

The rest of the people in the conference room at Gotoba Engineering's Tokyo headquarters nodded. The party to celebrate Ryuichi's safe return had taken place two weeks ago. Today's meeting had been called to discuss next steps. Gotoba's brain trust was assembled in the same conference room where the project first saw the light of day.

"After the prime-time spot aired, we received more than thirty-five hundred applications from individuals wanting to go into space. There were over fifteen hundred inquiries from national and local governments, universities, research institutions, travel agencies, broadcasters, web dailies, and news agencies. Everyone knows the fare per person is two hundred million yen."

Gotoba nodded with satisfaction. "It must be frustrating that you can't service all that demand. You'd be halfway to covering your costs already."

"Yes," said Reika. "But we're in no position to take applications yet."

"That's true. Gotoba Engineering staff will be the only passengers for a few years. But I have to say, Yaenami has guts. I could never have done that." Gotoba shrugged. This was the difference between him and Ryuichi; otherwise they seemed to resemble each other. Besides the fact that Gotoba was sixty-one and Ryuichi forty-one, the older man could leave the work to his people and derive satisfaction from their success.

"NASA hasn't come out with a plan for space tourism yet. We're still ahead, and the ball's in our court." He looked around the table. "Can we push harder? Move the timeline up?"

Takasumi Iwaki, head of Gotoba's Mobile Engineering Division, spoke. "This is not the time to panic. The project's on track, but we still face a huge number of challenges. Without people on the surface, we can't put the solar furnace into service and start producing cement. And we can't put people on the surface till TGT successfully sends *Apple* to the moon and back."

"Hmm." Gotoba looked at Tetsuo Sando. "What do you think NASA's planning?"

"They haven't released much in the way of specifics. Lunar Generator 1 is near Eden Crater. That will give them electric power, but all they did was attach a landing module to a unit developed for the Mars program. We have next to no information about other engineering equipment they might be developing. But we do know that six years from now—which parallels our timeline—they plan to have a lunar base with a hundred people. They're probably working round the clock on development."

"If they're cobbling something together, they won't be much of a threat." Gotoba chuckled, but Sando just gazed back at him like an aging philosopher with an ominous presentiment. He shook his head. "The Americans thought through every element of Sixth Continent more than thirty years ago."

The room buzzed with exclamations of disbelief. Sando continued drily, "Since we began this project, I've been reviewing the history of space exploration. Take lunar concrete. The Universities of Arizona and Illinois were working on this problem in the eighties. In 1988, the American Society of Civil Engineers held a major conference on construction in space. NASA has support from hundreds of external organizations in the U.S. They've been in existence since 1958, and their base of technology and experience is very, very broad. If necessary, they can use their accumulated expertise and call on many outside organizations to create heavy machinery and production facilities in a very short period of time." Sando paused, then said, "To be frank, I would not want to make an enemy of NASA."

"You're too pessimistic, Sando." Gotoba grinned. "We have a trump card: TROPHY."

"A trump card? No." Sando shook his head. "NASA has thirty Titan X heavy launch vehicles on order from Lockheed Martin for the Mars missions. With that capacity alone they could put 250 tons of payload into lunar orbit."

"Interesting," said Gotoba. "But we have *Apple*, which is better than anything NASA can offer. Their shuttle has a history of failure. They've lost three of them."

"Yes, three of the original shuttles. The supershuttle has a spotless record, and NASA has eight of them. If they wanted to, they could use that space fleet to put seventy people in low earth orbit in little more than two weeks. And their experience with the Apollo program means that putting people into lunar orbit would pose no challenge. Establishing a temporary presence on the surface would also be easy. Mars Ambassador 1 is on its way back to Earth as we speak. It could just as well be rerouted to the moon."

Sando removed his glasses and began polishing them. "This reminds me of my grandfather's stories of the Great Pacific War."

"You mean it gets worse?" growled Iwaki.

"NASA has a sponsor with unlimited financial resources: the U.S. government."

"Enough of this pessimism!" Gotoba pounded the table. He looked at Reika. "We have a powerful sponsor of our own. Right?"

"Yes," answered Reika. "We are prepared to fully fund the project." Reika began tapping out figures on her wearcom. "So far, investment includes three billion yen for the evaluation of Kunlun Base. Forty-three billion yen for fifty-two Eve launch vehicles. Thirty-three billion for twenty Adam launch vehicles. Eighteen billion in development costs for both vehicles. Fifteen billion to develop *Apple*. Roughly twenty billion for the engineering equipment and other project elements. Adding promotion and personnel expenses, the total comes to 130 billion."

"And the budget is 150," said Gotoba.

"Correct. So far we've recouped around three billion from broadcasting and publishing rights and reservation deposits. But this figure will grow substantially. And we are negotiating for additional bank financing."

"You see?" Gotoba turned to the room. "We're going to be fine. From here on out we'll be in our element. The Americans may be multiarmed and hydra-headed, but they've never built a base in the Himalayas or at the bottom of the ocean. Let's give them a run for their money!"

Iwaki and Sando nodded. Gotoba didn't need to prove anything by going into space. He could lead by force of personality alone.

———◆◆◆◆———

OVER THE NEXT six months, while the construction of Sixth Continent continued on schedule, NASA showed the world what it could do. The Americans launched fifteen heavy-lift rockets in rapid succession, inserting large payloads into lunar orbit. They established a power-generation capability and landed twenty-five rovers and five scrapers on the surface. The rovers acted purely as transport vehicles, and the scrapers simply removed regolith and permafrost from the surface. NASA's engineering equipment lacked the sophisticated capabilities of Gotoba's multidozers. But their conservative design was robust. Lack of time to develop anything better was doubtless a factor, but NASA had apparently decided that for construction on the scale they were planning, using many machines with basic functionality was the optimum approach. America's boundless industrial strength had enabled it to surpass Japan and Korea, Germany and France, its mother country England, and the mighty Soviet Union. At this rate, it seemed NASA would quickly catch up to and surpass the progress on Sixth Continent.

Eden Entertainment's response to these developments was muted, especially compared to their earlier splashy promotion campaign. They did not issue any particular comment. The media looked to Tae Toenji, whose guiding role in the project had been an open secret for some time, but she had withdrawn to her home in Nagoya and not been seen since. Some of the tabloids speculated that, having overreached herself, this mere teenager had taken flight at the decision by NASA, the world's preeminent space agency, to compete with ELE. But there was another and just as widely held opinion: Tae had another trump card up her sleeve and was waiting for the right time to reveal it.

In point of fact, there was some truth to this speculation—but only some. In the summer of 2030, more of that truth would come to light.

THE NEWLY RISEN full moon cast a yellowish glow over the dark bulk of the Makino-ga-ike Forest. The Toenji mansion was surrounded by trees that reduced the noise of traffic from the nearby highway to a distant murmur. On the south-facing third-floor terrace, a figure in robe and slippers was hunched over a tube of about equal height, watching the night sky.

"Grandfather?"

Sennosuke Toenji turned to see his granddaughter open the sliding glass door and step out onto the terrace, clad in pajamas.

"Did you finish your phone call?" he asked.

"I wanted to talk a little longer, but I didn't want to take too much of Josh's time. He told me to go to bed."

"He sounds like a considerate friend."

"He's probably just worried the phone is tapped. If the media finds out he's my friend, they'll be pounding on his door."

Sennosuke said nothing for a moment. "Come take a look."

"Yes, Grandfather."

Sennosuke stepped away from the telescope. Tae sat down next to it. It was a Newtonian reflector. Its tube, twelve centimeters in diameter, topped an equatorial mount on a wooden tripod. The telescope was rustic in design and manufacture, without a tracking drive, cold CCDs, or other electronic devices. Other than the tube and tripod legs, all the fittings were bronze. It had the appearance of a well-loved object.

Tae looked into the eyepiece. A circle of silvery white light struck her retina. Once she had blinked and allowed her eyes to adjust, the bright semicircular moon came into view. The telescope's secondary mirror cast a faint shadow over the center of the image, but the lunar surface was in sharp focus—an intricate mixture of faintly yellow-tinged mountains and dark basins. Tycho's white rays spread starlike from the crater. The surface was a profusion of overlapping craters of all sizes. It was the lunar southern hemisphere.

"I wonder if we can see the multidozers," said Tae.

"I doubt that."

"Maybe we should put beacons on them?"

"I doubt you could see them even then. They'd be lost in the light reflected from the surface. If they had lasers, you might be able to see them."

"Then let's be sure to fit them with lasers."

"Can you make out the crater?" asked Sennosuke.

The moon glided out of her field of view, then immediately returned. Tae looked up and saw Sennosuke making tiny adjustments to the telescope. He did not need to look through the scope to correct its orientation.

"I couldn't use this without your help," said Tae.

Sennosuke placed his hand on the tube with a nostalgic look. "I've been doing this for sixty years, you know. This used to be my only pleasure. I saw Sputnik and Halley's Comet with this. I wanted to see the plume from the crash of Lunar Prospector, but now I know why I couldn't."

"Why not?"

"You know—those threads. I hear they may have cushioned the force of impact and made the plume smaller. Once there's a way to get to Eden Crater, I'd like to go see for myself."

"I wonder if you'll live that long, Grandfather."

Sennosuke smiled warmly and patted the girl's head. "I'm glad I decided to make your dream come true. Now that we've come this far, it really looks like I might be able to go."

"Then I'll welcome you to my Eden."

"What about Kiichiro?"

Tae looked away, sullen. "He wouldn't come even if I asked."

"Not even via engraved invitation? You never know. Your father might actually be interested."

"No way. I'll never let him set foot in *Apple*." She obstinately shook her head. "He's the one I'm trying to get away from."

"That's too bad." Sennosuke fell silent. He was the only one who knew the truth—that Tae's father was the reason she had left Japan at an early age. He had showered money and education on her, but not the one thing she wanted most in the world. Nor was she able to hide her genius and wealth from the acquaintances she made in her travels: they ended up either flattering or avoiding her. She had no true intimates. Sennosuke was far too old to be a friend to Tae. All he could do was keep a careful watch over her from a distance.

Tae's baffling tendency to advance various outlandish proposals seemed to be her way of compensating for a lack of emotional sustenance. When she'd first said she wanted to go to the moon, that she wanted to build a wedding palace, Sennosuke had not known quite what to make of it. Even though Sixth Continent was just a means of luring people to the moon, he'd still doubted the wisdom of trying to do so in the first place.

But when he considered his granddaughter's upbringing, he felt he somehow understood. If she took charge of such a large project, the project itself would become the center of attention, and her immense wealth would fade into the background. Watching couples being joined at her wedding palace would help compensate for her loneliness. And if she succeeded, she'd be able to get back at her father.

Yet it was all so heartbreaking—to pursue such a wonderful, imaginative goal all out of loneliness. Tae had participated at least a little in his stargazing hobby, and he was happy she was able to share in the simple delight of looking at stars in the night sky just as any other teenager might.

"Tae, there's something I'd like you to do for me." Sennosuke had decided that what he was about to say was best for his granddaughter. "If you're willing to make room for me on *Apple*, then I'd like to yield my place to your father. I'm probably too old to go anyway. Let's invite him together, you and me."

She paused before answering. "I don't want to. If you can't go, I'll use it for something else."

"Something else?"

"A workstation with a cryptanalysis program, and a parabolic antenna."

"What would you do with that?"

"Search for messages from extraterrestrial life-forms."

Sennosuke was mystified. "You don't have to go all the way to the moon to do that. What's this all about?"

Tae's explanation tumbled out in a rush. "The frequencies you can detect from Earth are limited—the ionosphere and the atmosphere get in the way. No one has launched a satellite to search for extraterrestrial life. But there are several proposals for detecting signals from unknown life-forms. If you have the right hardware, you can run the software. If the life-forms are reasonably close to our solar system, they'll probably be sending signals toward planets that look suitable for life. But we may not be able to catch those signals from Earth. From the moon, we can monitor all frequencies without interference. I know this is kind of sudden—" She looked up at Sennosuke. "But it was always my intention, from the beginning."

"You could have at least told me."

"I didn't want you to worry…you know, about my not having a friend in the world."

Sennosuke thought for a moment. "So, 'from the beginning' means not just the search for extraterrestrials, but…this whole project…"

"Yes. I want to make friends. Sixth Continent, the wedding palace—everything is part of that plan."

Sennosuke was speechless. He thought he'd understood what his granddaughter wanted. And that was that; he'd merely imagined that he understood. Her goal hadn't been to make people happy. It was all nothing more than a search for friendship, and to go to such unheard-of lengths to do so meant that, in a sense, she had given up hope of ever actually succeeding.

Sennosuke knew there was no point in raising doubts now that things had proceeded this far, but he could not restrain himself.

"Do you really think there are extraterrestrials out there?"

"There are. There are no grounds for thinking there aren't. The theory of extrasolar planetary formation was revised twenty-five years ago. In the Milky Way alone there could be more than a hundred million Earth-like planets. With that many planets, it's unthinkable that there wouldn't be any close to our solar system."

"I see. But why not search with a satellite?"

"Would you greet them with a satellite? I mean, if they actually came? If you were back in the Edo period, Grandfather—in Nagasaki—and the first Dutch ship sailed into the harbor, would you go out to greet them in a splendid ship or in a rowboat? Which boat would get you recognized as a representative of the shogun?"

"And a satellite is the rowboat."

"It is compared to the International Space Station. I want to build something even better. A magnificent Dejima Island. A place any visitor will immediately recognize as an international port."

"But why do you have to go so far to search for friendship? Why, young Aomine, for example—he's important to you, isn't he?" This was Sennosuke's ace in the hole, but Tae's expression didn't change. She simply shook her head.

"This is no reflection on Sohya. He doesn't treat me as anyone special. I don't know why. If he knew my goal was to search for friends, I think he'd help me. We'd look for them together."

"And have you ever felt an emotion called jealousy?"

"Until I could scream. Those around me have so much that I don't. But I think Sohya will put up with me."

"Tae…" Sennosuke sighed. "I didn't realize you were so intent on this. I think we need to sit down and rethink things calmly. You needn't go to such lengths to find friends. I know it sounds extreme, but you could cancel this whole project, cut your ties to ELE, and live as a normal young woman…"

"Yes, that does sound extreme." Tae wrapped her arms around the telescope. She picked it up, walked to the edge of the terrace, and held it out over the railing. "Grandfather? Could you bear to part with this?"

"I don't know what you're getting at."

"You saw this in a shop in Hong Kong. You fell in love with it. It cost you three months' wages. You've replaced the mirror coating every year for sixty years. Am I right?"

"I'd hate to part with it. But I could if I had to."

"I could if I had to, too. But I'd really hate it." With a troubled smile, Tae put the telescope back on the terrace. "I don't want to lose the life I'm living. I think I'd have a hard time without money. I couldn't read books, or buy clothes, or fly all over the world."

"Too used to all that to give it up now, are you?"

"Yes. To be honest, it feels good having lots of people working on something at just a word from me."

She's a Toenji, thought Sennosuke, though he didn't want to say it. The same drive had enabled him to build Eden Entertainment. His son Kiichiro, ELE's president, had the same temperament.

"All right. Do what you want to do. You don't have to see your father if you don't want to. The two of you would probably just fight anyway."

"Thank you, Grandfather." Tae walked up to Sennosuke and hugged him. He put his arm around her shoulders and squeezed her tight. "I'm so glad we had this talk. Things are going to get a little bumpy soon, and I needed some encouragement."

"What's going to happen?"

"Maybe something like a battle."

"Well, that won't do. Shall I lend a hand?"

"Not yet. I have a strategy. But I'll probably need your help."

"You can count on me." He stroked her hair.

Tae's wearcom chimed softly. She looked at the display.

"Another phone call?" asked Sennosuke.

"It's my personal news feed. Whenever something about Sixth Continent pops up, I get an alert." She read the text streaming across the display, then happily said, "Aha! Just what I was waiting for."

"Your battle?"

"No, this is good news. It sounds like NASA is running into problems with that 'Liberty Island' of theirs. Their rovers are down."

"It's not right to celebrate the misfortunes of others, you know."

Tae selected a video from the wearcom's menu and hit play. "But, Grandfather, if the Americans don't slow down a bit, it'll be hard for us to win. Look at them. They're so confident." The tiny screen showed a press conference in the United States. A distinguished-looking American was delivering an impassioned statement.

❖

"WE HAVEN'T ABANDONED Mars."

Von Kármán Auditorium, Jet Propulsion Laboratory: the scene of hundreds of press conferences announcing dazzling achievements in space exploration. NASA Administrator Richard Ringstone was speaking forcefully.

"We simply redirected Mars Ambassador to swing by Venus. We used the same roundabout route on the outbound leg."

Several reporters stood with raised hands. Ringstone pointed to one of them.

"Mally, from AOL. I understand that a lot of the equipment designed for use on Mars is not usable on the lunar surface. Doesn't that represent a significant waste of NASA resources?"

"Not at all. The equipment will be preserved for future Mars missions. Even with the delays this revised strategy will entail, establishing a foothold on the moon offers long-term advantages. We're fortunate that Japanese private enterprise has been so aggressive. They've demonstrated that water exists on the surface in an easily recoverable form. Factoring that water into our Mars exploration plans should make it easier to achieve them in the long run."

Ringstone pointed to a full-scale mock-up of Viking 1, America's first Mars orbiter, standing in a corner of the auditorium.

"That's not all. Our lunar base will serve as a refueling point for missions to other planets. It could be used to build spacecraft themselves—even manned spacecraft. It can be a refueling depot, a production facility, and a home port for space missions."

"Zhang, from Xinhua News Agency. NASA's Lunar Generator 1 landed next to the crater where Japan's Sixth Continent consortium is constructing a base of its own. Is it NASA's intention to piggyback on the success of Japanese industry?" The question was provocative, but Ringstone was unruffled.

"That's a groundless assumption. The moon does not belong to Japan. It belongs to all of humanity, and its resources cannot be monopolized by any one nation. We have an inalienable right to be there." Ringstone looked stern but then broke into a smile. "Of course, we're thankful for what they've done. If they find themselves in some kind of trouble, NASA will be happy to lend them a hand. If they lose their way, we'll politely give them directions." Ringstone's self-assurance was magisterial. And why not?

As the NASA administrator's bald head reflected the lights from dozens of flashing cameras, he gave an elegant bow.

"NASA's moon base will be named Liberty Island. Hitch your wagons, everyone. The next continent is a big one."

———

SIX MONTHS HAD passed since NASA had broadcast its declaration of war to the world. From time to time, Tae replayed Ringstone's press conference to strengthen her resolve.

"Overconfidence is the enemy. NASA is the best of the best." She looked up at her Eden, floating in the night sky, and whispered to herself, "Americans are so talented at making friends... far more than I am."

[2]

THE GASOLINE-POWERED Chevrolet sped through the early-summer sunlight of Pasadena and through the gate of NASA's Jet Propulsion Laboratory at the foot of the San Gabriel Mountains.

The driver, a blond woman in a fiery scarlet suit, jumped out and strode quickly into the Space Flight Operations Facility. As she hurried toward a room next to mission control, she was inputting data into the wearcom embedded in her sunglasses with her left hand.

In her mid-thirties, Caroline Cadbury was operations administrator for NASA's Liberty Island Unmanned Engineering Phase. She yanked open the door of the Unmanned Operations Support Room and bellowed, "What's going on? *All* the boys are down?"

Her team sat at their bank of consoles. They swiveled to look at her. One stood up: a tall, beefy man who looked more like a truck driver than a NASA controller. He was pale.

"That's right, Carol. All twenty-five rovers and five scrapers."

"What the hell happened? Did you have them playing football?"

"No. There were no collisions. We were operating by the book." Joseph Lambach waved his hands apologetically. He was the "driver" for the engineering equipment, though with the two-way communications delay he could not control their speed and direction in real time. The rovers' AI programming let them move independently. Lambach's job was to assign objectives—ordering the vehicles to move a certain boulder, grade a site to a certain shape and dimensions, and so on.

"If there wasn't a collision, what happened?" Caroline was boiling with frustration. With her good looks, men tended to underestimate her, but this morning her fury was not showing her off to best effect.

Lambach winced. "We have a power supply problem. The charging stations are down. The rovers can't recharge their fuel cells. They've all gone into sleep mode."

"Show me the telemetry and any suspicious-looking video. Craig! Conference me with the rover tech supervisor at LPL!"

Craig initiated a call to the University of Arizona's Lunar and Planetary Laboratory. Caroline threw herself into a chair and started reviewing the telemetry data on her wearcom.

"I don't understand. All the chargers are off-line. But we have five stations and five solar arrays. Everything's networked. The only way this could happen would be if all five bridges were cut or all the arrays destroyed. Even a meteor strike should've left two or three stations online. Do we have video?"

Her display switched to video. She used the wearcom's controller, hanging like a pendant from the frame of her glasses, to page through the images. "I don't see any evidence of damage," she muttered.

"It's a long shot, but the circuits may have been damaged. The rovers' motherboards were designed for Mars. It has an atmosphere. It's farther from the sun. The circuits weren't shielded for the intensity of the solar wind on the moon. But everything went fine during the simulations."

"Even so," said Caroline, "the vehicles have redundant control. Self-diagnostic telemetry doesn't indicate any problems. Wait a minute—what's this?"

Caroline marked the image on her display. One of the solar arrays, a long panel on an aluminum frame extending horizontally over the surface. The panel was nearly vertical. NASA had not had time to experiment with Sixth Continent's spring-loaded deployment techniques. Instead, they used conventional rigid panels, tugged open in sections by a small rover, like an accordion. The panels had been proven on the ISS, and the rover had been developed for the Mars missions.

The image Caroline had selected showed dark mottling over the silver surface of the panel, as if it had been blackened with candle soot. "This looks like dust contamination. How did it happen?"

"Carol, I have Arizona," said Craig.

"Plug me in." The face of an LPL research scientist came up. Caroline didn't waste time with greetings. "We think the solar array may have been contaminated with regolith. Did you run simulations on anything like that in your moon garden?"

"Panel contamination? I'll check right away."

LPL's "moon garden" was a large-scale mock-up of the Liberty Island site, identical in every respect to the actual terrain, using lunar regolith stimulant. The use of simulated environments for each of their space missions with identical hardware and terrain was a time-honored NASA practice. When a problem developed far off in space, NASA used these environments to grasp the details of the problem and develop responses. By using a twin of the *Apollo* spacecraft, they had been able to mount a successful rescue effort when *Apollo 13* was stricken on its way to the moon. For the Mars Pathfinder rover tests, NASA had built a "Mars garden" based on data collected twenty-one years earlier by the Viking orbiter.

LPL's moon garden was populated with rovers and recharging stations. Progress on the lunar surface was being faithfully replicated. Five minutes later, the scientist was back.

"All vehicles are keeping well clear of the arrays. The landers touched down a safe distance from the panels, so we wouldn't expect to see contamination from that source."

"Then what did that? There's no wind on the moon. Show me the map." A view of the garden appeared on Caroline's lenses, with current rover locations and past routes superimposed. The rovers were indeed keeping well clear of the solar power arrays. Lambach had just finished running a calculation of trajectories the regolith might have taken after being kicked up by movement across the surface, but his analysis also indicated that this was not the source of the contamination.

"I don't understand. Did someone…?" Caroline pressed a finger to her chin, lost in thought, then suddenly looked up. "Joe! Get me a smaller-scale map."

"A standard surface map?"

"No, something that includes the Japanese base. There's one on their website. I want to see the two maps superimposed."

Lambach downloaded Sixth Continent's map and resized it to mate with the map of Liberty Island. When the controllers saw the result on the monitors, the room fell silent.

"When the hell did they do this?"

Sixth Continent was under construction on the Earth-facing side of Eden Crater. Since the moon maintained one face toward Earth, a base built on that side would have a fixed sight line for communications.

But NASA faced the same constraints. To harvest Eden's ice, they would have to source power from outside the crater, and unless they deployed multiple communications satellites in polar orbit, they would have to build on the side facing Earth. This meant that Liberty Island and Sixth Continent would have to be relatively close to each other.

The problem was, how close? The merged map showed that the distance between Sixth Continent and Liberty Island had shrunk to a mere two hundred meters. To make things worse, the closest modules to Sixth Continent were Caroline's five solar arrays.

"It was them! Their operations sprayed regolith onto our site! They contaminated our array and shut down our power. Didn't they notice they were doing this?"

"When we deployed the panels, Sixth Continent was at least a kilometer away." Lambach traced a line on the map with his finger. Caroline nodded.

"I know. That's why we figured it would be safe to put the arrays there. There was nothing on their website about plans to build any closer."

"At the time, no. Siting a permanent landing area depends on the terrain. They can't make a final decision till they've been working on the surface for a while."

"Great. So all they thought about was picking a spot where their own arrays wouldn't be contaminated, and they put their landing area right next to us."

"Not exactly. We didn't notice they were so close. They probably didn't notice either. No one's using IFF transponders up there. As far as the Japanese are concerned, our rovers could be terrain features. And vice versa."

"This is all academic. They created the problem. We're going to lodge a complaint— " Caroline paused, took a deep breath, and counted to five.

"But…before we do that, we need to think of a solution."

"Anger management?" said Lambach.

"I'm trying. I can't afford to do anything hasty on this project."

For Caroline, being tapped to direct unmanned operations on the surface—in effect, to be Liberty Island's Phase One administrator—was a huge professional coup. The reason for her selection was, of course, NASA's change in direction: the Mars project had suddenly been replaced by a lunar research base. In the process, the head of the Mars faction had lost influence. Caroline, whose support for the moon faction within NASA had relegated her to a subordinate role, suddenly found herself in the spotlight.

Caroline was well aware that her promotion was based on chance political developments. She did not want to lose her composure. That would only prompt people to doubt her abilities.

"Those panels were designed for Mars. All we did was change the power settings. Mars has sandstorms, so Wolf's team must've planned for contamination. What was the recovery protocol?"

"The assumption was that the panels would be scoured by the same sand that contaminated them. In the Martian ops plan, the panels were to be oriented at the optimum angle to promote autodecontamination."

"So what are the odds that our panels might decontaminate the same way? They're within ten degrees of vertical. Couldn't the regolith just drop off?"

This was a question with no easy answer. Caroline put out calls to LPL and research facilities across the United States. The answers came from NASA's Glenn Research Center in Cleveland and from Northrop Grumman in New York.

Glenn Research Center had the world's largest space environment simulation chamber, and their staff had deep experience in the effects of exposure to vacuum conditions. GRC's response: friction between regolith particles thrown up from the surface had probably generated a static charge, causing them to stick to each other. The charge would persist in the airless environment.

Northrop Grumman's response came from a staff member who had worked on the design and construction of Apollo lunar landing modules. The smallest regolith particles were as fine as flour. In the moon's one-sixth gravity, there was little chance they would drop off the panels of their own weight. The astronauts who walked on the moon couldn't prevent regolith from contaminating the O-rings on their EVA suits. This prevented them from removing their suits inside their lander, and after lifting off from the surface they had to struggle to avoid carrying dust particles into the command module. The only way to decontaminate the panels would be to have a human on scene to dislodge the regolith by pounding on the rear of the panels.

Caroline was hardly surprised by this analysis, but she had still hoped a solution might be found. Now that hope had been dashed.

"Back to square one," she said with a sigh. She bit her lip in frustration but wasn't ready to give up. As Grumman had noted, with humans on-site there would be any number of options for removing the regolith. Simply waiting for Liberty Island's manned phase would solve the problem. The overall project would be delayed, not stopped.

Still, she wanted to solve this immediately if at all possible. NASA's members were steeped in the legacy of their predecessors, whose originality, ingenuity, and adaptability had enabled them to resuscitate dying probes in the far reaches of space. If Method A was unsuccessful, they tried Method B or C. If those didn't work, they kept searching, racking their brains until they found a way. This unshakable determination had come to be known as "the right stuff." NASA owned it, and Caroline was a rightful heir to that legacy. She thought she had it; she hoped she did.

The next step was a brainstorming call between her staff in the Unmanned Operations Support Room and personnel from a cross section of other departments in JPL. Several solutions were proposed and immediately shot down. Use the minirover that deployed the arrays to shake off the regolith? The rover was not designed to perform gyrating motion or finely calibrated acceleration/deceleration. Proposal rejected. Try the same thing with one of the transport rovers? Too much power. The rover would probably topple the panels, and it lacked sensors to warn when that was about to happen. Proposal rejected. Haul one of the landers to the array location and use its small amount of remaining propellant to direct a blast of thrust at the panels? With no atmosphere, the force of the thrust stream would be very hard to calibrate. If the engine were fired too close to the arrays, it would destroy them. Proposal rejected. Alternate joule heating with radiative cooling by applying intermittent current to the panels, causing the surface to expand and contract? Excessive current could overheat the distribution circuits. In any case, there was no power source. Proposal rejected.

"This is not acceptable. Come on, people! This is NASA!"

Silence descended on the conference. Finally Lambach spoke. "Carol, there is a way. It's very simple."

"Then why hasn't someone proposed it?"

"Because we're NASA. Because we want to solve this on our own. The solution I'm talking about is right next door."

"I see." Caroline was silent for a moment. "The Japanese. You want to ask them to solve the problem for us."

"Yes," said Lambach quietly. "Their multidozers are capable of shaking our arrays without knocking them over. Of course, their equipment was built to completely different specifications. The problem we're facing doesn't allow for much direct human intervention. We'll have to leave it to the AI, and that makes it even more challenging. But it's not impossible if we share data. And one of the guys at Johnson told me *Frontier* helped them on one of their missions. If we bring that into the discussion—"

"That's not on the table. We're not going to do these guys a favor, say 'no strings attached,' and then show up later to collect the bill."

"Then we won't bring it up." Lambach reached for the hotline to NASA headquarters in D.C. "Let's ask Ringstone to summit with the head guys on the Japan side. It'll be risky for them to use valuable gear in an unscheduled operation. But I think Ringstone can convince them." He started to pick up the phone.

"Wait." Caroline put her hand over the receiver. She had removed her sunglasses. Her blue eyes were shining. "Not yet. I've got to think this through."

"Carol, this isn't defeat. If we succeed, you'll be praised for making a wise call."

"I know. But...I wonder what Wolf will say."

"Carol?" Lambach looked at her with concern.

Dr. Wolfgang Valkhoven had been mission director of the Mars project. Just a year ago, it had been NASA's flagship mission for the first half of the twenty-first century—a tremendous undertaking on which to stake their—and America's—reputation. Now the mission had been completely eclipsed by Liberty Island. The five billion dollar Mars Ambassador's failure to make a landing on the surface was just one factor in that eclipse. Political factors had also dimmed Valkhoven's star, including a failed presidential reelection bid by the mission's chief booster.

In the wake of these events, Caroline and the members of the Liberty Island project had risen in NASA, but it was mostly because Valkhoven's team had lost power and another team had had to step up to the plate. They had been liberated from the shadows. It was a tremendous stroke of luck.

But those who had replaced them in the wings were full of resentment. Naturally the chief representative of this faction was Wolf Valkhoven himself. If he and his allies could have their way, they would be back onstage, and they were waiting expectantly for Caroline to stumble. To seek help openly from the Japanese would be political suicide. But—

"I think Wolf would understand," said Lambach.

"You've got to be kidding." Caroline shook her head in disbelief.

"We're cogs in a machine, Carol," Lambach said quietly. "You, me, and everyone here. Our missions have gotten too large for any one person to take all the credit or all the blame. All we can do is be good cogs and try to keep this giant machine from falling apart. The politicians and the bureaucrats decide where the machine goes."

"I'm aware of that. Wolf suffered more than any of us because of those people. How could he approve of our going to the Japanese for help?"

"*Because* he suffered." Lambach nodded, as if he were trying to convince himself. "We've got to solve this here, at our level. Sixth Continent is on scene, and they have capabilities we don't. If we call on them, we can recover from this problem. Don't you see? We're the ones who make the call here. Not the politicians or the bureaucrats." He paused. "Wolf is a scientist, same as us. He'll understand. If his nose gets bent out of shape, I'll talk sense into him."

"You expect me to believe he'll see the Japanese as colleagues?" Caroline's mouth opened in stark disbelief. "Whatever gave you that idea? His project—which just happens to be frozen at the moment—is a lot more important to him. Anyway, the real question is whether *I* can see the Japanese as colleagues."

"Carol, I don't think personal animus has a place here—" Lambach stopped in midsentence. When he had signed on to work with this aggressive mission manager, she had told him a bit of personal history. She had also asked him to keep it confidential.

Caroline fixed him with a cold stare. "They didn't have a manned spacecraft of their own, so they bought my father's seat on the shuttle. And now they've rendered our arrays unusable. Please tell me where I've gone off the rails, Joe."

"I'm sorry, Carol. I misspoke." Lambach waved his hand, as if to wave away his earlier words, but he did not yield. "As mission administrator, which is more embarrassing—having a project canceled for political reasons or losing it because of an accident? Look at this objectively. Are you really going to pass on an option that could help us recover?"

Caroline stared at him for a long moment. "So you're asking whether I'll be able to face myself, much less everyone else." She looked down for a long moment, then put her sunglasses back on.

"All right. As long as there's something we can do about it, let's not waste time."

"Yes, ma'am." Lambach nodded with relief and picked up the hotline.

———

"MR. AOMINE, YOU have an outside call."

The speaker in the ceiling repeated the announcement. Sohya slid out from under a multidozer and wiped metal dust from his face with a cloth. "Sorry, I'll be right back."

"Leave her to me. I'll have this wrapped by the time you get back." The maintenance engineer closed the lid of the dozer's motherboard compartment and waved a hand in assurance.

Sohya exited through double metal doors, then an air lock. The magnetic shielding chamber was paneled with metal plates to screen out all geomagnetic and electromagnetic energy. This allowed tests on multidozer performance under different simulated conditions. Naturally, his wearcom would not function inside the chamber.

Sohya was in the multidozer manufacturing facility and proving ground at the foot of Mount Fuji. The facility was also central control for the dozers already on the surface. On top of his responsibilities for directing surface operations, Sohya was helping to improve the next generation of multidozers currently under construction.

Once outside the chamber, Sohya stepped into a nearby data processing center. All the terminals were busy, so he had to take the call on a bench in the corridor. He found Tae smiling back at him from his wearcom monitor.

"Hello, Sohya. Are you busy at the moment?"

"I was just about finished anyway," said Sohya. "Starting with Dozer 8 we're going to use slightly thinner shielding. That will allow us to increase its leverage."

"Sounds good. Listen, I couldn't get hold of Mr. Iwaki. I need someone who knows the front line," said Tae. Obviously this wasn't a personal call. Sohya was about to make a joke about his disappointment on that score, but what she said next banished that thought instantly.

"We're conferencing with Ringstone at NASA."

"NASA? You're joking!"

"Mr. Gotoba and Mr. Yaenami are waiting too. We're just about to start."

"But, Tae—"

Sohya's wearcom display divided into five cells, each with a face. He hurriedly composed himself.

"Hello, Administrator Ringstone. This is Tae Toenji speaking." Her accent was polished King's English, belying the fact that she'd learned the language in California.

"Greetings to all of you in Japan," answered Ringstone. "I'm calling with an important request. This discussion is off the record, so I would appreciate your candid opinion. First, let me introduce Caroline Cadbury from JPL. Caroline is operations director for the unmanned phase of Liberty Island."

"Hello, everyone." The same bald American Sohya had seen on the web yielded the floor to a blond woman. In a businesslike tone she began outlining NASA's problem. When she had finished, she looked up from her documents and spoke directly into the camera. "I'd like to emphasize that this problem was caused by the proximity of your landing sites. I hope you will fully bear in mind your responsibility as you consider our request."

"Carol, let's set that aside for the moment," Ringstone said with an uneasy chuckle. Then he turned to his audience. "We're prepared to render you assistance if you encounter problems. We regard this as an obligation, given our preeminent position in space exploration."

Ryuichi broke in, "You sounded pretty preeminent in that press conference."

"You saw that? Well, that puts me in a difficult position." Ringstone rubbed his pate, then slowly executed a formal bow, Japanese-style. "We would deeply appreciate your assistance. As humans, and as fellow strivers toward the stars."

"Mr. Ringstone, we need time to confer," said Tae.

"I understand. I hope you'll hurry." Ringstone's and Caroline's faces were replaced with the caption ON HOLD.

"Well then," said Gotoba. "First question: can we actually help them? What do you think, Aomine?"

Sohya returned to the present. He had been preoccupied with Caroline's steely expression.

"Um…yes. As far as I can tell from Cadbury's explanation, I think it's possible. The multidozers' power cables can easily extend two hundred meters. They have a macro for shaking our soft panels. With a little reprogramming, we could use it."

"Their panels are built from different materials. Are you sure you can dislodge the regolith just by shaking them?"

"If it doesn't work, we can clean it off."

"With what—a cloth or something?" asked Ryuichi.

"We could blow it off. The regolith contains titanium. That's a very hard metal. Wiping the panels free of regolith would damage them. We have a small spray module for cleaning the dozer video lenses. It's a metal container with a heating element, like a teakettle. We can generate as much vapor as we need by charging it with permafrost. We'd have to program the dozers to manipulate the module to reach the panels—that's a lot of area to cover. Tricky, but not impossible."

"I see," said Gotoba. "It's just a question of whether we want to spend the time."

"Basically, yes," said Sohya.

"So which benefits us most: investing time and resources to help NASA or leaving them to their own devices, cold as that might seem."

Ryuichi didn't wait for Gotoba to finish. "Let's help them." Gotoba looked intrigued.

"Your reason?"

"Number one: publicity. If we help NASA, it will be as effective as airing ten commercials. Two: we'll put them in our debt. We have no way of knowing what kind of problem we might run into at some point. It would be good to have them in our corner."

"Are you sure they'll be willing to repay the favor? What we really need is for them to slow the pace of construction on Liberty Island. They're certainly not going to do that."

"Fine," said Ryuichi. "It would be better for them to do well— even if they are competitors—than dump cold water on this space boom. NASA's success will have a halo effect on Sixth Continent."

"I'm not sure I share your optimism," said Gotoba.

"Then why did we let the rest of the world get a peek at TROPHY? I bet NASA will be building their own version soon, though it will take them a while to figure out the details. I welcome that."

Gotoba chuckled. "You make it sound very appealing. Ms. Toenji, what's your take on this?"

"I agree with Mr. Yaenami. As Sixth Continent's publicity director, helping NASA wouldn't be worth ten commercials—

it'd be worth a hundred. I'm thinking of having footage of our multidozers working on Liberty Island intercut with video of Ringstone thanking us for our help."

Sohya couldn't keep silent. Tae's triumphant expression was too much for him. "Excuse me, everyone. Have you forgotten what NASA did for *Apple 3*? Are we going to repay them by turning their misfortune into an ad campaign?"

"Aomine, this is not your issue." Gotoba gave him a sharp look. Sohya felt a stab of fear. Naturally he was just on the call to render a technical opinion, not to participate in high-level decision making. But he couldn't help himself.

"You saw Cadbury's face. She was in agony having to ask us for help. No wonder, when you consider NASA's legacy. It's like having to ask for help from a child who's just learning to walk. I think we should be satisfied with putting them in our debt, not running around telling—"

"Aomine—" Gotoba began to reprimand him, but Tae cut in.

"Sohya." She spoke coldly, with narrowed eyes. "Don't you understand? If they win, Sixth Continent will be in a real predicament." Sohya couldn't think of an answer. He opened a two-way channel to Tae.

"Tae, please. I'm in the same position as Cadbury. I know what she's going through. We're not senior people. We're on the front line, putting heart and soul into our work. We don't want political agendas to destroy what we're doing. If we go public with this, the media will crucify her."

"Sohya…" Her image on the wearcom display was tiny, but Sohya saw the change that came over her. "So gentle, as always."

"You mean 'weak,' right? But still."

"If only everyone were like you," murmured Tae. Then she sighed. "All right. Just this once." She returned to conference mode.

"Sorry for the interruption. After some thought, I think we should avoid publicity at this time."

"Really?" said Gotoba. "And help them for nothing?"

"Help, yes. But I don't think it will be for nothing. Sixth Continent is facing problems of its own. When the time comes for those problems to be addressed, this incident may prove important."

Gotoba's and Ryuichi's expressions suggested they understood what Tae meant. Sohya had no idea what she was talking about.

"Is everyone okay then?" Tae spoke as if she were closing the conference.

"I'm fine."

"All right then."

With that response from Ryuichi and Gotoba, Tae reopened the line to NASA.

"Mr. Ringstone, we've made a decision."

"And that is?"

"Sixth Continent will assist Liberty Island. In addition, please rest assured that we will not publicize this matter."

"Well…we're grateful for that," said Ringstone with evident surprise. Caroline's eyes opened wide with astonishment. "It will save us some face," continued Ringstone. "But are you sure you want to do this? It involves some risk of damage to your modules."

"We're aware of that. In that case, we'll take responsibility."

"That's very gallant of you. Is this *bushido*, by any chance?"

Tae smiled. "That's what you Americans always say. There haven't been any samurai in Japan for 160 years." Then she seemed to recall something. "Ms. Cadbury?"

"Yes?"

"I have a message from our unmanned operations director: 'Let's give it our best shot.'"

"…I understand."

"Well, that's all. We can take up the details in a separate call."

"Thanks again, Ms. Toenji," said Ringstone. He gave a two-finger salute and rang off, followed by Gotoba and Ryuichi.

"I owe you one, Tae." Sohya dipped his head in thanks.

"You certainly do."

"I'll take you to dinner next time. But I hope NASA and Sixth Continent can keep supporting each other."

"I *said*, 'Just this *once*.'"

"Tae?" She didn't answer at first. Then she looked away and murmured hoarsely, "You have to choose me."

"What?"

She hung up.

If Tae were reaching out to him, the timing was certainly strange. Sohya shook his head and began reading a news flash streaming across his wearcom.

━━●━◆◆━●━━

THE NIGHT AIR, heavy with the smell of the desert, parted before Caroline's speeding Chevy. The speedometer already showed eighty, but she gunned it harder. She half expected to see the highway patrol in her mirror, but she didn't care. What she needed now was a stiff drink.

"How dare he say, 'Let's give it our best shot'!"

Tae's "message" from Sohya was the last thing Caroline wanted to hear from someone Japanese. When she was a child, her father, a biologist, had been selected to fly aboard one of the original space shuttles. Entry into the elite corps of astronauts was a rare distinction and a source of tremendous pride for her father. But he was bumped from the crew just before his flight—by a Japanese astronaut. NASA was gearing up for its exploration of Mars and was eager to generate income from the shuttle. Japan had no manned spacecraft of its own. The agendas of both countries dovetailed.

Caroline's father waited patiently for his next opportunity, but luck was not with him. The transition from the original shuttle to the supershuttle began soon after that, and NASA's launch schedule was focused on shakedown and testing missions for the new spacecraft. Test pilots were given priority, and in the process of waiting, her father had lost his qualification to fly. A slight arrhythmia, undetected before, had worsened.

So he went back to his old job as a university scientist, where he was still making solid research contributions. But Caroline would never forget the night he had taken the call from the chief of the astronaut office, and how old and defeated he had looked afterward. The careers of father and daughter had both been buffeted by powers beyond their reach.

"These people bumped my father off the shuttle. Now I have to bow down to them?"

As she muttered to herself, she suddenly saw the gleam from a pair of eyes in the beam of her headlights. With a shock of fear, she hit the brake hard. She was doing over ninety. The car instantly went into a spin. She had a brief vision of the landscape spinning around in her headlights before she was off the highway and flying through the air over a ditch that paralleled the road. By some miracle the Chevy refused to flip over. It came to a halt in the scrub.

Caroline looked shakily around her. The highway stretched away into the California wilderness, deserted. There were no cars. She hadn't hit anything. The Chevy seemed undamaged. She sat in the driver's seat, shivering and wiping cold sweat from her forehead.

When she had collected herself, she looked up to see a number of animals the size of puppies in her headlights. They were standing on their hind legs, staring at her. Prairie dogs.

Perhaps they were blinded by the light or just curious. Caroline couldn't tell. Their calm gazes brought to mind Lambach of all people.

Wolf, the Japanese, Caroline and her people—they were all on the same quest.

"Come to your senses, girl!" she said out loud.

She honked the horn to scatter the prairie dogs, then stamped on the accelerator. The Chevy's rear wheels whined as they hit the road.

[3]

ON AUGUST 1, 2030, the United Nations International Court of Justice in The Hague issued a temporary injunction ordering Japan's government to freeze Tenryu Galaxy Transport's operations. TGT was operating under the administrative authority of JAXA, Japan's space agency.

The day before, Tae and Sennosuke had departed for Canada, as much to escape the summer heat of Nagoya as to conduct PR for Sixth Continent. Ryuichi was in Taiwan, negotiating expedited delivery of vital microchips. The first person to get word of the injunction was the president of Gotoba Engineering & Construction, during a visit to TGT's Nagoya headquarters.

"So you see, if we could develop an Earth–moon tugboat, it could operate with fuel produced on the moon. That would reduce the mass we have to carry up from Earth by even more."

"He's right. And taking passengers to the moon would only require one Eve launch vehicle, instead of two."

Shinji and Reika were tag teaming their presentation to Gotoba in one of TGT's conference rooms. They were an unlikely pair, but when Shinji had come up with the tugboat concept as a way of reducing costs, Reika had seen the potential and jumped on it. Both had been given a fairly free hand by their bosses, which made it easier to coordinate cross-company on ideas like this. All they needed was Gotoba's buy-in, so Shinji collared Gotoba during his visit to TGT's Nagoya plant. Reika hurried over from ELE to seize the opportunity.

Gotoba was cautious at first but began to warm to the idea. "Well, you two, I think that's an excellent plan. Of course, you'll have to figure out how to shoehorn tugboat production into the current manufacturing queue. It's already tight as a drum."

Gotoba's wearcom rang. "Excuse me," he said, and took the call. The exchange was short and he mostly listened, but his expression changed quickly. He hung up and seemed deep in thought. Shinji and Reika sat waiting for his signal to return to the discussion. Instead, Gotoba looked up and said, "The International Court of Justice wants to put Sixth Continent on hold."

"That's impossible!" said Reika.

"This is a serious problem. I'd like to talk to Yaenami and Chairman Toenji. Can you contact them for me?"

Reika and Shinji immediately began trying to contact their respective bosses, but both came up empty-handed.

"I'm sorry," said Shinji. "Yaenami is in the middle of a meeting with his chip supplier to see if we can get them to bump Intel and move our order up. I'll have to deal with this problem until he can tear himself away."

"Same problem," said Reika. "Our chairman and Ms. Toenji are in the middle of a presentation at the Ottawa City Hotel."

"It can't be helped, then. The three of us will have to coordinate an immediate response. I don't think we have time to spare."

Shinji and Reika nodded. Gotoba forwarded the documents he'd received to their wearcoms. For the next few minutes, they read through the documents carefully.

Finally Gotoba said, "According to this, the plaintiff is the U.S. government. Japan is the defendant. The basis for the complaint is the Moon Treaty, specifically the clause that prohibits exploitation of the moon for commercial purposes. There are a few things here I don't understand. Ms. Hozumi, do you have any legal background?"

"Some." Reika immediately began sourcing information on her wearcom. In a few moments, she downloaded data on international laws and treaties, the Court of Justice, and the Agreement Governing the Activities of States on the Moon and Other Celestial Bodies, also known as the Moon Treaty. "I'm ready," she said.

Gotoba smiled. *Faster than my legal eagles*, he thought. "All right, I have a question. Why is the complaint directed at Japan and not the project partners?"

"The International Court of Justice only handles disputes between nations. Also, Article 14 of the Outer Space Treaty of 1967 makes national governments responsible for the activities of private companies in space. Japan's government is responsible if a Japanese company violates some aspect of the agreement."

"We should've followed Ms. Toenji's suggestion and put a private flag on the moon, instead of a Japanese flag. Maybe we could've avoided this."

"Unfortunately, we're still taking suggestions for Sixth Continent's logo," said Reika. The three of them chuckled. Japan's government had pointedly requested that the nation's flag be placed on the moon. When the flag was being packed at ELE for launch, Tae had nearly ripped it to pieces in a fit of pique. The story was legend among Sixth Continent insiders.

"Hmm...so the target is really us, and the government is named in the complaint as a matter of form. What about the Moon Treaty?"

"It's an international treaty from 1979, prohibiting any commercial exploitation of the moon or other celestial bodies by any government, corporation, or individual. We're harvesting ice in Eden Crater for the purpose of building a commercial installation. That clearly puts us in violation of the treaty."

"Hey, hold it a second." Shinji looked at his wearcom. "I'm pretty sure almost nobody, maybe fewer than ten countries, signed that treaty. Let's see...America...Japan...Yes, neither one signed it."

"Now I remember," said Gotoba. "We looked into this when we started the design process. Any kind of construction activity involves getting dozens of permits approved, or you can't proceed. But Japan never signed the Moon Treaty. We decided it wasn't an issue."

"I'm afraid that was a hasty judgment," said Reika. "Laws concerning outer space are based on treaties and customary law. Customary law can be very tricky. International customary law is based on the concept that a customary practice becomes law if it continues long enough, even if the practice belongs to a culture without a well-developed legal system. The Moon Treaty itself can be considered as having the nature of customary law. Nations that never even signed the treaty may have a responsibility to abide by it."

"So customary law would make it illegal to drain the Pacific Ocean? Not that there's actually a law against it," said Shinji.

"Basically, yes."

"So the court is saying the treaty applies to Japan," said Gotoba. "What happens if we just ignore the injunction?"

"The International Court of Justice has no enforcement capacity, so we don't need to worry about being arrested. But…under Article 94 of the UN charter, if we ignore the injunction, the plaintiff can take the matter to the UN Security Council."

"The Security Council?" Gotoba looked appalled.

Shinji gulped. "Would they send peacekeeping troops?"

"No, of course not," said Reika. "They might threaten to, but that's all. But it would still be terrible for our corporate image."

"Well, we can't have that." Gotoba folded his arms.

"Mr. Gotoba, we still have some options," said Reika. "The court's injunction is temporary. We can recover from this."

"Yes, I'd forgotten that." Gotoba breathed a bit easier. "All right, I think I have the picture. We can't ignore this, but it's not insoluble. Our three companies should mount a counterresponse. I'd like to leave the details to the experts. Who's going to take this on?"

"ELE's legal team will handle this," said Reika. "If we need support, we'll call on Gotoba's legal department for help."

"Our opponents are the court and the U.S. government, but the Japanese government is going to put pressure on us not to embarrass them."

"Mr. Gotoba, can we look to you to handle them?"

"Leave it to me. I hope I'll be able to call on your chairman's influence."

"Of course."

"Well, there you are. Let's make sure they know we're not going to roll over for NASA."

The space tugboat discussion was shelved for the moment. Everyone stood up hastily. Shinji still seemed worried. "Why is America bringing this complaint anyway? We just gave NASA some assistance last month."

"The Americans do things by the book," said Gotoba. "They won't admit any linkage there."

"I don't know…It just doesn't sound like NASA to me." Shinji stood shaking his head as he watched them go.

ELE, GOTOBA, AND TGT, not the Japanese government, were the real force behind construction on the moon. ELE's senior counsel formed a defense team and took up the challenge of contesting the International Court's ruling.

The team's first move was to challenge the basis for the injunction, since neither plaintiff nor defendant were signatories to the Moon Treaty. But this move was rejected by the court, which ruled that the treaty had universal application, just as humanitarian law applied to all nations.

Sixth Continent objected to this ruling on the basis of intertemporal law, which requires that juridical facts be evaluated in light of laws in force at the time. The Moon Treaty did not anticipate that one day corporations might build facilities on the moon for the benefit of all humanity. Its restrictions were out of date. But Sixth Continent's plan to charge huge fees for travel to the moon was seized on by the court as demonstrating that the base was hardly intended for humanity's benefit.

The defense team next tried to challenge America's qualifications for bringing a complaint against Japan. They cited Section 11.3 of the Moon Treaty, which states: "Neither the surface nor the subsurface of the moon, nor any natural resources in place, shall become the property of any State, non-governmental entity or person." NASA was, after all, harvesting surface ice. Why couldn't Sixth Continent do the same?

The court rejected this move like all the others, citing Section 6.2 of the treaty, which states, "the States Parties shall have the right to collect on and remove from the moon samples of its mineral and other substances. Such samples shall remain at the disposal of those States Parties which caused them to be collected and may be used by them for scientific purposes." Since NASA planned to use Liberty Island as a base to explore Mars and other planets, their installation was obviously scientific.

The legal headwinds were stiff. The United States seemed to be pulling out all the stops to support their complaint with a formidable combination of lawyers, documentation, and funding. There was no indication that the Americans were actually attempting to bribe the court's fifteen judges. But they were obviously aiming for an early victory and were using every means available to put pressure on the court. The judges took less than a month to consider and dispose of every argument Sixth Continent mounted.

Public opinion was split in favor of Sixth Continent, but nearly everyone thought the Americans would ultimately prevail. The heads of Gotoba Engineering and ELE used their connections to obtain a reasonable level of support from Japan's government. But diplomacy was one thing, courtroom argument another. When it came to the actual legal battle, there was little chance that Sixth Continent could prevail against the United States, which saw everything in terms of cold logic.

Ryuichi Yaenami was not foolhardy enough to waste time and energy helping fight a battle outside his area of competence. Adam 5 successfully delivered its mysterious payload to the lunar surface. But whatever it was, it was not scheduled to go into operation until a month after it reached the moon. Furthermore, Sixth Continent would not reveal its purpose. TGT's refusal to supply details fanned speculation that Adam 5 might have blown up before reaching the moon. Reporters descended on Ryuichi for comment. Once again his character was on display, even in his silence. All he did was repeat, "No comment," without hinting why. This steadfastness earned him praise in some quarters, but overall, criticism of TGT only grew stronger.

The life force of Sixth Continent was like a candle in a gale.

———————

THE BAROMETER IN the Liberty Island Unmanned Operations Support Room was dropping.

At the eye of the storm sat Caroline Cadbury, on a chair in a corner of the room, looking fixedly downward. Her exact expression was concealed behind her sunglasses, but she'd already bitten the heads off the last eight members of her team who'd been foolhardy enough to try to speak to her. The ninth was quietly taping a sign to the wall behind her as a warning to others:

HURRICANE CAROLINE

FORCE 12 WINDS

Indeed, Caroline's mind was a swirling vortex of conflicting thoughts.

Sixth Continent was about to have its oxygen supply cut off. Caroline was struggling with the same doubts that had assailed Shinji: strangling Sixth Continent suited senior politicians in the U.S. government, but it was not something Caroline or her team would have wanted. Still, with NASA's rivals seemingly about to retire from the field, she should've been feeling elated. But her personal "right stuff" was having major problems with the situation.

What was it, ultimately, that was essential to face that hostile environment known simply as "space"? Undermining rivals with legal maneuvers couldn't possibly be part of it. America's early space program was indeed driven by competition with the

Russians. But even at the height of the space race, the men who led the charge—the seven legendary Mercury astronauts—simply wanted to fly. The competition was nowhere on their radar screen.

Should NASA actually take steps to banish its opponents from the field? Or should it proceed as if they did not exist?

"Oh, of all the…What am I going to do?"

Just then her wearcom display lit up: incoming call. At first she ignored it, but then she noticed the caller ID: SOHYA AOMINE, ACTIVE TASK FORCE CHIEF, GOTOBA E&C.

"Sohya…?" After a moment, she had it: this was the Sixth Continent engineer who had sent her words of encouragement. Almost despite herself, she took the call.

"This is Cadbury."

"It's Sohya Aomine."

He appeared on the display: an Asian man with black hair and a placid, youthful face. Japanese, like the people who had destroyed her father's dream! Giving in to her emotions, Caroline answered tartly, "What do you want?"

"My boss has asked me to negotiate something with you."

"*Negotiate?*"

"Yes. Sixth Continent needs NASA's help."

"Wonderful. We're rivals, you know. You're asking me to help you?"

"Hear me out and I'm confident you will." Sohya's voice was calm and soothing. *Why are these people always so damn difficult to deal with?* thought Caroline. *How can I yell at someone who talks this way?*

"So what is it you want to negotiate?"

Sohya began explaining. After several minutes, Caroline leapt to her feet. Her chair fell over with a crash. The team looked at her, braced for the worst. She broke her silence with a shout.

"*What?* Sixth Continent is equipped for that? Well, so what? That doesn't offer us much…You're joking! You're willing to give us TROPHY?"

Craig came half out of his chair at the mention of TGT's engine. This timid-looking controller, whose wearcom was integrated into his Coke-bottle glasses, was a Boeing-trained rocket engineer with a consuming interest in TROPHY technology.

"Carol! What was that about TROPHY?"

"Hold on, Craig." Lambach put a large hand on Craig's shoulder and gently pushed him back into his chair. Caroline kept talking feverishly into her sunglasses.

"Yes, I get it. That gives us a way to move. My boss? Don't worry, I'll convince him. He was a Rockwell test pilot. He was in line to fly one of the shuttles. Offer him a chance to fly on *Apple*, like TGT's president. Yes, I'm sure he'll approve...Yes, leave it to me!"

Caroline reached up a finger and rang off, then took off her sunglasses. Her sky blue eyes were shining. "Get me Ringstone!"

"Carol, what's going on?" said Lambach.

"We're going to help Sixth Continent!" Lambach picked up the phone. Caroline jerked it away and impatiently hit the call button. Craig stared at her, mystified.

"I thought you weren't a big fan of the Japanese," he said. "And what was that about TROPHY?"

"I'm willing to convert if we can get that technology. Even if we can't...Hello? This is Cadbury at JPL. I need to speak to Ringstone—now."

Craig watched his boss and shook his head. "Is she on something?"

"Your guess is as good as mine." Lambach shrugged. "Hurricanes go where they have to."

———◦◦◦———

IN THE HAGUE, final arguments regarding the Sixth Continent injunction were under way in the spacious courtroom of the International Court of Justice. Throughout the process, the superiority of the American position had been obvious. Special Assistant to the President Jim Lord, representing the United States, sat on the plaintiff's side of the room, wearing a confident smile.

The fifteen judges were drawn from as many countries. The chief justice of the court was an Australian jurist named Melville. She looked out over the courtroom and said in ringing tones, "We shall now hear final arguments from the defendant. Richard Ringstone, please take your place on the witness stand."

Commotion rose in the gallery and the plaintiff's section of the courtroom. Lord's mouth opened in surprise—Ringstone, NASA's administrator, was the last person he'd expected to see as a witness for Japan.

Ringstone was sworn in and sat down. Melville said, "The Court has been advised that you are here to present newly ascertained facts of relevance in this matter. What are those facts?"

"Sixth Continent is a scientific installation," said Ringstone.

"A *scientific* installation?" Lord said.

"That's right, Mr. Lord. Sixth Continent incorporates a SETI module. The module is already in operation. It was carried to the moon a month ago, on the last launch before the injunction was delivered."

"Utter nonsense. The defendant is obviously clutching at straws," Lord said to Melville.

"It's not nonsense. I was alerted to this by my subordinate at JPL. I personally investigated the module they are using. I can confirm that it is indeed an apparatus for detecting intelligent signals from deep space. Sixth Continent is a scientific facility. As such, Section 6.2 of the Moon Treaty applies to its activities, as it does to NASA's activities at Liberty Island. Sixth Continent has a right to make use of the moon's resources."

"Why are you here, Mr. Ringstone?" Lord was beginning to lose his temper. "What are you doing testifying against the interests of your own country? I would expect you, as NASA administrator, to adopt a rather different yardstick of behavior!"

Melville broke in. "Mr. Lord, this is not a forum for debating where the interests of the United States lie."

Lord grudgingly fell silent. Ringstone continued in a firm tone.

"Maybe it is time to consider the interests of the United States of America. We need a competitor. With a strong opponent, we show what we're really capable of. I believe Sixth Continent is the best opponent we could ask for. Yet at the same time, we at NASA don't see ourselves in competition with anyone. We act on behalf of humanity, to look far into space, to touch the stars. We don't play political games to achieve our objectives." So saying, Ringstone gave one of his trademark bows and stepped down.

The sound of applause rose like a wave—from the Americans in the gallery. Ringstone's testimony had struck home. Lord's pale complexion turned a deep shade of scarlet.

"Madame Justice, I wish to address the court."

"Proceed."

"I've tried to restrain myself from pointing this out to the court, but I can no longer continue to do so. I wish to draw your attention to the manipulation of this process by the government of Japan. Japan is ultimately responsible for the activities of Sixth Continent. They've even planted their national flag on the base. They refuse to exercise control over Sixth Continent's operations, yet they skillfully conspired to bring a representative of NASA here to testify in support of their position. I find this truly deplorable. I would like the court to affirm that Japan bears full responsibility for Sixth Continent's actions!"

The justices looked uneasy. Lord was reopening an issue that had already more or less been settled. Until now, the Americans had consistently taken the position that the Japanese government was only nominally overseeing Sixth Continent. In effect, Lord was asking the court to take the entire process back to square one.

"Madame Justice, may I speak?" Tae Toenji raised her hand. She had traveled to the Netherlands to be present on this final day of arguments. Since she was funding the project, she was seated with the defense team. Melville nodded.

Tae rose to her feet. "Madame Justice, would it be possible to bring Sixth Continent's home page onto the courtroom monitor?"

"Yes, I believe so," said Melville and motioned to the clerk of the court. "Would you please?"

The clerk opened a browser on the courtroom monitor. Tae gave him the address, and in a moment Sixth Continent's home page came up. The home page had a real-time webcam feed from the multidozers. Japan's rising sun flag was planted in the regolith, a crossbar on the pole holding it taut. Tae asked the clerk to freeze the image.

"Enhance, please." The clerk zoomed in on the flag. Tae murmured sadly, "I hate to say this, but I have no choice…All right, you can stop there."

The image of a red circle on a white ground filled the screen. Everyone in the courtroom craned forward to get a better look. Jutting from the top of the sun disk was a tiny, curved stem.

"This is the flag of Eden, not Japan. It's a red apple on a white field."

A hush fell. Tae's voice rang through the courtroom.

"All the equipment and facilities of Sixth Continent are the personal property of me and my grandfather, Sennosuke. We are not associated with Japan's government, either in name or in fact. I was unwilling to have the national flag represent my Eden, so before it was taken to the moon, I modified it. That, Madame Justice, is an apple."

"This…this is sophistry…" Lord stammered.

"Is it, Mr. Lord? How many of your arguments so far, as well as ours, have been anything but rhetoric? Let's drop this pointless war of words. Don't you think the best way to conclude this process—for both of us—would be for the justices to rule on this matter now?" She smiled, the smile that had charmed the world. Lord's mouth was moving, but no words came out.

Melville announced, "This concludes final arguments. The court will recess for thirty minutes. We will then hand down our verdict!"

The room began to buzz. Journalists jumped up and ran outside. In the gallery, Sohya looked over at Caroline.

"I smell an upset win. I have to say, Ringstone's speech was great. I can't believe you convinced him to do it."

"He's fifty-five, but he says he still wants a chance to go into space," said Caroline. "With TROPHY technology, we can develop our own scramjet and build a low-G lift vehicle that can take people with arrhythmia like Ringstone into space. That's all I had to tell him. Of course, we won't disclose the TROPHY deal till this whole issue blows over." She looked over at Tae, who was congratulating the members of the defense team. "Impeccable timing, getting the SETI module up when you did. That girl is really something. I'm impressed."

"That's a compliment, especially coming from you."

"But it doesn't mean we're buddies." Caroline stood up. She looked down at Sohya defiantly. "Ringstone meant what he said. NASA doesn't have rivals. We're pioneers. That's what we've always been and always will be. Today is special, and we're here together. After today, I wish you the best of luck. You'll need it."

"Thanks for that. We know you won't slow down just for us," said Sohya. He stood up and folded his arms across his chest with a smile. Caroline answered with a smile of her own and made no attempt to shake his hand. She spun on her heel and strode briskly out of the courtroom.

THE TELEVISION IN Ryuichi's office was an old flat-screen monitor from the beginning of the century. When he saw the news flash at the top of the screen—SIXTH CONTINENT VINDICATED—he sat back on the sofa and clapped.

"Shinji, we won! The verdict was unanimous!"

"Yes, yes, I know." Shinji was sitting opposite Ryuichi, slurping instant noodles out of a Styrofoam container and tapping away on a laptop. He nodded knowingly. "Aomine told me already.

Anyway, I'm the one who ordered their SETI module. I can't believe Tae had the foresight to realize we'd need it."

"Are you sure she launched that module just to create a legal trapdoor?"

"That must've been part of it. Anyway, I've never pretended to understand what she's thinking. Even Aomine gets jerked around by her. A SETI module on the moon is a cool idea though."

"You think so?"

"Why not? I mean, it can't fail. No one can prove it's a waste of time as long as there's no deadline."

Ryuichi snorted with amusement and peered at the laptop. Shinji had been working away at it all morning. "So what's cooking?"

Shinji turned the computer around so Ryuichi could see the screen. He finished the noodles in one titanic slurp. "Faifan fen," he said with his mouth full.

"Don't talk with your mouth full," said Ryuichi.

"Fokay...Ah, it's a proposal to modify the Titan X."

"Titan? That's one of theirs. It's based on an old ICBM design. Why modify it?"

"Since they're getting the plans for TROPHY, they might not need the last few Titans they have on order. I ran the concept past Ringstone before he left for the Netherlands. He sounded interested."

"What's the concept?" said Ryuichi.

"As configured, Titan X can put forty tons into low earth orbit. With a few modifications, it looks like we could use the third stage as a space tug. All we'd need to do is swap in a power plant with a longer service life. If we can include a few of these in the barter deal for TROPHY, it'd make things a lot easier going forward."

"Wow, that definitely sounds like a plan." Shinji had Ryuichi's full attention now.

"Yes, it's perfect. The tug will only be used between Earth and the moon, and it'll really expand the range of things we can do in space. Whatever the payload, all we have to do to get it to the moon is just take it outside Earth's atmosphere. We can park things in LEO and stop worrying about the best launch window. All pros, no cons."

"All pros, no cons…" Ryuichi said in a faraway voice. Shinji looked up. Ryuichi had spread both arms across the back of the sofa. He was staring at the ceiling.

"Everything these days feels like a dream."

"How so?" Shinji was mystified.

"Launching rockets to the moon like it was routine. I went up myself. To top it off, I've got NASA eating out of my hand. Remember that time you and I first met, in that beer place in Kanda? I never, ever thought we'd come this far."

"Me neither."

"I'm almost worried. It's like things are going too well."

"That doesn't sound like the Yaenami I know," chuckled Shinji. Ryuichi leaned across the table and looked at the waiflike face of his resident genius.

"It's all your doing. You deserve a bonus. What do you want?"

"I don't know. Okay, I'd like to go up too. LEO is fine."

"Is that all? In another fifteen years it'll only cost you a month's salary."

"A trip into orbit is more than enough. I want to see a TRO-PHY rocket coming up toward me. If I wait fifteen years, we'll probably be using a totally new engine."

"I get it." Ryuichi nodded. "You want to watch your carefully raised child fly from every angle."

"From low orbit I'll be able to see everything from liftoff to second-stage separation."

"Great, I'll make sure it happens." Ryuichi reached across the table and clapped Shinji on both shoulders. "Speaking of new engines to take us to the moon, shouldn't you be working on that? I'm counting on you!"

"I'd actually rather design something to take us to another planet."

"What a genius!" Ryuichi clapped his shoulders again and again.

"Hey, give me a break!" Shinji laughed.

CHAPTER 6
RISK MANAGEMENT AND DAMAGE CONTROL

[1]

THE LEAVES ENVELOPING the soaring office tower glowed crimson in the sunset over the Yoro Mountains. It was beautiful enough to take one's breath away.

Autumn, 2030. Eden Leisure Entertainment's headquarters was sheathed in Japanese maples flourishing on projecting ledges. On the twenty-third floor, their scarlet leaves framed a window and a man who stood gazing impassively from it.

The man's hair was parted neatly above his gold-rimmed glasses. Behind the glow reflected in their lenses, his eyes had a gentle softness. His features were clear-cut; age had only begun to touch his slightly hollowed cheeks. He stood on the green carpet of his enormous office like a tree nourished by the sun, feet planted shoulder width apart, spine straight, hands behind his back. A small badge with a logo of a red fruit in a treetop adorned his beige suit lapel.

ELE president Kiichiro Toenji was fifty-five years old. He was not admiring the sunset. He had turned his back on a visitor. The visitor's voice, coming from a sofa facing his desk, was pulsing with irritation.

"Why can't you be more flexible? One company sailing under two flags will only confuse our customers."

"Corporations have multiple brands all the time. Sixth Continent doesn't have to borrow Tokai Eden's design concepts," said Kiichiro, without moving a muscle.

"Then at least put a Sixth Continent banner at the top of our home page. Ninety-five percent of our visitors use the web to check the park schedule. You know that. Treating Sixth Continent like any other subsidiary just makes the rift between you and Tae that much more obvious."

"I'm surprised to hear you say that, Mr. Chairman. I think Sixth Continent's already made the rift obvious with their stance toward ELE. But that doesn't change the fact that Tae's moon base is not a core business. It's just part of our portfolio, like Eden Tourist or Vision of Eden Video. Our publishing division will probably show more profit in the long run. But this is academic. We agreed that she could draw on corporate resources, such as our publicity department, as long as Sixth Continent succeeded or failed on its own."

"Kiichiro, are you refusing to help your own flesh and blood?"

At the old man's sigh, Kiichiro's blank expression became, if anything, even more inscrutable. He adjusted his glasses on the bridge of his nose with a manicured fingertip. "I've faithfully followed the course you set."

"In what way?"

"'A paradise on Earth, a dream, a brief escape from reality—for everyone.' When you founded Paradise Tours, that was your company's motto. And in time, Paradise Tours grew into this enormous enterprise. Since I took over this office fifteen years ago, I've never forgotten that motto. Not for a single day."

"They're just words," said Sennosuke. "You don't know what they mean!"

"Don't I? I am a purveyor of dreams. It's you who has forgotten the meaning of those words. Sixth Continent will never be accessible to the public. It's not a place you can just decide to visit. It's a palace above the clouds for the superrich. If space travel is always going to be expensive, then the entire venture was ill conceived from the start."

"But the mere fact that there is such a place gives people hope for the future. Tae gets thousands of letters every week that prove it."

"Yes. She's dangling a dream of the future before the world. Her dream, the dream of a solitary young girl. I'm sure you understand the risks that entails. Offer a product strongly associated with a particular individual, and anything that damages that person's reputation damages the product. To make matters worse, Sixth Continent has no focus. Is it a wedding palace? A research facility? What happens if she ceases to be associated with it? The whole house of cards collapses. I doubt Tae herself understands why she's doing this. Her rationale for building a moon base changes depending on whom she's speaking to, the time, and the place. It's absurd."

"Kiichiro—don't you see why she's doing this?"

The son shook his head almost imperceptibly. "If I were unable to grasp the psychology of an eighteen-year-old, I'd hardly be qualified for this job. But to answer your question, yes, I know why she's doing it. And I can't give her what she wants."

"Is that why you allowed her to go ahead?" Sennosuke's shoulders sagged with sudden resignation. "Is this your way of trying to please her?"

Kiichiro was silent for a moment.

"I didn't expect the project to snowball the way it has. That was my error. But errors can be corrected. It's not too late to terminate the project. Once people begin living on the moon it will be impossible to pull the plug. Do we hemorrhage red ink and become an object of derision? Or worse, do we wait for some poor guest to lose his life and become a target of criticism? It's all too easy to see where this is heading."

"I didn't raise you to be so pessimistic. You've changed, but I saw it too late. Is it because of Shizu?"

Kiichiro whirled on him. "Shizu has nothing to do with it. That was an accident."

"So I understand. But it would be natural for you to feel responsible. She didn't have to be behind the wheel of that car."

"The dead do not assign blame. Nor do they forgive. Second thoughts are wasted thoughts. Please leave ancient history out of this, Mr. Chairman."

"Stop calling me that. I'm your father." Sennosuke was suddenly stern. "You said mistakes can be corrected. Give Tae the benefit of your experience. Sixth Continent is sure to be a roaring success. It will be a vehicle for her dreams and a hope for millions around the world. That's the kind of future you should be pursuing."

"We're talking past each other," said Kiichiro at length. He shook his head. "ELE's future is in my hands. I acknowledge your viewpoint. That is all, Mr. Chairman."

"Kiichiro…what she really wants—"

"Father." He raised a hand in warning and looked down at Sennosuke. The old man glowered at him.

"I take it back. Don't call me that again."

"I won't." Kiichiro nodded toward the exit. Sennosuke got up and strode out angrily. His son watched the door close, still impassive. He shrugged his shoulders lightly and touched the speed dial on his wearcom. His secretary answered.

"It's me. From now on, when the chairman visits, alert me before you admit him."

"Certainly, sir. Shall I issue him an ID card?"

"That won't be necessary. But things have changed. I'll need time to compose myself before seeing him."

"I see." The secretary needed no further explanation. "We're running short on time. You have a first-class seat on the maglev for tonight's dinner in Tokyo. I'm concerned about the traffic in Shinkiba. Shall we take the helicopter?"

"No. Let's stay with the maglev. I have some homework to do on the way there."

"How can I help?"

"I need a report on Sixth Continent's risk management from Central Planning. A summary of any factors that could negatively impact the project. Human, financial, technical, political, and anything else. There must still be someone in the division at this hour."

"Just a moment." There was silence for perhaps twenty seconds. "Yes, they can prepare a summary. The file will be ready in thirty-five minutes."

"Use level three—no, level four encryption. Passwords for the two of us only."

"Understood."

"Shall we be off then?"

Before he left his office, Kiichiro looked out the window. High above the setting sun was a sliver of moon. He stared at it intently.

The moon is too far. It's beyond the average person's reach. Perhaps in dreams...No. Father is wrong. The moon is no escape from reality. It's a harsh and unforgiving wasteland. Our future is here. On Earth.

He turned his back on the dying light and left the office.

THE IMPERIAL HOTEL, Tokyo.

A guard in a dark green military uniform was blocking the corridor. His insignia identified him as a member of the People's Liberation Army, Second Artillery Corps. Two men in suits stood in front of him, taking turns protesting, trying to gain admittance to the room he blocked. A few steps down the corridor, a middle-aged woman in a tailored suit was waiting with an irritated look.

One of the men waved a watermarked document in the soldier's face and whined, "Don't you understand? This is Tomoé Hayasaka, a member of the House of Representatives. We are her secretaries. She's a public figure. This document confirms your government's approval for this meeting. Please show us in immediately."

"I have no information on anyone named Hayasaka. Therefore, the National Heroes will not see her." The soldier shook his head obstinately. The other secretary started shouting.

"What's going on here? You'd better explain yourself!"

"The National Heroes are tired. My orders are to admit no one."

"Tired? Ms. Hayasaka went to great lengths to make these arrangements. At least let them know she's here!"

"Excuse me." A new voice. They turned to see a young man in an ill-fitting blue suit. One of the secretaries glared skeptically.

"Who are you? This is the Imperial Floor. Did you get on the wrong elevator?"

"I don't think so. Isn't this where Jinqing Jiang and Penghui Cui are staying? The Chinese astronauts? I'm here to see them."

"You? Go home. Ms. Hayasaka has an appointment."

"I see." The young man seemed surprised. He took a small object out of his pocket and held it out to the soldier.

"Could you just show them this? Ask them to call me later when they have a chance."

The object resembled a blue passport folder. The three visitors smiled condescendingly. Obviously this young man, whoever he thought he was, would get little satisfaction from the pigheaded soldier. But the soldier took one look at the folder and disappeared into the room behind him.

Moments later the door opened. Another young man, wearing a polo shirt, stepped into the corridor. The politician and her secretaries listened to the ensuing exchange, conducted in English, in disbelief.

"I was hoping you'd come! It's been five years. How've you been?"

"Just fine, Jiang. I'm glad you remember me," said Sohya.

"How could I forget a fellow astronaut? Here, this belongs to you." Jiang handed him the folder, and they shook hands warmly. The two secretaries stood dumbfounded.

"Who are you?" said one. "And what was that?"

"Oh, just an astronaut's notebook. Standard CNSA issue," said

Sohya with studied nonchalance. He turned back to Jiang. "Can you spare some time? Though I think these people are ahead of me."

"No, no problem. Let's—no, let's not go into the room. How about a walk outside? Show me a bit of Tokyo."

"Sure. I know just the place." They turned to leave, but the secretaries and the soldier blocked their path.

"Please wait, Mr. Jiang. Ms. Hayasaka has been waiting to see you."

"National Hero Jiang, it's dangerous for you to go out alone!"

Jiang smiled and said impishly, "My colleague is in the room. Why don't you negotiate with him? I'm in good hands with Aomine. He helped us deal with the meteor strike at Kunlun Base."

"He was there?" marveled the soldier.

"Yes. So I don't need an escort." The two young men headed for the elevator, leaving behind four people who looked as if they'd been bewitched.

———◦•◦•◦———

THE COMMUTER CRUSH thinned once the two men emerged from Ueno Station. Jiang sighed with relief. "So this is Tokyo rush hour. Maybe we shouldn't have gone out."

"Since you're a National Hero, you must be used to limos."

"No, that's worse. Imagine being stuck in traffic with Cui."

They laughed and waited for the light to change at the crossing to Ueno Park. Sohya looked off in the direction of the Imperial Palace. "Maybe I should've invited him."

"He wouldn't have come. You saw what happened five years ago."

"Is he still upset about having to stay the extra year?"

"You must be joking. When he got home he was a celebrity—the record holder for longest stay on the moon. He'd be embarrassed to be around you, that's all. So he didn't come."

"Then how did he feel about whatsername coming just to see him?"

"I doubt he was pleased." Jiang frowned. "I know what she's after. She's a member of that faction in your—what do you call it, House of Representatives? The group that's pushing space development."

"In that case, I would think they'd get along," said Sohya.

"Different agenda. For politicians it's just self-interest. A Japanese entrepreneur starts Sixth Continent and becomes an international celebrity. Politicians sit up and take notice. Space development gets them votes. But Sixth Continent isn't a government project. They can't take credit for it. So they cozy up to our astronauts. It gives them a few names to drop afterward."

"Is that what was happening? I guess I didn't do Cui much of a favor then." Sohya laughed briefly and looked at Jiang with admiration. "You see through everything, don't you?"

"It's not the first time this has happened. We're here for the Asian Space Agencies Conference, but we've already been dragged to all these different conferences and symposiums in different countries. There are always people with impressive titles who want to make contact. I don't like to be suspicious, but it gets to where you can't help it."

"Is that why you have a guard?"

"For that, and for reactionaries opposed to space development who might want to stir up trouble. But mostly it's to keep an eye on us. Did you see the insignia? Second Artillery Corps. They control our strategic missiles. They're worried we've gotten too Westernized and liberal from attending all these overseas forums. We might spill some of their secrets."

Jiang looked intently at Sohya. "Thanks to that guard, we haven't been able to see anything of Tokyo. I'm actually glad I got a chance to ride on a rush hour commuter train," he said.

Sohya laughed.

They emerged onto the tree-lined avenue leading to the National Museum of Western Art. A stone building, a bit like a miniature parliament, came into view. The building itself was unremarkable but flanked by two strange objects: a life-size model of a blue whale and a rocket perched on an orange launch rail. Sohya stopped in front of the rocket and motioned toward the building.

"This is the National Museum of Nature and Science. I thought you'd rather see this than a movie."

"A museum, huh? It's much smaller than the Palace Museum."

"Give me a break. Your population is twelve times larger than ours. I know you're proud of China, but reserve your judgment till you've seen it."

"Now that I think of it, the Palace Museum doesn't have a blue whale."

They sat down on the lawn in front of the rocket and stretched out on their backs, almost in unspoken unison.

"Well, no one will overhear us here. So what is it you want, Aomine?"

"Sorry. This wasn't just for old time's sake."

"Sixth Continent, right?" Jiang looked over at him. "We get the news in China too. You're one of the key people. And you need help, so you came to me. Am I getting warm?"

"Okay." Sohya held up his hands. He watched the families passing on the tree-lined drive as the breeze sent leaves spinning through the dusk.

"I'll get right to the point," he said. "We need Xiwangmu."

"Ah, yes. The world's finest lunar habitat module."

"How much do you know about Sixth Continent's construction plans?"

"Just what I see on the website," said Jiang, noncommittal.

"We'll be building with concrete. Until the main structures are in place, we'll need temporary quarters for people on-site. We need a solution." Sohya looked up at the rocket behind him. "Japan started launching pencil rockets after World War II. We worked hard to develop our space technology. That's a Lambda, the first Japanese launch vehicle to put a satellite in orbit. One hundred percent Made in Nippon. Later we borrowed some American technology, but today our rockets are completely homegrown."

"The rockets."

"Yes. Only the rockets." Sohya nodded. "Our manned space-craft technology is way behind. Developing a spacecraft has monopolized our resources. We haven't been able to keep the Phase Two habitats on schedule. On paper our plans for construction look foolproof, but once we start building we can't predict what problems we might run into. The Xiwangmu design is proven. We could learn a lot from it."

"Why don't you ask the Americans for help?"

"We owe them too much already."

"For what?"

"Our space tug is a modified Titan X second stage. We're hoping to start trial runs next spring. We plan to have it in service the year after that. The Americans are building up there too, you know. We can't afford to put ourselves any deeper in their debt."

Jiang chuckled. "What about the Russians? They have more experience building habitat modules than we do. Xiwangmu is just an extension of the Mir design."

"Russia is participating in ISS. They'll have their hands full as long as the station is operating. And they're in no position to irritate the U.S. by helping us."

"I see what you mean." Jiang folded his arms across his chest.

"Not only that, Xiwangmu is the only module we have any direct experience with. We need it. It's versatile. We think it would answer our requirements."

"You've got me cornered." Jiang shook his head wryly and glanced at Sohya. "Tell me something. If I wasn't a National Hero, would you still have come to see me?"

"What do you mean? Of course." Sohya smiled broadly. "I came to see you as a friend I met on a long journey. I'd be happy to show you all over Japan, not just to a museum."

"Okay." Jiang's eyes narrowed. He nodded several times. "Okay. I'll talk to the CNSA administrator. Would that do it?"

"That would be great. Our senior people are already talking to the National Space Subcommittee, but we could use some covering fire from a local source."

"Well, for the first time I'm glad they made me a National Hero."

Sohya clapped his shoulder in gratitude. "When do you think we could get them? You'd need six months or a year to build one, right? Do you think you could supply them in 2032, when we get the space tug into service?"

"If things go smoothly you can have them next month."

"No way!"

Jiang shrugged. "There are at least two units at China Great Wall Industry Corporation in Szechuan. We were going to use them to expand Kunlun Base. They were about a month away from launching on a Long March rocket. Then everything was frozen."

"What happened, anyway?"

"Budget problems. We'll reactivate the base eventually. The habitat modules were sealed and put in storage for when the time comes."

"When will that be?"

"I don't know. More than ten years, I'd guess. Maybe twenty or thirty. Not until nuclear fusion technology is ready."

"Nuclear fusion? Are you going to mine helium-3?"

"Yes." Jiang nodded confidently. "Kunlun's ultimate purpose was to mine helium-3 for pollution-free power generation. We finished the base, but fusion technology is far behind. Still, all we have to do is wait. Once the technology is perfected, we'll be in a good position to supply the fuel. We can mine enough helium-3 to supply Earth with power for a millennium. It's worth waiting thirty years. No need to get impatient."

"You're making our wedding palace sound like a kid's toy."

"Why not? It definitely sounds like fun." Jiang laughed. "If you can put those modules to use now, I don't see a problem. It'll be an investment. Maybe we can barter for access to your SETI data."

"SETI…That's not Sixth Continent's main purpose, though." Sohya was evasive. Jiang looked at him in surprise.

"Really? We were all excited when we heard about it. It's a brilliant idea."

"Brilliant? I wonder."

"Of course it is. Fusion may take thirty years, but meeting people from another star might be a century away. Pretty impressive to be planning that far into the future."

"All right. We'll share any SETI data we come up with on a preferential basis. This is Ms. Toenji's decision to make, but I can speak for her."

"Tae, that's right. How's she doing?" Jiang looked suddenly nostalgic.

"She's eighteen. Just as strong willed as ever. She's got all three partners wrapped around her finger."

"I can see why. I'd like to see her again."

"Unfortunately she's overseas right now. South Africa."

"Really? Too bad." Jiang looked up at the sky and sighed. Sohya got to his feet.

"Well, that's it. Maybe we better be getting back. Your guard will be worried."

"Don't be a party pooper. He can wait," said Jiang as he stood up. Sohya started back toward the station, but Jiang stopped him. "Hold it a minute, okay? Let's walk around the park first. This is Ueno, right? There's something I want to see—that statue of Saigo, the general who stirred up a rebellion against the government. If people tried to put up a statue of someone like that in China, the government would come and knock it down. I'd really like to see it."

"If you say so. But it's just him and a dog. Don't expect something grand, like one of those statues of Guan Yu. Actually, there's someone I'd like you to meet. His name is Tai. He's with TGT. I think you two would hit it off."

"Sure. Let's save it for later. First, let's go see Saigo!"

The men walked away through the autumn leaves like two old school chums deep in conversation.

———◆◆◆◆———

TAE SIGHED AND tossed the résumé back on the pile in front of her. She was sitting in a window seat on a South African Air Force Falcon SST transport plane. Reika, in the adjacent seat, plucked the folder from the pile and gazed at it sadly.

"Not even a chef from Le Grand Vefour?"

"He's not right."

"His restaurant has three Michelin stars."

"I don't care whether he's from Vefour or La Tour d'Argent. He's not right."

"I see. What about the others?"

"No one seems right for the job." Tae stared out the window. Reika reluctantly tidied the pile of folders and began perusing them again. Any gourmet would have been staggered by this collection of topflight résumés from famous restaurants in Paris, Milan, Beijing, and Tokyo.

These were the gleanings of Sixth Continent's global search for a head chef. Over three hundred professionals had responded to Tae's call for candidates to head the first "off-world restaurant." Famous establishments had even offered to open a branch on the moon. Yet for Tae, none of them were right. Reika was beginning to lose patience.

"I think we're wasting an opportunity here. If it were me, I'd be bowing in gratitude to these people just for applying."

"But we only need one." Tae looked out the window again at the featureless white landscape below. "The number of people the base can support is fixed. A wedding palace needs a big staff as it is, and we don't have room for two or three chefs. Someone who's an expert in just French or Chinese cuisine won't work. I want one person who can do it all. Someone versatile."

"I'd think a three-star chef could manage any kind of cuisine."

"First-rate chefs are sensitive and proud. They wouldn't tolerate the living conditions on the moon. They'd lose their edge. You're cooped up. Entertainment is limited. You're far away from home, and the culinary challenge is enormous…"

Reika had nothing to say. Tae had been there.

"We need someone tougher. Someone with all-around skills who can manage anywhere. Someone with the ability to keep surprising our guests."

"Is that why we came all the way here?" Reika leaned over and looked out the window. Below, Antarctica's Enderby Land was a single, glistening blue-white expanse.

The two women looked down on the snowfield—pure, without a single stone, much less any human presence. Reika was doubtful. "Is there really a chef down there?"

"Yes. I just hope he's surviving in this environment."

Tae had gone straight to the president of South Africa for a seat on the Falcon. The transport began to descend. It landed on a strip cut into the fantastically shaped snow ridges carved by the constant wind.

A parched, freezing blast struck their faces as the door opened. The pilot stayed in the cockpit. Hooded and swathed in heavy winter gear, Tae and Reika walked down the steps to find seven flimsy-looking, one-story prefab buildings, surrounded by several snowmobiles and thousands of supply containers. A sign stood just off the runway.

DOME FUJI

They were a thousand kilometers and three weeks by snowmobile from the Indian Ocean coast. Japan was carrying out its Deep Ice Coring project here.

Reika looked round at the unchanging colors from zenith to horizon—a bowl of blue sky over a blue-white ice sheet—

and said to Tae, "A top-class chef? In this place?"

"I'm telling you, he's here. See—here they come." She pointed. People were coming out of the buildings wearing bulky parkas that hid their shape and size. Everyone wore goggles. The only exposed skin was their cheeks, reddened by the wind or browned by the sun. Except for the location, they could just as easily have been Inuits.

A knot of six base members approached. One motioned for the others to stop and approached Reika and Tae alone. He stopped in front of Tae and peeled off his goggles. His face, covered with stubble and far from clean, was rough-hewn and weathered. His eyes widened in surprise.

"Are you the mogul with weird ideas who wanted to meet me?"

"I am indeed. Tae Toenji. And you would be Yoshihisa Kashiwabara?" So saying, Tae pulled back her hood. Her long black hair streamed out in the wind.

There was instant pandemonium. The group that had been hanging back gave a shout and rushed forward. They surrounded the two women and began babbling excitedly.

"It's really her! It's Tae Toenji!"

"You're eighteen, right? Out of high school yet?"

"Hey, this one's female too. She's good-looking!"

Reika shrank back. Tae looked wide eyed at the men.

"Welcome to Dome Fuji! C'mon, let's go inside!" The men crowded closer and began tugging at the women. Suddenly Kashiwabara pulled a kitchen cleaver from his parka. He held the flashing blade out menacingly.

"Back off and shut up! They're just ordinary people!" His colleagues seemed to come to their senses and fell silent. "What are you, teenagers?" Kashiwabara was furious. "You call yourselves scientists! What's gotten into you, Chief? You're as bad as the rest of them!"

"Um, sorry about that." The base chief, burnt darker than the others, turned out to be a woman in her forties. A ponytail fell to one side as she removed her hood. "Haven't seen a young person in I don't know how long. Guess I'm letting myself get carried away. But she sure is cute."

"Step aside," growled Kashiwabara. "These people are my guests." He put the cleaver away and bowed apologetically. "You'll have to excuse them. We almost never have visitors. Most of the year we're stuck in a freezing cellar staring at the same ugly faces day in and day out. After a while you forget how to act." He laughed. "Don't worry, I'm not crazy. I've fed this mob without a single case of food poisoning—not that anything's going to spoil in this climate."

Tae whispered to Reika, "See? It's him."

"But he looks like a barbarian." Reika shook her head, but Tae turned to the chef.

"Mr. Kashiwabara, I have a proposal for you. But first, I wonder if I could make a request."

"What?"

"I'd like to taste your cooking." Tae smiled playfully.

Kashiwabara took a step closer and squinted at her, puzzled.

"All we have is pouch food and freeze-dried."

"Yes, I know. I also know what a great chef you are. You're ex-Ichinose, right? The restaurant in Shimonoseki."

He grunted, "You know about that, huh? If that's why you came all the way to this godforsaken place, then we'd better get on with it. I'll give you a meal you won't forget."

Reika still looked doubtful. Tae grabbed her arm and started off after him.

＊＊＊＊＊

EVEN AFTER THE Falcon transport reached cruising altitude, Reika kept her palms against her reddened cheeks. "That was unbelievable. Everything started out frozen, but I've never had better sushi."

"Ichinose is a fugu restaurant. One slip of the knife and some-one could die of poisoning. Of course he's good. With skills like that he can do anything from French to Indian."

"But why is he in Antarctica?"

"Because he's good." Tae began tapping at her pendant wearcom. She seemed pleased. "When you live with the same people in a closed environment for a long time, it's stressful. People get on each other's nerves. That's how it was at Kun-lun. The same thing happened at Biosphere 2 in the 1990s. It happens on submarines and ships at sea. The best way to deal with it is with delicious food. Kashiwabara was chosen for Dome Fuji because of his culinary skills. He's there to help people get along."

"That makes sense," said Reika. "But why him? Why not some other chef?"

"You saw how he stopped the others from bothering us. He's fearless." Tae glanced at the pile of résumés. "Not many chefs would've been as bold as that. He has the patience to work exclu-sively with frozen and preserved foods. He creates meals no one can fault. He has the imagination to develop a culinary repertoire out of a limited range of ingredients. Don't you think those skills would be very useful for a base on the moon?"

Reika nodded. So this was what Tae had been seeking. The man had attributes one wouldn't expect to find in a chef from a top city restaurant.

"Now I understand. It's like he's already in training for Sixth Continent."

Tae nodded and looked at her wearcom. The display showed a template for a list of names, but at the moment it was empty.

It was a staffing list for Sixth Continent. The Bridal Depart-ment required a head chef, a sous chef, three banquet servers, a minister, a beautician, and a photographer: eight staff to con-duct the weddings and serve at the banquet.

Sending eight people to the moon would cost more than

a billion yen, but this was the minimum feasible number of staff. In fact, it really wasn't enough. To service a wedding on Earth with eighty guests would require at least twenty kitchen staff just for the banquet. Add a host, attendants for each set of in-laws, a train bearer, a drink server, four food servers, a manager and an assistant, and perhaps six people to act as receptionists and in backup roles. That meant something like forty staff members.

Weddings at Sixth Continent would have twenty guests, including the bride and groom. Much of the food preparation would be standardized. Still, eight staff was the bare minimum. The same people would also have to serve in hotel and housekeeping roles. They would be extremely busy.

But Sixth Continent would require more than just a bridal crew. Keeping the base functioning would require specialists in multiple disciplines—building and machine maintenance, hospitality, medicine, transport, communications, climate control, electric power. These specialists would be on call 24/7, so backup would be a must. Tae was planning for seventeen nonwedding staff.

The base would have a total of twenty-five staff. Add twenty wedding guests, a pilot, and four backup staff, and the base's occupancy would be maxed out.

Sixth Continent would be a specialized environment without precedent. Problems were inevitable. Each staff member had to be a trained professional—not only as a member of a lunar base but in terms of customer service. Visitors would be paying a fortune to make the journey. Justifying the fee based on hardware and transport costs alone would not be acceptable. Tae's guests would expect to be pampered.

Even with the right staff, intensive training would be needed before the facility was launched. Pulling this all together was Tae's job.

"This just keeps getting bigger..." she whispered.

In the beginning, it had been just her and her grandfather.

Since then it had grown far beyond that—Sohya, then Takumichi Gotoba, Ryuichi Yaenami, and the employees of three companies; people throughout Japan, throughout the world, had extended a hand to help. By now the number had grown too large to count.

None of these people were the kind of friends who would call her as she lay awake at night, unable to sleep. Even Sohya was different. But on some basic level, relationships with all these individuals brought Tae satisfaction. Being the driving force behind large numbers of people building a huge pyramid—this brought her pleasure. It helped ease her loneliness.

"Do your best, everyone."

She smiled and input the first name to her list.

"DR. TAI, WAKE up. Dr. Tai!"

Shinji was curled up on a sofa under a thin blanket. Someone was shaking his shoulder. He opened his eyes, groped around and found his glasses. He sat up and shivered.

"It's chilly in here."

"It's getting to where one blanket isn't enough. Look there."

The controller threw back the curtains. Shinji squinted against the sunlight flooding the Gotenba Ground Support staff lounge.

"First snow of the year, they say."

Mount Fuji loomed above them in the thin blue of sunrise. The volcano's summit was dusted with a crown of white that had not been there the day before.

Sixth Continent's Gotenba Ground Support complex, an expansion of the Multidozer Command Center, had started operating the previous summer. In the early years of the project, spacecraft tracking had been handled by TGT's Tsukuba Space Center, but eventually they would have to track multiple spacecraft in addition to supporting Sixth Continent itself. Tsukuba clearly would not be able to cope with all that traffic. GGS would be responsible for ground-based tracking and serve as Earth's link with the base.

Shinji rarely had a chance to return home. He was too busy shuttling between GGS and TGT headquarters in Nagoya. He swung his feet to the floor and put his arms through the sleeves of the lab coat he wore every day. He looked again at Fuji with its cap of snow.

"Did you get me up to show me this?"

"Of course not. Actually, there's good news and bad news. What do you want to hear first?"

"Give me the bad news. I always eat the stuff I don't like first."

"Dozer 6 is down. It's not responding to commands."

"Uh-oh. Let's get to the control room."

"Wait, we should wake up the others too."

"Let them sleep. The dozer isn't going anywhere."

There were half a dozen staff sacked out in the lounge. Shinji hushed the young controller and guided him into the corridor.

The center was quiet at this hour. Once the base was manned, these halls would be humming round the clock, but for now there were few personnel. The men's steps echoed as they traversed the long corridor.

"Dozer 6…That's the unit laying cable from the far side of the crater."

"Right, Dr. Tai. That will give us nearside power throughout the sun cycle."

"So what's the good news?"

"We connected the cable to the farside array before we lost the signal. It happened when number 6 was on its way back through the crater."

"Interesting."

The three controllers on watch at their monitors looked up as Shinji walked into the room. Nothing critical was in progress, so younger technicians from TGT and Gotoba were manning the stations. These three did not yet have much experience. They seemed relieved to see Shinji.

"Sorry to roust you out so early, Dr. Tai. We thought about contacting Tsukuba, but we weren't sure if this was important enough to disturb the flight director."

"When you're not sure, that's the time to contact the most senior person you can. But let me take a look. What's the problem?"

Shinji was a materials specialist, not an aerospace engineer, but his invention of TROPHY had made his genius widely known. One of the young controllers began explaining the problem.

"Dozer 6 didn't send an emergency signal. If its power cable had broken, it should still be responding with power from its fuel cell. One minute the signal was there, the next it was just gone."

"What about frequency displacement?"

"Frequency displacement?" The controllers looked at each other, caught off guard.

"The transmitter is potted in a block of acrylic. You could drop a dump truck on it and it wouldn't stop working," said one of the controllers.

"Yes, but what about temperature? If the chips are subjected to a drastic ambient temperature change, the transmission frequency could shift. It's 220 below in the shadow zone." Shinji looked around at the blank faces staring back at him. "You didn't think of that, did you? Try a recovery based on that assumption. The signals go through a repeater at the top of the nearside crater rim. Try tuning the repeater to find the dozer."

Somewhat doubtfully, the controllers began varying the repeater frequency. After a few minutes one of them shouted, "Got it! There's number 6's status signal!"

"Great," said Shinji. "How's it doing?"

"Green straight across. The AI's already guiding it to the near side."

"Then it didn't even need your help, did it?"

The controllers sighed with relief. "Sorry," one of them said to Shinji, looking apologetic. "This was such a minor problem. But how did you figure it out so quickly? This isn't your specialty."

"NASA ran into the same thing with Mars Pathfinder. It's not so unusual—hold on. Maybe there is a bigger problem." Shinji scratched his head. "The dozers are designed for that kind of environment. A transmission issue must mean the insulating shield is damaged."

"What can we do about it?"

"Not much. Dozer 6's generation doesn't have sensors to pinpoint an insulation breach. The only thing you can do is keep that dozer out of the shadow zone. The temperature outside the crater's only fifty below."

The controllers exchanged nervous glances, as if they expected to be held responsible for the damage.

"I wouldn't get too concerned," said Shinji philosophically. "We assumed we'd lose one or two machines during Phase One. Phase Two will start in plenty of time to get people on scene. Then we can do all the repairs we need." Shinji smiled. "Listen, why don't we get some breakfast? It's on me."

The controllers looked sheepish as Shinji touched the commissary's extension. "You got the farside array hooked up. Now we can operate throughout the month. Let's celebrate. Hello? Yes, can we get steak and eggs in the control room? For five. Yes, charge it to me."

In a few minutes, the room was filled with the aroma of hot coffee and Kobe beef. Shinji distributed the plates himself—the controllers had been up all night.

"We've got at least five years ahead of us. We should celebrate every little milestone."

We've got a long way to go, he thought as he poured himself some coffee. There were a huge number of challenges to meet before Phase One would be complete.

More solar panels to install. GPS satellites to put into lunar orbit for more precise positioning. Further spacecraft development and testing, including translunar injection, landing, and return to Earth. Electrolysis of water from permafrost. Generation, liquefaction, and storage of hydrogen and oxygen for rocket fuel. Space suit development and delivery of temporary habitats. Only after these hurdles were cleared could people begin living and working on the moon—the start of Phase Two.

That was not all. The Turtle landing "trucks" would have to return to lunar orbit using fuel synthesized on the surface, where orbital refueling drills would be run with the Titan X tugboat. Add experimental concrete production using a solar-powered kiln…

There was so much to do that parts of the project were already behind schedule. Phase One had been scheduled for completion by the end of next year—2031—but problems with the development of *Apple* had delayed them by six months. Phase Two now looked likely to begin in the spring of 2032.

Shinji sipped black coffee. The largely empty control room was filled with the sounds of quiet conversation. *Now it really begins. We'll have to make sure there are no more delays. I'll practically be living here.*

He was looking forward to it. Once Phase Two was on track, the lunar tug was operating, and people were traveling to the moon, Ryuichi would deliver on his promise: Shinji would be going into space too.

Eighteen months to go. For now, Shinji relaxed into the peace that surrounded him.

———◆◆◆———

MOUNT FUJI RECEIVED another dusting of snow. It melted, leaving the dark slopes naked again. At night, like a dragon, a procession of lanterns—climbers making the ascent to greet the rising sun—zigzagged up the mountain's massive bulk. Snow fell again. On the plain below the mountain, small white shapes moved to and fro. Dozers evolved and were shipped out, and the next generation evolved further. Tilt-rotors came and went from dawn till dusk. GGS had countless visitors. Some stayed for weeks.

Snow closed the trail up Mount Fuji; no lanterns snaked around the mountain. Spring came to the volcano, and the stream of visitors swelled to a flood. Huge satellite trucks topped with parabolic antennas stood in rows outside the Ground Support complex. Broadcast engineers scanned the skies outside their uplink trailers. The energy was palpable, like a high summer festival out of season.

May 2032. Japan's first manned spacecraft, *Apple 7*, was about to blast off for the moon.

The focus of attention for the media camped at GGS was a young man and a younger woman. This was history in the making—the first humans to pay a second visit to the moon.

The disheveled engineer who would ride into space with them attracted hardly any notice.

[2]

"IS THERE A problem?"

Tae blinked anxiously. She floated across the capsule to the pilot, who was staring bleakly at the environmental control panel. He nodded.

"The habitat module's CO_2 scrubber isn't functioning properly. The absorption filter might be partly blocked."

"Does this mean we can't go to the moon?" Tae paused, then rephrased her question. "Are we going to survive?"

"We'll be okay for at least a day or two. But even with the filter running flat out, we're generating more CO_2 than the scrubber can handle. Eventually it's going to get hard to breathe."

"Can you calculate when that will be?"

"I already have. The problem isn't so much the amount of time as the number of people aboard. With six people, the CO_2 will rise. Five or fewer, and we can probably maintain safe levels."

"So we do have a problem."

Three other passengers in the habitat module—Sohya and two engineers from Gotoba—looked worried. The sixth passenger, seated near a window, seemed remarkably unconcerned. "What's the problem? All we have to do is skip every sixth breath."

"Shinji…" Sohya floated over and gave him a playful slug in the arm. "This is no time for joking. You're having too much fun!"

Shinji looked up sheepishly. "Sorry, I'm kind of giddy right now. First time in space." He consulted his wearcom. "Let's think this through rationally. We've got three more hours to TLI. Either we fix the problem or we head back to Earth. There's no reason to panic. Gotenba's working on it as we speak."

Shinji's casual manner seemed to defuse the tension. *I'm glad we brought him along*, thought Sohya. They were orbiting at the same altitude Ryuichi had reached in *Apple 3*. But this mission was going all the way to the moon.

Like *Apple 3*, *Apple 7* included the four-meter diameter habitat module and the conical core module with its heat shield for reentry. Beneath the core was the descent module, resembling an insect with three landing struts. This module would take the core to the surface and, with its small engine, return it to lunar orbit.

The stack was perched atop the second stage of Eve XVIII, which would carry out the translunar injection burn. In a few hours, another Eve would launch with the return module. With a rocket engine, fuel, and life-support supplies, the return module would make its own way to the moon, where it would wait in orbit to dock with the core and take it back to Earth.

Something else would travel with them to the moon: Xiwangmu 6. With support from Jiang, TGT had convinced the Chinese government to sell the module. A week earlier, an Adam rocket had carried it into space. Now it was orbiting Earth, still attached to Adam's second stage, waiting for the signal to head for the moon.

Xiwangmu 6 could accommodate three crew members. The manned phase of Sixth Continent would begin by landing the habitat module on the moon. For Sohya and his two Gotoba colleagues, this was the beginning of a journey that was scheduled to last three months.

———◦·◦∗◦·◦———

WITH PUBLIC ATTENTION riveted on the ambitious mission, having a CO_2 scrubber fail first thing out of the gate was poor timing. The pilot, Toshiyuki Yamagiwa, and GGS examined and rejected a number of possible solutions to the problem.

Flight Director Hibiki, surrounded by his controllers, murmured, "How did we end up with the same problem as *Apollo 13*?"

Apollo 13 had suffered an oxygen tank explosion on the way to the moon and was forced to return without landing. During the struggle to survive in their crippled spacecraft, the astronauts had faced a series of problems. One was limited scrubber capacity, a problem they'd solved by modifying scrubbers from the command module and installing them in the lunar module, which was used as a "lifeboat" to bring the crew home.

"We're going to get slammed for not learning from experience," one of Hibiki's controllers said with a pained look.

"This isn't quite the same scenario," said Hibiki. "There's nothing wrong with the scrubber. Something's keeping it from doing its job."

The controller went back to his monitor. He suddenly groaned. "One of Gotoba's crew says he missed a handkerchief just after launch. I bet it's lodged in the scrubber intake."

"A handkerchief?" Hibiki was incredulous. "What are they doing letting stuff like that float around? It could go right into the filter!"

"Unfortunately, yes. The cabin airflow is designed to drive floating particles toward the scrubber intake—dust, hair, drops of perspiration. Stuff you don't want accumulating and interfering with breathing. A handkerchief is something else. They know passengers will play games in zero G, tossing small objects around. The intake is protected with a grille, but it obviously wasn't configured to stop a thin, deformable foreign object. That's going to have to be fixed."

"So why don't they just pull it out?"

"The air line snakes around the support ribs on the inner skin of the module. It's a single unit. Saves weight. They can't poke a rod down it, and they can't take it apart."

"Can't we detach the scrubber canister and hook it to an improvised air line, like they did on *Apollo 13*?"

"Not possible. *Apple*'s scrubbers use heat-regenerated metal-oxide sorbent material. No need for replenishment, but unfortunately it also means the canisters can't be swapped out without special tools, which of course they aren't carrying to save weight. Unintended consequences again."

"*Apollo 13* still applies," said Hibiki. "There's always the core scrubber."

"The core can only provide life support for six crew for twenty-four hours. That includes CO_2 scrubbing. But it's a week to the moon and back."

"All right, that's enough." Hibiki clapped his hands. The control room fell silent. "We're about out of time, people. We've got a decision to make. Getting the scrubber back up to full power is either going to be difficult or it's going to take a long time. The chances of getting that accomplished before TLI are pretty much zero. The only other option is to use the oxygen candles."

"But that will put us in Emergency Mode."

"That's what it's come to. We go to the candles, or we abort. Either way, we're not in a nominal operational posture." Hibiki turned to the Capsule Communications officer. "Tell *Apple* 7 it's their call."

Aboard *Apple* 7, the mood after Capcom delivered its message was grim.

"Emergency Mode…" Sohya shook his head.

"It's like a new ship springing a leak before it's out of the harbor," said Shinji.

"Well, I bet I know which option we'll choose," said Sohya. He looked at Tae. In a situation like this, the decision would be hers. "Use the candle and continue the mission, right? Aborting wouldn't be good for Sixth Continent's image."

"Well, yes," said Tae at length. "I'd like to avoid that if possible." She seemed to be pondering. "Whatever we do, we don't look good. Even if we continue, the world will hear we went to Emergency Mode. I'd prefer a third option."

"And that would be?"

"EVA to Xiwangmu 6."

There was a long silence. Yamagiwa stared at Tae in mild bafflement. He wasn't sure if she was joking or just foolhardy. "EVA isn't in the mission profile. If you want to advertise to the world that we're in trouble, that would probably be the best way to do it."

"On the contrary," said Tae. "We'd just be moving up the field testing of our Manna space suits. We were going to test them on the surface, but we should prove they're just as useful in zero G." Sixth Continent's Manna suits had not only been optimized for easy locomotion on the moon; they also looked chic, courtesy of the noted Italian designer Tae had recruited.

Yamagiwa frowned. "There's no air lock in this module. If one of us EVAs, we all have to suit up. There's no time for that."

"Exactly. So one of us goes into the core through the top hatch, seals it, puts their suit on, and exits by the side hatch. No one else has to suit up."

"But Xiwangmu is thousands of kilometers away."

"We do the EVA when we rendezvous for TLI. After that, whoever goes to Xiwangmu is just along for the ride. It's completely automated, no piloting skills required. I'll go if you want. There's a lot about Xiwangmu I don't like, but I'm sure I'll be comfortable with all that space." Tae smiled and pointed to the comm button. "Go ahead and ask Flight."

Yamagiwa looked skeptical but began contacting GGS. Tae saw Sohya's face. She frowned. "You think this is a bad idea."

"Sure do—it increases our risks without being absolutely necessary. The oxygen candle is safe and available, and everything else proceeds as planned. I can't see the point of an EVA."

"I'm telling you, it's not pointless. We trained for this in the neutral buoyancy pool. There'll be a tether too. It'll be easy."

"We've had one-twentieth of the training NASA astronauts get."

"Our suits are twenty times better. What do they call the outer shell, electroconformable? It's hard till you hit a switch, then gets really flexible. Way softer than those stiff Krechet M suits we used at Kunlun. I was so excited when we got them!"

Sohya was suspended from a handhold on the cabin wall. He leaned closer to Tae. "I've noticed something about you. Whenever you start talking like this, it means you're blowing smoke. You know this is dangerous, don't you? But it'll be good publicity, so to hell with the risks. How does that scan?"

Tae blinked several times, her optimistic expression frozen in place. It was a mask that betrayed no hint of what was going on behind it. Sohya knew he'd struck home.

He grinned. "I'm against it."

"What about the rest of you?" said Tae after a pause. "Wouldn't anyone like to be the first to EVA for Sixth Continent?"

The other passengers glanced at each other. The two engineers tentatively raised their hands.

"I say let's do it. I don't see it being any more risky than walking on the surface."

"I'd have to agree. I'm willing to go."

Yamagiwa was waiting for GGS to make a decision. He silently shook his head. Shinji raised his hand. "I'd like to go if you don't mind."

Sohya gaped in astonishment. "Shinji! Why?"

"It's what I came for. You do know why I'm here, don't you?" He smiled without a trace of irony. "Three for Xiwangmu on the surface. We know who they are. Tae is here for publicity, of course. The mission can't fly without its pilot. But me? I'm not doing anything special."

"Come on, Shinji—"

"No, I mean it. Okay, I'm supposed to be gathering TROPHY performance data. But the computer's doing it for me. I'm just warming the sixth seat. Hey, don't worry." He waved a restraining hand at Sohya. "I'm not complaining. I'm so happy I can barely sit still. This is my bonus from the boss for my work on TROPHY. Pretty soon I'll see what I came to see with my own eyes: Eve XIX, climbing to meet me." He winked at the other crew members. "Maybe I'll luck out, and she'll be coming up just about the time I'm out there. How's that for a ringside seat?"

The two engineers and Yamagiwa chuckled. There was something about Shinji one never quite got used to, something that made others want to help him.

Tae cocked her head slightly in thought. She nodded and touched Sohya's arm. "I think he's right. Don't you?"

Still, Sohya hesitated. "What does Ground Support say?"

"They're deliberating," said Yamagiwa. "No, wait a minute." Yamagiwa listened to his headphones. "They took it all the way to the top. Gotoba is neutral. Yaenami wants to go for it. Flight thinks it might be a viable option."

"That settles it," said Tae with a look of satisfaction.

"But—we'd have to go to TLI as soon as we make the rendezvous. They're calculating a new orbit that will let us rendezvous with Xiwangmu ahead of schedule. We're cleared for EVA, but only if we can rendezvous in time."

"Then let's get started," said Tae. "Shinji, you'd better get into your suit."

Shinji grinned and pushed off toward his locker. As he passed Sohya, he slapped him lightly on the back. "Don't worry. Tae's right."

"Look, Shinji…" For a split second, a look passed between the two men and Sohya understood. If Shinji hadn't volunteered, Tae probably would have gone, given the publicity potential. His self-effacing speech had prevented that without generating resistance. And if Tae was the first choice from a publicity angle, Sohya himself was number two. He and Tae were the media's chosen stars. Shinji had been concerned about his friend's safety as well.

"Pretty smooth," muttered Sohya.

"Wouldn't want you two to be separated," whispered Shinji.

He pulled his suit pack from the locker and gave Sohya and Tae a knowing wink. Sohya's jaw dropped in indignation. He started to speak, but Shinji waved him into silence. Then he disappeared through the narrow hatch into the core module.

———————

FOR ANY HOBBY you can name, there are people who go to extremes.

The spotter was middle-aged, and the bug had bitten him especially hard. Using the near-ubiquitous wireless Internet, he worked as a website designer from a dilapidated shepherd's hut in the Peruvian Andes. A telescope taller than he was stood in the center of the room. On clear nights he threw back the corrugated sheet metal that covered one side of the roof, eagerly scanning the heavens. He was a satellite spotter, dedicated enough to leave a home in the city to live year-round on this isolated mountaintop.

Night had already come to the Andes. As he worked at his computer, the spotter kept an eye on a live satellite feed from Gotenba Ground Support. The subcarrier channel at the bottom of the screen was datacasting mission-related information. He was anxious to get a glimpse of *Apple 7*; four times in the past week, he'd successfully identified Xiwangmu 6. Finding the Chinese module hadn't been particularly challenging given its size. But *Apple 7* would be much harder to identify, and the spotter had never tracked an object in this particular orbit, which would position the spacecraft for translunar injection. It was the kind of challenge he lived for.

The spotter glanced at the subchannel and froze. How many people were watching this obscure satellite feed at this precise moment—fewer than a hundred worldwide? He stared at the monitor, and he knew he hadn't imagined it: *Apple 7*'s orbital components were changing. The ship was altering course.

Work forgotten, he feverishly began collating the data. If his orientation was skewed, *Apple 7* might easily sail clean through his net.

The reason for the course change was quickly apparent: the rendezvous with Xiwangmu 6 had been moved up. But that meant he needed more data, because now there was something else to deal with: verification of the new orbit against that of other known objects. Over forty thousand objects large enough to spot, mostly space debris, were known to be orbiting Earth at various altitudes. If a large object turned up in an orbit similar to *Apple*'s, the spotter might end up tracking debris instead of the real thing.

The spotter loaded his translation software and patched the subchannel into his workstation for a closer look at the Japanese text streaming in from GGS. Sure enough, the Japanese were verifying the new orbit too. They had an even more urgent motivation. It would not do to have Japan's first moon mission collide with an errant piece of space junk.

The spotter said a silent thanks for the raw data coming in from GGS via the broadcaster's mobile earth station. It simplified his task considerably; all he had to do was consider the objects GGS was looking at. He was not surprised to see that several were expected to cross *Apple 7*'s path. The object that concerned him most was the size of a compact car, but GGS had already calculated the odds of a collision. The debris had a 0.002 percent chance of hitting *Apple 7*.

This made the spotter slightly uneasy. *Apple 7* had already shifted to its new orbit, so the dice had been rolled. Evidently the Japanese had decided the risk was acceptable. At odds of fifty thousand to one, a collision was not a realistic possibility.

What bothered the spotter were not the odds of collision. It was the possibility of a near miss. Fifty thousand to one was another way of saying the object would pass within a few kilometers of the six astronauts. At a distance of three hundred kilometers, with a short observation window, the spotter could easily become confused and miss his quarry.

Anxiously he began pulling information on the object's shape; that would give him an idea of its probable brightness. Brightness was the key to satellite spotting. His telescope was good, but even with the best amateur optics he could not make a visual identification based on shape alone. The objects were just too far away.

A moment later he was looking at the United States Space Command public website. The site included information on a variety of objects in earth orbit, from functioning satellites to satellites in mothballs or defunct, entire spent rocket stages, fuel tanks, and explosion and collision fragments. GGS would have the same data.

He punched up the object's profile. It was a Russian Cosmos satellite that had "broken up"—exploded—a year and a half earlier. The cause could have been anything from leftover fuel expanding into a gas and rupturing the tanks to a breached fuel cell. Whatever the reason, the satellite was now junk.

The spotter paused, something tugging at his memory. He knew this object. Before it had exploded, it had been well-known in the spotting community for its unusual brightness. Tracking it after it broke up with his thirty-five-centimeter reflector, he'd noticed that the central point of brightness was surrounded by a gaseous-looking halo of some sort, about the size of a full moon. This would be a cloud of smaller debris fragments, but it seemed strange that the fragments would stay close to the main body over several months instead of dispersing into different orbits.

Now he remembered. One night, with a group of friends—some of them dedicated comet watchers, others consumed by an interest in the planets—he'd spotted the object, and they'd all taken turns examining it, debating what the "cloud" might be. The most plausible theory pointed to a debris cloud embedded in splintered strands of some sort of plastic material, like the smashed remains of a wire-reinforced window. The satellite was almost certainly military, but the Russian Space Forces had issued no comment regarding its fate, so it continued to be a mystery.

This was not good news. If this object passed close to *Apple 7*, it would seriously complicate his observation.

Wait a minute… The spotter froze. *One-inch devils!*

Space debris are tracked by radar, which can't reliably detect objects less than ten centimeters across. Objects smaller than one centimeter would likely vaporize against a spacecraft's Whipple shield. Objects invisible to radar yet larger than one centimeter represented the biggest threat to spacecraft in low earth orbit. The only way to deal with them was to trust in luck and a prayer. If that debris cloud was thick with objects larger than one centimeter and less than ten…

A moment later the spotter was on his feet, lunging toward the ancient rotary-dial satellite phone on the wall of the hut.

———⟡———

"FLIGHT, YOU HAVE an outside call." The public affairs officer was responsible for liaison with the media concerning control room operations. Hibiki kept his eyes on his monitor.

"Busy."

"Apparently it's very important. 'Critical, urgent, life and death.'"

"What's that supposed to mean? Who is it?"

"I don't know. He had a thick accent, Spanish or maybe Portuguese. One of the satellite trucks put him through to us."

"You talk to him."

"Yes, sir." The officer took the call through his headset, struggling to get the voice recognition package in his wearcom calibrated to the man's excited stream of speech so it could be translated. As PAO, he was used to dealing with all types, and he made a polite effort to make appropriately sympathetic noises from time to time.

Suddenly he went pale. He tore off his headset and shouted, "Flight, he's saying Object 35665 is a collision risk!"

"We ran all the SOC numbers," said Hibiki, with barely a change of expression. "The crew is aware."

"He says the Standard Object Catalog is incomplete! Object 35665 is being followed by a cloud of debris with minimal radar signature!"

"What?" Hibiki turned to stare at the PAO, who was already rushing toward the Flight Dynamics station.

"That was a South American satellite spotter, an amateur. He says the object has a debris cloud that was never reported. The mission was classified. He swears it's trailing thousands of particles smaller than ten centimeters, held together by some kind of weblike structure. We've got to evade—immediately!"

"Get Roskosmos. I want to know everything about Object 35665. Capcom, tell the crew to suit up without delay. Hurry—closest approach in eighteen minutes."

A wave of quiet alarm spread through the control room. A minute later the GNC officer called out, "Flight! Object 35665 was a Russian Space Forces tethered satellite."

"A tethered pair?"

"A base and a subunit, originally linked with forty kilometers of carbon fiber cable. Eighteen months ago a fuel cell exploded, and one of the pair broke up. The explosion created a matrix of tangled fiber that trapped a certain amount of small debris. The Russians estimate the matrix contains around a thousand fragments, maximum five centimeters. This fits what the spotter says he observed."

"What's the diameter of this so-called matrix?"

The officer hesitated. "Apparently it's roughly spherical. Diameter is eight kilometers. Roskosmos estimates there are around a thousand debris pieces at least a centimeter across, but they can't say how many are bigger than that."

When Hibiki's next command came, his voice had a glacial calm, as if the temperature in the room had suddenly dropped.

"Tell Roskosmos we need an immediate orbital correction for 35665. If it's been in the same orbit for eighteen months, the subunit must've exploded. The base unit should still be responding to guidance commands."

"In that case, they would've deorbited it by now. Moscow says it isn't responding, but the attitude control system is still powered up and functioning. All they can do is wait for it to run out of fuel."

"Capcom, tell *Apple 7* to separate the core module from the stack and go to descent burn immediately."

"They can't, Flight. Dr. Tai's already opened the side hatch. He'd have to close it, repressurize, and get everyone into the core. That'd take half an hour."

"Tell him to fire the second stage manually. We can worry about the new orbit later. Anything's better than a collision."

"The ignition lock is engaged. The main engine can't be fired, even manually, for at least ten minutes after the hatch is closed. It's a safety feature to give the crew time to get into their flight couches and prepare for a burn."

"Override the safety system."

"That can only be done from the core control panel. Dr. Tai doesn't have the training—"

"DPS, explain the override procedure to him!"

The Data Processing systems engineer leapt over his console and sprinted over to Capcom. He began giving Shinji the override instructions, trying hard to keep the panic out of his voice.

The network officer called out, "Flight, TSC just confirmed backup request for Eve XIX."

Everyone froze. For the last few minutes, the fact that Eve XIX was on the pad and about to lift off had been driven from everyone's mind. GGS was responsible for all phases of flight except the launch itself, which was Tanegashima's primary responsibility.

"Shall we terminate the countdown?" asked the network officer. "This is no time to worry about putting the return module into orbit."

"Don't terminate," said Hibiki without hesitation. "Go to backup mode. Who knows, they might need an extra engine."

The controllers' faces tightened with anxiety. The flight director had just issued a prediction. *Apple 7* might find itself adrift. But if his assessment of the situation had just gotten worse, Hibiki showed no outward sign of it.

"Whoever's not on top of something right now should start making calls."

"To whom?" asked the PAO.

"Their next of kin." Hibiki swiveled in his chair and looked up at the bay window of the observation booth behind him. Sennosuke Toenji was standing with both palms pressed against the glass, staring wide-eyed at the mission screens.

YAMAGIWA AND SOHYA were both in their space suits, perspiring as they worked at the habitat module's control panel.

"Now we have to power off the attitude gyros," said Yamagiwa. "Can you do it?"

"Gyro off…no, the power's still on. The core won't hand off." Sohya was riffling through the operations manual with quiet desperation. Yamagiwa continued working the control panel, trying to use the module's small attitude thrusters to change the orbit, if only by a fraction. But Shinji was still struggling to manually override the main engine ignition lock. As long as he was preoccupied with that, the core would not relinquish control to the habitat module. Both men were at the limits of their patience.

"More unintended consequences. If this was *Apollo 13* we'd be able to improvise something," muttered Sohya.

"Apollo was a toggle switch jungle. If *Apple* hadn't consolidated everything in one panel, I probably wouldn't have qualified as pilot."

"All they had to do was give us a second control post. Now we're screwed!"

"Calm down," said Yamagiwa, putting a hand on Sohya's shoulder. "There's nothing we can do. Better do something about her though." He pointed to Tae, who was motionless next to one of the windows. She wasn't in her suit.

Sohya grabbed her floating suit pack and crossed over to her. "Come on, let's get this on you."

"…I don't want to."

"Feeling guilty?"

She stiffened. Sohya put a hand on her shoulder and turned her toward him.

"Get suited up—now!"

"But…"

"You can't help Shinji by exposing yourself to danger. What are you playing at?"

She glared at him, resentment smoldering deep in her eyes. Sohya said nothing but began assembling the suit around her—first the two halves of the torso shell, then the arm and leg tubes. He plugged in the power unit for the joints. For ease of movement, the joints were normally electroconformed to their wearer in a process that took a few minutes. There probably was no time for that, but the suit would still be pressurized. Tae angrily snatched the helmet from Sohya's hand and turned back to the window, as if searching for the invisible enemy stalking them.

"Put your helmet on," Sohya was about to say, but decided it would be pointless. He looked at Yamagiwa. "How much longer?"

"Six minutes, maybe a bit more. Dr. Tai, what's your status?"

Shinji was as nonchalant as ever. "Well, gentlemen, I'm afraid a manual system override and main engine burn at short notice is a bit beyond me. I don't want to make a mistake and send us straight into the Pacific."

"Shinji, don't give up! At least come back here!"

"I would if I wasn't in this suit. Can't fit through the top hatch, and there's not enough time to repressurize. I'm not giving up though. GGS just gave me another option, and it's a lot simpler."

"What is it?"

"Turn the stack end-on to the debris cloud. Use the second stage as a shield. There's no safety lock on the attitude thrusters, so I can do that right now. Here we go—better hold on to something."

The rest of the crew each took hold of a grip support. A few seconds later there was a jolt. White propellant gas from lateral thrusters at each end of the eighteen-meter-long stack began pushing in opposite directions. Eve's second-stage main engine moved until it was almost directly oriented toward the North Star. The thrusters continued firing in short bursts as *Apple 7* settled into its new attitude.

"I'm venting the second-stage tanks now in case they get hit. We won't be able to go to the moon, but that's all right. We wouldn't have been able to go even if I'd figured out the ignition override."

Sohya and the others watched as a huge cloud of vapor escaped from the far end of the stack. Shinji was venting the liquid hydrogen and oxygen into space.

"Shinji, is this going to work?" Sohya wasn't sure.

His friend sounded almost cheerful. "Leave it to me. I've got the main engine, the second stage, and the descent module between me and the debris. You're even safer where you are. The main engine is coated in my cermet. A machine gun couldn't punch a hole in it."

"But the debris has a lot more kinetic energy than a bullet—"

"The satellite is in polar orbit, heading south. We're orbiting at right angles to the equator. You guys are facing the south pole. It's the safest place to be. Besides, look at it this way. If a thousand ping-pong balls spread out in a bubble eight thousand meters across were heading for you, what're the chances you'd stop one? If we panic now, they'll have a good laugh at our expense when this is over."

"But those 'ping-pong balls' are tangled in a web of carbon fibers."

"Don't be so pessimistic, Sohya. It doesn't suit you." Shinji paused. "Remember what I said? Even blunders are valuable. Here's the proof. Whether we make it back or not, we'll be helping whoever comes after us. I don't think we need to get too worked up."

For the next minute or so, the only sound in their headsets was Shinji's labored breathing. Then he spoke again. "I'm going to rotate her just a bit more. I want to get a view of Earth."

The stack rolled slightly. Suddenly they heard him calling like an excited child.

"It's her! I can see her! See there, on the northern horizon? Here she comes!"

"It's Eve XIX," said Tae. Everyone crowded around the window. Below them, Japan extended over the northern horizon and out of sight. Out of the blue haze, from the southern tip of the archipelago, a tiny column of white was climbing into the atmosphere. The column quickly toppled over toward the horizontal, growing larger and longer above the Pacific.

"It looks like a dragon!" Shinji yelled, ecstatic. "Fly! Fly faster. Fly higher! To the stars!"

Eve XIX surged through the atmosphere with astonishing speed, trailing its white cloud. Even the atmospheric conditions were special; the dragon kept its tail even after the first stage separation. Eve soared over the equator and rose to meet them on an immense, sharply defined pillar of steam spawned by the combustion of liquid hydrogen and oxygen.

"Don't stop! Keep going! Come *on!*"

There was a sharp *bang!* and the habitat module shuddered violently. A sheet of orange fire flashed past the window. The stack started yawing slowly.

"Shinji! Shinji!" Sohya screamed.

No warning lights lit up. No buzzers sounded. In the habitat module, everything was quiet and secure.

In the core, there was only silence.

◆·•◦•·◆

"SECOND-STAGE TELEMETRY lost. Descent module nominal, core telemetry out. Habitat pressure and power normal, no signs of combustion. Life-support systems nominal."

"Are they still in their suits? Tell them to stay suited up and stand by," said Hibiki. He turned to the INCO officer. "The only way the debris could reach the core is through the descent module. Why is the core not responding if the descent module is undamaged?"

"The main engine was hit first. We lost telemetry from the core three one-hundredths of a second later. Maybe it was hit by secondary debris."

"The second stage was head-on to the debris. There's no way the core could have sustained a lateral strike. The impact probably knocked out the core's instrumentation. Keep hailing Tai!"

The controllers frantically began analyzing the telemetry. The one thing no one in space or on the ground could do was visually inspect *Apple*'s exterior, which forced the controllers to try to divine its condition from a jigsaw puzzle of data.

Then the network officer stood up. "Flight, Bangalore says they have a visual!"

"Bangalore?"

"Vardhana was within visual range. They had their cameras on *Apple*!"

"Tell them we're grateful. Main screen."

The Vardhana Orbital Experimental Facility's images were beamed from India's ISTRAC satellite via the Indian space agency's Bangalore uplink facility. Vardhana was several hundred kilometers from *Apple*, but the Indians had used the station's astronomical telescope. The images coming up on the screen were sharp and detailed.

The video showed bright flashes of light from the second stage and the core module. Then the entire stack began revolving slowly. Frame-by-frame playback did not yield any additional detail. Each second of video contained thirty frames, but the flashes were visible on only two. One frame was probably an afterimage. No debris was visible; even with unlimited resolution, imaging a small object moving at close to eight kilometers a second was impossible. Still, the images told them everything they needed to know.

"That's a lateral strike," said the Flight Dynamics officer. "That means the object was moving along a curved path, like a man rappelling down a cliff. The tether material must have snagged on the main engine. That could've swung a debris fragment into the core, like a tetherball. It would explain why the descent module was bypassed. But Dr. Tai—"

"He might be alive," said Hibiki.

Which meant he was probably dead.

"The habitat module was spared. Tell the crew to depressurize, open the core hatch, and see if they can locate Dr. Tai. And tell Tanegashima to get Eve XX on the pad as soon as possible. *Apple 8* is their only way home now."

"Flight...the media..." The PAO pointed to the observation booth. A knot of reporters was staring into the control room like vultures, armed with microphones and cameras.

"Tell them we confirm five crew safe." Hibiki spoke quietly. "We're working on number six. Nothing more."

"What do I tell them about the mission?"

"We're working on it!" Hibiki roared.

———————

ONCE THE HABITAT module was depressurized, the inter-lock disengaged automatically. The top hatch opened. Sohya wedged himself headfirst into the opening, as far as his suit would allow.

"Shinji!"

The interior of the core was roughly the size of a minibus, with two couches forward and four more in a row behind. Now it was wrapped in darkness. As Sohya's eyes adjusted, he could see faint blue light suffusing the cabin—earthlight. He felt a wave of horror. A ragged breach, about the size of the hatch, yawned in the hull to his right.

"Shinji...where are you?"

Sohya's shoulders were jammed in the hatch. No one had considered it might be necessary to pass through the top hatch in a space suit. He craned his neck, peering around the cabin.

He saw what he was searching for floating next to the window, opposite the breach. Shinji's eyes were visible through his visor, narrowed as if looking into the distance. He was smiling faintly. This was how he must have watched Eve XIX climbing into space. It was a look full of hope.

But the side of his suit had a sandblasted appearance, riddled with tiny holes. Whatever had hit *Apple* had vaporized on impact, and the plasma jet had caught Shinji full on.

He was dead.

Sohya reached out, but it was too far. He felt his strength draining away. "Shinji...goddamn it..."

"Sohya? Can you see him?" It was Tae.

"Why did this have to happen? He had so much left to do..."

"He didn't make it?" Tae's voice was maddeningly serene. Sohya slowly extricated himself from the hatch. He choked back his fury and radioed Capcom.

"Gotenba, *Apple 7*. Dr. Tai is dead. Tell his family he saved our lives."

"I'm so sorry." Tae bowed her head and placed a hand on Sohya's arm, but he felt nothing through his suit. Her next words were unfathomable.

"Gotenba, *Apple 7*. Please don't disclose this yet."

"*Apple 7*, say again?"

"The core module is crippled. Please launch *Apple 8* and advise ETA immediately."

"Tae, what are you saying?" Shinji stared down at her. She was furiously weighing her next move, eyes tightly shut.

After a long pause, Capcom came back. "*Apple 7*, Gotenba. It will take at least six days to prepare *Apple 8* for launch. You'll have to wait in orbit. What's this about a news blackout?"

"Six days. Understood." Tae opened her eyes. Her voice was firm. "Eve XIX will rendezvous with us soon. We'll jettison the return module and our damaged second stage. We'll dock the other end of the habitat module with Eve XIX's second stage."

"What are you talking about?" said Sohya.

"While we wait for *Apple 8*, we'll use a free return trajectory to go around the moon and back to Earth. You can announce Dr. Tai's death once we're on our way."

The communication circuits were silent. Those who were listening doubted their ears. Several seconds later a new voice spoke up.

"*Apple 7*, Gotenba. This is Flight Control. Ms. Toenji, your concept has a major flaw. Without the return module, you can't land on the moon."

"Understood. Even if we land using the descent module, it can't get us back to Earth. But we're not going to land. All we're going to do is loop around the moon. We just need the free return trajectory."

"Free return. Yes, you could do that." With the right trajectory, one second-stage burn would send *Apple* around the moon and back to Earth. Until *Apple 8* arrived, all they would require was Eve XIX's second stage and the habitat module. But Hibiki was still doubtful.

"What would that prove? We already did it with *Apple 6*."

"We're going to take Dr. Tai to the moon."

"You're not serious!" said Sohya.

"I am serious." Tae looked at him sadly. "We can't take him back. He's never going home. We can't pressurize the core, and we can't get inside with our suits on. *Apple 8* can't bring him back. The only thing we can do is undock the core and leave him behind. It should be somewhere fitting."

"But why the moon?"

"Didn't you hear him calling to Eve XIX? The stars were always his destination." Tae's eyes welled with tears. She clenched her fists. "We won't give up, just as he wished. We'll all go together."

Suddenly another voice crackled in their ears—trembling, but full of resolve. It was Ryuichi.

"I second that. Do it for him. He'll be happy, I'm sure. I just...I wish—" He broke off.

"Please carry out Xiwangmu's TLI as planned," said Tae. "We won't need it. We'll rendezvous with Eve XIX and take the next window."

"Tae, wait." Sohya grasped her shoulder. She looked away.

"Let me go."

"Is this more PR?"

Yamagiwa broke in. "Aomine, you don't have to— "

"Sorry. I do. I don't want to say it, but I'm the only one who will. Answer me, Tae. Is this really for Shinji? Or are you just trying to put the best face you can on this?"

"Well, what if I am?" Her gaze was unrelenting. "Is it wrong to try to accomplish something? If I cried, and felt terrible, and threw the whole project out the window, would that help Shinji?"

"You don't feel responsible? A few minutes ago you wouldn't put your suit on. Was that just for show too?"

"Would you please just stop talking?" She raised her hands halfway to her ears, as if she wished she could shut out his voice. She was trembling. "It was my fault. Transferring to Xiwangmu. This risky orbit. Everything was my idea. Could you please let me do something right for once?"

"Look, that's enough," said Yamagiwa firmly. He drew Sohya away from the girl. "She's right. We're spending millions of yen every second up here. Even with the accident—no, because of the accident—we've got to salvage something from this mission. I know how you feel, but don't take it out on her."

"I don't believe it. You too!"

"Think, Aomine. Think of the reception waiting for her when she gets back. We can't just stand by and let them tear her apart. We have responsibilities too."

Sohya was silent. A headstrong girl, a fatal accident—it was the kind of story the media would beat to death.

Yamagiwa crossed over to the core hatch. "I'm closing this now. We have to start getting ready."

"Wait," said Sohya. "I'll do it." Sohya put his hand on the hatch lever. He looked into the core for the last time.

"You're going ahead of us all, Shinji." He closed the hatch.

He turned back to the crew. Tae wasn't watching him. She was staring out a window, the one facing away from Earth.

Something about Tae had always eluded Sohya's understanding. He had worked hard to bridge that gulf. But now he knew that whatever it was that drove her was beyond his comprehension.

———— ·•◦•· ————

THE CORE MODULE carrying Shinji's body was released before *Apple 7* looped around the moon. The habitat module swung around the moon and back toward Earth, but the core with its descent module braked into orbit and dropped toward the surface. Like Xiwangmu 6's descent module, the module carrying Shinji in the damaged core had its own guidance system. On the way to the moon, GGS programmed it to touch down atop the rim of Eden Crater. Shinji would be the first of his species to bask in sunlight for unbroken eons.

Once back in low earth orbit, the crew docked with the waiting *Apple 8* core module. After that, there was nothing to do but transfer to the core and go home.

As they expected, their reception was anything but cordial.

[3]

THE MORNING AFTER touchdown, Sohya woke in the support center's dormitory to find himself in the eye of the storm. First came an emergency call from Iwaki, ordering him back to headquarters immediately. The agenda: begin investigating the cause of the accident. Prepare for a memorial service for Shinji. Draft a public statement explaining the sacrifice of two *Apple* spacecraft and three Eve launch vehicles. Revise the project schedule. Media strategy. And on and on.

Sohya rousted his two colleagues and told them to get ready to leave. Then he went looking for Tae, but she'd already boarded a tilt-rotor for Nagoya. As he rushed through breakfast with Yamagiwa, he had a feeling he'd been left in the lurch. And then there she was, on the television in the commissary.

The footage appeared to have been taped inside the tilt-rotor. First came her apology and condolences to Shinji's family, segueing into a crisp statement of determination to continue, "as Shinji would have wished." Next she emphasized that the mission had been hit by a chain of unfortunate accidents that would never be repeated and that she was ready to ride into space again at the next opportunity. Then she laid ultimate responsibility for the accident at the feet of the Russian government. She closed with a promise to add space safety and debris cleanup measures to her plan.

Sohya's openmouthed amazement at this assured performance was interrupted by another call from Iwaki. Sohya didn't wait for him to speak. "Did you see the TV just now? Tae's already gone to work."

"Already? She's late. While you guys were out there, the media was wall-to-wall Shinji Tai."

"We saw it. But I didn't think the coverage was that critical."

"They were focusing on his achievements and waiting for you to come back. The fact that Sixth Continent isn't using taxpayer money made it a little harder for them to find a hook. But now she's back. The fun's just starting."

"Great. And what should I do?"

"Listen, Aomine. Things have gotten a little complicated. Don't go to the airport. Come back by ferry and train. Stay away from headquarters, and *don't* go home. One of our subcontractors has an inn at Hakoné. You like hot springs, don't you? Get yourself up there. I'll rendezvous with you."

"What is this? What's going on?"

"The police paid us a visit today. They want a statement from you."

"The *police*?"

"Concerning a case of professional negligence resulting in death. They want to question you about Shinji's accident. Don't worry. It wasn't your fault, but we want you to stay out of sight till things cool down a bit."

"If it wasn't my fault, why do I have to lie low?"

"You idiot—do you think the police know anything about orbital physics or *Apple*'s design? If they get their hooks into you, you'll be testifying for years."

Yamagiwa cut in. "He's right, Aomine. I'd do what he says. You have too much on your plate. If you get mixed up with an investigation, you'll only be throwing fuel on the fire for the media. Get out of here while you can." Yamagiwa glanced out the window. A siren sounded faintly in the distance.

"And there they are." Yamagiwa held out a set of car keys to Sohya. "Here. Head for the car pool. They won't stop you in one of our cars."

Sohya hesitated. "What are you going to do?"

"I'm stuck either way. Either I land in jail or I'm on *Apple 9*. Pilots are useless in hiding."

"Good luck!" Sohya dashed out of the commissary, his two colleagues on his heels.

At first they drove toward the hydrofoil pier but thought better of it; too many tourists. Instead they doubled back to a small harbor, where they found a fisherman with a fast boat willing to take them to the southern tip of Kyushu, about four hours away.

On Kyushu, they took a roundabout route by taxi and train as far as Miyazaki. As they boarded the late-afternoon train north to Kokura, they started wondering if they might be taking things a bit too seriously. When they saw the news on the train, they changed their minds.

Top of the evening news was an in-depth report on Tae—an "exposé" of how a selfish rich girl had foisted a foolhardy and accident-plagued project on her hapless father's company. Obviously her stock was in the toilet as far as the media was concerned. Before the program broke for a commercial, the host announced the focus for the next segment: Tae's yes-man, Sohya Aomine…

It was time to move. They jumped off at the next station and caught a ferry for Shikoku. The station cameras would eventually allow them to be traced. They would have to stay away from the national railway.

They also switched off their wearcoms. It still might take the authorities a few days to get a warrant to track their signals, but then again the police didn't always follow the legal niceties.

Once on Shikoku, the men stayed at a youth hostel. The next day they started moving east across the island, taking local trains and scanning the newspapers and occasional public terminals for updates.

Like a dam venting pent-up floodwaters, the media unleashed a wave of bitter condemnation. Their main thrust—that Tae and Hibiki made serious misjudgments leading to Shinji's death, and that *Apple*'s designers displayed an astonishing lack of foresight in not allowing for the possibility that going through the top hatch in a space suit might save a life—was tame compared to their other accusations.

One station did an interview with Shinji's grieving parents—heavily edited—to highlight the perils of manned spaceflight. The next day, the station apologized for "selectively" editing the interview but would not disclose what was taken out. Sohya had listened as Shinji took a phone call of encouragement from his parents shortly before boarding *Apple 7*, so he could guess what had been omitted.

One webpaper did an investigative report that accused Tenryu Galaxy Transport of misusing public funds—specifically its infrastructure, which once had been state property—without any attempt to return some of its massive profits to the public. Concerning the privatization of Japan's space program two decades earlier and of TGT's years of struggle without public support, the report was silent.

This was the reaction from major media, those shapers of public opinion. When it came to the tabloid press, their articles could hardly be read without laughing. A bizarre love triangle between Shinji, Tae, and Sohya. Secret military links to NASA. Enormous kickbacks from China's space agency.

The three men left the train and trudged the final ten kilometers to the hot springs inn at Hakoné. When an exhausted Sohya arrived at his room late that night, Iwaki was waiting.

"Has everyone gone totally nuts?" said Sohya, throwing his bags on the floor. "Before, we couldn't do anything wrong. Now we're outcasts."

"That's the way this country works," said Iwaki, comfortably cross-legged at a low table. "It's fun to see people fail. If everything goes without a hitch for too long, the media gets fed up. Anyway, I'm glad you made it in one piece."

Iwaki poured him a beer from the refrigerator. Sohya downed it and sighed. "Now I feel human again. The past two days felt like being a criminal on the run."

"Relax. In a month, the media will move on. They're going after the wrong people."

"I just hope they don't forget Shinji. Nothing can bring him back."

"I know. Poor guy." Iwaki looked intently at Sohya. "Have you heard what Tae's been up to?"

"How would I?"

"Sounds like you don't care anymore. I sympathize, but don't let your personal feelings get in the way. She's really hanging in there."

"And how is she doing that?"

"Her public relations and TV commercials are hitting back hard. Two days after she got back she put a commercial out confirming that Sixth Continent would go on. The same channel aired a special later the same day, criticizing the project. Broadcasters are such pimps."

"Is that it?"

"I guess, if you think worldwide coverage isn't worth much. The reaction overseas has been positive. Experts in the U.S. and Europe have been pretty unanimous in saying there was no negligence. That kind of thing will start having an effect here soon. She's also suing the Russians for compensation. At least she's not accusing them of murder."

"Another lawsuit?" Sohya shrugged his shoulders.

"No. This time it's different. I doubt she thinks she can actually win. The Russians are steel-reinforced assholes. All the suit will do is get their back up, and they'll refuse to apologize. Remember the nuclear waste storage facility we built in Novaya Zemlya? They ask us to build it, then they sue us for supposedly violating their environmental regulations."

"So what's the point of going after them?"

"We've got cause. The UN Committee on the Peaceful Uses of Outer Space requires nations to clean up their space junk. But there's no way to enforce it. The Russians will probably say that dealing with all that debris isn't practical. I think that's what Tae's looking for."

"She wants to lose? That's new."

"She wants to focus the public's indignation on the Russians. She's going to highlight how uncaring they are."

Sohya downed another glass of beer. "I can't understand what she gets out of all this maneuvering. Is it a game for her?"

"I thought you knew the answer to that."

"Not after what happened up there."

"That could be a problem. We met at headquarters yesterday to decide whether to proceed with this project. The decision was unanimous: we proceed. We need our communications conduit with our sponsor more than ever now."

"Is that what I am, a conduit?" Sohya shook his head. "What does TGT say?"

"Business as usual. They're still on board. We can make money here on Earth, but TGT's only business is in space. Did you hear Yaenami's statement?"

"Yeah. I think he was a little premature." Sohya sipped a fresh beer. "And too optimistic. I was checking the news on the way up here. There's this new organization pushing the debris issue, questioning the whole idea of space development. Every time anyone puts something in space, it creates more junk, and that just makes going into space more dangerous. They're saying we're going to choke on our own trash. Once we cross the threshold and the debris cascade starts, junk will collide with junk, generating so many more fragments and collisions that low earth orbit will be blanketed with one-inch devils. How did they put it? 'Space development is inherently self-limiting.'"

Iwaki glanced at him sharply, but Sohya was staring at the floor. "It's not like this just started." Sohya shook his head. "Why are they making an issue of it now? They're either out of touch or just trying to make trouble."

"They're making a lot of trouble, my friend." Sohya looked up, puzzled. Iwaki frowned as he peeled an edamame.

"They started getting their message out right after Shinji was killed. Of course the whole thing is nothing new to us, but it's news to the public, and it frightens them. These are the people Sixth Continent is trying to appeal to."

"What are you so worried about? The whole thing is just as stupid as the rest of the flack we've been getting."

"You know, Aomine, I'm not sure if you really grasp what's going on here." Iwaki shook his head and looked at the wall clock. "He should be out of the bath soon."

"Who? The other guys are asleep already."

"Sennosuke Toenji."

Sohya put his glass down. "What's the chairman doing here?"

"He's not the chairman anymore. I'm here because he is. You think I came down here just for you guys?"

Footsteps were already coming down the corridor. The sliding door opened, and the portly old man, wearing a cotton kimono and slippers, paused on the threshold and bowed deeply.

"Mr. Aomine. I see you've arrived safely. I'm just a private citizen now. I may need to rely on Gotoba Engineering's kindness and support for some time. Allow me to thank you."

"I don't understand." Sohya looked from Sennosuke to Iwaki, stunned.

"Mr. Toenji was fired this morning by ELE's president," said Iwaki. "As of now, he's unemployed."

"But—what about the project?"

Sennosuke sat down at the table, looking grim. "It's going

forward, at least for the moment. Now it's up to me to finance it, though my bank account is not quite that large."

"Your *bank account*? The budget's 150 billion. How can you pay for that?"

"Including the money ELE has spent so far, which I'm afraid I'll have to repay, I can provide 130 and change. That's everything I have."

Sohya was staggered that one person could control so much wealth, but that wasn't important now. "So how are you going to get another twenty billion?"

"The banks seem willing to help us. If so, we'll be able to make the budget."

Iwaki had the same grim expression as the old man. "But of course, we'll have to pay it back. We can't expect any more help from ELE. In other words, we'll be flying without a safety net. We can't make any more mistakes."

No more mistakes? That was totally impossible. Sohya felt a cold void opening beneath his feet. Sixth Continent had been destined to be a string of problems; it had to be. There certainly had been many setbacks so far, large and small. Sohya was not privy to the financial details, but with every new obstacle they faced, the line between black ink and red moved up and down like a dinghy in heavy seas. What he did know was that right now, their projections showed them barely breaking even. The next shock might send their ship straight to the bottom of the ocean. And that was just the money side of the problem.

"What about Tae?"

"She's in the same situation," said Sennosuke. "She doesn't represent ELE anymore. She's using her network of connections for everything from PR to suing the Russian government. We haven't announced any of this yet. We will soon though."

"How can she do all that by herself?" Sohya suddenly felt cold sober. Sennosuke leaned toward him.

"I have a favor to ask, Sohya. Watch over her, please. Support her. She needs it more than ever."

"That group you were talking about," said Iwaki. "It's called Joyful Homeland. At first glance they don't look like much, but their arguments are based on hard science, and they have a lot of influential people behind them. Pretty soon they're going to start threatening Sixth Continent's base of support. And they have a backer: Kiichiro Toenji. He wants to make sure ELE isn't tarnished by everything that's happened. So he jettisoned Sixth Continent."

"Sohya, do you know Eden Leisure Entertainment's motto?" asked Sennosuke. "'Paradise on Earth.' It was my idea. Somehow it sounds like someone else's motto now. But for seventy years, we've tried to show the public an ideal world. It may surprise you to learn that people whose business it is to bring an ideal world to the public can't be dreamers themselves. In fact, they have to be brutally pragmatic. We brought our ideal world to the public by shouldering the burden of reality for them. I instilled this in my son from the beginning, and he's doing what I taught him. He's never been a dreamer. He's convinced that reality and ideals are incompatible. That's what enables him to do his job. It's thanks mostly to Kiichiro that ELE has grown to its present size. In fact, that's the problem. It's too big. ELE is so good at creating ideal worlds it's trapped by its own success."

Sennosuke rested his fists on his knees and spoke haltingly. "Sixth Continent is a dream of people…who are in the business of making dreams reality. It's the real thing. There's no guarantee we can make everyone happy. But my son thinks that dream is a threat to ELE."

"And he's washing his hands of it while he still has the chance. Now it's up to Tae—and you," said Iwaki. Sennosuke nodded sadly.

"So thanks to her own father, Tae is an outcast," said Sohya.

"Unfortunately, you are correct." Sennosuke put his hands on the table in front of him and lowered his head. "My granddaughter's back is against the wall. If she doesn't have someone she trusts to give her support, she's going to fall apart. Sohya, we need your help."

Sohya was speechless. The mission had left him disillusioned and fed up. But now her single-minded pursuit made a little more sense.

There was nothing he could say. He was completely hemmed in by his own feelings.

THE TAXI PULLED into the graveled driveway of the mansion on the shore of Lake Makino and stopped at the entrance. Tae was waiting, wearing a beret and lugging a suitcase almost larger than she was. She maneuvered it into the backseat and was about to get in when a voice called to her.

"Where do you suppose you're going?"

Kiichiro was standing at the columned entrance to the Toenji mansion. This place, and her father, had never felt as if they belonged to her. But she turned to look at him, almost against her will.

"Are you going to stop me?"

"Do you want to be stopped?"

"Why are you always like this?"

"I'm just trying to respect your wishes."

"How kind. Have you turned over a new leaf?" She stared daggers at him. "I'm not your toy. And neither was Mother."

"That was an accident. How many times do we have to drag that swamp?"

"We don't. I've heard enough." She raised her hand in farewell.

"Wait!" Kiichiro stepped toward her. "Sixth Continent will fail."

"You mean you'll make it fail. I was impressed. You not only paid off the board, you created an 'independent' group to harass us. A textbook example of a conspiracy. You taught me something new."

"The board backed me 100 percent! Everyone in the company—"

"What about Reika? She quit, didn't she? Do you know where she is? Tanegashima. If everyone had her guts, ELE would be deserted."

"The threat from debris is real. It killed a man."

"I know what he would say if he were alive. Challenges are something to face, not run away from. And TGT has the solution."

"You actually think they can neutralize the danger? Do you have the funds for that?"

"It doesn't concern you."

"Tae—"

"Don't talk to me." She looked at him icily. "You never even met him. Now he's dead, and you're using him to further your agenda. It's disgusting. I have nothing left to say to you."

"Tae!"

"Goodbye." She got into the taxi. The car drove slowly through the gates.

Kiichiro slammed his fist into a column. In the taxi, Tae's face was buried in her hands. Her beret had fallen to the floor.

[4]

EDEN CRATER, THE lunar south pole. White multidozers shuttled back and forth under the sun, fulfilling their tasks. Several hundred meters away, in the darkness of a smaller crater, the only source of heat was a single linear motor.

The Turtle squatting here was different from its compatriots. It bore a machine, a powerful computing unit in a shielded oblong container, topped by a fifteen-meter parabolic antenna that scanned the heavens with exquisite deliberation.

Something had drawn the machine's attention. The antenna was motionless now, pointing toward a distant star. A signal, an anomalous stream of energy emerging from the cosmic background, had stirred the machine's circuits into activity.

Wavelength: sixty megahertz. Flux density: fifty millijanskys. No antenna on Earth could have caught this whisper from space. The atmosphere would have masked it.

The machine began running a transform analysis. The signal might be something unremarkable: perhaps the radiation signature of a stream of hot gas, accreting from one star to another in a distant binary system. The machine searched for matches between the signal and known natural sources. It found none.

Could the signal be intelligent, from beyond the solar system?

The machine was inorganic, free of preconceptions. Without a tremor of anticipation or interest, it initiated its verification subroutine.

If the signal were intelligent, its maker would want someone to notice; it should persist long enough to reliably detect and interpret. But five minutes later, it disappeared. The diagnostic software could discern no pattern in that strange signature.

The machine consigned its findings to the database. The parabolic antenna resumed its slow revolving scan.

Forty minutes later, another signal flashed from Eden Crater toward the star. The machine did not detect it. Its antenna was pointed skyward.

CHAPTER 7
SECOND ENVIRONMENTAL ASSESSMENT AND NEW CONSTRUCTION PLAN

[1]

THE DESCENT MODULE'S engine was small but innovative, capable of fifteen successive ignitions without reconditioning. On November 24, 2032, it fired once to leave lunar orbit and once more to touch down outside Eden Crater.

The square hatch of the core module opened forty minutes later. A figure in a sleek green space suit with a compact life-support backpack emerged from the cone and cautiously climbed down a ladder to the surface. His left foot touched the hard-packed surface first, followed by his right. He released the ladder and slowly turned to survey his surroundings.

Ten long shadows—six multidozers, two moon rovers, and a pair of carpenter robots—stretched from both sides of the graded road surface that even now was being extended from the landing site. In the distance, to his right, was a glistening array of solar panels. In the opposite direction lay the regolith-shrouded bulk of Xiwangmu 6.

These were the first sights that met thirty-one-year-old Sohya Aomine's excited gaze on this, his second trip to the moon.

He looked down. The landing pad was an immaculately packed disk of black regolith, like a freshly scrubbed stone porch. His insulated boots left no impression.

"What a beautiful welcome." Those were his first words.

One by one, three more space-suited figures clambered down to the surface—Yamagiwa and two Gotoba engineers. Six months had elapsed since *Apple 7*'s tragic mission. Sixth Continent was a year behind schedule. Now, at last, they were here.

"The contrast between light and shadow is unbelievable," said Yamagiwa. First words, but not for the history books. It wasn't that they were indifferent to the historic nature of their mission—they simply didn't much want to be noticed. In fact, they had done everything they could to stay inconspicuous. The main focus of Sixth Continent's publicity was another mission taking place at this same moment. That was the mission Tae had chosen.

"Do you wish she were here too, Sohya?" Yamagiwa put his hand on Sohya's shoulder.

He shook his head inside his Manna suit. "It was her decision. Her mission has a higher profile. At least we hope it does."

"This mission is at least as important."

"Technically, sure, but…" Sohya looked at the descent stack. Their first landing was a major step forward; there was no doubt about that. Instead of a standard hydrazine-fueled engine, they would be using LOX and hydrogen extracted on the surface to return to orbit, something never attempted and, indeed, impossible till now. The new descent engine was temperamental but had a longer operating life. If everything went well, they would travel back and forth between lunar orbit and the surface without ever depending on Earth for fuel again.

"All this new technology is not of much interest to our customers," said Sohya. "No one cares what the bus they're on is using for fuel."

"I'd stick to the science and let Marketing do their job."

"Just remember, if they don't come, Gotoba and TGT go down

together. We don't have the kind of financial backing we used to."

Having completed his walk-around check of the descent stack, one of the engineers joined them. "Not only that, but our costs keep going up, thanks to that stuff." He pointed toward Earth, or rather, to the space around Earth. Yamagiwa shook his head.

"Phase E is a service to humanity. If the mission goes well, we should be seeing contributions from space agencies around the world."

"I think you're being optimistic," said Sohya.

"Let's quit jawing and get to work." Yamagiwa clapped his gloved hands and frowned when he realized they made no sound. "First we have to get Xiwangmu's environmental control system booted up. Multidozer repair, regolith decontamination, fuel synthesis—we've got a mountain of work to get through."

"I'm going for a drive first," said Sohya.

"You're kidding. You're not setting a very good example for the rest of us, Mr. Site Supervisor." Yamagiwa was about to say more when he noticed the direction of Sohya's gaze.

"I want to pay my respects." He was looking up at a tiny, glinting point of light atop the crater rim, which was the height of a low range of hills. "You go ahead. I'm going to leave some flowers and a picture of his parents."

Sohya climbed back into the core. When he returned with a small package, Yamagiwa was checking over one of the rovers. He got in and patted the passenger seat.

"Come on, let's get moving."

"You're going to drive me there?"

"This is what I do. We have to test this thing, you know."

Yamagiwa stared straight ahead, as if impatient to start right away. He would stay on the surface with the first team as another cost-cutting measure to keep the number of Eve launches to a minimum. He was eager to prove he could be just as useful on the ground as in space. With an extra team member, work would proceed more quickly, but one of the four crew members would have to spend his sleep periods in the core module.

"All right. Drive carefully."

"Roger that." Yamagiwa nodded and pushed the starter switch. The rover sprang forward.

———

APPLE 10 WAS in low earth orbit, crossing over the Horn of Africa.

"I have a visual fix. Standard Object 38124. Type: spherical, attached valve. Metal finish. Looks like a thruster pod. Object is within size limits."

"Orbital analysis complete. Puffball is in range."

"Proceed," said Tae.

The image on the monitor, magnified by a zoom lens, showed a gigantic spherical object lit ash blue by earthlight. The sphere jogged into its new path with a nimbleness that belied its size. A few minutes later, light gleamed briefly at the edge of the sphere and a cone of fire seemed to pierce its semitransparent interior. An instant later the light winked out.

The navigator scanned his array of monitors. "Fragmentation complete. Vaporization 2 percent. Maximum fragment axis, eight millimeters. Good job."

"That makes twenty. How much fuel do we have?" asked Tae.

"Forty-two percent. Maybe ten more objects."

"Then let's go to the next probable orbit."

"Roger. That's three and a half orbits from now, five hours and fifteen minutes." The three crew members relaxed and floated upward from their flight couches.

Apple 10's mission, one of a series planned for Phase E(xtra), was a process of patiently eliminating one piece of space junk after another. The core module, equipped with a sensitive video camera and image processing system, was orbiting near the "puffball," a huge sphere designed to break space debris into harmless fragments. From a distance, it looked like a two-hundred-meter sphere of steel wool. A closer look would have revealed multiple vortices of fine wire twisted into larger strands like lily yarn. Each strand was perforated with one-centimeter holes.

The puffball's perforated strands wound from the surface toward the core in a uniform, weblike spiral. At the center of the puffball was a propulsion module with six-axis thrusters. The thruster exhaust gas flowed out through the web into space.

The puffball's unique feature was the nested arrangement of its strands. The entire sphere could be compressed to a diameter of five meters and carried inside the payload shroud of an Adam rocket. Its mass was exactly one hundred tons, Adam's maximum lift capacity. Once in orbit, the shroud was jettisoned, and the puffball elastically expanded to two hundred meters.

TGT's strategy was based on careful planning. Flying along in a spacecraft and simply scooping up the debris would seem to be the most straightforward approach, but this was quickly shot down. To creep up on each piece of debris would call for precise synchronization of relative orbital speed. The huge amount of fuel that would consume made this approach unworkable.

The solution was to ignore relative speed and rely on position and timing. This meant the debris would be approaching with a relative velocity of several kilometers per second—not something to stop with a rubber bumper. At that velocity, whatever intercepted the debris would also be destroyed. Materials like aluminum, advanced ceramics, or Kevlar wouldn't stand a chance. The awesome kinetic energy would be instantaneously converted to heat. Beyond a given impactor size, no obstacle could stand up to that kind of blowtorch. Anything in the way would be vaporized or blown apart.

Anything massive enough to withstand such impacts would be too heavy to loft into orbit, yet the interceptor could not be too small either. If they miscalculated and the backstop wasn't tough enough, the resulting breakup would simply create more orbiting junk.

TGT's answer was a three-dimensional woven structure known as the puffball. Its steel strands were not designed to cushion the shock of impact; space debris would penetrate faster than any network of strands could respond by deforming. Instead, the debris vaporized the strands and broke apart as its kinetic energy was rapidly converted to intense heat. The plasma jet would punch a tunnel through the strands, but the puffball would stay intact. After penetrating a few tens of meters, the debris would either be vaporized or reduced to trapped fragments. The only fragments able to escape would be under a centimeter in size, including shattered strands, and would pose relatively little risk to spacecraft.

The puffball could gobble up debris as much as a meter across, limited only by the fuel for its thrusters. Once that was almost exhausted, it would fire one last time, deorbit, and burn up in the atmosphere.

One problem remained: how to locate the debris. Pieces larger than one centimeter but smaller than ten—the so-called one-inch devils—were invisible to radar. U.S. Space Command was rumored to have the capability to detect these tiny killers, but their technology was classified. In any case, ground-based radar systems had their limits. The South American spotter's discovery of a debris cloud around the Russian satellite was a fluke.

The puffball needed an escort to locate the objects and guide it to them. Optical sensing was the optimal approach: there was no atmosphere in orbit to attenuate visible light, and its short wavelength compared to radar was better for detecting small objects. Monitoring was automated with high-resolution CCD sensors and computerized image analysis. The system scanned the entire horizon every two minutes as *Apple* moved through its orbit. From 350 kilometers up, *Apple* could scan 2,200 kilometers of horizon. Orbits would be calculated for any debris detected; objects in high or eccentric orbits were out of reach but did not pose a significant collision risk. Some debris had complex orbits that could not be evaluated. There was nothing to do but let these objects go.

Once a piece of debris was designated for fragmenting, simple pursuit was not an option if fuel was to be conserved. The debris was only followed long enough for its orbit to be calculated. Then a new orbit for *Apple* would be worked out, one using the least amount of fuel. This might mean orbiting Earth several times before the final encounter.

The crew returned to the habitat module. The hours till the next encounter would be filled with work. Clearing low earth orbit of debris yielded no profit, so the habitat module was crammed with microgravity projects waiting to be tended by the crew.

The navigator made his way to a workstation where his task was to cast ultrahard drill bits using a steel-aluminum-silica alloy. The bits had been ordered by a machine tool company.

"These things sell for 150,000 wholesale," muttered the navigator. "If we make a thousand, that's 150 million. Our share is fifty million. But this mission is costing us three billion. It's like trying to fill a swimming pool with an eyedropper."

Tae was adding hot water to freeze-dried food pouches. "Just keep at it. Reika went to a lot of trouble to get that order."

Microgravity manufacturing was nothing new. The real profit was in taxpayer-subsidized scientific work, but such projects were typically years in the planning, and there had been no time for lengthy negotiations. The only projects they could take on were those where the manufacturing process could be implemented immediately. Reika was now a TGT employee and had searched high and low for accessible work of this kind.

But being in the subcontracted manufacturing business meant dealing with clients who pushed hard for lower prices. To make things more difficult, ISS and Vardhana had already had years to establish their grip on this market, so the only way to get clients was to offer deep discounts.

The pilot pushed off from a handrail to float toward another workstation. The navigator yelled in frustration. "You just spilled my alloy! I was in the middle of pouring."

"There goes fifty thousand. Sorry, I'll be careful. But this whole thing shakes every time we move."

"Just let me know, okay?"

Apple's habitat module was not designed for microgravity manufacturing. Compared to the much larger modules used by its competitors, its smaller mass made it vulnerable to tiny vibrations that caused transitory gravity fluctuations, enough to impair the functioning of the equipment.

"Maybe we should rethink this whole operation," said the pilot, dejected. "We can't solve this on our own. We should be investing in getting the base completed."

"We'll do nothing of the sort. Phase E is vital for attracting customers." Tae gave him a steely look. "You know what Joyful Homeland is saying. They've turned us into a poster child for the problems with space development. We're going to generate more debris with our launches—over a hundred before Sixth Continent is complete. With enough objects, you get a collision cascade, and the Kessler syndrome kicks in. Debris hitting other debris will create so many fragments we won't even be able to put satellites into orbit. Unfortunately, the science says they're right, or pretty close to it. We've got nowhere to hide. We lost 20 percent of our reservations in the past six months." She pointed out the window. The silvery gray puffball loomed a few hundred meters away. "That's the only way we can neutralize people's fears."

"But we can't clean up all of it."

"Trying is better than nothing. When you buy a car, you go for the eco-friendly model even though one car, or even a whole car company, isn't going to make a dent in the world's pollution."

"But how do we cover the costs? Phase E wasn't in the budget."

"Don't worry. It's not a problem." Tae smiled. The pilot returned to his task. He didn't seem convinced.

Tae wasn't convinced either. In fact, she was extremely worried. Phase E was putting serious pressure on Sixth Continent's finances. At this rate, they would run out of funds before the base was complete. To make things worse, construction was running a year behind schedule. Even her supporters were beginning to voice doubts.

But this was no time to give up. If she threw in the towel now, she'd have to go crawling back to her father. Proving him wrong was the whole point of being here.

Tae stopped, looked out into space, and made her decision.

"I'm going to EVA for the next rendezvous." Her two crew members stared in disbelief. "Be sure and get me in the frame when the debris hits. If we just shoot the puffball in action, it might make some people even more nervous. With me in the frame, we can prove that the debris is nothing to be scared of. It's just another problem we're solving."

"It's too dangerous! You might get hit by a fragment even from a distance of several hundred meters. If something a millimeter across—"

"I'm going to EVA." She went to her locker and opened it. "I want you to shoot me changing into my suit and going through the core hatch too. I want everyone to see the redesign. I want them to understand that what happened to Shinji can't happen again." She unzipped her jumpsuit and wriggled out. She was no longer the skinny little girl who traveled to the moon on Sohya's lap. The navigator gulped and went to fetch the camera.

Tae pulled her thermal undergarment on. "I'll do whatever it takes," she muttered. "I have to rely on myself now."

———◉✦◉———

RYUICHI YAENAMI GAVE a low whistle of admiration. "It's like a chapel in here." He was in an office in Akasaka in the center of Tokyo. The building was elegant, sheathed in ivy.

"Miss Toenji insisted. This is the gateway to Sixth Continent. Couples who visit need to be in the right mood." Reika was leaning with her back against the entrance. When she stepped away, Ryuichi saw that the inside of the door was faced with a mirror. The Sixth Continent logo and its motto—BE FRUITFUL AND MULTIPLY, AND FILL THE MOON—were etched into the glass.

The walls of the office were faced in dignified red brick, interrupted at intervals by slender, Renaissance-style alabaster columns. The furniture was white cast metal. The window opposite the door was stained glass, with a representation of the Virgin Mary. The carpet was scarlet. The room was only fifty square meters, but the atmosphere was simple and refined.

"This office is all she has now," said Reika. "We're trying to compensate for the size with nice decor. We don't want to spend more on staff, so Tae and I are managing everything."

Yaenami glanced toward an elderly woman working at a laptop at the rear of the office, partially shielded by a few potted plants. An elegant shawl draped her shoulders.

Reika lowered her eyes, embarrassed. "I'm sorry. I'm with TGT now, but I'm spending most of my time here."

"Don't be so formal. You're not an employee. You're my partner. If you think being here is best, go ahead."

Reika whispered *Ryuichi* and looked at him gratefully. He quickly adopted a serious expression, but there was a twinkle in his eye.

"Maybe we should get married on the moon."

"You can't be serious. It's very expensive."

"Okay, okay—just kidding. People are canceling, but we're still overbooked. I don't think I can wait that long." He looked suddenly pensive. "But I'd like to visit Shinji."

"I would too." Reika had seen a lot of the two men's friendship over the last six years. In some ways, Ryuichi had been closer to Shinji.

"You know…it would be nice if we could at least have the wedding portrait taken right away." Reika looked shyly at the floor.

She was thirty-six. She wanted to be photographed in her dress, and soon; who knew how long it would be before they could travel to the moon?

She had complete command of the millions of line items in Sixth Continent's budget. Her take-no-prisoners approach to budget austerity had earned her a fearsome reputation as a cost cutter at TGT and Gotoba. But right now she was blushing furiously and digging at the carpet with her heel.

Yaenami laughed awkwardly. "Taking a wedding picture is the kind of thing you do when the time comes."

"All right."

"But let's go to city hall after we're through here."

"What?"

Without allowing time for this to sink in, Ryuichi nodded toward the old woman. "Aren't you going to introduce me?"

"Oh…Yes, of course. That's Ms. Halifax. She's helping with the office work. Dorothy?"

The diminutive woman removed her spectacles, rose, and approached them. Her silver hair was carefully coiffed. She smiled at Ryuichi and extended her hand. "Good day, Mr. Yaenami. I'm Dorothy Halifax."

They shook hands. Ryuichi was charmed. "Pleased to meet you, Ms. Halifax. May I call you Dorothy?"

"Of course. You know, Reika never stops talking about you."

"Dorothy!"

The old woman chuckled. "She's so cute. A bit too old to be shy, though." Reika blushed. Dorothy winked at her.

Ryuichi cleared his throat. "Did you know Reika before this?"

"Oh no. Tae asked me to help out. I put her up when she was going to school in California. It was Sennosuke's idea. I've known him for half a century. We met in Hong Kong."

"She's very helpful." Reika had recovered her composure. "Students from sixteen countries have stayed with her. She's good at advising young couples. Her husband is a Catholic priest, so she knows a lot about religion. Sixth Continent will be hosting couples from all over the world."

"Then we'll need her advice," said Ryuichi, smiling at the old woman. "Experienced wedding consultants are hard to find."

Dorothy's eyes sparkled. "That's just my hobby. Let's take a look at my real work."

She went to her desk, sat down in front of an ancient laptop, and typed a password with her index fingers. Ryuichi and Reika watched over her shoulder. The computer and its operator were old; the software was anything but.

Data began scrolling up the screen, splitting off into red and blue icons representing compressed data. The icons formed up into opposing ranks, like a game board covered with carefully arranged pieces. They moved forward, jostling each other. Lines began busily extending across the gaps, connecting icon to icon in apparently random fashion. The connections made the icons pulsate; some grew larger and brighter, while the others shrank or disappeared completely, sometimes reappearing, sometimes not. The disappearance of some icons also seemed to give rise to new ones. After a few minutes, the blue icons were gradually overwhelmed by the red.

"What is this?" asked Ryuichi.

"The blue icons are positive factors. The red are negative. This is a risk-management simulation for Sixth Continent. The future can be predicted by assigning numerical coefficients to different factors affecting the project. It's not terribly precise, of course. But as fortune-telling goes, it's reasonably effective."

"Dorothy was a professor of computer science at Caltech before she retired," interjected Reika.

"I like that. But red just won. Does that mean we're on the brink of disaster?"

"Yes, it looks that way. Unless the right steps are taken, the project will probably fail." Dorothy's matter-of-fact tone stunned Ryuichi into silence. She clicked on a red tile, and a window with data opened beside it. "Take this risk factor, for example. This is the influence posed by the dangers associated with space travel. One person has already died. That accident has greatly activated this factor and strengthened its influence. Something very positive must be found to oppose it, or it will never be neutralized."

"What about our publicity? We revised our safety protocols. We reengineered the core module. We could advertise that more."

"In that case, here's what happens." Dorothy created another blue icon with a few keystrokes and linked it with the red icon. The connection pulsated, and the red icon began to shrink, as if its vital force were ebbing away. But after a few moments the balance seemed to shift, and the blue icon withered and disappeared.

"Some influence. Not much," murmured Dorothy. "The media is fickle. They'll forget about the accident soon. But over the long term, I'm afraid it won't work. The danger will be back in the news. Overemphasizing the safety factor via publicity simply makes everyone more aware of the risks."

"What should we do?"

"Let's try this." Dorothy created another connection, this time between the same red icon and another red icon. After resonating for a few moments, they both disappeared.

"Negative destroys negative. Admit the danger instead of trying to minimize it. For example, disclose the failure rate for Eve. Tell the public there's a statistical probability of one catastrophic failure in fifty launches."

"*What?*" Ryuichi slammed his fist on the desk. Reika retreated a step, alarmed. He suddenly had the look of a demon. "Shinji gave his life for that rocket! He poured everything he had into it. We have no business scaring the public with risk factors that are out of our hands!"

"Out of your hands. Yes, that's precisely what I mean. I wonder if it's fair to conceal that sort of thing?"

Ryuichi was practically nose to nose with her, trembling with anger beyond his control. The old woman's eyes were placid as a mountain lake. "I'm sure some *would* be frightened, just as they feared airplanes at the beginning of the twentieth century. Now millions of people use them every year. I believe everyone knows that airplanes sometimes fall out of the sky."

"Sixth Continent is different. Customers will be going for a once-in-a-lifetime event—a wedding! Even if we tell them there's an escape system, just thinking about it will scare them away!"

"People use airplanes for their once-in-a-lifetime honeymoons. Are they scared when they see the life jackets under their seats?" Dorothy playfully poked Ryuichi's forehead with a fingertip. "Tell the world. Make it common knowledge."

Ryuichi grunted doubtfully, but his anger had left him. He straightened up. Dorothy turned back to the laptop.

"That was just an example. There are lots of other problems. Here's one." She selected another red icon. A window opened next to it: an image of a man on a balcony, raising his hand to a huge crowd below. He was wearing robes trimmed in gold.

"The pope, Pius XIII. He's critical of your attempt to colonize the moon. The Bible says nothing about the moon being given to humanity by God. Western powers used the teachings of the Church to justify their colonization of other peoples. The pope fears a resurgence of that madness. You may find it difficult to conduct Catholic weddings at Sixth Continent. I doubt Catholics would pay large amounts of money to be married in a place their Holy Father has denounced."

"I'm sorry. I don't know the first thing about this," said Ryuichi.

"You Japanese are an interesting people. You're willing to swear an oath before a god you don't even believe in. I wonder if you understand the real meaning of the wedding ceremony."

Her voice had a slight edge. Ryuichi hung his head, a bit too theatrically perhaps.

"I'm afraid you're right."

"At least you're willing to admit it. That's a very admirable trait. Reika, I think you've chosen well."

"Of course!" Reika came and stood next to Ryuichi. Dorothy smiled warmly. She typed something on the laptop's keyboard.

"I've made some small adjustments to your parameters, Ryuichi. Still, it's not enough. We need more positive factors, or honestly, your chances for success are quite slim. And the cost of the orbital cleanup could pose a dire threat to your financial health. It's not something poor Tae can handle on her own."

"We have to do something about the religious issue too," said Ryuichi. "The pope's words influence a billion believers."

"Well, if you were only catering to Japanese customers, my husband could help you."

Ryuichi raised an eyebrow. "You said he was a Catholic priest. Since when are priests allowed to marry?"

"Oh dear, I'm afraid I've been indiscreet." Dorothy cocked her head and laughed uncomfortably. "Well, I believe you'll be meeting him soon enough. Perhaps you should ask him yourself. I could tell you the story, but it's slightly embarrassing, to me anyway."

Ryuichi looked to Reika for a clue, but she shook her head, baffled. Suddenly Dorothy clapped her hands. "I just remembered something important. Ryuichi, you'll have to get authorization to establish an embassy."

"Why would we do that?"

"For your marketing. Some of your customers will want to legally register their unions there. You'll need a government representative. How were you going to deal with that?"

"Hm…I don't know. An embassy, eh?"

"Or maybe a consulate. I'm not sure. You can't send just anyone though. One of your staff will have to be authorized by the Foreign Ministry. It could be complicated." Dorothy looked at the couple and winked. "I'm sure you won't want to wait that long though."

"You heard?"

"Of course. You might have picked a more romantic setting. A place where you could both be shy about it."

"I'm too old to be shy." So saying, Ryuichi suddenly swept Reika off her feet into his arms.

"Ryuichi, what are you doing?" she said in shocked surprise.

"Dorothy, I'm looking forward to meeting your husband. Thanks again for everything!"

"Omedeto gozaimasu!" Dorothy said, in passable Japanese.

Dorothy waved as Ryuichi left, carrying Reika in his arms.

———⊶⊷———

"GET OFF OF there, you rascals. This isn't a playground!"

The old priest was bald, with a semicircle of blond hair. The children jumped down from the stone plinth and scattered. One of them toppled the large stone sitting on the plinth as he jumped. They left it on the ground and scampered off, hooting with derision.

"It's Xavier! He's gonna get us! The chrome dome priest!"

"Little buggers." Aaron Halifax smiled and watched the children run through the shrine gate and away down the stone steps. Sennosuke frowned.

"They shouldn't do that. You're too easy on them."

"Think so? At least they ran off. They know they've incurred God's wrath." He squatted and picked up the fallen stone. It was about the size of a baby's head and shaped like a crescent, its weathered surface mottled with lichen. Clearly the stone had been worked by hands that had vanished centuries, if not millennia ago. He hefted it back into place.

"There we go. They know this is sacred. They like to scare themselves by knocking it over. Even in this day and age, children haven't lost their innocence. Don't you think that's a miracle?"

"But that stone is your principal image. Getting it knocked over isn't very auspicious."

"'Principal image' is a Buddhist term. This stone houses Tsukuyomi no Mikoto, the Shinto moon god. The deity also resides at Ise Grand Shrine."

Aaron straightened up and looked toward the southern sky above the cryptomeria forest surrounding the shrine. "Ise doesn't have branch shrines, so our founder brought the deity here on his own initiative, if you take my meaning."

"Shinto is all rather mysterious to me."

"It can be very hard to understand. Still, it's an interesting way of looking at the world. Very accommodating. It's the religion of your ancestors. Don't you think you should know more about it?"

"Uh-oh, here comes the sermon." The two old men laughed and continued their stroll across the open hilltop in the early winter sunlight. Tsukiyama Shrine was deep in the mountains of northern Mie Prefecture. Aaron was the head priest.

As a Shinto shrine, Tsukiyama was unusual. There was no main building, only the stone plinth where the principal deity was enshrined. The shrine grounds also served as a park for the surrounding villages, and littering was rampant. The two men walked slowly around the grounds, stooping to pick up the odd bit of trash.

"Is that why you converted to Shinto from Catholicism? Because it's accommodating?"

"Well, I haven't returned to the laity, at least not yet. Maybe my letter of excommunication just hasn't caught up with me here in the mountains." Aaron seemed wholly at peace. "I was ordained in the diocese of Los Angeles. As a young man I hadn't the slightest doubts about my faith. But then something happened that plunged me into despair: love." Aaron gathered up another scrap of litter. "I met Dorothy. Naturally, Roman Catholic priests are forbidden to marry. For the first time I was confused. 'May God Almighty bless you and make you fertile, multiply you that you may become an assembly of people.' It suddenly made no sense that this path was closed to me. Of course, I knew the Church's teaching on celibacy for priests in great detail. But once the seed of doubt was planted, those teachings seem tinged with sophistry. I was hungry for a faith that offered space for me as a human being. Then I discovered Shinto."

"But didn't you find it...incomprehensible?"

"It is incomprehensible, in some ways. Maybe that's why it's flexible enough to encompass the whole of life. Shinto finds a spiritual essence residing in all things: the sun and moon, mountains and rivers, water and fire. Everything has this essence, the myriad gods that populate our world and what lies beyond it. Is there any other faith so wild, so lacking in reason and discrimination? Shinto might pick out a tree or a stone by the roadside as an object of worship. I was stunned to discover such a primitive religion thriving in a nation built on science and technology."

"Of course, the original practices were shaped by the ruling classes," said Sennosuke. "The ritual forms and practices changed a lot after Buddhism arrived in Japan. Then there was State Shinto during the war."

"Yet Shinto survived it all, absorbing everything without being changed. Christianity is based on the Bible. It wouldn't occur to anyone to make changes to the story of the life of Christ or write a new god into it. But Shinto is flexible enough to change. Taoism is a bit similar, but not quite the same. The urge to worship is very strong in Shinto. The object of veneration might be the fire on the hearth, even the location of a toilet. You Japanese are a strange people to worship such things."

Sennosuke stroked his beard. "So you fell in love with this strange faith and came to Japan."

"Yes. I studied for two years at Kogakkan University, passed the Association of Shinto Shrines' qualifying exam, and became a priest. I had a hard time—even my wearcom was no help in deciphering the ancient texts."

"Were you happy with your decision?"

"I was. Dorothy hated it. We had a huge blowup. I was supposed to come back and marry her, and instead I ended up staying here, putting the cart before the horse. But the fact is I didn't study Shinto just so I could be with her. Anyway, we agreed that I'd visit

California four times a year. It was a near thing, but I convinced her." He chuckled. "Thanks to a few lucky connections, I was assigned to this shrine. I didn't see it at first, but it's perfect for me. The deity here is the moon god, but it's just a stone without the slightest adornment. Simple nature worship."

Aaron looked toward the curved stone resting on its plinth in the center of the open space. He walked over to it and stood on the west side.

"During the annual festival, we hold a ceremony here for the rising moon. I was quite nervous the first time. I'm not Japanese, after all, and I wondered if I was even qualified to do it. But I needn't have worried." He looked off into the sky. A thin crescent floated just above the trees, faint against the bright blue.

"When I saw the moon that night, I had a spontaneous experience of wonderment. Thanks to the moon, grains fruit, tides move, women ovulate. The moon looks down on us from on high, but it's so close compared to the stars. Its power flows down on us all. All you need to worship it is to be human. I can easily understand why the people of ancient Japan looked up and revered it."

The two men stood gazing quietly at the crescent in the sky. Like most Japanese, Sennosuke did not hold any deep religious faith; for him, Aaron's view of the world held a certain freshness. Still, there was a fundamental difference between that worldview and his own. The Japanese veneration of the spiritual in everything, including the moon—often referred to with honorifics in Japanese—was something quite ordinary, simply a part of life, and very different from the serious way Westerners seemed to approach matters of faith. Sennosuke was struck anew by this curious fact, like seeing the rough surface of a stone come to light again after years covered over with moss.

"Perhaps space travel will be easier for the Japanese than for the rest of us," said Aaron abruptly.

"Why would that be?"

"You can create gods wherever you find yourself. You don't have to go to the trouble of figuring out the correct direction to face while praying, the way Muslims do. Wherever you go, a guardian deity is waiting for you—on the moon, Mars, Jupiter, Alpha Centauri. And you can have a deity for your rocket engines, your communications equipment, or your spacecraft."

"Sounds a little too convenient."

"Why not? A drowning man will create a deity to save himself, if he has to. The God of Christianity won't look after rocket engines. But you can find the sacred in anything. You can call up that spirit of reverence when you need it."

"I think you're giving us too much credit." Sennosuke sighed. "Most Japanese have lost that sense of reverence. They could probably benefit from one of your sermons."

"Uh-oh, here it comes."

"That's why I'm here today. It's time to discuss—"

"Sixth Continent?" Aaron's gray eyes rested lightly on Sennosuke. "You want me to conduct weddings there."

"Yes."

"I had a feeling that was the reason for this visit. I understand you've been busy dealing with the police. This is probably not a good time for you to be taking a trip to the mountains. Frankly, I was planning to turn you down. It seemed to me that you could do better than a dropout priest."

"I'm sorry to hear that."

"I said 'was.'" Aaron giggled like a boy. "Until you were fired. I take it separate priests for Shinto and Catholic ceremonies are beyond your means?"

"It's embarrassing, but you're right."

"Then I'm the man for the job. I'd be delighted to go."

"Really? That's wonderful!" Sennosuke grabbed Aaron's hand and began shaking it enthusiastically. Aaron tried to extricate himself.

"Don't forget, the Vatican may not permit it, given my switch to Shinto. There'll be complaints of some sort, I guarantee it."

"You leave that to me. I promise I'll handle it somehow."

"Then it's settled." They shook hands. The elderly American in traditional shrine vestments and the old Japanese in a tailored suit made a strange pair.

"How soon should I start getting ready?"

"Oh, not for three years. There's no rush."

"I see." Aaron glanced away. "You know, there's something I wanted to ask you. I can't get anyone to explain it to me."

"What's that?"

"Why does everyone around here call me 'Xavier'?"

A smile spread slowly across Sennosuke's face until he was grinning broadly. "It's a term of affection."

"I don't understand."

"It's the name of a very famous priest who came to Japan a long time ago."

Aaron stared at him, perplexed. Sennosuke chuckled for a moment, then Aaron remembered that the founder of the Jesuit order had visited Japan in the sixteenth century.

THE LOAN OFFICER walked into the senior managing director's office and pulled up short. His boss had a habit of stabbing at figures he didn't like with the tip of his finger. He was doing it now.

The loan officer spoke cautiously. "I see you received the updated numbers for Sixth Continent."

"They want six billion. Look at these ratios. Are you sure this is prudent?"

The loan officer would have preferred that this particular application not go so high in the bank's hierarchy, but the amount involved made it inevitable. "Sixth Continent is independent of ELE now. But Gotoba Engineering and Tenryu Galaxy Transport have indicated they will proceed with the project. Their ties with

Sixth Continent are very tight. With a hundred billion already invested, I don't see much chance of them pulling out. The earnings projection was independently audited by three firms. Two of the auditors came back and said the projections appeared reasonable. The other said it was impossible to assign any certainty to the numbers. Too many things could happen. The media has eased off its attacks, which is helping the reservation numbers. I don't see significant risk in extending additional credit."

"The media's a temporary problem. I wish I could say the same for this. Take a look." He pushed a newspaper across his desk.

"'Joyful Homeland'?" The loan officer was puzzled. "Is it some kind of religious cult?"

"It's a bona fide pressure group. Scientists, university professors, economists, critics, politicians. Even some well-known lobbyists."

"What's their goal?"

"They say Sixth Continent's orbital debris will seriously interfere with other uses of space. Furthermore, trying to clean up even part of this stuff will sink them financially. A lot of the current funding is going to pay for Phase E."

"I'm sorry. I'll prepare a uses of funds statement immediately."

"Don't bother. I've already done it." The director stabbed another paper with his finger. "Their own projections don't promise much more than break-even performance. One more unforeseen problem could sink them. If that happens, even support from their partners might not be enough. Do you want a repeat of what happened twenty years ago?"

The loan officer frowned. The bank had briefly been a ward of the state after nearly collapsing due to bad loans. It had been a black day in Japan's economic history. Public opposition to the rescue had been intense; people were fed up with taxpayer assistance to banks that could not manage their appetite for risk.

"We're into these people for more than enough. No more. In fact, I want them to come up with more collateral for the loans they do have."

"That would be their physical assets on the moon, sir—materials and equipment. If they default, I don't see how those assets could be recovered." The loan officer was perspiring. He had personally hoped to see Tae succeed. Her project seemed to offer some kind of hope for the future, even if he would never be able to go to the moon himself.

But the senior managing director dealt in facts, not dreams. "NASA is building something similar nearby. I don't know if we could transfer the equipment to them, but I'm sure they'd find a use for at least some of it. If Sixth Continent defaults, we sell the assets to the Americans."

"We'll go anywhere to repossess. Even the moon," said the loan officer wryly.

"Moneylenders have never been popular. We're not in the business of selling hope for the future. Better get that through your head too."

"Yes, sir."

As he left the office, the loan officer realized the meaning of that "too." The senior managing director had also been young once.

[2]

THE SPRING OF 2033 saw a string of small successes at Eden Crater.

A synchronized array of forty heliostats at the top of the crater rim focused sunlight on a kiln that revolved much like a cement mixer at the base. The mirror array raised the temperature in the kiln to over 1200 degrees, sintering the churning material into alumina cement clinker. The roasted clinker was transported by multidozers to the crushing module, and from there to the block assembly area, where permafrost catapulted over the crater rim by the bulk shooter was ready for mixing. The permafrost/cement mixture was poured, still frozen, into forms preloaded with a carbon fiber reinforcing lattice. The regolith embedded in the water ice matrix acted as aggregate for the cement. External tensioning rods stretched the carbon fiber lattice while pressure was applied to the form itself. This prestressing would reduce the tendency of the finished blocks to crack under tensile stress. It was essential if the concrete structures were to be pressurized safely.

The heliostats were then trained on the blocks. Eventually the kiln and block assembly would each have its own array of mirrors, but for the moment Sixth Continent was making do with one.

The solar heat applied to the forms melted the permafrost, initiating the cement's hydration reaction and causing the concrete to progressively harden. The blocks were then left to cure for three days at constant temperature and humidity. Unless curing was carefully controlled, the concrete would not reach its potential strength.

The forms were then lifted off by a dozer. Each milky white block was three meters long by one square—on the lunar surface, a mass of 1.2 tons. As the first block emerged from its form, Sohya and his team moved in to inspect it.

Sohya hesitantly touched the surface of the block. It was free of bubbles or pores, as smooth as if it had been polished. It almost looked as if it could reflect the stars. On Earth, a block like this would attract no special notice. Here, on the rugged surface of the moon, it seemed as beautiful and priceless as a jewel in its flawless symmetry.

The most important component of Sixth Continent—concrete—was now a reality. Eighty percent of the work would consist of the manufacture of these massive cuboids, which seemed to radiate a gravitas far weightier than metal. For several minutes, the four men moved silently around the block in wonder, brushing it with the tips of their gloves.

The first block was carried by a multidozer and placed on foundation piles at a location pinpointed by laser from polar orbit. All further construction would proceed using this block as a reference point. Sohya anchored the white granite plaque brought from

Earth to the side of the block. This was the cornerstone of Sixth Continent. The date was March 15, 2033.

Later that day, a party was held simultaneously on the moon and at Gotenba Ground Support. Sohya toasted Iwaki with a glass of sake.

"To progress. Tomorrow we start construction of the base."

"To progress," said Iwaki. "Listen, we've decided to hold off on spraying the ice blanket. We'll be sticking with block placement for the time being." Iwaki's face was oddly devoid of expression. He was referring to the repeated spraying of liquid water on the completed surface of the structures. The resulting layer of ice would act as an additional seal against the vacuum and provide enhanced shielding from cosmic rays.

"Why put it off? The ice has to be applied in stages. If we delay it, it will change the whole timeline. What's up?"

"We just don't want to lock ourselves in…Listen, I'd better explain later. Have another one for me."

With ice spraying off the schedule, they decided to begin the next day with liftoff testing for the Turtles and orbital fueling of the Titan X tugboat. The tugboat was the second stage of a rocket designed to launch NASA satellites, modified in the Unitd States with a lower-output engine for extended operational life and an adaptor port for refueling. The tugboat reached lunar orbit under NASA control. This would be the first time the Japanese had direct access. They called on Liberty Island to help with the handover.

The Americans had rerouted their large Mars Ambassador spacecraft to the lunar south pole and were rapidly expanding the base with inflatable structures. Liberty Island would serve as a planetary research facility and did not need concrete structures. Instead, it was steadily building a platform where JPL's ground-based functions for tracking and controlling unmanned planetary probes could be fully replicated.

NASA astronaut Henderson—the same astronaut who had rendered assistance to Ryuichi in *Apple 3*—arrived at Xiwangmu 6 with a portable control panel for the tug. While he maneuvered the tug in orbit above the surface, Yamagiwa sat at another control panel, guiding the Turtle to its docking position. Managing this delicate operation was impossible from Earth given the three-second signal delay. In effect, Yamagiwa and Henderson were standing in for GGS and Johnson Space Center.

After a few tense moments, the spacecraft were successfully docked. The Turtle began transferring liquid oxygen and hydrogen to the tug. The astronauts wiped the perspiration from their foreheads and shook hands.

"That was a beautiful approach, Mr. Yamagiwa."

"I couldn't have done it without your help, Commander Henderson. Thanks for familiarizing yourself with the control console on short notice—we were planning to do this a bit later."

"I had to pull an all-nighter to tell the truth. But she's all yours now. Are you sure you can handle it on your own next time?"

Sohya had taped the entire procedure. He lowered his video camera and gave the two men the high sign. Then he looked from one to the other. "You guys were really in sync there. Do you know each other?"

"A bit," said Henderson. The two men wagged their eyebrows and laughed. Sohya didn't know that Henderson had been commander of the shuttle *Frontier*.

"Now Sixth Continent has a free ride from low earth orbit all the way to the lunar surface with the fuel you're synthesizing here. If my bosses weren't so stubborn, Liberty Island could benefit from it too."

"We'd love to have you use it," said Sohya, "but we don't have much fuel on hand yet. Our ice-spraying operation was delayed, so we have to move on to fuel synthesis earlier than we planned. We've produced plenty of oxygen for the base, but we don't have the facilities to store much liquid hydrogen—with the tanks we have, it would slowly leak away. On the other hand, shutting down the electrolysis unit loses us time too. This schedule change is a pain in the ass."

"That's not a problem," Henderson said casually. "Any kind of storage tank will work. Put it in the shadow zone. The temperature is close to the boiling point for hydrogen there."

"I see…That's great advice. Thanks. I'll get Gotenba to work out the details."

"Glad to be of assistance." Henderson waved as if to say *no problem*. "What's up with the ice blanket? Have you run into something?"

"I'm not sure. Gotenba doesn't want to seal the blocks in position yet. I don't know why. There's no way we'd move them once they're in place."

"I would say not." Henderson shook his head ruefully. "It might be on the off chance that you end up having to sell the blocks to NASA. We sure could use them at Liberty Island."

"What 'off chance'?"

"If you guys can't pay your creditors, say. One of the senior people at Johnson made a comment to that effect. He said your equipment and materials were put up as collateral for your loans. If you default, your banks might end up selling them to us."

Yamagiwa and Sohya gaped in surprise. "Did you hear anything about this?"

"No. The guys back on Earth aren't telling us everything."

"They probably don't want to demoralize you," said Henderson. "Look, I'm sorry. I probably shouldn't even have mentioned it."

Seeing their increasing bewilderment, he hastened to reassure them. "Seriously, I wouldn't worry about it. Don't forget, the Moon Treaty is still in force. As far as the UN Court of Justice is concerned, this is a SETI research facility, not a commercial operation. Converting what you have here into loan collateral probably wouldn't stand up in court."

Yamagiwa sighed. "I hope so. You know, John Swigert had to worry about the IRS while he was fighting for his life on *Apollo 13*. Even up here, we can't get away from the bullshit back home."

"Well, we'd best leave that sort of thing to our bosses on Earth.

Worrying about it won't do us any good." Hoping to change the subject, Henderson looked around the interior of Xiwangmu. "It's strange. Here I am, an American astronaut, visiting a spacecraft designed by the Russians, built by the Chinese, and operated by the Japanese." He smiled. "It's got to be some kind of miracle."

"Just hard work," said Sohya. "There are no miracles in space." Henderson was about to say something, but Sohya's expression stopped him. There had been no miracle for Shinji.

Henderson nodded. He moved toward the air lock. "Good luck. Hope to see this place completed soon. Don't let the bickering back home get under your skin. NASA's rooting for your success."

"Good luck to you too, Commander."

Henderson waved farewell and disappeared into the air lock.

For the next two months, block production proceeded smoothly. A Turtle made six trips into lunar orbit and back. Sixty tons of supplies arrived from Earth aboard the tug and were brought down to the surface. But on its seventh journey into orbit, the Turtle's engine exploded. A round-trip took three burns—one to climb into orbit and two to return to the surface—so the engine had managed a total of twenty ignitions before giving out. This was three more than expected, which meant this test to failure could be counted a success. The explosion had been anticipated, and the side of the habitat module facing the landing pad had been shielded with regolith by the multidozers. The only collateral damage was the loss of a few panels on the solar array.

At some point the tug's main engine would also fail. No engine yet developed had an unlimited operating life; the next challenge was to determine a safe schedule for replacing the engines before they failed. Otherwise the tug could not ferry humans to the moon.

Every success produced a new challenge. This alternating cycle of progress and challenges was something Tetsuo Sando had anticipated. Every problem that arose was reported to Gotoba for resolution by its team of engineers.

At the end of May, the first team wrapped six months of work on the surface and prepared to return to Earth. This first six months on the surface had been filled with hurdles, but they had pressed ahead and managed to complete all their objectives. They had planned to wait for the arrival of the second team before departing but were told that the launch had been delayed at the last minute by bad weather. Gotenba ordered them home on schedule.

But when they emerged from the core on the runway at Tanegashima, they saw that all the launch pads were empty.

———◦•◦•◦———

"TAE, ARE YOU here? Tae!"

Sohya was knocking on the door of a house near Nagoya International Airport. After a minute, Reika Hozumi peeked out.

"Sohya, how did you find this place?"

"Ryuichi. Tae's wearcom isn't responding. Is she here?"

"Yes, but…"

"He only told me after I'd looked everywhere else. I've got to see her." He brushed past Reika into a corridor that gave onto a spacious living room. Tae was sitting on a sofa in the corner of the room, wearing her usual monotone ensemble. She was leaning back on the cushions with her eyes closed.

Sohya advanced toward her. "What's the deal? Things are falling apart. This is no time to go underground."

"Sohya, don't. She's exhausted." Reika tried to pull him aside. "She just got back from Guyana this morning. Before that she was in Riyadh, and Paris before that—"

"I just got back from the moon. I've been gone six months. I can barely walk on this planet anymore."

"You don't know how hard she's been working!"

"Reika." Tae waved a hand and leaned forward. She ran her fingers through her tousled black hair and sighed. "I'm fine."

"But—"

"It's all right. Sohya should know everything." She kept her eyes on the floor. "Sit down." Perplexed, Sohya sat beside her. "I was in Paris to ask the ESA for help," she said, still staring at the floor.

"What kind of help?"

"They told me to talk to their sponsors. So I flew to Riyadh. I talked to Arabsat. ESA launches their satellites."

"What did you need help with?"

"But Arabsat said they only launch geostationary satellites. They're not part of the problem. So I went to Guyana. To ESA's Phaedra launch center. If the sponsors wouldn't talk to me, I thought maybe the people at the space center would."

"I still don't follow you."

"I wanted a partner to help with Phase E." Tae looked up at him. Her eyes were welling with tears. "Almost all the debris belongs to the world's space agencies. It didn't come from us."

"Why talk to Arabsat? What about the Americans? Or the Russians? Most of the junk is theirs."

She shook her head. Sohya suddenly remembered that she'd sued the Russian government after Shinji's death. That had gone nowhere though, and she'd had nowhere else to turn.

"It's no good. I went all over the world. They just slammed the door in my face."

"But why did you have to go to all that trouble? Sixth Continent is a private venture. We've already done everything we can to deal with the problem. Even if we can't solve it single-handedly, it's great PR."

"Of course it is. We told the world! But it's no use." Tae's voice was filled with despair. "We can't beat them!"

Sohya drew back. He'd never heard her wail like this. "Joyful Homeland is attacking us with numbers," she continued. "Real numbers. They're right. Our PR isn't working. The only way we can fight back is with numbers of our own. But we don't have any."

Sohya wasn't sure how to respond to this litany. He said

to Reika, who was leaning against the back of the sofa, "What's Phase E accomplished so far?"

"We've eliminated 112 pieces of debris with five puffballs. We certainly proved the effectiveness of the approach."

"But it's nothing compared to the forty thousand objects larger than ten centimeters that are still out there," Tae whispered, her voice trembling. "Getting rid of them all would take almost two *thousand* puffballs. It's completely hopeless."

"Is that why you're hiding here?" Sohya tried to keep the edge out of his voice. Reika shook her head.

"We knew we could never eliminate all the debris on our own. The problem is we can't even clean up the debris that Sixth Continent is generating. Phase E isn't going to have much effect if it can't accomplish that."

"So—can it?"

"We need to launch two more puffballs. If we can launch two more, we can clean up everything over ten centimeters in the orbital band that Sixth Continent is using. TGT is modifying their designs. Future spent boosters will automatically deorbit and burn up. So once the cleanup is done, we won't be generating any more junk."

"That doesn't sound so bad."

"Each mission costs three billion yen," murmured Tae. "We don't have the funds. No one will lend to us. Joyful Homeland has made sure the banks don't see a future in Sixth Continent."

Suddenly Henderson's statement about collateral made sense to Sohya. But it still didn't explain why Tae had to go into hiding.

"Reika, I'd like to talk to her alone."

"All right. I'll make a fresh pot of coffee." Reika gave Tae a look of concern and left the room.

"We haven't had a chance to talk like this for a year," said Sohya. "Not since Shinji died." Tae didn't answer. She stared at the floor. "There's something I need to ask you. I want you to tell me the truth."

"What is it?"

"What do you want?"

She looked at him, puzzled. He peered at her steadily. "You seem to be taking the long way around to happiness. I have no idea what it is you really want. I asked you eight years ago. I'm going to ask you again. Why are you doing this?"

Tae's lips were dry. They moved fitfully, but the words would not come. At length she said, "I...I want friends."

"Friends."

"Yes. I'm going to wait on the moon for visitors from another world. Sixth Continent will be there to welcome—"

"That's the first time I've heard that. So that's what the SETI package is for. Okay, I'm sure you're telling the truth. But that's not why you're doing this. You don't know yourself, do you? It's all just a means to an end."

"An end? What end?"

"You're obsessed with Joyful Homeland. They're no bigger than the other challenges we've faced. But your father is behind them. That's why they bother you so much. It didn't hit me till I heard you talking just now."

Tae pressed her lips together grimly. She shook her head.

Sohya spoke softly. "I'm right, aren't I?"

"No. You're wrong."

"Am I? I don't know what happened between you and your father. But everything points to him. People all over the world think you're a genius, but it's never made you smile. There's only one person you care about, but he won't give you what you want."

"I'm twenty-one years old! What do I need approval for?"

"Age doesn't mean a thing. Let down the barriers for once, Tae. Sixth Continent is all about getting approval from your father— isn't it?"

"My mother is dead. It was his fault!"

This was unexpected. "Are you sure of that?"

Her shoulders were trembling. She closed her eyes. "There was an accident. At the park. People were hurt."

"What happened?"

"It was one of the rides. A design problem. Twelve people were injured. Of course someone senior, a company representative, had to visit them in the hospital. But the whole management team was overseas, except my mother. So she had to go to the hospital. A truck hit her car on the way there. She died instantly."

"So it was an accident, right?"

"Maybe. But it was the kind of role my father always shoved off on her. He would never have gone to the hospital himself." She shook her head. "All he cared about was his own convenience. I hate him. He wouldn't even take time off for a proper wedding ceremony—"

"Tae, listen to me." Sohya gently grasped her shoulders. "You're building a wedding palace for your mother and father."

He watched her. Her eyes were wide-open now, brimming with baffled tears. He put a hand on her cheek. It was burning.

"Try to remember. There must have been a time when your parents were happy together. That's what you want to recapture."

There was no answer. She blinked several times, staring into some far distance. All her life she had been marching determinedly away from her past. Now her mind was retracing those steps.

At last she regained her voice. "No…it can't be. It's not true…"

"Relax. Take some time and think about it. We'll figure out Phase E later. I have an idea."

Tae groaned, as if she were about to faint. Her eyes were blank. She was shaking. Sohya quietly moved away from her. Some space inside her that she had walled up long ago was breaking open. Only she could gaze into that darkness. He would just have to wait for her to return when she was ready.

The front door jerked open. Sohya half expected to see Reika. Instead, it was a man in a tailored beige suit. He jumped to his feet.

"What are you doing here?" he shouted.

"You must be Sohya Aomine. I recognize you. I'm Tae's father."

"How did you find this place?"

"Your wearcom. You've been spending too much time with my daughter's bodyguards. Very careless. They had everything we needed to trace it."

"Mr. Toenji! Please don't do this!" Two ELE security men emerged from the kitchen with Reika firmly in their grip. Obviously they were familiar with the layout of the house. "She can't see you now! She's under tremendous stress!" cried Reika.

"That's why I had to come." Kiichiro brushed past Reika and strode into the room. He went over to Tae and looked down at her coldly.

"Come, Tae. Look at me. You know it's no use. You've reached your limit. It's time for you to come home and let go of Sixth Continent once and for all."

"Mr. Toenji, you should be ashamed." Sohya stepped protectively in front of Tae. "Is this how you deal with your daughter? Is force the only language you understand? Can't you understand why she's going to so much trouble to stay away from you?"

"This matter doesn't concern you. I'll deal with you later, after—"

"Tae!" Reika cried out and broke free. She ran over and grabbed her hand. "Are you all right?"

Sohya turned to see the girl slumped over, eyes closed. Her breathing was shallow and rapid. Something was wrong. Sohya felt her forehead; it was on fire.

"Call an ambulance. She's burning up!"

"I'll do it!" Reika ran for the phone.

"Wait," said Kiichiro. "I'll take her." He motioned to his security detail. "Get the helicopter." He looked at Sohya and Reika. "I need you to go to her place and bring a change of clothes."

"She doesn't have a place!" said Reika. She pointed to a large suitcase in the corner of the room. "That's everything she has now. She's living like a nomad out of that one suitcase!"

"I'll take her to the hospital then. Bring the suitcase in your car."

Sohya put his arms around Tae and looked up at Kiichiro. "You don't have the right to take her."

"What are you talking about?"

"Leave her. But when she's better, you owe her an apology!"

"What in the world would I apologize for?" Kiichiro reached out to pull her away from Sohya.

"A fatal traffic accident!"

Kiichiro's hand jerked back. Sohya could only have heard about the accident from Tae. Perhaps this young man knew his daughter better than he imagined.

He motioned to the security detail at the exit. They parted to let Sohya through as he carried Tae in his arms like a fragile doll. Kiichiro did not follow. He stood and watched them go.

[3]

TAE HAD NOT dreamt for years. When she was able to sleep, she slept deeply, her heart barred against that inner world. She rarely experienced the twilight zone between dreams and wakefulness.

She opened her eyes slightly. A flood of colors struck her retinas. *Oh. This must be a dream*, she thought.

Eyes open wider, coming awake, she realized it was no dream. She was surrounded by flowers—a wall of them, from the floor to higher than her head.

"What...?"

"Well, good morning." A nurse was standing next to the bed, making notes on a clipboard. She smiled. "We have a limit on flowers in the room, but the man who brought you here asked us to bring everything in. How are you feeling?"

"I think I'm dreaming."

"You like flowers?"

It's not that, Tae was about to say, but she couldn't find the words. It wasn't that she disliked flowers. The nurse began replacing her IV bag.

"It's been three days since you collapsed. Fatigue from overwork, plus jet lag, aggravated by a cold. You almost developed pneumonia. You shouldn't have been running around the world without vaccinations either. We're going to conduct more tests. You'll be here for a few more days."

"When can I leave? If I don't get back to work, everyone will—"

"Everyone is just fine," said the nurse. "You're famous, Ms. Toenji."

She tried to sit up. The nurse skillfully eased her back onto the pillows and inserted a thermometer in her ear. "A hundred and one. Still high. You need more rest. Tomorrow if you have an appetite, we'll start you on soft food. Until then you'll just have to be patient." The nurse rearranged the bedcovers and left the room.

Tae looked around. The number of bouquets was truly unbelievable. Those at the bottom were probably from TGT and Gotoba. So the next layer would be from partners and affiliates. Wouldn't it? She plucked a tiny card from a bouquet nearby.

Take care of yourself, moon Princess. A.B. Navamukundan, KL.

She didn't recognize the name. Someone in Malaysia? The next card was from another unknown sender. And the next. And the next. Some were from individuals, some from companies with no connection to Sixth Continent. There were even a few from foreign politicians.

Then it hit her: her condition had been announced to the world. How was she going to deal with this? It was hardly good for Sixth Continent's image for people to know that its prime mover had—

Sixth Continent's image?

Hundreds of bouquets. An ocean of compassion. Best wishes from people she'd never met.

Tae looked around the room in a daze. She would never have expected such an outpouring of support. She'd never paid attention to fan mail and automatically filtered messages that didn't appear important. She'd never thought of the effects of her publicity except in terms of numbers—approval ratings, audience share…

Now she was surrounded by pure affection no numbers could convey. As the reality sank in, she felt overwhelmed. She sank deeper into the pillows and closed her eyes. Sohya's voice echoed in the darkness. "A means to an end…"

I'm using these people. And Sohya.

Tae's fever roared back. She fell into a deep sleep.

———◆·✦·◆———

SENNOSUKE STEPPED OUT of the limousine and almost lost his footing. Two strong arms supported him from either side.

"Are you all right?" said Ryuichi.

"Sorry about that. I strained my back at the beginning of spring. Once you reach ninety-three, things start falling apart, it seems."

"Come now, the base won't be complete for another three years. A year of that is our fault, of course," said Gotoba.

"Not just yours," said Ryuichi. "I'm forty-five, you're sixty-five. If we don't get on with it, we won't be able to go into space either. Let's get this project finished as soon as possible."

"The question is whether it will be finished before I retire." The three men laughed. Each wore an expression of resolve—none wanted to be the first to forgo a trip into space because of his age.

The men left the car and driver behind and walked across a concrete roadway as wide as a six-lane highway. On the opposite side was an enormous, featureless building. Up close, it was so long that its ends were hard to make out. This was just part of TGT's Tobishima facility.

The men stood in front of a single door set into the vast expanse of wall. "What is it you wanted to show us?" asked Gotoba.

"If you've only seen Eve and Adam on a video monitor," said Ryuichi, "you don't know what a rocket is really like. I want you to experience the real thing."

"That's how you convinced Aomine," laughed Gotoba. After witnessing the TROPHY test, Sohya had returned to headquarters fired with such enthusiasm that people wondered if TGT had brainwashed him.

"After you." Ryuichi opened the door. Inside, the vast building was awash with the flat, white illumination of LCD lights. Immediately before them was a squat tube the size of a microbus, lying on its side. A line of twenty tubes stretched off in both directions.

"This is the HAB. Hybrid Assist Booster."

"A new engine?"

"Nothing new about it. That's our selling point." Ryuichi walked up to one of the engines and laid his hand on it.

"You're familiar with the solid boosters strapped to Eve and Adam? They use conventional polymer-binder fuel. HAB uses solid *and* liquid fuel. The booster can be extinguished and reignited—no, let's leave out the technical explanations. I'm not sure I understand it myself."

"Good," said Sennosuke. "I have no idea how these things work either. 'Paraffin fuel binders'? 'Mandelbrot set cross sections'? It's like a foreign language." He was reading from a plaque on a stand in front of one of the engines.

"Shinji was so good at explaining this sort of thing," said Ryuichi quietly. "This was his final design. He thought it was his best. The point is it's for export. As you've probably heard, the old Diet resolution against exporting rocket technology has just been repealed. These engines will be heading out the door soon."

"You said they'd sell because the design isn't new?" asked Sennosuke.

"The concept has a long history. Like TROPHY, people have been trying to develop an engine like this since the last century. Shinji made the design safe. These boosters could be used with the Eve launch vehicle—they're reliable enough for manned applications. Of course we won't be doing that since we've already manufactured all the boosters we'll need for Sixth Continent." He turned to Gotoba. "How are your multidozer sales? I heard you were selling them for extreme environment applications."

"We're selling a few. If our bid for the Euphrates dredging project wins, we should be able to recoup our development costs."

"So both our companies have sources of income besides Sixth Continent. Can I interest you in a little philanthropy?"

"I knew this wasn't just a factory tour." Gotoba's expression indicated he'd been expecting this.

"Reika and our finance people have been working hard. With eight billion in additional funds, we can finish the base. That includes the remaining costs of Phase E. I'd like to propose that Gotoba and TGT jointly provide the funds."

Sennosuke raised his hand. "Just a moment, Mr. Yaenami. It pains me to hear this. You don't need to go that far."

Ryuichi ignored him. "I know what you're thinking, Mr. Gotoba. Construction companies aren't supposed to subsidize their own projects. You could withdraw from the project and make a profit elsewhere. So I won't insist. This is a personal appeal."

"It won't be easy to convince the board."

Ryuichi was not expecting this response. He'd expected hesitation, quite a bit in fact. But Gotoba's answer meant he had agreed.

"I've been president of the company long enough. The board might kick me out before the project is complete, but it's worth betting my seat on."

"Mr. Gotoba, are you sure?" asked Sennosuke.

"I can't afford eight billion. That's half the net profit we're expecting from this project. I might be able to swing a billion. But let's consider all the options."

"I thank you, sir!"

"No need for that. People in our industry hate to withdraw from something once they've taken it on. If it's necessary to get things completed, we're willing to give a bit extra." Gotoba waved his hand magnanimously.

Ryuichi ran his fingers through his disheveled mane and murmured, "The question is how much of the other seven billion TGT can come up with."

Sennosuke shook his head and bowed deeply. "I don't know how to thank you—either of you. I wish there were some way I could."

Ryuichi shook his head and smiled. "The space business has always been full of pitfalls. People make a fortune in the information or entertainment industries and apply their wealth to space development. Then the costs go sky high, they lose their fortunes and have to give up. Frankly, I've been expecting bankruptcy since I joined this project."

"If only I were still chairman of ELE…No, I'm too old to be calling the tune now. I just hope I can keep helping Tae."

"We never should've allowed her to bear so much responsibility."

The three men nodded sadly. Ryuichi and Gotoba were both seasoned executives; they had never blindly assumed Tae could handle the job. They had accepted her because of her abilities and her value as a symbol of the project. Even after ELE had washed its hands of Sixth Continent, they had agreed to her remaining its symbol. But working herself into the hospital could only be regarded as a blunder on her part, both as an executive and an adult. "We need someone who can take over some of her responsibilities. We're the ones who are supposed to be helping her, after all," said Ryuichi.

"But where can we find someone who's as capable as she is and acceptable to her as well?" The three men exchanged resigned glances. Ryuichi's wearcom chimed. He stepped away for a moment.

"Excuse me…Yes, it's me. Clients? I'm busy. From Seattle?" His expression changed. Without ending the call, he said to his visitors, "You're not in a hurry, are you? I'd like you to join me in a meeting."

"Concerning what?"

"Something good, I have a feeling. A representative from Blue Origin is in my office. The private space development company in Seattle."

"Private enterprise building launch vehicles?" said Sennosuke. "I didn't know there were such companies in America—"

Ryuichi wasn't listening. He was already running for the door.

KIICHIRO WALKED QUICKLY through the lobby of Nagoya University Hospital. He noticed an old man wearing traditional white and light blue priest's robes talking to someone at the counter. As he walked past, toward the patient's wing, the man addressed him.

"Mr. Toenji?"

Kiichiro turned and saw that the man was looking at him. After a moment he realized with a start that this was a Shinto priest with gray eyes—a foreigner.

"Excuse me?"

"My name is Aaron Halifax. You're Mr. Toenji, aren't you. Your father is a personal friend of mine."

"Sennosuke?"

"Yes. You're here to see Tae. So am I. Shall we go together?"

"As you wish." Kiichiro was hardly pleased, but he could think of no reason to refuse. They walked down a long corridor marked with tape of different colors. The corridor was busy with nurses and patients in automated wheelchairs. Kiichiro kept three or four paces ahead.

"You have good news, I see," said Aaron.

"What makes you think that?"

"Someone with bad news wouldn't be in such a hurry. It must be something that will please your daughter."

"You think I'm here to please her?"

"You're her father."

"I'm afraid my domestic affairs are private."

"My apologies. I had the feeling you needed some advice."

"May I ask who you are?" Kiichiro stopped in the middle of the corridor, genuinely irritated. Aaron smiled calmly.

"Can't you tell? I'm a priest. I'd be happy to perform the sacrament of reconciliation for you. If you need a confessor, I'm at your disposal." Kiichiro saw that Aaron was holding a small cross. He narrowed his eyes in suspicion.

"You're a clergyman?"

"I am a Catholic priest. The seal of the confessional is inviolable, of course." With that, Aaron slipped through a door that opened off the corridor. Kiichiro followed him, about to say more, and found himself in a large linen closet.

"You love your daughter, don't you?"

"Of course." Kiichiro glanced around at the shelves of folded towels in bewilderment.

"And is she happy?"

"I'm afraid not."

"Then she does not feel your love. You should consider how you communicate it. Are you making a sincere effort to let her know how you feel?"

"I do…I mean, of course I am."

"You're certain?" asked Aaron quietly. Kiichiro felt a sudden constriction in his chest. What was he doing here? What were these questions? First that young friend of Tae's, now this old man.

"My daughter…runs away from me. I try to stop her, but—"

"You don't want her to leave."

"No."

"You want love."

Kiichiro blushed. Aaron touched him gently. "No need to feel embarrassed. It's normal to want the love of one's offspring. But you realize love can't be forced, don't you? God enjoins us to love one other, not to be loved."

"…Yes." Kiichiro nodded.

Aaron smiled. "Thank you, you have confessed."

"What?" Kiichiro looked startled.

"Your penance is complete. You know what to do. Don't force it. If love doesn't come today, it will tomorrow, or the day after."

"What do you mean?"

"Don't hurry. Take things a day at a time." Aaron patted his arm and left the room. He headed toward the lobby.

"You're not coming?" called Kiichiro.

"Give my regards to your daughter. Tell her I'm looking forward to becoming an astronaut." He rounded the corner and disappeared.

For a few moments Kiichiro stood uncertainly in the corridor, then nodded and set off for Tae's room. He felt as if he'd just experienced something unreal. Yet Aaron's words lingered in his mind. *Your penance is complete.*

Had he really done penance? Lost in thought, he walked past Tae's room without noticing. A nurse called to him. He doubled back and knocked on the door.

"Tae? It's me."

"Come in." Her voice was unexpectedly casual. Feeling slightly disarmed, he opened the door and was astonished to see the flowers surrounding the bed. "What happened?"

"Everyone's been so kind. They're very pretty, but the ones at the bottom are starting to wilt. I'm going to have to do something. By the way, Sohya was the one who told them to bring them all in here."

She was smiling cheerfully. It was positively disconcerting. He approached the bed hesitantly and noticed that each of the bouquets had a handwritten card attached.

"Are these all from individuals?"

"Not every one. Some are from fan clubs around the world. I don't know any of these people. But look at them all. I've been doing a lot of thinking."

"About what?"

"So many people are wishing us success, regardless of the space debris. I thought I could control our image with publicity. Now I feel so embarrassed. The first thing I do at the next press conference will be to thank everyone for this."

The old enmity had left her voice. Or was she was just hiding it? She was far more at ease than Kiichiro, who had come girded for another confrontation. Now the opportunity to go on the attack before being attacked seemed to have slipped away.

Tae picked up her wearcom from the bedside table and looked steadily at Kiichiro. "People are even making contributions."

"Really?"

"So far we've gotten donations from more than thirty thousand people. It's about five hundred million yen. I'm going to use the money for Phase E. Some of the contributors requested that anyway. It really helps."

"Did you publicize your financial situation?"

"Yes, we did. Moody's and S&P both dropped us in their ratings a bit, but I'm not going to worry about it." Tae smiled. Like a flower.

She's changed, thought Kiichiro. *I don't know how or why, but she doesn't seem obsessed anymore. It's as if a burden has been taken from her. She was never able to accept positive feedback like this before.* Support had changed her—support from countless anonymous people. Tokai Eden had never received this much positive feedback from its guests.

"What brings you here?" asked Tae. Her question brought Kiichiro out of his reverie. Why *was* he here?

"I have good news."

Given what he had come to say, Kiichiro had been expecting to deliver his announcement with a tinge of sarcasm. Now he was mystified to find that his bitterness had dissolved.

"Actually, three pieces of good news. Reika Hozumi at TGT advised me of the first. Eight private space development companies in the United States, including Blue Origin, want to license the right to manufacture puffballs. They want to develop the expertise to sell orbital cleanup services to NASA."

"Really?" Tae sat up excitedly. "Blue Origin developed their own TROPHY engine with information released by TGT. This must be their way of thanking us!"

"Number two: NASA is seriously considering paying private

companies for orbital cleanup work. Not only that—the Indian and European space agencies have announced they will start cleanup operations within a year. China and India are rivals, so that may be why China has just announced a joint effort with Russia to do the same thing."

"Why is this happening all of a sudden? When I talked to those agencies, they were all so unfriendly." Tae's eyes were wide with astonishment.

Kiichiro shook his head. "You're still naive. There's no short-term benefit from cleaning up the debris, but the national space agencies know there's a long-term benefit to solving the problem. Still, no one wanted to be the first mover, so they were all hanging back. It's inevitable. Once the main orbital bands are clean, whoever uses them will enjoy safer spaceflight, lower launch costs, and lower insurance premiums. Everyone has been waiting for someone else to grasp the nettle. If nothing is done, private industry is sure to go after NASA in a few years anyway, and they'll have no choice but to deal with it. But they wouldn't be likely to base their timing on Sixth Continent's image problem."

"So my timing was bad."

"Of course. You confused their interests with your own. In fact, moving ahead after a push from you would only make them look worse for not acting earlier."

Kiichiro felt a strange joy welling up inside him. He and Tae were talking instead of fighting. This simple pleasure, an everyday event between parent and child, was something he hadn't experienced for many years. Tae's eyes were shining. "What's the third piece of news?"

"Joyful Homeland is disbanding. The response from the space agencies makes it no longer necessary. Three years from now, when Sixth Continent is complete, low earth orbit should be safe for manned commercial spaceflight. There'll be no need to keep humanity tied to Earth."

"Was that your decision?"

"I founded the group, but I don't control it. Its main advantage was that its arguments were firmly based in reality. But reality has changed."

"Father!"

Kiichiro was so surprised he almost retreated a step. Tae grasped his hands tightly. She could hardly speak from excitement.

"Father, I…I was thinking…I have a favor to ask of you. It's kind of strange…I mean, sort of late…or maybe impossible…" Her voice died away. He squeezed her hand.

"Calm down now. Tell me."

"I want you and Mother to have a wedding on the moon!"

She clung to his hand so determinedly that Kiichiro was almost pulled off balance. He was pondering the meaning of her request when Aaron's words echoed in the back of his mind. *Now I understand. We were both talking past each other, not listening. All it did was make sure neither of us understood the other.* Now was the time to start listening.

"I don't think that's possible," said Kiichiro.

Tae was stunned. For a moment she looked fearful. Kiichiro smiled.

"I think Sixth Continent is bit too grand for your mother and me. And so many people are waiting to go there. Let's leave the moon to those people. The earth is fine for us."

"Does that mean—"

"Of course I'll do it. I've no one else's feelings to consider. I wish you'd taken more notice of the fact that I never remarried, Tae." Kiichiro drew her toward him. She relaxed and closed her eyes.

"Thank you, Father." She looked up at him questioningly. "So…you're not against Sixth Continent anymore?"

"It seems I have no choice but to lend you my support. Your distant and nearly unreachable moon palace has captured the public's imagination in a way our paradise on Earth never did. ELE will back you again. This time, I'll guide the project."

"No, I don't want that." She drew away. "Everyone's relying on me. No matter what problems are waiting, I want to see them through myself."

"This whole thing is bigger than you can handle now. Before you overwork yourself again—" Kiichiro stopped. He was giving orders. *That's going to take some time to change, after all.* He exhaled and relaxed. "All right. If you need something, let me know."

Instead of rejoicing, Tae looked puzzled. Perhaps she'd also been expecting another test of wills. At length she nodded, cautiously. "Thank you. I'll do my best."

"I'm sure you will. Good luck."

Father and daughter looked at one another awkwardly. They had reached a compromise, but it would take getting used to.

———◆•◆◆•———

AFTER HER FATHER left, Tae lay limply in bed. In a few moments, her situation of a week ago had been altered in ways she could never have imagined.

When Sohya had pointed out that everything she was doing was for approval from someone she thought she hated, she'd plunged into a deep depression. She hadn't been willing to admit she could act so illogically. But finally she had admitted it and had fought her way through the depression. That led to a reconciliation with her father. It pained her to think how shallow she'd been. Doubtless there were more discoveries like this waiting for her, things she was sure she understood about herself but did not.

It was Sohya who had seen clearly into her confused heart. He understood her better than she did herself. Yet what did she know about him? For eight years he'd given her support whenever she needed it. Yet in all the time she'd known him, had she ever really tried to *know* him? She could only remember shrugging off what he'd said or disagreeing with him. She'd never initiated a frank discussion about anything, yet he'd never given up on her. For the first time, Tae felt a genuine yearning to see him—to be with him and start a new friendship.

She touched his speed dial on her wearcom. No answer. She called Gotoba. Because Sohya had not been able to do a proper handoff to the second team before returning, he'd already left with them for another stint on the moon. He would not be back for at least three months.

"Sohya…"

She heaved a dejected sigh. A tear ran down her cheek and fell on the pillow.

[4]

REIKA WAS ABOUT to enter Sixth Continent's offices in Aka-saka when the door opened and a couple in their forties emerged, gazing fondly at each another. She stepped aside and watched them go.

Inside, she found Dorothy filing documents. The couple had signed a contract. Even in this era, Japanese didn't feel comfort-able entering into agreements without affixing their personal seal to a paper document.

"How many is that?"

"One hundred and eighty-nine. They said they hadn't been able to afford a proper wedding when they were young and wanted to do it right. About half our customers are like them. It makes sense. It's not exactly cheap."

"Make sure you put that in box C-2 before you forget. I don't want to tell one of our couples that we lost their contract during the move."

"I'd gotten rather fond of this place, I must say." Dorothy looked round the office, sighed, and filed the folder of documents in a box. Sixth Continent was moving into bigger offices at ELE's Tokyo branch.

ELE was giving them more than just office space. It had positioned Sixth Continent as a major company venture and was contributing significant funding and staff. The credit rating agencies had issued new opinions, ranking Sixth Continent's debt even higher than before Tae had collapsed. The attitude of the banks was starting to change. Those assets on the moon were beginning to look very safe after all.

"Dorothy, we've got some bad news. Adam 20 was hit by a lightning strike just after launch. It didn't reach the correct orbit, so Gotenba gave the autodestruct command. Fortunately the problem wasn't due to a malfunction."

"Ryuichi said something like this would happen sooner or later. Let's check the computer."

Dorothy sat down at her laptop and launched the risk simulation. Hundreds of red and blue icons rose out of a black background. Reika watched intently as a red icon, representing the negative effects of a failed launch, linked to all the other icons. Apparently the accident would impact the entire project. But nothing happened; the other icons seemed hardly affected.

"See? That's the benefit of full disclosure. Sixth Continent has carried out forty launches. Our warnings about an impending failure have had their effect. The accuracy of the prediction is almost a plus. Good."

"How can it be good? The rocket and payload were worth two billion." Reika sighed.

"Don't worry so much. The payload was insured. ELE is backing us again. Every time there's a failure, the designers go to work and the safety margin improves. We need more failures if you ask me."

"Dorothy, you can't be serious!"

"Now if we can just have a crash with Eve, it will help publicize our launch escape system...Oh my." A new icon had appeared on the screen. It was yellow.

"What's that?" said Reika.

"A wild card. Positive or negative? I don't know. Gotenba is updating the simulation all the time. This is something new."

"I want to know what it is!"

"All right, don't get impatient." Dorothy clicked on the icon. A video opened in a small window. The image was jerky, taken by a handheld camera. It showed a black sky and a circle of light traveling across a sparkling surface. There was no sound.

"It's from the crater," said Dorothy. The video showed two space-suited figures. One was pointing to what appeared to be a home brew metal detector. A crude wand or antenna extended from a small box. The astronaut was bringing the antenna close to the surface and raising it again. The camera zoomed in on the box. A small LCD screen with digital readout was affixed to the box with suit-repair tape. The data changed with the distance from the box to the ground. The two women watched the changing numbers, mystified.

The video was replaced by a mixture of text and mathematical formulas. Dorothy scrutinized it for a moment and leaned back in her chair. "Physics and higher mathematics are not my specialty. What is this, I wonder?"

"It looks like they're picking up radio emissions from under the permafrost in Eden Crater. Or maybe it's radioactivity, like a uranium deposit."

"Whatever it is, the impact on Sixth Continent is unknown." On the screen, the video was playing back in a loop. They watched as the readout changed with the distance from the surface.

BOOK III

FINAL SHAKEDOWN, 2036–2037

CHAPTER 8
ARCHITECTURE, OPERATIONS MANAGEMENT, AND ADDITIONAL CONSTRUCTION

[1]

THE DAWN KNIFED through the gap in the distant mountain range. The two-week lunar day had begun.

The sun did not rise; it moved sideways. The triple array of solar panels at the western edge of the base were first to receive its light. The sparkling panels extended for hundreds of meters, like a castle's first line of defense.

Next to emerge from darkness were the arched roofs of the three habitat wings—single-story white structures with small windows that housed Sixth Continent's guests and the base crew. The design was not only optimized for pressure containment, it contributed to the aesthetics of the buildings. A repeating band of inverted semicircles fashioned from ice—a decorative Lombard corbel table—wrapped the building where the roof and walls met. The decoration was created with a numerically controlled sprayer program, the brainchild of one of Gotoba's architectural designers.

Then sunlight slowly unveiled the massive bulk of the Great Hall. The habitats extended from the hall on an east/west axis, like

367

transepts. This was Sixth Continent's largest building, its footprint as large as the habitat wings combined. It housed a banquet room for thirty, a kitchen, a bridal room, and most of the base's sports and entertainment facilities.

East of the Great Hall stood the cathedral, topped with a twenty-meter spire. Soft light fell on the altar through a stained glass window in the arched end wall of the chancel. The mood was more solemn than lavish.

Gotoba's designers had taken full advantage of architectural forms dictated by the environment—simple shapes, arched roofs, few windows—and created an echo of the Romanesque style. The beautiful cathedral, a pinnacle of science and technology optimized for the lunar environment, embodied the beauty of a grand building of the Middle Ages. To the cathedral spire the architects had added echoes of the Gothic, the style that succeeded the Romanesque. Form followed function: the tower concealed a gravity-fed water tank with enough pressure to service the entire base. The weight of the spire reinforced the high-ceilinged cathedral by bearing down on the roof.

A week later, as sun and Earth drew closer on the horizon, the entire complex was bathed in sunlight. East of the cathedral was SELS, the Sealed Environment Life Support module. Air, water, electrical power, heat, ventilation, and waste disposal were all produced and controlled here. Drawing on the experience of Kunlun Base, conduits for water, oxygen, and other life-support elements were carefully encased in spaces between the blocks that formed the walls of the buildings, concealing the conduits and guaranteeing their structural integrity. Maintenance was performed by robots that scuttled through the conduits. Bidirectional loop circulation ensured that vital life support would be maintained even with temporary blockages.

Where it could be carried out efficiently, waste was recycled. Unrecycled waste was not discarded in the open, as at Kunlun. It was compressed and neatly stored in trenches. This waste contained elements not available on the moon, and the day would come when they could be recovered.

East of SELS was Xiwangmu 6, the cement production sector, and the collection area for permafrost from the bulk shooter. The equipment in this area would eventually be moved or dismantled. For now, it was concealed by a wall of blocks that protected the base from regolith contamination from Liberty Island.

The spaceport was situated at the eastern edge of the base. Once the port was completed, the Turtles were lined up nearby, like aircraft beside a helipad. The port was a graded site three hundred meters across. Its array of red and blue landing lights were a dazzling beacon for arriving visitors.

The base was divided into distinct zones, with each in functional relation to its neighbor. Preventing regolith contamination was an absolute priority, so the spaceport and permafrost collection areas were far from the Great Hall. Between these areas and the main building was the SELS module, which did not need careful shielding from contamination. The living quarters were located away from sectors where accidents might occur.

Finally, at the greatest possible distance from potential accidents and contamination were the solar arrays. The arrays were the only part of the base visible from the habitat windows. Beyond them, in the daytime, stretched the white lunar surface. During the lunar night, Earth's blue and white globe floated on the horizon against a background of stars.

Sixth Continent's layout had another purpose as well: to create a sense of excitement in arriving visitors.

"IT'S BEAUTIFUL..."

Tae looked down at the gleaming lights of the spaceport rising to meet them. The descent module's engine fired again, easing the spacecraft onto the landing pad. After a few minutes the side hatch opened. The six passengers moved through an air lock into a pressurized compartment without the need for space suits. Once they were safely aboard, the container lowered itself to its chassis, and the robot shuttle set off for the Great Hall.

Scenery flowed by the shuttle windows—first the screening wall, with construction equipment visible through gaps, then SELS, and finally the cathedral and the Great Hall. The views changed smoothly from barren and industrial to elegant and timeless. As they approached the facade of the cathedral, Tae and the other passengers gasped with amazement. It was covered with a majestic mural depicting the Garden of Eden.

This gradual change of aspect and psychological impact from the spaceport to the Great Hall had been Tae's concept, but she was struck with emotion as she experienced it for the first time. She also felt a twinge of fear.

"So, Ms. Toenji—what do you think?" A journalist named Sumoto thrust a pen mic toward her. The camera in his sunglasses showed a beautiful young woman sitting across the shuttle aisle, looking out the window. Tae tucked her hair behind an ear but kept her eyes on the scenery.

"I'm grateful. None of this would've been possible without the support of so many people. It's been a long road."

"Construction has taken four years longer than you originally planned. How do you feel now that it's almost finished?"

"Happier than words can say."

The reporter was hoping for something meatier. He leaned forward, held the mic closer. "You seem a little nervous. Can you tell me about that?"

"Careful, Mr. Sumoto." The reporter glanced at the old man next to him just as the shuttle jerked sharply and stopped. Before the reporter could brace himself, he pitched forward and landed facedown in Tae's lap.

"I've never had a man in my lap before," said Tae with a laugh. Sumoto began apologizing profusely.

"Did you forget the prelaunch briefing? It's hard to keep your balance in this weak gravity." The old man smiled and helped the reporter up. Sumoto scratched his head with embarrassment, muttered something about "first off the boat," and headed for the exit.

For a moment Tae and Aaron were alone. "You're scared, aren't you? And not about being on the moon," he said.

"Yes, I am scared. I haven't seen him since he took me to the hospital."

"Don't worry. When you see each other again, you'll both know."

The cathedral facade loomed over them. They could hear the boarding tube extending from the Great Hall, then the interlock and the door opening. There was a slight breeze as the pressure equalized. A recorded voice said, "You have arrived at Sixth Continent. Please be sure to take all your belongings."

The pilot, Sumoto, and two women here to join the base staff exited the shuttle. Tae stood up, twitched her nose, and sniffed the air. She looked puzzled, then smiled. "It smells like a church. Stone and burning candles."

"The base manual says that's concrete and the odor-neutralizing system."

"Whatever it is, it doesn't smell like a ramen shop. He remembered…"

Aaron helped Tae through the hatch. They walked through an inflated tunnel and entered a space that could have been the lobby of a luxury hotel.

Structural colors—minute surface treatments that reflected light like butterfly wings—had been used on the walls instead of pigments, which would have offgassed as they dried. The shimmering surface texture was wholly unlike concrete. Shallow niches in the walls were skillfully lit to suggest depth. Ivy nurtured from seeds wound up toward the ceiling, framing a huge statue of a peaceful figure that could have been either a saint or a bodhisattva, carved from concrete. The floor was tiled with fused regolith particles; the surface was pitted, with a soft effect like dark cork.

Tae stared skeptically at the ivy and the sculpture. *That statue might have to go*, she thought, but Aaron and Sumoto stood looking at it with awe.

"Welcome to Sixth Continent, Ms. Toenji." Lined up to greet her were the base crew in functional white jumpsuits and the bridal crew in dark blue formal wear.

"Greetings, everyone," said Tae.

February 10, 2036. Six months before its grand opening, Sixth Continent was welcoming its creator.

———◦•✦•◦———

"WHOA! THAT'S HOT!"

The pot on the stove belched a geyser of boiling soup. Sohya ducked. The bearded chef rushed over and turned down the heat.

"What the hell are you doing? Don't come crying to me if you scald yourself!"

"Sorry. I didn't think it would boil up like that."

"The low gravity keeps vapor from circulating. The bubbles build up in the bottom of the pot and blow all at once. How many times have you been here anyway?"

"This is my sixth trip. But we never had pots or a proper kitchen before. Anyway, how come you know all this? You just got here."

"Dome Fuji was at thirty-eight hundred meters. If you don't watch out, a pot lid can blow off at that elevation." Kashiwabara shook his head and began cleaning up. He had actually arrived three months before to begin developing the menus for Sixth Continent. His Antarctic experience had been invaluable; he had quickly factored in the effects of low gravity on the cooking process. In the kitchen, Kashiwabara's word was law.

Now he was adding generous amounts of salt to the potage. "If you can't even watch a pot for me, you're not going to be of much use here."

Sohya's eyes widened as he saw how much salt the chef was using. "Um, isn't that going to be a little too sal—"

"Three days of weightlessness dulls the taste buds. Now get out of here. You have visitors to greet."

"That's why I was hiding out here," grumbled Sohya as he headed for the door.

He walked out of Kashiwabara's kingdom into the banquet hall just as a bow-tied maître d' was pouring champagne onto the floor. The man hurriedly set the bottle on one of the round tables. A two-meter fountain of champagne promptly shot into the air. "What's this?" said Sohya, surprised.

"I wish I knew," said the maître d', sadly holding his trouser cuffs out of the pool on the floor. "I opened it as usual. But when I tried to pour, it overshot the glass."

"I told you, it's because of the low—"

"I know, I know. But it's not second nature yet. What a waste. That was vintage Krug."

"You were at Les Caves Taillevent, right? You've got a reputation to preserve, Mr. Kiwa."

"True—but I'm no sommelier."

Sosuke Kiwa had been maître d'hôtel at one of Tokyo's finest French restaurants. Rumor had it that on at least one occasion he had waited on the emperor himself. But the moon was giving him problems. Sohya was helping him wipe the floor when a wail came from the bridal room next door.

"Help! I can't move!"

Sohya rushed in and found Kanna Mikimoto, another member of the bridal crew, wearing a wedding dress and walking furiously in place, as if on a treadmill. Sohya rolled his eyes.

"Okay. What are you doing?"

"I'm not doing anything! I'm just trying to walk, but I'm not getting anywhere."

Sohya went behind her and lifted the long hem of the dress. She immediately took a few stumbling steps forward. "Oh—what did you do?"

"That dress has a better grip on the floor than your shoes do. You don't weigh enough."

"What should we do? We don't have a train bearer."

"Maybe we can sew some dozer bearings into the hem to cut the friction. They might rattle on the floor though." He looked askance at Mikimoto, who had come with stellar bona fides as an assistant Shinto priest of Usa Shrine, second only to Ise Grand Shrine in the Shinto hierarchy. "Why are you playing bride at a time like this anyway?"

She laughed nervously. "I've worn the Shinto-style white kimono before, but never the dress." Sohya stared at her with incomprehension. "At least I found a problem before we used it."

"Go ahead and make the alterations. Just don't wear it out, okay?"

"Yes, sir." She left the room. Sohya sighed. Limited staffing was forcing everyone to wear multiple hats. Mikimoto would assist Aaron during Shinto weddings. Kiwa the maître d' would double as concierge and interpreter for English, French, and German. Yamagiwa was heading the base crew. He had also been approved by the Foreign Ministry to act as a one-man Japanese consulate.

Tae wanted her employees to have comfortable working conditions, but that was not realistic, especially before the base was even fully staffed. No one was getting enough sleep; it would have been unfair for Sohya to bear down too hard for the occasional mistake.

Sixth Continent had entered Phase Three. Structural work was nearly complete. Staff training and operational testing of the base's control systems were in full swing. During the past two years, Sohya had spent more time here than on Earth, overseeing construction and installation of interior fittings.

The amount of work still facing them was truly daunting. Sohya was either on the surface directing construction or back on Earth running from one Gotoba department to another till all hours of the morning. Gotoba's engineers had to rely on simulations—Sohya was the only one with a detailed sense of the actual operating conditions. He was solicited for advice on everything: bolt strength and odor-control design, the firmness of the chairs and the pressure in the washlet. A certain amount of discontent was sparked by his seemingly monopolizing all opportunities for travel to the moon. Then something happened to silence the criticism.

Sohya was at Gotoba headquarters when, due to a software glitch, an ice sprayer ended up sealing one of the lunar construction crew into a habitat work space. Dismantling the structure with multidozers would have taken far too long. The fastest option was to use carpenter robots to drill through to him, but that would still take three days. The astronaut was equipped with nothing more than a hand drill and a medical kit. There was just enough breathable air in the space where he was trapped, but the battery on his suit's CO_2 scrubber would not hold out for long.

The flight surgeon's recommendation was to use the drill's battery to keep the CO_2 scrubber working. The astronaut would also take enough morphine to slow his respiration while he waited for rescue. But Sohya intervened. A large dose of morphine without close medical monitoring would be dangerous. Instead, he proposed using all available battery power to keep the astronaut warm. Sohya waved off the flight surgeon's worries about CO_2 and insisted that his plan be followed.

The astronaut was none the worse for wear when he was rescued seventy hours later. The space where he was trapped had been scored with fine lines to generate structural colors. This effectively increased the wall area by several times, and the concrete itself had CO_2 absorption properties. Sohya had noticed during construction that CO_2 concentrations seemed to rise only slowly in such spaces. He knew the astronaut had a margin of safety even without the scrubber.

This incident proved the wisdom of having at least one crew member with as many hours of on-site experience as possible. Sohya's knowledge was indispensable. Unfortunately, it also guaranteed that he never had any time off.

Sohya was tired. The theater dome was still under construction, so he made his way into the cathedral to find some quiet. He sat down in one of the pews. A few moments later Yamagiwa walked in.

"There you are, Aomine. Everything ready for the big dinner?"

"Can we push it back an hour? We've still got a skeleton crew. It's total chaos in the dining room and the kitchen."

"I've got to get over to SELS. The software thought all that extra body heat was a fire. Now the oxygen generator's shut down. I have to recalibrate the system."

"I'll never laugh at Kunlun again. Did the guests notice anything?"

"I persuaded our journalist friend to check out his quarters. But our special guest—"

"Speak of the devil." Sohya stood up. Tae was framed in the door behind Yamagiwa, clad in her usual monotone ensemble. She doffed her beret and bowed, hands crossed formally over her thighs.

"Hello, Sohya. It's been a long time."

The way she leaned forward at the hips was as graceful as a narcissus. She straightened up and gave Sohya a slightly questioning up-from-under look. Her skirt billowed behind her as she walked slowly toward him in the one-sixth gravity. A gentle puff of some restrained floral fragrance reached him. Tae was twenty-four. She was no longer a girl.

He struggled to speak. "Um…yes, it's been a while."

It was their first meeting in two years and eight months—and where it was happening left Sohya slightly flustered.

[2]

THE DISCOVERY IN July 2033 of a technological phenomenon of nonhuman origin—an artificial radio signal emanating from Eden Crater—created an uproar on Earth, at least in certain quarters.

The most vocal were the self-styled "contactees." For years, they'd maintained that the lunar south pole was a secret UFO base. Aliens had been using it for millennia as a jumping-off point for Earth, where they had disguised themselves as humans and were waiting for the right moment to launch a global coup. The

CIA and the KGB (the latter had ceased to exist decades earlier, though the contactees refused to believe it) were working behind the scenes to hide the truth from the public. But a Japanese rogue agent had entered the crater and triggered the signal. The contactees demanded that the truth—which Sixth Continent and Liberty Island had obviously been constructed to conceal—be revealed.

All available information about the signal had been made public, but the fringe groups weren't listening. In a typical incident, TGT security had to detain a woman they found searching for a door in the first stage of an Adam rocket. She was planning to hitch a ride to the moon and return with proof that aliens were here.

The media always treated paranormal phenomena, including flying saucers, with humorous disdain. After their initial reports on the discovery, they went silent. Aliens were right up there with ghost stories and the Loch Ness monster. Treating the signal as news rather than variety show fodder went against their instincts, and the fact that it was unintelligible made it even harder for them to decide how to handle it.

An exchange between a veteran news anchor and a radio astronomer on one of the late night talk shows highlighted this dilemma. The anchor opened with a blunt question.

"Was this an alien signal?"

"Well, that's something we just don't know yet."

"But it wasn't man-made, and it wasn't natural. Correct? Then it must be aliens signaling Earth—"

"The signal wasn't aimed at us. It was directed toward a point in the southern skies: minus twenty-two degrees galactic longitude, minus fifty degrees latitude."

"What's in that direction?"

"In that *exact* direction? As far as we know, nothing."

"Then what about the electro-neutral grid—ENG, is it? The fibers found just beneath the lunar surface. What were they trying to accomplish?"

"We don't know much about that either."

"This is getting very hard to pin down. Let me just break in here and say what I think. If I'm wrong, interrupt me, all right? A signal is sent from the moon's south pole. No space agency or military organization admits to having sent it. So it wasn't sent by Earth. But Sixth Continent and Liberty Island are right next door, and that's how it was discovered. Here's my point: if you're going to build a TV station on Earth, do you build it in the middle of the desert or on a ship in the middle of the ocean?"

"Well, that depends on the broadcast frequency and output. If the station uses the megahertz band or higher, and if there are relay stations—"

"That's not what I'm driving at. You build the station where your viewers are. In a city, right?"

"I suppose, yes."

"Now, judging from where the signal was sent, it's as if someone had anticipated that humans would build something in that area. So wouldn't that mean we were meant to take notice?"

"I wouldn't know. I'm not the one who sent the signal."

"But you're a scientist—don't you have an opinion?"

"Along with the rest of the scientific community, I'm just not in a position to say what the purpose of the transmission might be. Of course, I have my own personal opinion, or perhaps it's a hope—but I'm afraid I'd better not speculate."

The anchor made a few more attempts to draw his guest out further before giving up. He closed the program with a look of indigestion. The media expected scientists to quickly determine at least the purpose of the signal, if not its meaning. After all, humans did not send radio signals without a reason. If someone credible would just stick their neck out and offer an opinion, the media could follow up with investigation and coverage—"alien signals" certainly weren't bad for ratings. But as things stood, all they had to go on was the barest of conjectures. After the initial reports, media coverage rapidly declined, and the interest of the general public declined with it.

Scientists of all kinds, however, were enthusiastically studying the signal. Radio astronomers jumped in, even though their specialty was natural emission sources, not artificial signals. Communications engineers, linguists, and SETI researchers were following their own lines of inquiry, but the exogeologists and electrical engineers had a head start over everyone. For seven years, they had been working with ENG samples brought back by Serpent, though without much success.

It had long been rumored that the fibers comprised some sort of machine fabricated from elements in the regolith. The reason this conjecture did not receive more open support was that no scientist had any idea of how such a machine could work. Only once had ENG shown any evidence of functionality: a sample held at JPL actually generated a small percentage of new fibers. This took place after a magnitude seven earthquake rocked California, with JPL at the approximate epicenter.

Attempts to image the fibers using electron or atomic force microscopes were equally unsuccessful. At low magnification, ENG showed a structure roughly similar to plant cells. But when magnification was raised to the nanometer level, the microscopes lost calibration. A research group in Canada demonstrated that ENG was absorbing the energy directed at it by the microscopes. The mechanism of energy storage was unknown, and no one had been successful in coaxing their sample to emit a signal.

Researchers at Liberty Island did determine that the way the fibers were intertwined could potentially contribute to signal emission and modulation. They went to work after the signal was discovered by Sohya and his crew. Careful radar mapping of ENG density beneath the floor of Eden Crater revealed thousands of rodlike aggregations of fibers about two and a half meters long. The Americans speculated that these structures could act as primitive dipole antennas. Their length was consistent with the signal's frequency. When an alternating current was passed through them, they emitted radio waves.

Sohya's team only managed to record forty seconds of the transmission before it ended. They first noticed the signal when it interfered with their transceivers. In fifteen minutes they had rigged a crude receiver and recorded part of the signal. It consisted of a long series of unmodulated pulses with only two amplitudes. Since the recording was just a fragment, it was no surprise that it could not be deciphered.

If ENG could be used to transmit signals, it could also receive them. Was the Eden Signal a response to another signal of some kind? Sixty-megahertz radio waves had never been detected outside the solar system. This frequency corresponded to one of the spectrum absorption lines of oxygen, which made Earth's atmosphere opaque to the signal. A few communications satellites operated close to that frequency, but none had receivers capable of detecting a signal that was a hundred billion times weaker than a terrestrial TV broadcast. No radio telescope in orbit was observing at frequencies anywhere near sixty megahertz.

Only one antenna caught the signal that had started it all—the SETI module Tae had sent to the moon. The five-minute transmission slept in the machine's memory, forgotten till prompted by a query from Earth.

Nevertheless, this incoming signal was just as unintelligible as its reply from Eden Crater. Opinion was not unanimous, but most SETI researchers were forced to conclude that whatever its meaning, it was not meant to be decoded. Otherwise it would have been accompanied by a key.

Somewhere in space, a signal had been sent, to which ENG had responded. The signals had been intended for sender and receiver alone. The rodlike structures beneath the surface would not make very efficient antennas. Assuming the goal was interplanetary communication, a conical or parabolic antenna would have been far more effective. Why multiple dipoles?

There could be only one reason: by modulating the phase of signals emitted by individual rods, the direction of transmission could be varied even with a fixed array, like phased-array radar installations, which were stationary and did not need to sweep the skies. Apparently ENG was not designed to aim its signal in one particular direction. Multiple dipoles were robust, flexible enough to transmit in any direction, and could be assembled with minimal resources.

Some proposed that ENG might be a life-form carried in the ice from comets, capable of communicating across the galaxy in response to intelligent signals. But this hypothesis was eventually rejected. ENG did seem to have the ability to grow, a purposeful structure, and a certain capacity to adapt to its environment. But no scientist could devise a model whereby any life-form could have extracted metallic elements from the regolith and assembled itself into such a structure. A seed would be required. Planting seeds meant intentionality. The entity that had planted the seed must be the source of the signal.

This is what the radio astronomer had hesitated to say on national television. To do so would have invited a barrage of questions. Why plant the seed in Eden Crater? Why not on Earth? Why send one signal and then go silent? Without answers, the conjecture—which for many scientists represented a hope—would simply have been ridiculed.

Sixth Continent was preoccupied with construction and could not spend time doing research. Liberty Island produced no further findings. Life on Earth went on as usual. People reacted just as they had to evidence of life in a meteorite from Mars discovered in Antarctica: it was interesting but not astonishing. After all, ENG was not trying to invade Earth. It was not made of pure gold. It didn't announce the coming of Armageddon.

But there were a curious few who were like people expectantly awaiting a letter. They at least felt a tremor of excitement. Now they were certain that a writer of letters existed, even if the message had not been addressed to humankind.

Liberty Island's scientists kept working to solve the puzzle.

Ironically, while Sixth Continent had discovered ENG, they were in no position to follow up. This difference between the two bases was gradually turning into a source of conflict.

———◦•••◦———

SELS MODULE, EARLY morning, February 12. The interior was a maze of machinery, piping, and conduits, similar to a chemical plant. Sohya and the module supervisor were peering into the water electrolysis tank.

"See? Those electrodes are broken," she said.

"You're right. Almost half of them are toast. That couldn't have happened during liftoff. They must be defective. Do we have replacements?"

"No. We weren't expecting to need them. We'll just have to wait for the next tug."

Sohya checked his wearcom and frowned. The screen was blank. "Battery's dead. I've had this too many years. I left the charger back on Earth."

"I've got one in my cabin. Want me to charge it for you?"

"Yeah, could you do that for me?"

The supervisor put Sohya's wearcom in her pocket and ran some calculations on her own unit. "At this rate, we'll be below nominal oxygen levels in two weeks."

"If we use the SFOG candles, we'll need more of those from Earth too. What about the greenhouse? Can we squeeze some O_2 out of that?"

"The spirulina culture? It doesn't generate much oxygen."

A simple greenhouse had been rigged on the module roof using leftover construction materials. Too small to grow plants for food, it was being used to cultivate spirulina, a strongly photosynthetic bacteria. Cultivating plants to absorb CO_2 and purify the air would eventually be more efficient than chemical methods.

"Use the heliostats to increase the solar energy to the greenhouse. That should give us more output."

"That might be a good idea. I'll rerun the numbers."

"The heliostats should be free." Sohya used the communication pad on the wall to call the Control Center. While he waited for a response, the supervisor gave him the high sign. The spirulina would close the oxygen gap.

The answer from Control was not promising though. "Who's using them?" said Sohya. "Some kind of experiment? Liberty Island?"

"Oh no. I forgot about that." The supervisor winced. "Remember last month we agreed to lease the heliostats?"

"No one told me about that. Anyway, it's a life-support issue. Control, connect me with Liberty. I'll talk to them directly."

The monitor went dark for a moment before a woman's face came up. Sohya was astonished. "Carol, is that you?"

"Well, hello, Sohya. How's everything in your neck of the woods?" Caroline Cadbury put her trademark sunglasses on her forehead.

"What're you doing here?"

"What else? Working. We have far better control over our rovers from here than we do from JPL. The lack of signal lag lets us do so much more."

"I'm glad you're here. Listen, we need our mirrors back."

"Sohya, your system control supervisor notified me earlier about the electrodes. He was hoping we might have some spares. You've got a long wait till the next tug arrives." She smiled—was that a hint of satisfaction? "It's not critical. You have at least three other options I can think of off the top of my head. I suggest you use one."

"Those mirrors are ours!"

"Right now they're ours. You made a deal. If you want to renege, better let Washington know."

"Carol!"

The screen went dark. After a short conversation with Control, Sohya hung up. "Damn it! Control is more interested in ENG research than they are in this base. They suggested we just pull some oxygen from the fuel vault. In fact, they invited me to go get the tanks myself." He noticed Tae standing in the entrance to the compartment. "You're up early. It's not even four yet."

"Jet lag. I was in Vancouver till just before liftoff. I'm sorry to bother you, but—"

"No, it's okay. I'm finished here."

"Really? Good." Tae smiled and came closer. "You were talking to Liberty Island just now, weren't you? What's going on?"

Sohya briefed her on his exchange with Cadbury. "NASA is keen to investigate ENG, but our permafrost harvesting is getting in the way, and things have been a little tense. They think the grid's two-kilometer radius is significant, that the samples on Earth are too small to replicate its behavior. They think there must be some kind of critical mass effect."

"So why do they need our mirrors?"

"They haven't told us. Maybe they just want to slow us down. Without the heliostats, we lose a lot of flexibility. We could use some extra income, so somebody must have decided to lease the mirrors to generate additional—" He broke off and stared at her. "Was that you?"

"Hm? Oh, yes. Yes…that was me." She glanced away, embarrassed. "But I wanted to hear what you had to say."

The SELS supervisor picked up a tool kit and smiled nervously. "Well, I think I'm done here, so I'd better leave you two to carry on."

"Not so fast. You forgot to close the tank lid," said Sohya. He called Control again. "This is Aomine. I'm taking a rover into the crater to retrieve some oxygen. Tae Toenji will be going with me." He turned to her. "You haven't seen ENG firsthand, have you?"

"No."

"Great. Better hit the restroom before we go."

Tae hurried out, looking excited and happy. The SELS supervisor gave a low whistle. "You really know how to handle her."

"You think so? This is as far as I've gotten in the eleven years I've known her." Sohya laughed and shrugged his shoulders.

THE ROVER SKIDDED wildly as it climbed the bright white slope of the crater rim. Sohya corrected with the joystick. Tae squealed in surprise and clutched his arm.

"Sohya! I almost fell out!"

"It's like a roller coaster, isn't it?" He laughed and opened the throttle all the way. The rover's maximum speed was eighteen kilometers per hour. There was no cabin. The chassis hugged the ground, countering any tendency to roll. The suspension was springy, and a jerk on the control stick would instantly induce a skid. It was a bit like being in a sports car. The rover was powered by a thin superconducting cable extending from the cathedral spire. Taking it out for a spin during breaks was a popular activity with the base crew.

At the top of the ridge ahead, forty oblong shapes like yacht sails were spaced at intervals—the heliostats, each with four square meters of mirrored surface, remotely controlled. Moving in tandem, they could send a concentrated beam of light to any point in Sixth Continent. Together they could generate about two megawatts of solar power.

"It looks like Liberty's moving them," said Sohya. The mirrors were rotating very slowly, tipping toward the sun. "I wonder what they're doing?"

They were almost at the top of the rim. "Could you stop when we get up there?" asked Tae. "I want to check out the view."

"I was planning to. I have to change the cable anyway. And there's something else." Sohya pointed to *Apple 7*, just coming into view. He could hear Tae's throat catch. The blackened hole in the core module was clearly visible. "I always stop there to pray for safety."

At the top of the ridge Sohya got out, swapped the power cable into a distributor box, and attached a new cable. Tae got out of the rover. The ten-meter-high heliostats extended in both directions. She walked along the ridge. To her left lay the base and the outer slope of the crater rim, bathed in light. To her right was an abyss of darkness. As she got closer to *Apple 7*, she could see offerings left by other visitors: canned fruit, sake, books. There was no marker.

"Is he still inside?"

"Of course. If we buried him he wouldn't be able to see the stars. His body won't decay." Sohya had finished swapping the cables. He placed his palms together and bowed his head.

"Don't you mean he wouldn't be able to see Earth?" asked Tae.

"Wasn't it you who said the stars were his destination?"

She didn't answer but leaned against him. Through the glazing on her visor, he could just make out a tear tracing down her cheek.

"You didn't cry when he died."

"I know. It's strange. It's taken me till now."

"What changed?"

"We left him all alone for half a year. I wonder if we did the right thing."

"He's not alone anymore."

Sohya started back for the rover. Tae swung round—startled at first, then embarrassed. Somehow she'd expected him to be angry with her. He motioned from the rover. "Let's go. I want to get there by five thirty."

She looked at the core again, then toward the stars that would be Shinji's forever. At the base of the gentle slope in the sun-washed desert, her palace seemed close enough to touch. Beyond lay a smaller crater. The distances were deceiving. The SETI crater was more than a kilometer away, but it looked startlingly close. A fiery disk and a thin crescent of blue and white hung in the blackness above the horizon.

Sohya was right. The view was superb. Shinji would have many visitors. Tae was almost to the rover when a voice came on the comm.

"Aomine? It's Yamagiwa. Look, this isn't exactly urgent, but I've got something to pass on to you. Johnson Space Center—"

"Aomine here. I'm going to radio silence for a while. I'll contact you on the landline from the vault. ETA is 0530 hours." He started the rover over the ridge and into the crater.

"What? Aomine, repeat, please."

Sohya switched off the transceiver. He took a comm cable from behind the seat and connected it to a jack on Tae's backpack, then to his own.

"Why did you switch off? Is that okay?"

"No. But I wanted to be able to talk without people listening in."

They looked at each other in silence. Suddenly the darkness swallowed them. They were in the shadow zone. Sohya switched on the floodlights, which cast a sharp-edged cone of light on the downslope ahead. The inner surface of the rim was steep; on Earth it would have been a difficult descent even on foot. Sohya steered cautiously as they headed downward.

"I was worried for so long," said Tae abruptly.

"About what?"

"I thought you were angry with me. For what happened to Shinji."

"It wasn't your fault. If it was, then I'm just as much to blame. Okay, I was angry with you at first. But later I realized I was really angry at myself."

"So you're angry."

"How could I not be? But it's over."

"I'm sorry." A small voice. Sohya turned his head inside his helmet to look at her. "When he died, I didn't mourn. Not really."

"I know."

"I'm not asking you to forgive me. But it's really hitting me now. I just wanted you to know that."

"I saw you crying." He reached over and drew her close. She stiffened, then relaxed against him.

"Thank you, Sohya."

"It's okay. Don't worry anymore."

She rested her helmet against his shoulder. They hadn't been alone since she'd arrived two days ago. In fact, they'd hardly been alone together in the past eleven years. Sohya broke the silence. "You've changed."

"Do I seem different?"

"It's the way you act. You're not as pushy. The old Tae would have been obsessed with collecting money for Phase E. She would have driven a far harder bargain with Liberty Island for the heliostats too."

"Was I really so pushy?" Judging from her voice, she was blushing. She didn't seem so self-assured now. Sohya was happy to see a spontaneous reaction for a change.

"You're more genuine. What happened? Was it your father?"

"I still can't relax around him." *Back into her shell,* thought Sohya. Then she added, "But we're both working on it, trying to get closer to each other. That's huge progress."

"So what I said to you that day at Reika's was right?"

"I guess. All I could think about was doing something really big and showing my father up once and for all."

"It's good that you finally realized that. But what now? How are you going to keep motivated enough to see this project through?"

"That's something I'm a little concerned about." Her voice was suddenly tired. "It doesn't belong to me now. It belongs to thousands of people. I'm wondering whether it makes sense for me to keep leading the project. I'm getting more help than I'm giving."

"Sounds like advice from your father."

"Yes…Yes, it does." She looked up at him. "What about you? Do you have the energy to see this through?"

"Are you joking? The Apollo missions were like mountaineers building cairns to show other climbers the way. Sixth Continent is a permanent base camp. I want to show the world what we can do."

"I envy your confidence."

"You said it yourself. People really can live on the moon. It's not like Antarctica. It's the real Sixth Continent."

"But what will I have to live for once it's finished?"

"You need another goal." The rover swayed as it reached the crater floor. Its floodlights pierced far into the darkness. Tae noticed the color of the surface; it was different here, like a winter snowfield surrounded by a ring of mountains. Far off to the left, the beacon of another vehicle was moving rapidly away, toward Liberty Island.

Sohya trailed a fingertip across the permafrost as it moved past underneath him. "Unravel the secrets buried in this crater. Wouldn't that be a challenging new goal?"

"But Liberty Island is already moving full speed."

"I don't think they'll find all the answers. Five or ten, maybe twenty years from now, Sixth Continent will be a major research facility. Maybe we'll even mine the helium-3 that the Chinese are going after. There are so many things we can do."

"And where will you be in twenty years?"

Sohya didn't answer. He was Sixth Continent's construction supervisor. Once construction was finished—what then?

A simple declaration of their true feelings would have bridged the gulf between them. They both knew it, but they had let too many opportunities to say what needed to be said slip away. They had known each other too long. Now neither of them could imagine how honesty might change things, and it scared them both.

They pressed ahead in silence. A few minutes later Sohya halted the rover. They were at the edge of a hundred-meter depression in the crater left by permafrost mining. He played the floodlights over their surroundings. The dragonlike bulk shooter, off-line and inactive, squatted a short distance away near the rim. A single multidozer stood motionless in the pit below.

Sohya advanced down the slope. Moments later, the multidozer moved out of the pit, as if yielding to them, and headed rapidly away. A notch with a vertical wall about three meters high had been cut into the far side of the pit, and a massive frame surrounding an aluminum door was set into the wall of the cut. Sohya stopped nearby and climbed out of the rover, leaving the floodlights on.

"This is the vault. We store hydrogen and oxygen in spent fuel pods here. Don't try to open it with your hands." He unreeled his suit tether and hooked the end under the bottom edge of the metal slab. It lifted up and inward like a garage door. Beyond was a sloping passage leading down into darkness. They walked into the tunnel.

Seconds later, forty points of light flashed into brilliance above the rim of the crater. The area around the entrance grew brighter. But Sohya and Tae were already inside.

[3]

THE TUNNEL DESCENDED at a shallow angle for twenty meters. At the end, a room five meters square by two high had been carved out of the permafrost. Twenty or so spherical metal tanks were lined up on the floor, each nearly a meter in diameter.

Tae looked at the smooth walls enclosing them. "This must have taken a lot of time. Was all that work really necessary?"

"Long-term storage on the surface is slightly risky. A micrometeor might puncture a tank. The carpenter robots dug this after they finished shaping the blocks for the buildings. We wanted to keep them busy."

Tae laughed. "No point in letting them goof off." She looked closer at a nearby wall. Lit by small spotlights set like epaulets into the shoulders of her suit, the fibers made the coffee-colored permafrost sparkle. "So this is how it looks." She reached out to touch the wall. Sohya pulled her gently away.

"It's 220 below in here. Touch that wall and the cold could penetrate your glove and freeze the end of your finger. Is your heater on max?"

"I think so. It's pretty noisy."

"Don't squat down either. You want to keep the joints in your suit open so the heat can circulate. Now let's get some of these tanks out of here."

Sohya was about to hook the end of his tether to a handcart propped against the wall when Tae said, "Shouldn't you contact Yamagiwa?"

"You're right. Totally slipped my mind."

She absently reached for her wearcom pendant before she realized it was inside her Manna suit. She checked the comm pad in the suit's left forearm. "There's no signal."

"The fibers block any signal. That's why we have this." He pointed to a small interface box in the ceiling. It was connected to a cable that ran down the wall and back up the shaft toward the entrance. He reached up and connected their cables to the box.

"Control, Aomine. We've reached the vault. All conditions nominal. Sorry for being out of touch."

"Aomine! Are you all right?" It was Yamagiwa. He sounded worried.

"We're fine." Sohya glanced at Tae in surprise. "What's going on?"

"We thought something might've happened to you. You're underground, right? Did you notice anything on the way there?"

"No, not a thing."

"That's odd, because Liberty Island is focusing the heliostats right at you."

For a moment Sohya doubted his ears. "In the shadow zone? How? The sun is on the far side of the mirrors. They can't send light down here."

"Unfortunately they can, if the heliostats are tipped at the correct angle. The output is limited but still strong enough to kill you if you get in the way."

"But what's the point?"

"It's some sort of experiment. They didn't let us in on it. The problem is we can't contact them."

"Hold that thought, Yamagiwa. I'd better look outside." Sohya unplugged the comm cable, motioned to Tae to stay put, and ran back up the shaft. He was more irritated than worried. *Liberty Island. Great timing, guys.*

The shaft door was closed. This *was* strange. Sohya was certain he'd left it open. It wasn't there to keep anyone out; it was to keep the shaft clear if the cut next to it collapsed. The up-and-over design was easy to open even if the frame was pinched by rubble. In the open position, it gave the entrance some protection against falling rock. Now it was closed. Had the wall above it caved in?

He felt a spike of fear but suppressed it immediately; panic would only make clear thinking harder. Liberty Island and Sixth Continent could send all the help they needed. If he called for assistance, someone would arrive in half an hour at most. If he did nothing, someone would come anyway. The only question was whether he could open the door himself.

Touching it with his glove was out of the question; in a few seconds, the cold would make even the tough covering of his gloves brittle enough to fracture when he moved his hands. One part of his suit could stand up to the cold: his insulated boots. Sohya gave the door a kick.

What happened next was a blur. He was thrown backward by a force that felt like some wild beast suddenly freed from its cage. He slid a short distance across the frozen regolith, but in an instant his reflexes put him back on his feet. He had no idea what had just happened.

The door was closed again. Sohya stared at it, dazed, and tried to remember. Some sort of blinding light had pierced his visor. For an instant, the door had opened wide. A gauzy substance, like a lace curtain, had been undulating outside. Then it had rushed toward him and knocked him off his feet.

Sohya had no desire to open that door again. He backed away as if it were the only thing between him and some wrathful spirit. He ran back into the vault. Tae was still standing there, looking at the fibers in the walls as if nothing had happened. Sohya plugged his cable in. She noticed him and asked, "Did you see anything?"

He ignored her. "Control, emergency! Something's happening outside the vault, some kind of energy release. We're trapped!"

"Aomine! Johnson confirms Liberty is running a large-scale heating experiment in the crater. They claim they had no advance notice either."

Sohya's and Yamagiwa's shouting overlapped. After a pause, Yamagiwa said, "What happened?"

"I saw something outside, a gas or maybe a vapor. It blew me off my feet as soon as the door opened."

"Are you all right?"

"I'm fine. The door seems to be keeping whatever is out there from entering the vault. What is it?"

Suddenly Sohya thought it might be better to disconnect Tae's cable. He wasn't sure he wanted her to hear what Yamagiwa was about to say. He reached for it, but she stared at him and shook her head.

"Ground zero for the experiment is right outside the vault. They've got the heliostats focused on the notch we made in the permafrost. It's the only place in the crater where there's a good-sized vertical cross section exposing part of the ENG. The solar energy is releasing huge amounts of vapor from the permafrost. Don't go outside for any reason."

"What do you mean? Tell the Americans to terminate the experiment!"

"That's what I tried to tell you. They're not responding. There was an observation team in the crater, but they've disappeared."

"The rover that was leaving when we entered the crater," murmured Tae.

Sohya's mind was racing, trying to derive a course of action from the information hitting him. "Then...override the controls and turn the mirrors away. Or send someone up the rim and redirect them manually."

"We can't go anywhere. We're bottled up here. There's a solar flare warning!"

"A solar—?"

"An X-class flare. The proton storm will make things extremely hazardous anywhere there's sunlight. I tried to tell you guys before you headed into the crater, but you cut the link!"

Sohya's spirits sank. Yamagiwa was right. He'd been trying to say something, but Sohya had had other things on his mind when he shut off the transceiver.

"Does that mean we're going to get cancer?" Tae was filled with apprehension.

"Not right away," said Yamagiwa. "An hour outside during a flare would expose you to a year's worth of radiation. Definitely not healthy. But that's the one thing you don't need to worry about, Ms. Toenji. You're in no danger in the crater. That's why I said it wasn't an emergency.

"Everyone here is safe behind concrete walls. But the Americans' inflatable modules don't provide much shielding. They're probably hunkered down in a shelter, waiting till it's safe to come out, which would explain why we can't raise them. But unless they hand off control to us, there's not much we can do. The heliostats can't be hacked into. The mirrors pack a lot of power. We didn't want them getting hijacked."

"But why would they head for their shelter without stopping the experiment?"

"Who knows? Maybe they wanted to finish what they started before we got Johnson to override them. Or maybe it's something they don't need to monitor in real time. We just don't know."

There was silence for a moment. "Sohya, stay calm. This is no time for panic. There's another problem." Yamagiwa's voice was eerily expressionless. "The surface of the permafrost will sublimate first. From what you describe, it sounds like that's already happening. But then the heat from the mirrors will penetrate the surface, maybe thirty or forty centimeters. At some point, heat will be coming in faster than the surface can radiate it away."

"Is the vault going to flood?" Tae asked.

"No. The vacuum still means direct sublimation from ice to vapor. And if that happens too fast…" There was silence for a few seconds. "There's going to be a detonation."

More silence. Sohya and Tae could hear someone giving Yamagiwa an update. Finally he spoke again. "We just reran the numbers. There's no mistake. It depends on how tight the beam is focused, but even in the best case, the vault is going to come down. Aomine, are you listening carefully?"

"I'm listening." Sohya looked at Tae. There was a firm set to her jaw and her gaze was steady, but she couldn't stop blinking. He put both hands on her shoulders and squeezed. "Are you okay?"

"I think so."

Yamagiwa's voice was cautious. "I want you to keep everything I've told you in mind. A lunar eclipse is under way as we speak. The Earth is moving between you and the sun. It's going to cut off the light from the heliostats. The eclipse may be your key to getting out of this."

"Did it just start? The light was bright as hell a few minutes ago," said Sohya.

"Earth's umbra touched the moon at 0531, but that was up near the equator. It hasn't reached the south pole yet. The eclipse is going to be total, but just barely. Right now the moon's apparent diameter from Earth is 33.2 arc minutes. The umbra's diameter is 91.8 arc minutes. The south pole is going to pass just inside the southern edge of the umbra. That'll be totality, but it will only last a short time. Even then, light scattering through Earth's atmosphere will make things look red. It won't be completely dark."

"So that's when we make a break for it. When do we go? How long till totality?" Sohya was almost shouting with tension now.

No answer. They waited. Ten seconds. Twenty seconds. Sohya was afraid to say anything, in case he talked over Yamagiwa. A drop of sweat ran into his left eye. Spurred by the stinging, he whispered into his mic.

"Yamagiwa?" Silence. "Yamagiwa! Answer me! Control, do you read?"

There was no answer. Tae touched his elbow and pointed to the comm cable. The tip of her finger traced the cable to the box, then across the ceiling and down to the floor where it went up the shaft.

Sohya's voice was almost a squeak. "The cable..." Something— the focused sunlight or a cave-in—had probably cut it.

"Goddamn it!" He ripped the comm cables out of the box and punched the wall of the vault twice for good measure. "How much bad luck can we have? Why the hell didn't he just tell us right away when to run for it?"

"He probably thought we needed the whole picture." Tae's voice came softly over the transceiver link. Her voice was trembling, though she was trying to keep it steady. "He wanted us to know the background first so we wouldn't panic. So everything would make sense."

"Tae..." He looked at her. She stared straight back, blinking tears out of her eyes.

"It was the only way he could handle it. Sohya, please be calm. I really, really need you to be calm now."

"Calm? Of course I'm calm..." His voice died away. He was embarrassed; he wanted to hide. For a few moments, his desire— his desperation—to protect her had made it impossible to think straight. The only way to short-circuit the panic was to admit it. "I'm sorry. You're right. I almost lost it there for a second."

"I think you're okay now." She smiled behind her visor and embraced him. "I'm scared too. You've always protected me. I want to do the same for you. More than anything I've ever wanted." He could feel her trembling through the shell of her space suit. "I love you, Sohya."

Her eyes were closed. Her head fell back in her helmet, and her mouth opened slightly. At first Sohya was astonished, then he felt something breaking free at last, something he'd been quietly nurturing for eleven years. He closed his eyes.

"I love you too, Tae."

They were unable to kiss, but everything that needed saying had been said. Their embrace lasted a long time; there was no reason to let go. They were going to die—

No. I will not give up. We've found each other. We are not going to lose this.

"Tae, we've got to think. Maybe there's something we can do."

They parted and gazed at each other, feeding for a moment on each other's resolve. Tae spoke first. "Maybe we should crack the door a little and see what's happening?"

"Too dangerous. By now the permafrost's probably crumbling. It took a lot of strength to open the door the first time. If we do it again, we might bring the wall down." He thought for a moment. "Can we dig out from a different direction? We could use our suit heaters to melt the ice."

"I don't think we have enough battery power. Mine's dropping fast as it is, just from regulating the temperature. I wonder—if they can't go outside, wouldn't they send multidozers up the ridge to knock the mirrors down?"

"Maybe they're doing that right now. Problem is we don't know. We've got to try something on our own."

"What about this fuel? Could we ignite it and tunnel out that way?"

"The oxygen's solid at this temperature—just barely, but it's frozen. We'd have to melt it first. Same problem: if we use up too much battery power, we'll freeze too."

For several minutes they discussed other ideas, all unworkable. They lapsed into silence. Finally Sohya murmured, "We'll just have to try and guess when totality's occurred and make a break for it then."

"Can't we calculate it?"

Sohya blinked in bewilderment. "But neither of us knows anything about celestial mechanics."

"Maybe we don't need to. We'll need your wearcom."

Sohya touched his forearm, then realized he'd left his wearcom back at the base. "I don't have it with me. Damn it—I think my software library had an application we could have used."

"Our comm pads can do simple calculations. Try to remember what Yamagiwa said. The eclipse started at five thirty, right?"

"Yes…0531."

"And the apparent diameter was 33.2 arc minutes. The Earth's umbra was 91.8 arc minutes. What time does that add up to?"

"It's not clock time," said Sohya. "It's a section of a circle. One arc minute is a sixtieth of a degree. Apparent diameter is how big the moon looks from Earth, and the size of the earth's shadow relative to the moon. If those are the figures, maybe we can work something out. We need to know how long the eclipse will last. Totality will be at the halfway point."

"Right!" Tae's eyes were shining.

"The length of the eclipse depends on how fast the moon orbits the earth, so we need the orbital speed. I know that: it's 1.68 kilometers per second."

"What's the moon's diameter? I think it was about thirty-five hundred kilometers."

"Closer to 3,476. So an object 3,476 kilometers wide is moving at 1.68 kilometers per second."

"The diameter of the umbra is 91.8 arc minutes. So how many kilometers wide would it be?"

"I think we can use ratios. Divide 91.8 by 33.2 and multiply by 3,476."

She punched in the numbers. "It's 9,611 kilometers!"

"So the moon is going to cross a shadow 9,611 kilometers wide, and it's going to do it at 1.68 kilometers per second."

"Let's see…No, wait. The eclipse starts when the umbra hits

the moon's edge, but it's not over till the other edge leaves the shadow. So we have to add one moon diameter to the diameter of the umbra. That's…13,087 kilometers. That's how far the moon has to go before it's completely out of the shadow."

"Right—if the moon is passing straight through the center of the umbra. But it's going to skirt the south edge. That means we're not going to be in shadow for very long, just like Yamagiwa said. One circle inside a bigger circle. Listen, calculate these numbers. We can use the Pythagorean theorem."

Tae input the numbers Sohya gave her. "The answer is 11,560 kilometers. Then I divide that by the orbital velocity?"

"Right."

"That's 6,881 seconds. Half of that is 3,440 seconds. That's when totality will be reached. Add that to 0531…it's 0627."

They looked at the display on her comm pad as if it were some exotic animal. "We did it," said Sohya.

"Are you sure this is right?"

"The procedure was right. But if we overlooked some parameter, it's going to be wrong. We better go through everything once more independently." For the next few minutes, they worked the figures repeatedly.

"Same answer," said Tae finally. They exchanged worried looks. They were amateurs at this kind of calculation. If they'd made a mistake, it would cost them their lives.

Sohya looked at his comm pad again. His expression hardened. If they were right, they were almost out of time.

"Tae…I trust you."

"I trust you too, Sohya."

"Then let's get out of here." They walked up the tunnel to the entrance. Tae watched her time readout intently. The seconds dragged by.

"Now."

Sohya kicked the door. It swung upward easily. He grabbed her hand and ran out onto the surface. The pit was thick with mist, suffused with faint orange light from the heliostats. Ice particles—diamond dust—sparkled in the dimness and drifted slowly downward. A reddish orange glow was visible above the rim in the direction of the base. Earth's atmosphere was bending the sun's long red wavelengths and sending them into the umbra.

"We were right!" Sohya shouted with joy. Tae lifted her arms and spun around happily. The wall of permafrost over the door began to sag. They saw the outline of an object half-submerged in the permafrost. It was the rover.

"We have to get away from here! Run!"

They kicked off in a kind of skip that should have carried them several meters, but they couldn't seem to make much headway. The surface of the pit was soft and spongy. It was like a bad dream—they could run hardly faster than on Earth, and their Manna suits were not made for sprinting. Tae stumbled and fell to her hands and knees. In an instant Sohya was at her side, pulling her up again. They felt the ground heaving, as if an enormous serpent were uncoiling beneath their feet. A few moments later they reached the rim of the pit and left the zone of reflection from the now-dimmed heliostats. What they saw in the darkness beyond, faintly visible, caused them to halt in astonishment.

Under the glittering stars, thousands of golden points of light were pulsating all over the ice in a regular rhythm. At the same time, the moon began to emerge from Earth's umbra. Unfiltered sunlight bounced off the heliostats and into the pit, cutting through the mist. The heat sent the drifting ice crystals spinning upward again. Seconds later, the vapor flowed over the edge of the pit and rushed outward in all directions at terrific speed.

Sohya took one look over his shoulder, grabbed Tae, and moved to shield her with his body. But before they could drop to the ground, the hurtling cloud threw them violently into the air.

For an agonized instant, Sohya felt as if his internal organs were tearing loose. Then the pain was replaced by a delicious sensation of floating. He heard Tae's stifled scream. They could both see the lunar surface racing beneath them from what looked like fifty or sixty meters up. Even in one-sixth gravity—even with the hard carapace of their Manna suits—falling from this height at this speed would pulp their bodies like the contents of a can of food dropped off a cliff. As they described a perfect parabola through space, Tae and Sohya embraced.

Something lifted them from both sides. Their direction of flight changed and began rising steeply, like a bird taking flight. There were no birds on the moon...Even before the reality of what was happening penetrated Sohya's brain, he was already shouting.

"Henderson!"

"And Hardin. Say, I don't think I know this one," said Henderson casually.

The two NASA astronauts were straddling Rocket Comet mobility units like outsize witch's brooms, gripping Sohya and Tae from either side. The shoulders of their white hard-shell suits bore an insignia of a crimson arrow against a dark blue field of stars.

"Hurricane Cadbury sent us to find you."

Sohya helped Tae clamber up behind Hardin. He got behind Henderson and held on to his backpack. The American mobility units seemed completely unaffected by the additional mass, the change in center of gravity, and the force of the vapor cloud pushing up from below. They set off in perfect formation, curving higher over the crater. Sohya could only look down with wonder and relief.

"One of your multidozers stopped outside our flare shelter half an hour ago, so we went outside to investigate. It told us there were people in the crater. We had no idea anyone would be out after that warning was issued. We had to wait for totality though."

Sohya slumped with fatigue. "We barely figured out when to make a run for it. We almost ended up roasting inside our suits. What was the point of sending sunlight into the crater?"

"There's something very interesting about ENG. It uses elements in the regolith to grow, and to do that it needs energy. But there's almost no energy in the shadow zone—no heat, no electromagnetic gradient, no sunlight. If it can grow in the shadow zone, we thought giving it more energy would result in some interesting changes."

"But they tried that already with samples on Earth."

"Yes, in Earth's gravity. What about the moon's gravity? The one time ENG grew on Earth was after an earthquake, when the local gravitational field changed. But we couldn't get the samples we had at Liberty Island to grow either. There's only one difference between our sample and ENG in the crater: the mass."

"So you gave the mother colony a big shot of energy just to see what would happen? What is it with you Americans and brute force anyway?"

"It's worked for 250 years." Henderson laughed. "Still, we're glad you're safe. Now we need to see the effect—"

Tae shouted, "What's that?" They looked down where the fuel vault had been. What was taking place before their eyes could only be called construction. Hundreds of golden pillars thrust upward from the surface. Golden beams extended to link them. Walls formed between pillars and beams. Like time-lapse photography, terraces, roofs, and towers formed with dizzying speed, radiating out from a central spire thirty meters in diameter, like the roots of a huge tree.

Suddenly the growth stopped. The light from the heliostats lost focus, divided into forty squares of light, and raced away across the ice. The experiment had been terminated. Eden's brief noon was over. In its wake was a majestic work in progress rising fifteen meters above the ice, stretching for five hundred meters on its long axis, gleaming weakly in the darkness: a Sagrada Família created by some nonhuman intelligence. They floated over it in silence.

"Is that a cathedral?"

Tae's astonished question were the only words spoken for some time.

CHAPTER 9
PERMANENT SETTLEMENT—AND BEYOND

THE MAJESTIC TONES of the synthesized pipe organ filled the cathedral. The bride and groom entered. People in the pews turned to watch. There was a wave of applause. The bride wore a princess-style dress and walked slowly up the scarlet carpet on the arm of her tuxedoed groom.

The couple stopped before the altar where the priest was waiting. The applause subsided, and for a moment the only sound was the whisper of the ventilation. Then the organist launched into a spirited hymn. The guests looked at their leaflets and joined in, calling for God's blessing. Some sang haltingly; others seemed to know the words from memory.

The priest called the assembly to prayer. Then he spoke to the bride and groom, who stood before him with their heads bowed.

"In Genesis, the Lord says: 'Be fruitful and multiply, and fill the earth and subdue it.' Humanity did, and all of Earth is under our dominion. Now we have reached out and taken the moon unto ourselves. Surely this is pleasing in the sight of the Lord, because He created us in His image. But with dominion comes responsibility. Where humanity would rule over God's earth, so too must we submit to His law. And where we would unify His heavens, so too must we submit to Him here also. As you would extend your love to the earth, so shall you extend your compassion to the stars. Only then can you be fruitful and multiply, and fill the moon, and subdue it. Surely the Lord will look upon your efforts and smile. It may be a somewhat ironic smile though."

There was muffled laughter. Aaron ended his sermon with a solemn prayer and began the exchange of vows.

"Ryuichi Yaenami, do you take Reika Hozumi for your lawful wife, to have and to hold from this day forward, for better or for worse, in sickness and in health, to love and to cherish, till death do you part?"

"I do." The groom's confident answer boomed through the cathedral.

"Reika Hozumi, do you take Ryuichi Yaenami for your lawful husband, to have and to hold from this day forward, for better or for worse, in sickness and in health, to love and to cherish, till death do you part?"

"I…do…" Her voice was faint. A few of the guests were crying.

"You will now exchange rings as a symbol of your vows."

The organist gave each a silver ring. They took one another by the hand, slipped on the rings, and kissed. Ryuichi embraced his diffident bride passionately. Some of the guests reddened and looked away.

———◆◆◆———

STAR ROAD.

That was the name they gave to the titanic ramp that sloped toward the stars out of Eden Crater. Thanks to ENG, the cost of escaping lunar gravity had fallen to nearly zero. Miraculous as it was, the ramp was also a windfall for Sixth Continent. Takumichi Gotoba contributed his unexpected profits to fund a series of weddings for employees from ELE, TGT, and Gotoba Engineering.

Invited to Ryuichi and Reika's wedding were not only friends and family, but neighbors: crew members from Liberty Island and astronauts from Kunlun Base. China had announced that the base would soon be fully operational again.

The stand-up reception was held in the banquet hall. Under the soft light of paper lanterns, the room echoed with conversations in a dozen languages.

"There you are, Aomine!"

Sohya and Tae were standing together—Sohya in a spotless white crew jumpsuit, Tae in a dark blue silk dress. Jinqing Jiang pushed his way through the crowd, raised his glass, and greeted Tae in Japanese.

"Jiang! It's good to see you." Sohya toasted him in return. Jiang had made the journey from Kunlun Base in a modified resupply vehicle.

"This whole place is quite an accomplishment. I envy you guys."

"I hear Xiwangmu 7 will be coming to Kunlun soon. I plan to drop by when I get the chance."

"Be my guest, but we'll put you to work." Jiang slapped a puzzled Sohya on the back. "Helium-3 mining will be a huge effort. We're starting next year. The State Council just announced it. Kunlun's the only base in the northern hemisphere. We're going to be doing a lot of digging, my friend."

"Maybe China will be the world's biggest energy producer in ten years."

"More like twenty. But we'll get there." Jiang seemed very confident. Then Sohya's smile froze; he saw another Chinese astronaut approaching.

"Hello, Cui."

Penghui Cui towered impassively over him for a moment before smiling and extending his hand. "We heard about your quick thinking in the crater. Even professional astronauts might not have made it out of that one. But you didn't give up."

Sohya shook his hand. "Thanks. I wish you guys luck. Let us know if there's any way we can help."

Cui's grip was firm. He beamed. "Well, we'd better see what's for dinner. The buffet looks impressive." The two astronauts started making their way toward the food.

"I'm not surprised. All they get at Kunlun is Chinese," said Tae. Sohya burst out laughing.

Someone tapped him on the shoulder. He turned to see a woman in a gold dress flashy enough to show up even the bride. With her was a heavyset, bearded man in jeans and a print T-shirt.

"That's an amazing dress," said Tae. "The design is wonderful."

"Made it myself." Caroline Cadbury plucked a glass of champagne from a tray skillfully maneuvered around the room by Mikimoto. She took a sip. "I didn't have a thing to wear at Liberty Island. I made this out of micrometeoroid film. I feel a little like Sputnik."

"I didn't know you were a seamstress."

"I'd be glad to make one for you. What're your measurements?" Caroline started eyeing her.

"Oh, um, I'm fine with this dress…"

"Relax and enjoy yourselves," said Sohya. "There's plenty of food." As if on cue, Kashiwabara emerged from the kitchen, followed close behind by Kiwa, who was carrying a tureen.

"Careful, now—that soup's a lot hotter at the bottom!" he shouted.

"I can handle the soup, thanks," said Kiwa, rolling his eyes and pushing the chef back into the kitchen.

Sohya shook his head sadly. "This is our tenth reception. He's got to start trusting the service people."

"Maybe he's used to doing everything himself," said Caroline. "Listen, we have to get back to the Island. Hope to see you over there soon." She put her glass down and strode away.

"What's the hurry?" called Sohya.

"Star Road. I'm not much for partying. I can't hang out here while the rest of my people are working."

Lambach laughed. "After all the time you spent working on that dress?"

"Now, now. Watch your manners. Come on!" She disappeared into the crowd.

Lambach shrugged. "Sorry about that. I think she's jealous."

"Then we're honored," said Sohya.

"I'd better go. Oh, I almost forgot. This is for you. Just our way of saying thanks for inviting us." He held out his wearcom and smiled.

"Hm?" Sohya did the same. Lambach transferred the file and left them. Tae peered at Sohya's wearcom.

"What is it?"

"Some kind of report. I'll take a look at it later."

They walked slowly around the room. Along with Sixth Continent staff and space agency people like Jiang and Caroline, several female friends of the bride as well as her parents mingled. Reika's friends and family were the only "civilian" guests, but they seemed very much at home, laughing and chatting as they strolled lightly around in the low gravity.

The oldest guest of all sat near the wall, wearing a string tie with a jade clasp and warming a wine glass in his hands. Sohya and Tae went over to greet him. "Are you tired, Mr. Sando?" asked Tae.

"Oh no, I'm fine. I'm having a wonderful time, thanks to Gotoba. And Mr. Toenji gave me his seat on *Apple*." He smiled peacefully.

Gotoba and Sennosuke had yet to visit the moon. *Both of them should be here*, thought Sohya, but each had his own reason for refusing. The last time Sohya and Tae had seen him, Sennosuke had only recently begun using a wheelchair. "Twenty years ago I took Tae all over the world. Now that she has someone else to take care of her, I can relax."

"Grandfather, why don't you let me take you to the moon?" Tae had asked.

"I don't need you to take me anywhere. I can still walk anytime I want." He was almost out of the chair before Sohya and Tae hurriedly restrained him.

Gotoba had offered his seat on *Apple* in a company raffle; it went to someone from the Sapporo office. "The boss keeps saying he'll only come here if he pays for it himself," said Sohya. "Well, it's going to get a lot cheaper soon."

"I doubt he'll come," said Sando. "He wants our younger engineers to get hands-on experience. Developing the moon is going to take a lot of work. He says it's time for the next generation to take over. Oldsters on the verge of retirement shouldn't be taking up space on *Apple*. That means I shouldn't be here either. You know, I've got a pacemaker." He pointed to his string tie. "I thought it would be a good way to demonstrate the reliability of our launch vehicles, to show that an old man with a heart condition can go to the moon. I'm here as a guinea pig."

"Mr. Sando, you're not a guinea pig."

"Someone has to do it. Besides, old people like to travel." He winked. "Don't worry, I'm not exerting myself. Now go have some fun, you two."

The bride was throwing frequent glances in their direction from the head table, but Tae steered Sohya over to Aaron. With an appropriately solemn expression, the old priest was methodically tucking into a plate of cheese with a pair of chopsticks.

"Thanks for such a lovely ceremony, Aaron."

"Hello, Tae. You choreographed things beautifully."

"I think those vestments look better on you than the Shinto robes did."

"It was Ryuichi's request. Reika wanted a Shinto ceremony."

"Sorry about that last-minute change."

"Don't worry. My wish for the couple's happiness is the same in either religion. But I can only conduct Catholic weddings for non-Catholics. When I go home on the next rotation, you should get some real priests."

"But you *are* a real priest," said Sohya.

Tae laughed. "We're looking for people from other religions to officiate. Couples of other faiths will have to wait till there's someone up here who can marry them. Still, I'd like you to conduct the Catholic weddings."

"It'll be difficult to get devout Catholics to come here for a few years. The Vatican still doesn't approve."

Tae looked disappointed. "A few years? Will they approve someday?"

"A friend in Rome says Star Road has the Vatican tied up in knots. There's nothing in the Bible about God creating aliens." He smiled mischievously. "The archbishops and cardinals are racking their brains trying to square the existence of life on other planets with the Church's teachings. But I'm sure they'll find a way to integrate it into doctrine, just as they did with evolution. And if they can do that, they can accept people living on the moon. Then Catholics can marry here without any conflict."

"Will it take a long time?"

"It took the Church 350 years to apologize for Galileo's persecution. I wouldn't hold your breath. But once they sanction marriage on the moon, they won't rescind the decision." Aaron nodded toward the head table. "That's enough theology for now. Go say hello to the bride. She's waiting."

Sohya and Tae approached the head table. Reika was bare shouldered in a snow-white dress and appeared to be on the verge of tears.

"Congratulations, Reika," said Tae.

"Do I look strange? I think I'm too old for this dress. It's so embarrassing—"

"Don't be silly. You look beautiful. You must be very happy." Tae wasted no time handing her a handkerchief. Reika daubed at her eyes.

Sohya raised his glass. "Ryuichi, congratulations. Now I understand—this is why you decided to come on board with Sixth Continent, right?"

"Come on. Meeting Reika was a stroke of luck, pure and simple. We registered our marriage a while ago. I wasn't going to let her get away. I've paid my respects to Shinji as well, so I'm a happy man."

Forceful as ever, Ryuichi was also flushed. Evidently he'd been enjoying the wine. He leaned forward. "Listen, Aomine, you should be sitting here too. Isn't it about time?"

"What? Um, well, I don't know…" He stammered and looked at Tae, who returned his gaze thoughtfully.

Someone else was at the head table: Kiichiro Toenji. "Ryuichi's right. If Tae were getting married too, it would save me a trip."

"Father! Please, it's our decision to make."

"Really? After all that pressure you put on me?" he said, unruffled. Tae had extracted his promise to hold a proper wedding ceremony in honor of her mother, but later she'd realized it was unfair. Surely her mother would have wanted Kiichiro to remarry if at all possible.

"As your father, I have a right to say this. Don't think you can keep putting it off forever. Being busy is no excuse. Ryuichi and I are busy too, preparing for the next phase of construction."

"He's right, Tae," said Reika. "Don't wait. The time goes so quickly!"

"You couldn't be more convincing," laughed Sohya.

"Sohya, you're terrible!"

Everyone chuckled. A strobe flashed; Sumoto was covering the event with a trio of cameras around his neck and a camcorder. "Smile, everyone. Sixth Continent's founders in one place. This will make great publicity!"

Tae tugged Sohya's sleeve. "Publicity is not what I'm in the mood for," she whispered.

"Then let's get out of here."

"Hey, I'm the man of the hour here!" said Ryuichi, stepping in front of the camera. He winked at Sohya. "You should get going."

They left the hall as the other guests looked on.

THE GREENHOUSE ON the roof of the SELS module was now large enough to allow the cultivation of trees. Sohya and Tae stole inside and sat down under a kenaf tree. Tae took off her heels.

"Do your feet hurt?"

"Not in this gravity. But its feels better barefoot."

"I'm glad I wasn't dressed up. Yaenami was ready to turn us into sacrificial lambs."

"I don't know about you, but I was ready to be sacrificed." She looked at him and smiled.

They gazed through the glass walls of the greenhouse toward Eden Crater. The ceiling and walls toward the sun were leaded glass to attenuate the radiation flux, but the glass on the crater side was transparent. Through it they could see a structure of such titanic scale that it might have been a hallucination. Rising up out of the crater and extending for ninety kilometers directly west was an enormous golden ramp. The end of the ramp was lost in the distance. Cargo containers of different sizes moved ceaselessly up it, rapidly shrinking to the size of poppy seeds and accelerating before being lost to sight.

A year ago—six months before Sixth Continent opened— ENG had emerged from the ice and built the kernel of Star Road. After a detailed investigation, its function was clear. Embedded in the surface of the nascent ramp were tens of thousands of small, coiled structures, regularly distributed on their long axis.

The discovery provoked astonishment. This was exactly the structure needed to accelerate a magnetized object. The ramp pointed west, in the direction of the moon's rotation.

ENG was poised to grow into a mass driver on a titanic scale. Such a structure could accelerate objects to escape velocity and beyond without the use of fuel. The seed sown in Eden Crater was ready to complete its growth.

It was human nature to want to finish the structure and see if it could be put to use. Naturally this aroused fierce opposition on Earth. The intelligence behind ENG and its mechanism of growth was a complete enigma. Meddling with it would be like inviting a chimpanzee to play with a nuclear warhead. Star Road was not something ephemeral like a radio transmission. It was a real object, perhaps a terrible weapon designed to send a destructive device toward Earth.

That possibility could not be ruled out. But after further consideration, opposition faded. Heat and light provided the energy for ENG's growth, but only on the moon. Further tests showed that the fibers grew in as little as 1 percent Earth gravity, but not in true weightlessness. Furthermore, there was no growth above one-third G. This meant ENG was designed for minor planets, moons, or asteroids, but not for Earth.

If they were hostile—even if they had only planned to utilize the earth for some benign purpose—the Architects who had started it all could easily have modified ENG for Earth's environment. With its extreme efficiency in converting energy into growth, an Earth-based ENG could have shaped its surroundings in any way the Architects desired. But they had sown their seed on the moon.

There were questions about that as well. ENG was planted not in the full light of the sun, but in the eternal darkness of the shadow zone. That meant it required something else: water. Yet the earth offered far more water than the moon, water without limit. The only conclusion that could be drawn was that ENG had been deliberately sown where it would not encounter life. The message from the southern skies reinforced this conclusion. ENG's creators had deliberately chosen a frequency that would not penetrate Earth's atmosphere, though they could easily have determined that Earth's atmosphere contained oxygen if they'd wanted to communicate with Earth. Clearly they did not want their message overheard.

Such actions suggested an intention to preserve Earth from harm. Gradually, fewer people worried that tampering with this creation of a mysterious intelligence might trigger some sort of retribution. Common sense dictated that where there was food, there would be an eater—that was the definition of life. Refraining from doing so when presented with the opportunity was a hallmark of benevolent intelligence. This was the ultimate reason to trust the Architects.

Just before Sixth Continent formally opened, scientists at Liberty Island once more exposed the structure to sunlight. At that point it was still within the shadow zone; Caroline's team cautiously used only 1 percent as much solar energy as before. The structure immediately resumed its growth. In less than a month, it was complete.

As ENG emerged into the sunlight, it had all the energy it needed to grow. But when the ramp reached ninety kilometers, growth suddenly ceased, and electricity from solar energy immediately began flowing through the coils in the ramp. When a storage container studded with magnets was placed on the ramp, it accelerated past the moon's escape velocity and was hurled into interplanetary space. The ramp had no other function and displayed no further growth, though it now had access to unlimited solar energy. Whoever the Architects were, they were not ENG itself. ENG was a tool.

The two bases immediately put this useful implement to good use. Still, the debate continued: Why this structure? Why on the moon? Two things were clear: the Architects did not possess ultra-advanced technology, otherwise they would not have chosen a mass driver to escape from the moon's gravity; and they had not yet been to the moon, otherwise they would have left a complete structure behind instead of merely its seed.

This suggested that the Architects might not be so very different from humankind. The mass driver accelerated objects at a constant three gravities. If the Architects were planning to use it, that meant their physical structure was roughly similar to that of humans in terms of structural strength. If they were capable of withstanding greater stress, Star Road would have been shorter, with higher acceleration. This was likely an intelligent species with reasoning processes analogous to humans and bodies at least somewhat similar. Would they return to visit their creation? Because of humanity's actions, Star Road had emerged earlier than planned. Would this prove to be a mistake?

Tae rested quietly, her head on Sohya's shoulders. Idly, he called up Lambach's report and began glancing through it. Suddenly he stood up.

"What's wrong?" Tae saw he was looking not toward the crater, but at his wearcom.

"I don't believe it. This report is an analysis of signals between Star Road and the Architects over the last few months. They've been communicating quite a bit."

"Did Liberty crack the code?" Tae was now looking excitedly at the wearcom.

"No, but the interval between exchanges indicates the distance to the Architects: only five trillion kilometers, about half a light year. Not only that, their transmissions are Doppler shifted. This says that when the first message was sent, they were moving toward us at about two thousand kilometers a second. That would get them here eighty years from now. But the Doppler shift of the last transmission was much greater. Now they're moving close to ten thousand kilometers per second, about 3 percent light speed. They'll be here in fifteen years, give or take. They'll need time to decelerate when they get closer, of course. But we'll be around when they arrive."

"Star Road must've told them it's ready and waiting. They moved up their schedule."

"Yes, but why bother?"

"Because now they know about us too. So that means they're coming to meet us…"

"There's no other reason for them to hurry," Sohya said. "It's what you or I would do if we were late for a meeting. Without our intervention, ENG would have grown anyway, just far more slow-ly, in time for the Architects' arrival. And extrapolating growth rates back from before Liberty Island's first experiment, it looks like ENG was only planted 150 years ago. It's too much of a coin-cidence—the Architects acted because they were aware of human activities on Earth."

"But why take the trouble to physically come here? Are we sure they just want to communicate? We can't decode their signals, and they didn't exactly make it easy for us to notice them. They haven't acknowledged the signals we've sent in the same direction. Maybe we're like fish in an aquarium, and they're just stopping by to check up on us? In any case, once they get here, what do we do?"

"Maybe we should get ready to welcome them."

Tae looked suddenly somber. "I hope we can do it peacefully. Some people will say we should arm ourselves to the teeth. And Star Road just makes it easier."

"We can't be certain they'll come in peace, you know."

Tae looked toward the ramp. "I have to admit I'm a little scared. Maybe we should at least think about preparing some sort of defense."

"What happens if there's a misunderstanding? You know how easily a minor falling-out can poison a relationship."

Tae blushed. She'd been needlessly estranged from her father for years. The same thing had almost happened with Sohya.

He put his arm around her. "Don't worry. The Architects know they're dealing with an intelligent species. They know we were capable of waking up Star Road. Now they're hurrying to meet us. Maybe they're worried that we've hijacked their creation, but if they have the power to build something like that, they could've designed ENG to defend itself as soon as we started messing with it. So far their technology has been used only to create, not de-stroy. I think they'll be worthy of our respect."

"Sohya…" Tae looked up at him, a twinkle in her eye. "You re-ally believe we can make friends with them, don't you?"

"We've got to try. It may not be easy. Just like in any relationship—you meet, communicate, maybe misunderstand each other, and you figure out a way to overcome that. Eventually you get to know each other really well. You go from total stranger, to acquaintance, to friend—"

"To lovers," Tae whispered, and smiled. "And there'll be a kind of marriage between humans and Architects. Sixth Continent is just the place for that."

Sohya laughed. "That's right. Sixth Continent will be the new world. This is where the adventure starts." He looked down at her. "Maybe Ryuichi was right. Maybe it's our time too."

She pinched him. "We promised to wait till we can both live here permanently, after the base is expanded. But I'm not Reika. I'm can't wait fifteen years!"

"I can't either. We'll be the first couple to marry and settle here. It's just a little longer."

"Then again—we could do it now." She looked at him mischievously. Sohya's eyes widened with surprise. She pulled him down onto a soft bed of ferns.

Their children would be born here, and their grandchildren. Their descendants would encounter beings from another star and build a new world. Their day would come, just as it had for Sohya and Tae.

Not yet, but soon.

ABOUT THE AUTHOR

Born in 1975 in Gifu Prefecture, ISSUI OGAWA is rapidly becoming known as one of Japan's premier SF writers. His 1996 debut, *First a Letter from Popular Palace*, won the Shueisha JUMP Novel Grand Prix. *The Next Continent* (2003), a two-volume novel (complete in this single-volume Haikasoru edition) about settlement on the moon, garnered the 35th Seiun Prize. A collection of his short stories won the 2005 Best SF Poll, and "The Drifting Man," included in that collection, was awarded the 37th Seiun Prize for domestic short stories. Other works include *Land of Resurrection*, *Free Lunch Era*, *Fortress in a Strange Land*, *Guiding Star*, and *Lord of the Sands of Time* (Haikasoru 2009). Ogawa is a principal member of the Space Authors Club.

HAIKASORU
THE FUTURE IS JAPANESE

LOUPS-GAROUS BY NATSUHIKO KYOGOKU

In the near future, humans will communicate almost exclusively through online networks—face-to-face meetings are rare and the surveillance state nearly all-powerful. So when a serial killer starts slaughtering young people, the crackdown is harsh. And despite all the safeguards, the killer's latest victim turns out to have been in contact with three young girls: Mio Tsuzuki, a certified prodigy; Hazuki Makino, a quiet but opinionated classmate; and Ayumi Kono, her best friend. As the girls get caught up in trying to find the killer—who just might be a werewolf—Hazuki learns that there is much more to their monitored communications than meets the eye.

THE STORIES OF IBIS BY HIROSHI YAMAMOTO

In a world where humans are a minority and androids have created their own civilization, a wandering storyteller meets the beautiful android Ibis. She tells him seven stories of human/android interaction in order to reveal the secret behind humanity's fall. The tales Ibis tells are science fiction stories about the events surrounding the development of artificial intelligence in the twentieth and twenty-first centuries. At a glance, these stories do not appear to have any sort of connection, but what is the true meaning behind them? What are Ibis's real intentions?

SLUM ONLINE BY HIROSHI SAKURAZAKA

Etsuro Sakagami is a college freshman who feels uncomfortable in reality, but when he logs on to the combat MMO *Versus Town*, he becomes "'Tetsuo," a karate champ on his way to becoming the most powerful martial artist around. While his relationship with new classmate Fumiko goes nowhere, Etsuro spends his days and nights online in search of the invincible fighter Ganker Jack. Drifting between the virtual and the real, will Etsuro ever be ready to face his most formidable opponent?

ALSO BY ISSUI OGAWA

THE LORD OF THE SANDS OF TIME

Sixty-two years after human life on Earth was annihilated by rampaging alien invaders, the enigmatic Messenger O is sent back in time with a mission to unite humanity of past eras—during the Second World War, in ancient Japan, and at the dawn of humanity—to defeat the invasion before it begins. However, in a future shredded by love and genocide, love waits for O. Will O save humanity only to doom himself?

VISIT US AT WWW.HAIKASORU.COM